Praise for *USA TODAY* bestselling author Lynne Graham

"The second-chance romance is a heartbreaking page-turner. Graham's ritzy settings are ideal, her little-boy co-star coaxes smiles and her couple's tumultuous relationship enthralls."
—*RT Book Reviews* on *The Secret His Mistress Carried*

"Graham's desert romance is superb. Her dark, intensely handsome, aristocratic hero and innocent with-a-bite heroine are a perfect fit. Their tongue-lashings are spectacular, the lovemaking is as hot as the desert at mid-day and her exotic locales give the read a modern *Arabian Nights* feel."
—*RT Book Reviews* on *Zarif's Convenient Queen*

Praise for *USA TODAY* bestselling author Abby Green

"Green's romance is a nonstop roller coaster of emotions between its flame-haired Irish heroine and her prideful Italian hero. The Italian countryside is the perfect setting for their tumultuous relationship. The heroine's inventive ploys to avoid marriage are outlandishly ingenious."
—*RT Book Reviews* on *Delucca's Marriage Contract*

"Green's lust-at-first-sight to love story is sensational. Her charming, broken hero and determined heroine rule every page with their palpable sexual tension, lively repartee and viscerally carnal love scenes."
—*RT Book Reviews* on *Rival's Challenge*

USA TODAY bestselling author **Lynne Graham** was born in Northern Ireland and has been a keen romance reader since her teens. She is very happily married to an understanding husband who has learned to cook since she started to write! Her five children keep her on her toes. She has a very large dog who knocks everything over, a very small terrier who barks a lot, and two cats. Visit her on the web at lynnegraham.com.

Books by Lynne Graham

Harlequin Presents

Leonetti's Housekeeper Bride
The Secret His Mistress Carried
The Dimitrakos Proposition
A Ring to Secure His Heir
Unlocking Her Innocence

The Notorious Greeks

The Greek Demands His Heir
The Greek Commands His Mistress

Bound by Gold

The Sheikh's Secret Babies
The Billionaire's Bridal Bargain

The Legacies of Powerful Men

Ravelli's Defiant Bride
Christakis's Rebellious Wife
Zarif's Convenient Queen

A Bride for a Billionaire

A Rich Man's Whim
The Sheikh's Prize
The Billionaire's Trophy
Challenging Dante

Visit the Author Profile page
at Harlequin.com for more titles.

Lynne Graham
& Abby Green

Jewel in His Crown
& The Call of the Desert

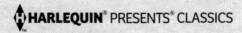

HARLEQUIN® PRESENTS® CLASSICS

ISBN-13: 978-0-373-60239-1

Jewel in His Crown & The Call of the Desert

Copyright © 2016 by Harlequin Books S.A.

The publisher acknowledges the copyright holders
of the individual works as follows:

Jewel in His Crown
Copyright © 2011 by Lynne Graham

The Call of the Desert
Copyright © 2011 by Abby Green

Recycling programs
for this product may
not exist in your area.

This edition published by arrangement with Harlequin Books S.A.

For questions and comments about the quality of this book,
please contact us at CustomerService@Harlequin.com.

Printed in U.S.A.

www.Harlequin.com

CONTENTS

Lynne Graham

———

Jewel in His Crown

CHAPTER ONE

THE BEAUTIFUL BRUNETTE lay in the tangled bed sheets watching her lover get dressed. Prince Raja al-Somari had black hair and exotic dark golden eyes. Exceptionally handsome, he was pure leashed power, muscle and magnetic attraction. He was also a wild force of nature in bed, she reflected with a languorous look of sensual satisfaction on her face.

As his mistress, Chloe, one of the world's top fashion models, certainly had no complaints. But then Chloe was excessively fond of rich men, money and fabulous jewellery. Her prince from the oil-rich country of Najar in the Persian Gulf was staggeringly wealthy and he delivered on every count, so naturally she didn't want to lose him. When a plane crash had killed the bride in the arranged marriage being planned for Raja, Chloe had breathed a secret sigh of relief for such an alliance could well lead to the end of the most profitable relationship she had ever had. And even if another arranged marriage lurked on the horizon, Chloe was determined to hold onto her lover.

Raja watched Chloe finger the glittering new diamond bracelet encircling one slender wrist as if it were a talisman and his mouth quirked at her predictability. Although the demands of his position had made it difficult for him to see her in recent months, Chloe had subjected him to neither tantrums nor tears. Like most Western women he had met since his university days in England, she was as easy to placate as a child with a shiny new toy. In return for the complete discretion he demanded from his lovers, he was extremely generous but he never thought about his bed partners when he was away from them. Sex might be a necessity to a man of his appetites, but it was also simply an amusement and an escape from the weight of responsibility he carried. As acting Regent and ruler of conservative Najar, he could not openly enjoy a sex life without causing offence.

Furthermore, Raja was always aware that he had much more important issues to worry about. The recent appalling plane crash had devastated the people of Najar and its neighbour and former enemy, Ashur. The future of both countries stood on the edge of catastrophe. For seven years war had raged between oil-rich Najar and poverty stricken Ashur and when peace had finally been brokered by the Scandinavian state leading the talks, the two countries had added a more personal cultural twist to the agreement before they were satisfied that the peace would hold firm. That twist had been an arranged marriage between the two royal families and joint rulership that would ultimately unite Najar with Ashur. Having spent most of his adult life as a businessman before serving his country, Raja had accepted that he had to marry Princess Bariah of Ashur. That she was a widow well into her thirties while he was still in his twenties he had accepted as his royal duty to put the needs of his country first.

And his country and his people did desperately *need* a fresh blueprint for a lasting peace.

Unfortunately for all concerned, a tragedy had lurked in the wings of the peace accord. A fortnight earlier, Bariah and her parents had died in a plane crash. Shorn of its entire ruling family in one fell swoop, Ashur was in deep crisis and the court officials were searching frantically through the Shakarian family tree for a suitable heir to the throne who could take Bariah's place as Raja's bride and consort.

His mobile phone buzzed and he lifted it.

'You have to come home,' his younger brother Haroun told him heavily. 'Wajid Sulieman, the Ashuri court advisor, is already on his way here. According to his aide, he is very excited so I expect that means they've found another bride for you.'

It was the news that Raja had been waiting for, the news that honour demanded he hope for, but he still had to fight the crushing sensation of a rock settling on his chest to shorten his breathing. 'We must hope for the best—'

'The best would be if they *couldn't* find anyone else to marry you!' his youthful sibling opined without hesitation. 'Why are you letting yourself be forced into an arranged marriage? Are we still living in the Dark Ages?'

Raja's lean bronzed features were as impassive as he had learned to make them in the presence of others. He rarely spoke without consideration. His wheelchair-bound father had taught him everything he knew about kingship. 'It is necessary that I do this.'

'Trouble?' Chloe asked, blue eyes bright with curiosity as Raja set down the phone and lifted his shirt.

'I have to leave immediately.'

Chloe scrambled out of bed and pressed her lithe pale body to his. 'But we were going out tonight,' she protested, looking up at him with wide, wounded eyes while being careful to look and sound hurt and disappointed rather than accusing, for there was very little Chloe didn't know about keeping a man happy.

'I'll make up for it on my next visit,' Raja promised, setting her to one side to resume dressing.

He was trying not to wonder *who* the Ashuri representatives had found for him to marry. What did the woman's identity matter? Hopefully she would be reasonably attractive. That was the most he could hope for. Anything more would be icing on the cake. He suppressed the thought that he was as imprisoned by his royal birth as an animal in a trap. Such reflections were unnecessarily dramatic and in no way productive.

His private jet whisked him back to Najar within hours and his brother was waiting in the limo that met him at the airport.

'I wouldn't marry a stranger!' Haroun told him heatedly.

'I do it gladly for you.' Raja was grateful that his kid brother had no such future sacrifice to fear. 'Right now, after a long period of instability, tradition is exactly what the people in both countries long to have back—'

'The Ashuris are broke. Their country is in ruins. Why don't you offer them a portion of our oil revenues instead?'

'Haroun!' Raja censured. 'Watch your mouth. Until

we find a feasible framework for this peace agreement we all need to practise great diplomacy.'

'Since when has the truth been a hanging offence?' Haroun argued. 'We won the war yet you're being bartered off to a bunch of boundary thieves, who were still herding sheep when our great-great-grandfather, Rashid, was a king!'

Conscious that many Najaris would agree with his sibling, for the war had sown deep enmity and prejudice between the people of both countries, Raja merely dealt the younger man an impatient appraisal. 'I expect a more balanced outlook from a young man as well educated as you are.'

At the royal palace, the grey-haired and excessively precise Ashuri court advisor awaited Raja's arrival with an assistant and both men were, indeed, wreathed in smiles.

'My apologies if our timing has proved inconvenient, Your Royal Highness. Thank you for seeing us at such short notice.' Bowing very low, Wajid wasted no time in making small talk. A man on a mission, he spread open a file on the polished table between them. 'We have discovered that the only legal and marriageable female heir to the Ashuri throne is the daughter of the late King Anwar and a British citizen—'

'A British citizen?' Haroun repeated, intrigued. 'Anwar was ruler before Princess Bariah's father, King Tamim, wasn't he?'

'He was Tamim's elder brother. I recall that King Anwar made more than one marriage,' Raja remarked. 'Who was the lady's mother?'

The older man's mouth compressed. 'His first wife

was an Englishwoman. The alliance was brief and she returned with the child to England after the divorce.'

'And what age is Anwar's daughter now?' Haroun was full of lively curiosity.

'Twenty-one years old. She has never been married.'

'Half English,' Prince Raja mused. 'And still very young. Of good character?'

Wajid stiffened. 'Of course.'

Raja was not so easily impressed. In his experience women who coveted the attentions of a prince were only looking for a good time and something sparkly to sweeten the deal. 'Why did King Anwar divorce her mother?'

'She was unable to have more children. It was a love match and short-lived,' the older man commented with a scornful compression of his lips. 'The king had two sons with his second wife, both of whom were killed during the war.'

Although Wajid was repeating information he was already well acquainted with, Raja dipped his head in respectful acknowledgement for a generation of young men who had been decimated by the conflict that had raged for so long. As far as he was concerned if his marriage could persuade bitter enemies to live together in peace, it was a small sacrifice in comparison to the endless funerals he had once been forced to attend.

'The name of Anwar's daughter?'

'The princess's name is Ruby. As her mother chose to leave Ashur, the royal family took no further interest in either mother or daughter. Unfortunately Princess Ruby has had no training or preparation for a royal role.'

Raja frowned. 'In which case she would find the lifestyle and the expectations very challenging.'

'The princess is young enough to learn quickly.' The court advisor rubbed his hands together with unfeigned enthusiasm. 'Our advisors believe she can be easily moulded.'

'Have you a photograph to show my brother?' Haroun questioned eagerly.

Wajid leafed through the file and extracted a small photo. 'I'm afraid this is several years old but the most recent photograph we have.'

Raja studied the slender blonde in the miniskirt and T-shirt, captured outside the Ashuri cathedral in their capital city. It was a tourist snap and the girl still had the legginess and slightly chubby and unformed features of adolescence. Her pale colouring was very unusual in his culture and that long blonde hair was exceptionally attractive and he immediately felt guilty for that shallow reflection with his former fiancée, Bariah, so recently laid to rest. But in truth he had only met Bariah briefly on one formal occasion and she had remained a stranger to him.

Less guarded than his elder brother, Haroun studied Princess Ruby and loosed a long low whistle of boyish approval.

'That is enough,' Raja rebuked the younger man in exasperation. 'When can I hope to meet her?'

'As soon as we can arrange it, Your Royal Highness.' Not displeased by the compliment entailed in Haroun's whistle of admiration, Wajid beamed, relieved by Raja's practical response to the offer of another bride. Not for the first time, Wajid felt that Prince Raja would be a king he could do business with. The Najari regent accepted his responsibilities without fuss and if there was one thing he knew inside out, it was *how* to be royal. A young woman blessed with his support and guidance would soon learn the ropes.

'*PLEASE*, RUBY,' STEVE PLEADED, gripping Ruby's small waist with possessive hands.

'No!' Ruby told her boyfriend without hesitation. She pushed his hands from below her sweater. Although it didn't appear to bother him she felt foolish grappling with him in broad daylight in a car parked in the shadiest corner of the pub car park.

Steve dealt her a sulky look of resentment before finally retreating back into the driver's seat. Ruby, with her big brown eyes, blonde hair and fabulous figure, was a trophy and he was the envy of all his friends, but when she dug her heels in, she was as immovable as a granite rock. 'Can I come over tonight?'

'I'm tired,' Ruby lied. 'I should get back to work. I don't want to be late.'

Steve dropped her back at the busy legal practice where she was a receptionist. They lived in the same Yorkshire market town. A salesman in an estate agency, Steve worked across the street from her and he was fighting a last-ditch battle to persuade Ruby that sex was a desirable activity. She had wondered if Steve might be the one to change her mind on that score for she had initially thought him very attractive. He had the blond hair and blue eyes she had always admired in men, but his kisses were wet and his roving hands squeezed her as if she were a piece of ripening fruit for

sale on a stall. Steve had taught her that a man could
be good-looking without being sexy.

'You're ten minutes late, Ruby,' the office manager,
a thin, bespectacled woman in her thirties, remarked
sourly. 'You need to watch your timekeeping.'

Ruby apologised and got back to work, letting her
mind drift to escape the boredom of the routine tasks
that made up her working day. When she had first
started working at Collins, Jones & Fowler, she had
been eighteen years old, her mother had just died and
she had badly needed a job. Her colleagues were all
female and older and the middle-aged trio of solicitors
they worked for were an equally uninteresting bunch.
Conversations were about elderly parents, children and
the evening meal, never gossip, fashion or men. Ruby
enjoyed the familiar faces of the regular clients and
the brief snatches of friendly chatter they exchanged
with her but continually wished that life offered more
variety and excitement.

In comparison, her late mother, Vanessa, had had
more than a taste of excitement while she was still
young enough to enjoy it, Ruby recalled affectionately.
As a youthful catwalk model in London, Vanessa had
caught the eye of an Arab prince, who had married
her after a whirlwind romance. Ruby's birthplace was
the country of Ashur in the Persian Gulf. Her father,
Anwar, however, had chosen to take a second wife
while still married to her mother and that had been the
ignominious end of what Vanessa had afterwards referred to as her 'royal fling'. Vanessa had got a divorce
and had returned to the UK with her child. In Ashur
daughters were rarely valued as much as sons and

Ruby's father had promptly chosen to forget her existence.

A year later, Vanessa, armed with a substantial pay-off and very much on the rebound, had married Curtis Sommerton, a Yorkshire businessman. She had immediately begun calling her daughter by her second husband's surname in the belief that it would enable Ruby to forget the family that had rejected them. Meanwhile Curtis had sneakily run through her mother's financial nest egg and had deserted her once the money was spent. Heartbroken, Vanessa had grieved long and hard over that second betrayal of trust and had died of a premature heart attack soon afterwards.

'My mistake was letting myself get carried away with my feelings,' Vanessa had often told her daughter. 'Anwar promised me the moon and I bet he promised the other wife he took the moon, as well. The proof of the pudding is in the eating, my love. Don't go falling for sweet-talking womanisers like I did!'

Fiery and intelligent, Ruby was very practical and quick to spot anyone trying to take too much advantage of her good nature. She had loved her mother very much and preferred to remember Vanessa as a warm and loving woman, who was rather naive about men. Her stepfather, on the other hand, had been a total creep, whom Ruby had hated and feared. Vanessa had had touching faith in love and romance but, to date, life had only taught Ruby that what men seemed to want most was sex. Finer feelings like commitment, loyalty and romance were much harder to find or awaken. Like so many men before him, Steve had made Ruby feel grubby and she was determined not to go out with him again.

After work she walked home, to the tiny terraced house that she rented, for the second time that day. Her lunch breaks were always cut short by her need to go home and take her dog out for a quick walk but she didn't mind. Hermione, the light of Ruby's life, was a Jack Russell terrier, who adored Ruby and disliked men. Hermione had protected Ruby from her stepfather, Curtis, on more than one occasion. Creeping into Ruby's bedroom at night had been a very dangerous exercise with Hermione in residence.

Ruby shared the small house with her friend Stella Carter, who worked as a supermarket cashier. Now she was surprised to see an opulent BMW car complete with a driver parked outside her home and she had not even contrived to get her key into the front door before it shot abruptly open.

'Thank goodness, you're home!' Stella exclaimed, her round face flushed and uneasy. 'You've got visitors in the lounge...' she informed Ruby in a suitable whisper.

Ruby frowned. 'Who are they?'

'They're something to do with your father's family... No, not Curtis the perv, the *real* one!' That distinction was hissed into Ruby's ear.

Completely bewildered, Ruby went into the compact front room, which seemed uncomfortably full of people. A small grey-haired man beamed at her and bowed very low. The middle aged woman with him and the younger man followed suit, so that Ruby found herself staring in wonderment at three downbent heads.

'Your Royal Highness,' the older man breathed in a tone of reverent enthusiasm. 'May I say what a very great pleasure it is to meet you at last?'

'He's been going on about you being a princess ever since he arrived,' Stella told her worriedly out of the corner of her mouth.

'I'm not a princess. I'm not a royal anything,' Ruby declared with a frown of wryly amused discomfiture. 'What's this all about? Who are you?'

Wajid Sulieman introduced himself and his wife, Haniyah, and his assistant. 'I represent the interests of the Ashuri royal family and I am afraid I must first give you bad news.'

Striving to recall her manners and contain her impatience, Ruby asked her visitors to take a seat. Wajid informed her that her uncle, Tamim, his wife and his daughter, Bariah, had died in a plane crash over the desert three weeks earlier. The names rang a very vague bell of familiarity from Ruby's one and only visit to Ashur when she was a schoolgirl of fourteen. 'My uncle was the king...' she said hesitantly, not even quite sure of that fact.

'And until a year ago your eldest brother was his heir,' Wajid completed.

Ruby's big brown eyes opened very wide in surprise. 'I have a brother?'

Wajid had the grace to flush at the level of her ignorance about her relatives. 'Your late father had two sons by his second wife.'

Ruby emitted a rueful laugh. 'So I have two half-brothers I never knew about. Do they know about me?'

Wajid looked grave. 'Once again it is my sad duty

to inform you that your brothers died bravely as soldiers in Ashur's recent war with Najar.'

Stunned, Ruby struggled to speak. 'Oh…yes, I've read about the war in the newspapers. That's very sad about my brothers. They must've been very young, as well,' Ruby remarked uncertainly, feeling hopelessly out of her depth.

The Ashuri side of her family was a complete blank to Ruby. She had never met her father or his relations and knew virtually nothing about them. On her one and only visit to Ashur, her once powerful curiosity had been cured when her mother's attempt to claim a connection to the ruling family was heartily rejected. Vanessa had written in advance of their visit but there had been no reply. Her phone calls once they arrived in Ashur had also failed to win them an invitation to the palace. Indeed, Vanessa and her daughter had finally been humiliatingly turned away from the gates of the royal palace when her father's relatives had not deigned to meet their estranged British relatives. From that moment on Ruby had proudly suppressed her curiosity about the Ashuri portion of her genes.

'Your brothers were brave young men,' Wajid told her. 'They died fighting for their country.'

Ruby nodded with a respectful smile and thought sadly about the two younger brothers she had never got the chance to meet. Had they ever wondered what she was like? She suspected that royal protocol might well have divided them even if, unlike the rest of their family, they had had sufficient interest to want to get to know her.

'I share these tragedies with you so that you can understand that you are now the present heir to the throne of Ashur, Your Royal Highness.'

'I'm the heir?' Ruby laughed out loud in sheer disbelief. 'How is that possible? I'm a girl, for goodness' sake! And why do you keep on calling me Your Royal Highness as if I have a title?'

'Whether you use it or otherwise, you have carried the title of Princess since the day you were born,' Wajid asserted with confidence. 'It is your birthright as the daughter of a king.'

It all sounded very impressive but Ruby was well aware that in reality, Ashur was still picking up the pieces in the aftermath of the conflict. That such a country had fought a war with its wealthy neighbour over the oil fields on their disputed boundary was a testament to their dogged pride and determination in spite of the odds against them. Even so she had been hugely relieved when she heard on the news that the war was finally over.

She struggled to appear composed when she was actually shaken by the assurance that she had a legal right to call herself a princess and then her natural common sense reasserted its sway. Could there be anything more ridiculously inappropriate than a princess who worked as a humble receptionist and had to struggle to pay her rent most months? Even with few extras in her budget Ruby was invariably broke and she often did a weekend shift at Stella's supermarket to help make ends meet.

'There's no room for titles and such things in my life,' she said gently, reluctant to cause offence by being any more blunt. 'I'm a very ordinary girl.'

'But that is exactly what our people would like most

about you. We are a country of ordinary hard-working people,' Wajid declared with ringing pride. 'You are the only heir to the throne of Ashur and you must take your rightful place.'

Ruby's soft pink lips parted in astonishment. 'Let me get this straight—you are asking me to come out to Ashur and live there as a princess?'

'Yes. That is why we are here, to make you aware of your position and to bring you home.' Wajid spread his arms expansively to emphasise his enthusiasm for the venture.

A good deal less expressive, Ruby tensed and shook her fair head in a quiet negative motion. 'Ashur is not my home. Nobody in the royal family has even seen me since I left the country as a baby. There has been no contact and no interest.'

The older man looked grave. 'That is true, but the tragedies that have almost wiped out the Shakarian family have ensured that everything has changed. You are now a very important person in Ashur, a princess, the daughter of a recent king and the niece of another, with a strong legal claim to the throne—'

'But I don't want to claim the throne, and in any case I do know enough about Ashur to know that women don't rule there,' Ruby cut in, her impatience growing, for she felt she was being fed a rather hypocritical official line that was a whitewash of the less palatable truth. 'I'm quite sure there is some man hovering in the wings ready to do the ruling in Ashur.'

The court advisor would have squirmed with dismay had he not possessed the carriage of a man with an iron bar welded to his short spine. Visibly, however, he stiffened even more. 'You are, of course, correct when you say that women do not rule in Ashur. Our country has long practised male preference primogeniture—'

'So I am really not quite as important as you would like to make out?' Ruby marvelled that he could ever have believed she might be so ignorant of the hereditary male role of kingship in Ashur. After all, hadn't her poor mother's marriage ended in tears and divorce thanks to those strict rules? Her father had taken another wife in a desperate attempt to have a son.

Placed in an awkward spot when he had least expected it, Wajid reddened and revised up his assumptions about the level of the princess's intelligence. 'I am sorry to contradict you but you are unquestionably a very important young woman in the eyes of our people. Without you there can be no King,' he admitted baldly.

'Excuse me?' Her fine brows were pleating. 'I'm sorry, I don't understand what you mean.'

Wajid hesitated. 'Ashur and Najar are to be united and jointly ruled by a marriage between the two royal families. That was integral to the peace terms that were agreed to at the end of the war.'

Ruby froze at that grudging explanation and resisted the urge to release an incredulous laugh, for she suddenly grasped what her true value was to this stern little man. They needed a princess to marry off, a princess who could claim to be in line to the throne of Ashur. And here she was young and single. Nothing personal or even complimentary as such in her selection, she reflected with a stab of resentment and regret. It did, however, make more sense to her that she was only finally being acknowledged in Ashur as a member of the royal family because there was nobody else more suitable available.

'I didn't know that arranged marriages still took place in Ashur.'

'Mainly within the royal family,' Wajid conceded grudgingly. 'Sometimes parents know their children better than their children know themselves.'

'Well, I no longer have parents to make that decision for me. In any case, *my* father never took the time to get to know me at all. I'm afraid you're wasting your time here, Mr Sulieman. I don't want to be a princess and I don't want to marry a stranger, either. I'm quite content with my life as it is.' Rising to her feet to indicate that she felt it was time that her visitors took their leave, Ruby felt sorry enough for the older man in his ignorance of contemporary Western values to offer him a look of sympathy. 'These days few young women would be attracted by an arrangement of that nature.'

Long after the limousine had disappeared from view Ruby and Stella sat discussing the visit.

'A princess?' Stella kept on repeating, studying the girl she had known from primary school with growing fascination. 'And you honestly didn't know?'

'I don't think they can have wanted Mum to know,' Ruby offered evenly. 'After the divorce my father and his family were happy for her to leave Ashur and from then on they preferred to pretend that she and I didn't exist.'

'I wonder what the guy they want you to marry is like,' Stella remarked, twirling her dark fringe with dreamy eyes, her imagination clearly caught.

'If he's anything like as callous as my father I'm

not missing anything. My father was willing to break Mum's heart to have a son and no doubt the man they want me to marry would do *anything* to become King of Ashur—'

'The guy has to be from the other country, right?'

'Najar? Must be. Probably some ambitious poor relation of their royal family looking for a leg up the ladder,' Ruby contended with rich cynicism, her scorn unconcealed.

'I'm not sure I would have been so quick to send your visitors packing. I mean, if you leave the husband out of it, being a princess might have been very exciting.'

'There was nothing exciting about Ashur,' Ruby assured her friend with a guilty wince at still being bitter about the country that had rejected her, for she had recognised Wajid Sulieman's sincere love for his country and the news of that awful trail of family deaths had been sobering and had left her feeling sad.

After a normal weekend during which her impressions of that astounding visit from the court advisor faded a little, Ruby went back to work. She had met up with Steve briefly on the Saturday afternoon and had told him that their relationship was over. He had taken it badly and had texted her repeatedly since then, alternately asking for another chance and then truculently criticising her and demanding to know what was wrong with him. She began ignoring the texts, wishing she had never gone out with him in the first place. He was acting a bit obsessive for a man she had only dated for a few weeks.

'Men always go mad over you,' Stella had sighed

enviously when the texts started coming through again at breakfast, which the girls snatched standing up in the tiny kitchen. 'I know Steve's being a nuisance but I wouldn't mind the attention.'

'That kind of attention you'd be welcome to,' Ruby declared without hesitation and she felt the same at work when her phone began buzzing before lunchtime with more messages, for she had nothing left to say to Steve.

A tall guy with luxuriant black hair strode through the door. There was something about him that immediately grabbed attention and Ruby found herself helplessly staring. Maybe it was his clothes, which stood out in a town where decent suits were only seen at weddings and then usually hired. He wore a strikingly elegant dark business suit that would have looked right at home in a designer advertisement in an exclusive magazine. It was perfectly modelled on his tall, well-built frame and long powerful legs. His razor-edged cheekbones were perfectly chiselled too, and as for those eyes, deep set, dark as sloes and brooding. *Wow*, Ruby thought for the very first time in her life as she looked at a man....

CHAPTER TWO

WHEN PRINCE RAJA walked into the solicitor's office, Ruby was the first person he saw and indeed, in spite of the number of other people milling about the busy reception area, pretty much the *only* person he saw. The pretty schoolgirl in the holiday snap had grown into a strikingly beautiful woman with a tumbling mane of blonde hair, sparkling eyes and a soft, full mouth that put him in mind of a succulent peach.

'You are Ruby Shakarian?' the prince asked as a tall, even more powerfully built man came through the door behind him to station himself several feet away.

'I don't use that surname.' Ruby frowned, wondering how many more royal dignitaries she would have to deflect before they got the hint and dropped this ridiculous idea that she was a princess. 'Where did you get it from?'

'Wajid Sulieman gave it to me and asked me to speak to you on his behalf. Shakarian is your family name,' Raja pointed out with an irrefutable logic that set her small white teeth on edge.

'I'm at work right now and not in a position to speak to you.' But Ruby continued to study him covertly, absorbing the lush black lashes semi-screening those mesmerising eyes, the twin slashes of his well-marked ebony brows, the smooth olive-toned skin moulding his strong cheekbones and the faint dark shadow of stubble accentuating his strong jaw and wide, sensual lips. Her prolonged scrutiny only served to confirm her original assessment that he was a stunningly beautiful man. Her heart was hammering so hard inside her chest that she felt seriously short of breath. It was a reaction that thoroughly infuriated her, for Ruby had always prided herself on her armour-plated indifference around men and the role of admirer was new to her.

'Aren't you going for lunch yet?' one of her co-workers enquired, walking past her desk.

'We could have lunch,' Raja pronounced, pouncing on the idea with relief.

Since his private jet had wafted him to Yorkshire and the cool spring temperature that morning, Prince Raja had felt rather like an alien set down on a strange planet. He was not used to small towns and checking into a third-rate local hotel had not improved his mood. He was cold, he was on edge and he did not relish the task foisted on him.

'If you're connected to that Wajid guy, no thanks to lunch,' Ruby pronounced as she got to her feet and reached for her bag regardless because she always went home at lunchtime.

The impression created by her seemingly long legs in that photo had been deceptive, for she was much smaller than Raja had expected and the top of her head barely reached halfway up his chest. Startled by that difference and bemused by that hitch in his concentration, Raja frowned. 'Connected?' he queried, confused by her use of the word.

'If you want to talk about the same thing that Wajid did, I've already heard all I need to hear on that subject,' Ruby extended ruefully. 'I mean…' she leant purposefully closer, not wishing to be overheard, and her intonation was gently mocking '…do I look like a princess to you?'

'You look like a goddess,' the prince heard himself say, speaking his thoughts out loud in a manner that was most unusual for him. His jaw tensed, for he would have preferred not to admit that her dazzling oval face had reminded him of a poster of a film star he recalled from his time serving with the Najari armed forces.

'A goddess?' Equally taken aback, Ruby suddenly grinned, dimples adorning her rounded cheeks. 'Well, that's a new one. Not something any of the men I know would come up with anyway.'

In the face of that glorious smile, Raja's fluent English vocabulary seized up entirely. 'Lunch,' he pronounced again stiltedly.

On the brink of saying no, Ruby recognised Steve waiting outside the door and almost groaned out loud. She knew the one infallible way of shaking a man off was generally to let him see her in the company of another. 'Lunch,' Ruby agreed abruptly, and she planted a determined hand on Raja's sleeve as if to take control of the situation. 'But first I have to go home and take my dog out.'

Raja was taken aback by that sudden physical contact, for people were never so familiar in the presence of royalty, and his breath rasped between his lips. 'That is acceptable.'

'Who is that guy over there watching us?' Ruby

asked in a suspicious whisper, long blonde hair brushing his shoulder and releasing a tide of perfume as fragrant as summer flowers into the air.

'One of my bodyguards.' Raja advanced with the
relaxed attitude of a male who took a constant security presence entirely for granted. 'My car is waiting
outside.'

The bodyguard went out first, looked to either side,
almost bumping into Steve, and then spread the door
wide again for their exit.

'Ruby?' Steve questioned, frowning at the tall dark
male by her side as she emerged. 'Who is this guy?
Where are you going with him?'

'I don't have anything more to say to you, Steve,'
Ruby stated firmly.

'I have a right to ask who this guy is!' Steve snapped
argumentatively, his face turning an angry red below
his fair, floppy fringe.

'You have no rights over me at all,' Ruby told him
in exasperation.

As Steve moved forward the prince made an almost
infinitesimal signal with one hand and suddenly a big
bodyguard was blocking the younger man's attempt to
get closer to Ruby. At the same time the other bodyguard had whipped open the passenger door to a long
sleek limousine.

'I can't possibly get into a car with a stranger,' Ruby
objected, trying not to stare at the sheer size and opulence of the car and its interior.

Raja was unaccustomed to meeting with such suspicious treatment and it off balanced him for it was
not what he had expected from her. In truth he had

expected her to scramble eagerly into the limo and
gush about the built-in bar while helping herself to his
champagne like the usual women he dated. But if the
angry lovelorn young man shouting Ruby's name was
typical of the men she met perhaps she was sensible
to be mistrustful of his sex.

'I live close by. I'll walk back home first and meet
you there.' Ruby gave him her address and sped across
the street at a smart pace, deliberately not turning her
head or looking back when Steve called her name.

The prince watched her walk away briskly. The
breeze blew back her hair in a glorious fan of golden
strands and whipped pink into her pale cheeks. She had
big eyes the colour of milk chocolate and the sort of
lashes that graced cartoon characters in the films that
Raja's youngest relatives loved to watch. A conspicu-
ously feminine woman, she had a small waist and fine
curves above and below it. Great legs, delicate at ankle
and knee. He wondered if Steve had lain between those
legs and the shock of that startlingly intimate thought
sliced through Raja as the limo wafted him past and he
got a last look at her. A woman with a face and body
like that would make an arranged marriage tempting
to any hot-blooded male, he told himself impatiently.
And just at that moment Raja's blood was running very
hot indeed and there was a heavy tightness at his groin
that signified a rare loss of control for him.

Ruby took Hermione out on her lead and by the time
she unlocked the front door again, with the little black-
and-white dog trotting at her heels, the limousine was
parked outside waiting for her. This time she noticed
that as well as the bodyguard in the front passenger

seat there was also a separate car evidently packed with bodyguards parked behind it. Why was so much security necessary? Who was this guy? For the first time it occurred to Ruby that this particular visitor had to be someone more important than Wajid Sulieman and his wife. Certainly he travelled in much greater style. Checking her watch then, she frowned. There really wasn't time for her to have lunch with anyone and she dug out her phone to ring work and ask if she could take an extended lunch hour. The office manager advanced grudging agreement only after she promised to catch up with her work by staying later that evening.

As she stood in the doorway, Hermione having retreated to her furry basket in the living room, the passenger door of the limo was opened by one of the bodyguards. Biting her full lower lip in confusion, Ruby finally pulled the door of her home closed behind her and crossed the pavement.

'I really do need to know who you are,' she spelt out tautly.

For the first time in more years than he cared to recall, Raja had the challenge of introducing himself.

'Raja and you're a prince?' she repeated blankly, his complex surname leaving her head as soon as she heard the unfamiliar syllables. 'But *who* are you?'

His wide, sensual mouth quirked and he surrendered to the inevitable. 'I'm the man Wajid Sulieman wants you to marry.'

And so great was the surprise of that admission that Ruby got into the car and sat back without further comment. This gorgeous guy was the man they wanted her to marry? He bore no resemblance whatsoever to her vague imaginings.

'Obviously you're from the other country, Najar,' she specified, recovering her ready tongue. 'A member of their royal family?'

'I am acting Regent of Najar. My father, King Ahmed, suffered a serious stroke some years ago and is now an invalid. I carry out his role in public because he is no longer able to do so.'

Ruby grasped the fine distinction he was making. Although his father suffered from ill health the older man remained the power behind the throne, doubtless restricting his son's ability to make his own decisions. Was that why Raja was willing to marry a stranger? Was he eager to assume power in Ashur where he could rule without his father's interference? Ruby hated being so ignorant. But what did she know about the politics of power and influence within the two countries?

One thing was for sure, however, Raja was very far from being the poor and accommodating royal hanger-on she had envisaged. Entrapped by her growing curiosity, she stole a long sidewise glance at him, noting the curling density of his lush black lashes, the high sculpted cheekbones that gave his profile such definition, the stubborn set of his masculine jaw line. Young, no more than thirty years of age at most, she estimated. Young, extremely good-looking *and* rich if the car and the security presence were anything to go by, she reasoned, all of which made it even harder for her to understand why he would be willing to even consider an arranged marriage.

'Someone digs up a total stranger, who just happens

to be a long-lost relative of the Shakarian family, and you're immediately willing to marry her?' she jibed.

'I have very good reasons for my compliance and that is why I was willing to fly here to speak to you personally,' Raja fielded with more than a hint of quelling ice in his deep, dark drawl and he waved a hand in a fluid gesture of emphasis that caught her attention. His movements were very graceful and yet amazingly masculine at the same time. He commanded her attention in a way she had never experienced before.

An involuntary flush at that reflection warmed Ruby's cheeks, for in general aggressively male men irritated her. Her stepfather had been just such a man, full of sports repartee, beer and sexist comments while he perved on her behind closed doors. 'Nothing you could say is likely to change my mind,' she warned Raja ruefully.

Unsettled by the effect he had on her and feeling inordinately like an insecure teenager, Ruby lowered her eyes defensively and her gaze fell on the male leg positioned nearest to hers. The fine, expensive material of his tailored trousers outlined the lean, muscular power of his thigh while the snug fit over the bulge at his crotch defined his male attributes. As soon as she realised where her attention had lodged she glanced hurriedly away, her face hot enough to fry eggs on and shock reverberating through her, for it was the very first time she had looked at a man as if he were solely a sex object. When she thought of how she hated men checking her out she could only feel embarrassed.

The prince took her to the town's only decent hotel for lunch. He attracted a good deal of attention there, particularly from women, Ruby registered with grow-ing irritation. It didn't help that he walked across the busy dining room like the royal prince that he was, emanating a positive force field of sleek sophistication and assurance that set him apart from more ordinary mortals. Beside him she felt seriously underdressed in her plain skirt and raincoat. She just knew the other female diners were looking at her and wondering what such a magnificent male specimen was doing with her. The head waiter seated them in a quiet alcove where, mercifully, Ruby felt less on show and more at ease.

While they ate, and the food was excellent, Raja began to tell her about the war between Najar and Ashur and the current state of recovery in her birth country. The whole time he talked her attention was locked on him. It was as if they were the only two peo-ple left on the planet. He shifted a shapely hand and she wondered what it would feel like to have that hand touching her body. The surprise of the thought made her face flame. She absorbed the velvet nuances of his accented drawl and recognised that he had a beauti-ful speaking voice. But worst of all when she met the steady glitter of his dark, reflective, midnight gaze she felt positively light-headed and her mouth ran dry.

'Ashur's entire infrastructure was ruined and un-employment and poverty are rising,' Raja spelt out. 'Ashur needs massive investment to rebuild the roads, hospitals and schools that have been destroyed. Najar will make that investment but only if you and I marry. Peace was agreed solely on the basis of a marriage that would eventually unite our two countries as one.'

Gulping down some water in an attempt to ground

herself to planet earth again, Ruby was surprised by the willpower she had to muster simply to drag her gaze from his darkly handsome features and she said in an almost defiant tone, 'That's completely crazy.'

The prince angled his proud dark head in a position that signified unapologetic disagreement. 'Far from it. It is at present the only effective route to reconciliation which can be undertaken without either country losing face.' As he made that statement his classic cheekbones were taut with tension, accentuating the smooth planes of the olive-tinted skin stretched over his superb bone structure.

'Obviously I can see that nobody with a brain would want the war to kick off again,' Ruby cut in ruefully, more shaken than she was prepared to admit by the serious nature of Ashur's plight. She had not appreciated how grave the problems might be and even though the ruling family of her birth country had refused to acknowledge her existence, she was ashamed of the level of her ignorance.

'Precisely, and that is where *our* role comes in,' Raja imparted smoothly. 'Ashur can only accept my country's economic intervention if it comes wrapped in the reassurance of a traditional royal marriage.'

Ruby nodded in comprehension, her expression carefully blank as she asked what was for her the obvious question. 'So what's going to happen when this marriage fails to take place?'

In the dragging silence that fell in receipt of that leading query, his brilliant dark eyes narrowed and his lean, strong face took on a forbidding aspect. 'As the marriage was an established element of the peace accord, many will argue that if no marriage takes place the agreement has broken down and hostilities could easily break out again. Our families are well respected. Given the right approach, we could act as a unifying force and our people would support us in that endeavour for the sake of a lasting peace.'

'And you're willing to sacrifice your own freedom for the sake of that peace?' Ruby asked, wearing a dubious expression.

'It is not a choice. It is a duty,' Raja pronounced with a fluid shift of his beautifully shaped fingers. He said more with his hands than with his tongue, Ruby decided, for that eloquent gesture encompassed his complete acceptance of a sacrifice he clearly saw as unavoidable.

Ruby surveyed him steadily before saying without hesitation, 'I think that's a load of nonsense. How can you be so accepting of your duty?'

Raja breathed in deep and slow before responding to her challenge. 'As a member of the royal family I have led a privileged life and I was brought up to appreciate that what is best for my country should be my prime motivation.'

Unimpressed by that zealous statement, Ruby rolled her eyes in cynical dismissal. 'Well, I haven't led a privileged life and I'm afraid I don't have that kind of motivation to fall back on. I'm not sure I can believe that you do, either.'

Under rare attack for his conservative views and for the depth of his sincerity, Raja squared his broad shoulders, his lean, dark features setting hard. He was offended but determined to keep his emotions in check.

He suspected that the real problem was that Ruby rarely thought before she spoke and he virtually never met with challenge or criticism. 'Meaning?'

'Did you fight in the war?' Ruby prompted suddenly.

'Yes.'

Ruby's appetite ebbed and she rested back in her chair, milk-chocolate eyes telegraphing her contempt in a look that her quarry was not accustomed to receiving.

His tough jaw line clenched. 'That is the reality of war.'

'And now you think you can buy your way out of that reality by marrying me and becoming a saviour where you were once the aggressor?' Ruby fired back with a curled lip as she pushed away her plate. 'Sorry, I have no intention of being a pawn in a power struggle or of helping you to come to terms with your conscience. I'd like to leave now.'

On a wave of angry frustration Raja studied her truculent little face, his glittering eyes hostile. 'You haven't listened to me—'

Confident of her own opinion, Ruby lifted her chin in direct challenge of that charge. 'On the contrary, I've listened and I've heard as much as I need to hear. I can't be the woman you want me to be. I'm not a princess and I have no desire to sacrifice myself for the people or the country that broke my mother's heart.'

At that melodramatic response, Raja only just resisted the urge to groan out loud. 'You're talking like a child.'

A red-hot flush ran up to the very roots of Ruby's pale hair. 'How dare you?' she ground out, outraged.

'I dare because I need you to think like an adult to deal with this dilemma. You may be prejudiced against the country where you were born but don't drag up old history as an excuse—'

'There's nothing old about the way I grew up without a father,' Ruby argued vehemently, starting to rise from her chair in tune with her rapidly rising temper. 'Or the fact that he married another woman while he was still married to my mum! If that's what you call prejudice then I'm not ashamed to own up to it!'

'Lower your voice and sit down!' the prince ground out in a biting undertone.

Ruby was so stunned by that command that she instinctively fell back into her seat and stared across the table at him with a shaken frown of disbelief that he could think he had the right to order her around. 'Don't speak to me like that—'

'Then calm down and think of those less fortunate than you are.'

'It still won't make me willing to marry a stranger, who would marry a dancing bear if he was asked!' Ruby shot back at him angrily.

'What on earth are you trying to suggest?' Raja demanded, dark eyes blazing like angry golden flames above them.

More than ready to tell him what she thought of him, Ruby tossed down her napkin with a positive flourish. 'Did you think that I would be too stupid to work out what you're really after?' she asked him sharply. 'You want the throne in Ashur and I'm the only way you have of getting it! Without me and a ring on my finger, you get nothing!'

Subjecting her to a stunned look of proud incredulity, Raja watched with even greater astonishment as Ruby plunged upright, abandoned their meal and stalked away, hair flying, narrow back rigid, skirt riding up on those slender shapely thighs. Had she no manners? No concept of restraint in public places? She actually believed that he *wanted* the throne in Ashur? Was that her idea of a joke? She had no grasp of realities whatsoever. He was the future hereditary ruler of one of the most sophisticated and rich countries in the Persian Gulf, he did not need to rule Ashur, as well.

A BRISK WALK of twenty minutes brought Ruby back to work. A little breathless and flustered after the time she had had to consider that fiery exchange over lunch, she was still trying to decide whether or not she had been unfair in her assessment of Prince Raja. Waiting on her desktop for her attention was a pile of work, however, and her head was already aching from the stress of the information he had dumped on her.

At spare moments during the afternoon that followed she mulled over what she had learned about her birth country's predicament. It was not her fault all that had happened between Ashur and Najar, was it? But if Raja was correct and the peace broke down over the reality that their marriage and therefore the planned unification of the two countries did not take place, how would she feel about things then? That was a much less straightforward question and Ruby resolved to do some Internet research that evening to settle the questions she needed answered.

While Stella was cooking a late dinner, Ruby lifted

the laptop the two young women shared, let Hermione curl up by her feet and sought information on the
recent events in Ashur. Unfortunately a good deal of
what she discovered was distressing stuff. Her late father's country, Ashur, she slowly recognised, desperately needed help getting back on its feet and people
everywhere were praying that the peace would hold.
Reading a charity worker's blog about the rising number of homeless people and orphans, Ruby felt tears
sting her eyes and she blinked them back hurriedly and
went to eat her dinner without an appetite. She could
tell herself that Ashur was nothing to do with her but
she was learning that her gut reaction was not guided
by intellect. The war might be over but there was a huge
job of rebuilding to be done and not enough resources
to pay for it. In the meantime the people of Ashur were
suffering. Could the future of an entire country and its
people be resting on what she chose to do?

Sobered by that thought and the heavy responsibility that accompanied it, Ruby started to carefully
consider her possible options. Stella ate and hurried
out on a date. While Ruby was still deep in thought
and tidying up the tiny kitchen, the doorbell buzzed.
This time she was not surprised to find Najar's much-
decorated fighter-pilot prince on her doorstep again, for
even she was now prepared to admit that they still had
stuff to talk about. The sheer, dark masculine beauty of
his bronzed features still took her by storm though and
mesmerised her into stunned stillness. Those lustrous
eyes set between sooty lashes in that stunningly masculine face exerted a powerful magnetic pull. She felt
a tug at the heart of her and a prickling surge of heat.

Once again, dragging her attention from him was like trying to leap single-handed out of a swamp.

'You'd better come in—we have to talk,' she acknowledged in a brittle breathless aside, exasperated by the way he made her stare and turning on her heel with hot cheeks to leave him to follow her.

'It's rude in my culture to turn your back on a guest or on royalty,' Raja informed her almost carelessly.

With a sound of annoyance, Ruby whipped her blonde head around to study him with frowning brown eyes. 'We have bigger problems than my ignorance of etiquette!'

As the tall, powerful man entered the room in Ruby's wake Hermione peered out of her basket, beady, dark eyes full of suspicion. A low warning growl vibrated in the dog's throat.

'No!' Ruby told her pet firmly.

'You were expecting my visit,' Raja acknowledged, taking a seat at her invitation and striving not to notice the way her tight black leggings and shrunken tee hugged her pert, rounded curves at breast and hip. The fluffy pink bunny slippers she wore on her tiny feet, however, made him compress his handsome mouth. He did not want to be reminded of just how young and unprepared she was for the role being offered to her.

Ruby breathed in deep, fighting the arrowing slide of shameless awareness keeping her unnaturally tense as she took a seat opposite him. Even at rest, the intoxicating strength of his tall, long-limbed, muscular body was obvious and she was suddenly conscious that her nipples had tightened into hard bullet points. She sucked in another breath, desperate to regain her usual composure. 'Yes, I was expecting you.'

Raja did not break the silence when her voice faltered. He waited patiently for her to continue with a quality of confident cool and calm that she found fantastically sexy.

'It's best if I lay my cards on the table this time. First of all, I would never, *ever* be prepared to agree to a normal marriage with a stranger, so that option isn't even a possibility,' Ruby declared without apology, knowing that she needed to tell him that upfront. 'But if you genuinely believe that only our marriage could ensure peace for Ashur, I feel I have to consider some way of bringing that about that we can both live with.'

Approbation gleamed in Raja's dark gaze because he believed that she was finally beginning to see sense. He was also in the act of reflecting that he could contrive to live with her without any great problem. He pinned his attention to the stunning contours of her face while remaining painfully aware of the full soft, rounded curves of her unbound breasts outlined in thin cotton. Clear indentations in the fabric marked the pointed evidence of her nipples and the flame of nagging heat at his groin would not quit. Angry at his loss of concentration at so important a meeting, however, he compressed his wide, sensual mouth and willed his undisciplined body back under his control.

'I *do* believe that only our marriage can give our countries the hope of an enduring peace,' he admitted. 'But if you are not prepared to consider a normal marriage, what are you suggesting?'

'A total fake,' Ruby replied without hesitation, a

hint of amusement lightening her unusually serious eyes. 'I marry you and we make occasional public appearances together to satisfy expectations but behind closed doors we're just pretending to be an ordinary married couple.'

The prince concealed his surprise and mastered his expression lest he make the mistake of revealing that inflicting such a massive deception on so many people would be abhorrent to his principles. 'A platonic arrangement?'

Ruby nodded with enthusiasm. 'No offence intended but I'm really not into sex—'

'With me? Or with anyone?' Raja could not resist demanding that she make that distinction.

'Anyone. It's nothing personal,' she hastened to assure a male who was taking it all very personally indeed. 'And it will also give you the perfect future excuse to divorce me.'

Hopelessly engaged in wondering what had happened to her to give her such a distaste for intimacy, Raja frowned in bewilderment. 'How?'

'Well, obviously there won't be a child. I'm not stupid, Raja. Obviously if we get married a son and heir is what everyone will be hoping for,' she pointed out wryly. 'But when there is no pregnancy and no child, you can use that as a very good reason to divorce me and then marry someone much more suitable.'

'It would not be that simple. I fully understand where you got this idea from though,' he imparted wryly. 'But while your father may have divorced your mother in such circumstances, there has never been a divorce within my family and our people and yours would be very much shocked and disturbed by such a development.'

Ruby shrugged a slight shoulder in disinterested dismissal of that possibility. 'There isn't going to be a *perfect* solution to our dilemma,' she told him impatiently. 'And I think that a fake marriage could well be as good as it gets. Take it or leave it, Raja.'

Raja almost laughed out loud at that impudent closing speech. What a child she still was! He could only begin to imagine how deeply offended the Ashuri people would be were he to divorce their princess while seeking to continue to rule their country. What she was suggesting was only a stopgap solution, not a permanent remedy to the dilemma.

'Well, that's one angle but not the only one,' Ruby continued ruefully. 'I have to be very blunt here…'

An unexpected grin slanted across Raja's beautifully moulded mouth, for in his opinion she had already been exceedingly frank. 'By all means, be blunt.'

'I would have to have equal billing in the ruling stakes,' she told him squarely. 'I can't see how you can be trusted to look out for the interests of both countries when you're from Najar. You would have an unfair advantage. I will only agree to marry you if I have as much of a say in all major decisions as you do.'

'That is a revolutionary idea and not without its merits,' Raja commented, striving not to picture Wajid Sulieman's shattered face when he learned that his princess was not, after all, prepared to be a powerless puppet on the throne. 'You should have that right but it will not be easy to convince the councils of old men, who act as the real government in our respective countries. In addition, you will surely concede that you know nothing about our culture—'

'But I can certainly learn,' Ruby broke in with stubborn determination. 'Well, those are my terms.'

'You won't negotiate?' the prince prompted.

'There is no room for negotiation.'

Raja was grimly amused by that uncompromising stance. In many ways it only emphasised her naivety. She assumed that she could break all the rules and remain untouched by the consequences yet she had no idea of what real life was like in her native country. Without that knowledge she could not understand how much was at stake. He knew his own role too well to require advice on how to respond to her demands.

Royal life had taught him early that he did not have the luxury of personal choice. His primary duty was to persuade the princess to take up her official role in Ashur and to marry her, twin objectives that he was expected to achieve by using any and every means within his power. His father had made it clear that the need for peace must overrule every other consideration. Any natural reluctance to agree to a celibate marriage in a society where extramarital sex was regarded as a serious evil did not even weigh in the balance.

I'm really not into sex, she had confided and, like any man, he was intrigued. Since she could not make such an announcement and still be an innocent he could only assume that she had suffered from the attentions of at least one clumsy lover. Far from being an amateur in the same field, Raja surveyed her with a gleam of sensual speculation in his dark eyes. He was convinced that given the right opportunity he could change her mind on that score.

'Well, what do you think?' Ruby pressed edgily as she rose to her feet again.

'I will consider your proposition,' the prince conceded non-committally, springing upright to look down at her with hooded, dark eyes.

His ability to conceal his thoughts from his lean, dark features infuriated Ruby, who had always found the male sex fairly easy to read. For once she had not a clue what a man might be thinking and her ignorance intimidated and frustrated her. Like the truly stunning dark good looks that probably turned heads wherever he went, the prince's reticence was one of his most noticeable attributes. He had the skills of a natural-born diplomat, she conceded, grudgingly recognising how well equipped he was to deal with opposing viewpoints and sensitive political issues.

'I thought time was a real matter of concern,' Ruby could not help remarking, irritated by his silence.

A highly attractive grin slanted his wide sensual mouth. 'If you give me your phone number I will contact you later this evening with my answer.'

Ruby gave him that information and walked out to the front door. As she began to open it he rested a hand on her shoulder, staying her, and she glanced up from below her lashes, eyes questioning. Hermione growled. Raja ignored the animal, sliding his hand lightly down Ruby's arm and up again, his handsome head lowering, his proud gaze glittering as bright as diamonds from below the fringe of his dense black lashes. She stopped breathing, moving, even thinking, trapped in

the humming silence while a buzz of excitement unlike anything she had ever experienced trailed along
her nerve endings like a taunting touch.

His breath warmed her cheek and she focused on
his strong sensual mouth, the surge of heat and warmth
between her thighs going crazy. Desire was shooting
through her veins like adrenaline and she didn't understand it, couldn't control it either, any more than
she could defy the temptation to rest up against him,
palms spread across his chest to absorb the muscular
strength of his powerful frame and remain upright.
Eyes wide, she stared up at him, trembling with anticipation and he did not disappoint her. On the passage to her mouth his lips grazed the pulse quivering
in her neck and an almost violent shimmy of sensation
shot down through her slight length. His hand sliding
down to her waist to steady her, he circled her mouth
with a kiss as hot as a blowtorch. The heat of his passion sent a shock wave of sexual response spiralling
down straight into her pelvis.

Raja only lifted his head again when Hermione's
noisy assault on his ankles became too violent to ignore. 'Call off your dog,' he urged her huskily.

Grateful for the excuse to move, Ruby wasted no
time in capturing her snarling pet and depositing her
back in the living room. Her hands were shaking. Nervous perspiration beaded her upper lip. Ruby was in
serious shock from finally feeling what a man had
never made her feel before. She was still light-headed
from the experience, and her temper surged when she
caught Raja studying her intently. Consumed by a sense
of foolishness, she was afraid that he might have no-

ticed that she was trembling and her condemnation was shrill. 'You had no right to touch me!'

His lustrous dark eyes glinted like rapier blades over her angry face. 'I had no right but I was very curious,' he countered with a studied insolence that pushed a tide of colour into her cheeks. 'And you were worth the risk.'

A moment later he was gone and she closed the door, only just resisting the urge to slam it noisily. She was still as wound up as a clock spring. Men didn't speak to Ruby in that condescending tone and they rarely, if ever, offered her provocation. Invariably they tried to please her and utilised every ploy from flattery to gifts to achieve that end. Raja, on the other hand, had subjected her to a cool measuring scrutiny and had remained resolutely unimpressed and in control while she fell apart and she could only hate him for that: *she* had shown weakness and susceptibility, he had not.

Her phone rang at eleven when she was getting ready for bed.

'It's Raja.' His dark drawl was very businesslike in tone and delivery. 'I hope you're prepared to move quickly on this as time is of the essence.'

Taut with strain and with her teeth gritted, for it was an effort to be polite to him with her pride still stinging from that kiss that she had failed to rebuff, Ruby said stiffly, 'That depends on whether or not you're prepared to stand by my terms.'

'You have my agreement. While I make arrangements for our marriage to take place here—'

'Like soon...*now*? And we're to get married *here*?'

Ruby interrupted, unable to swallow back her astonishment.

'It would be safer and more straightforward if the
deed were already done before you even set foot in
Ashur because our respective representatives will very
likely quarrel about the when and the where and the
how of our wedding for months on end,' the prince informed her wryly. 'In those circumstances, staging a
quiet ceremony here in the UK makes the most sense.'

Infuriatingly at home giving orders and impervious
to her tart comments, Raja advised her to resign from
her job immediately and start packing. Ruby stayed
out of bed purely to tell Stella that she was getting
married. Her friend was stunned and less moved than
Ruby by stories of Ashur's current instability and economic hardship.

'You're not thinking about what you're doing,' Stella
exclaimed, her pretty face troubled. 'You've let this
prince talk you round. He made you feel bad but, let's
face it, your life is here. What's your father's country
got to do with you?'

Only forty-eight hours earlier, Ruby would have
agreed with that sentiment. But matters were not so cut
and dried now. Ashur's problems were no longer distant, impersonal issues and she could not ignore their
claim on her conscience. In her mind the suffering
there now bore the faces of the ordinary people whose
lives had been ruined by the long conflict.

Ruby compressed her generous mouth. 'I just feel
that if I can do something to help, I should do it. It
won't be a proper marriage, for goodness' sake.'

'You might get over there and find out that the prince already has a wife,' Stella said with a curled lip.

'I don't think so. He wouldn't be here if I wasn't needed.'

Unaccustomed to Ruby being so serious, Stella pulled a face. 'Well, look what happened to your mother when she married a man from a different culture.'

'But Mum was in love while I would just be acting out a role. I won't get hurt the way she did. I'm not stuffed full of stupid romantic ideas,' Ruby declared, her chin coming up. 'I'm much tougher and I can look after myself.'

'I suppose you know yourself best,' Stella conceded, taken aback by Ruby's vehemence.

Ruby couldn't sleep that night. The idea of marrying Najar's Prince still felt unreal. She could have done without her friend's honest reminder that her mother's royal marriage had gone badly wrong. Although Ruby knew that she had absolutely no romantic interest in Raja and was therefore safe from being hurt or disappointed by him, she could not forget the heartbreak her mother had suffered when she had attempted to adapt to a very different way of life.

At the same time the haunting images Ruby had seen of the devastation in Ashur kept her awake until the early hours. The plight of her father's people was the only reason she was willing to agree to such a marriage, she reflected ruefully. Even though she was being driven by good intentions the prospect of marrying a prince and making her home in a strange land filled her to overflowing with doubts and insecurity.

In recent years she had often regretted the lack of excitement in her life, but now all of a sudden she was being confronted with the truth of that old adage: *Be careful of what you wish for....*

CHAPTER THREE

THE SALESWOMAN DISPLAYED a ghastly, shapeless plum-coloured suit that could only have pleased a woman who had lost interest in her appearance. Of course it was not the saleswoman's fault, Ruby reasoned in growing frustration; it was Raja's insistence on the outfit being 'very conservative and plain' that had encouraged the misunderstanding of what Ruby might be prepared to wear at her wedding.

'That's not me, that's really not my style!' Ruby declared with a grimace.

'Then choose something and quickly,' the prince urged in an impatient aside for he was not a patient shopper. 'Show some initiative!'

Raja did not understand why what she wore should matter so much. After all, even in her current outfit of faded jeans and a blue sweater she looked beautiful enough in his opinion to stop traffic. Luxuriant honey-blonde hair tumbled round her narrow shoulders. Denim moulded her curvy derrière and slim thighs, wool cupped the swell of her pouting breasts and emphasised her small waist. Even unadorned, she had buckets of utterly natural sex appeal. As he recognised the swelling heaviness of arousal at his groin his lean dark features clenched hard and he fixed his attention on the wall instead.

Show some initiative? Dull coins of aggravated red blossomed over Ruby's cheekbones and her sultry pink mouth compressed. Where did someone who had so far dismissed all her helpful suggestions get the nerve to taunt her with her lack of initiative? It was only an hour and a half since she had met her future husband at his hotel to sign the various forms that would enable them to get married in a civil ceremony and he was already getting on her nerves so much that she wanted to kill him! Or at the very least kick him! A high-ranking London diplomat had also attended that meeting to explain that a special licence was being advanced to facilitate their speedy marriage. Raja, she had learned, enjoyed diplomatic immunity. He was equally immune, she was discovering, to any sense of fashion or any appreciation of female superiority.

Stalking up to the rail of the town's most expensive boutique, Ruby began to leaf through it, eventually pulling a red suit out. 'I'll try this one on.'

The prince's beautifully shaped mouth curled. 'It is very bright.'

'You did say that a formal publicity photo would be taken and I don't want to vanish into the woodwork,' Ruby told him sweetly, big brown eyes wide with innocence but swiftly narrowing to stare intently at his glorious face. He was gorgeous. That fabulous bone structure and those dark deep-set eyes set below that slightly curly but ruthlessly cropped black hair took her breath away every time.

The saleswoman took the suit to hang it in a dressing room. With fluid grace Raja lifted his hand and let his thumb graze along the fullness of Ruby's luscious lower lip. His dark eyes glittered hot as coals as he felt that softness and remembered the sweet heady taste of that succulent mouth beneath his own. Tensing, Ruby dealt him a startled look, her lips tingling at his touch while alarm tugged at her nerves. As his hand dropped she moved closer and muttered in taut warning, 'This is business, just business between us.'

'Business,' the prince repeated, his accent scissoring round the label like a razor-sharp blade. Business was straightforward and Ruby Shakarian was anything but. He watched her sashay into the dressing room, little shoulders squared, hair bouncing, all cheeky attitude and surplus energy. He wanted to laugh but he had far too much tact. He didn't agree with her description. Business? No, he wanted to have sex with her. He wanted to have sex with her very, very much. He knew that and accepted it as a natural consequence of his male libido. Desire was a predictable response in a young and healthy man when he was with a beautiful woman. It was also a positive advantage in a royal marriage. Sex was sex, after all, little more than an entertaining means to an end when children were required. Finer feelings were neither required nor advisable. Been there, done that, Raja acknowledged in a bleak burst of recollection from the past. He had had his heart broken once and had sworn he would never put it up for a woman's target practice again.

Even so, once Ruby was his wife Raja had every intention of ensuring that the marriage followed a much more conventional path than she presently intended.

Obviously he didn't want a divorce. A divorce would mean he had failed in his duty, failed his family and *failed* his very country. He breathed in deep and slow at that aggrieved acknowledgement, mentally tasting the bite of such a far-reaching failure and striving not to flinch from it. After all there was only so much that he *could* do. It was unfair that so much should rest on his ability to make a success of an arranged marriage but Raja al-Somari had long understood that life was rarely fair. The bottom line was that he and everyone who depended on them needed their prince and princess to build a relationship with a future. And a fake marriage could never achieve that objective.

Over the three days that followed Ruby was much too busy to get cold feet about the upheaval in her life. She resigned from her job without much regret and began packing, systematically working through all her possessions and discarding the clutter while Stella lamented her approaching departure and placed an ad in the local paper for a new housemate. The day before the wedding, Hermione, accompanied by her favourite squeaky toy and copious instructions regarding her care and diet, was collected to be transported out to Ashur in advance. The memory of her pet's frightened little eyes above her greying muzzle as she looked out through the barred door of her pet carrier kept her mistress awake that night.

The wedding was staged with the maximum possible discretion in a private room at the hotel with two diplomats acting as official witnesses. Accompanied only by Stella, Ruby arrived and took her place by Raja's side. His black hair displaying a glossy blue-black sheen below the lights, dark eyes brilliant shards of light between the thick fringe of his lashes, Raja looked impossibly handsome in a formal, dark pin-stripe suit. When he met her appraisal he didn't smile and his lean bronzed features remained grave. She wondered what he was thinking. Not knowing annoyed her. Her heart was beating uncomfortably fast by the time that the middle-aged registrar began the short service. Raja slid a gold ring onto her finger and because it was too big she had to crook her finger to keep the ring from falling off. The poorly fitting ring struck her as an appropriate addition to a ceremony that, shorn of all bridal and emotional frills, left her feeling distinctly unmarried.

It was done, goal achieved, Raja reflected with considerable satisfaction. His bride had not succumbed to a last-minute change of heart as he had feared. He studied Ruby's delicately drawn profile with appreciation. She might look fragile as a wild flower but she had a core of steel, for she had given her word and although he had sensed her mounting tension and uncertainty she had defied his expectations and stuck to it.

One of the diplomats shook Ruby's hand and addressed her as 'Your Royal Highness', which felt seriously weird to her.

'I'm never ever going to be able to see you as a princess,' Stella confided with a giggle.

'Give Ruby time,' Raja remarked silkily.

Colour tinged Ruby's cheeks. 'I'm not going to change, Stella.'

'Of course you will,' the prince contradicted with unassailable confidence, escorting his bride over to a floral display on a table where the photographer awaited them. 'You're about to enter a different life and I believe you'll pick up the rules quickly. Smile.'

'Raja,' Ruby whispered sweetly, and as he inclined his arrogant, dark head down to hers she snapped, '*Don't* tell me what to do!'

'Petty,' he told her smoothly, his shrewd gaze encompassing the photographer within earshot.

And foolish as it was over so minor an exchange, Ruby's blood boiled in her veins. She hated that sensation of being ignorant and in the position that she was likely to do something wrong. Even more did she hate being bossed around and told what to do and Raja al-Somari rapped out commands to the manner born. No doubt she would make the occasional mistake but she was determined to learn even quicker than he expected for both their sakes.

Chin at a defiant angle, Ruby gave Stella a quick hug, promised to phone and climbed into the limousine to travel to the airport. She would have liked the chance to change into something more comfortable in which to travel but Raja had stopped her from doing so, advising her that while she was in her official capacity as a princess of Ashur and his wife she was on duty and had to embrace the conservative wardrobe. His wife, Ruby thought in a daze of disbelief, thinking back to the previous week when she had been kissing Steve in his car. How could her life have changed so much in so short a time?

But she comforted herself with the knowledge that she wasn't *really* his wife, she was only pretending. Boarding the unbelievably opulent private jet awaiting them and seeing the unconcealed curiosity in the eyes of the cabin staff, Ruby finally appreciated that pretending to be a princess married to Raja was likely to demand a fair degree of acting from her. Instead of kicking off her shoes and curling up in one of the cream leather seats in the cabin, she found herself sitting down sedately and striving for a dignified pose for the first time in her life.

Soon after take-off, Raja rose from his seat and settled a file down in front of her. 'I asked my staff to prepare this for you.' He flipped it open. 'It contains photos and names for the main members of the two royal households and various VIPs in both countries as well as other useful information—'

'Homework,' Ruby commented dulcetly. 'To think I thought I'd left that behind when I left school.'

'Careful preparation should make the transition a little easier for you.'

Ruby could not credit how many names and faces he expected her to memorise, and the lengthy sections encompassing history, geography and culture in both countries made distinctly heavy reading. After a light lunch was served, Ruby took a break and watched Raja working on his laptop, lean fingers deft and fast. Her husband? It still didn't feel credible. His black lashes shaded his eyes like silk fans and when he glanced at her with those dark deep-set eyes that gleamed like polished bronze, something tripped in her throat and strangled her breathing. He was drop-dead gorgeous and naturally she was staring. Any woman would, she told herself irritably. She didn't fancy him; she did *not*.

Raja left the main cabin to change and reappeared

in a white, full-length, desert-style robe worn with a headdress bound with a black and gold cord.

'You look just like you're starring in an old black-and-white movie set in the desert,' she confided helplessly, totally taken aback by the transformation.

'That is not a comment I would repeat in Najar, where such a mode of dress is the norm,' Raja advised her drily. 'I do not flaunt a Western lifestyle at home.'

Embarrassment stirring red heat in her cheeks, Ruby dealt him a look of annoyance. 'Or a sense of humour.'

But in truth there was nothing funny about his appearance. He actually looked amazingly dignified and royal and shockingly handsome. Even so his statement that he did not follow a Western lifestyle sent an arrow of apprehension winging through her. What other surprises might lie in wait for her?

A few minutes later he warned her that the jet would be landing in Najar in thirty minutes. When she returned after freshening up he announced with the utmost casualness that they would be parting once the jet landed. She would be flying straight on to Ashur where he would join her later in the week.

Ruby was shattered by that unexpected news and her head swivelled, eyes filled with disbelief. 'You're leaving me to travel on alone to Ashur?'

'Only for thirty-six hours at most. I'm afraid that I can't be in two places at once.'

'Even on what's supposed to be our wedding night?' Ruby launched at him.

The prince shut his laptop and shot her a veiled look as silky as melted honey and somehow that appraisal made her tummy perform acrobatics. 'Are you offering me one?'

The silence simmered like a kettle on the boil. Her cheeks washed with heat, Ruby scrambled to her feet. 'Of course, I'm not!'

'I thought not. So, what's the problem? The exact date of our marriage will not be publicly announced. Very few people will be aware that this is our wedding night.'

Ruby almost screamed. He was not that stupid. He was seriously not that stupid and his casual reaction to her criticism enraged her. She breathed in so deep and long she was vaguely surprised that her head didn't lift off her shoulders and float. 'You're asking me what the problem is? Is that a joke?'

Raja uncoiled from his seat with the fluid grace of a martial arts expert. Standing very straight and tall, broad shoulders hard as a blade, Raja rested cool eyes on her, for he was not accustomed to being shouted at and he was in no mood to become accustomed to the experience. 'Naturally I am not joking.'

'And you can't see anything wrong with dumping me with a bunch of strangers in a foreign country? I don't know anyone, don't speak the language, don't even know *how* to behave,' Ruby yelled back at him full volume, causing the steward entering the cabin with a trolley to hastily backtrack and close the door again. 'How can you abandon me like that?'

The prince gazed down at her with frowning dark eyes, exasperated by her ignorance. Clearly she had no concept of the extensive planning and detailed security arrangements that accompanied his every movement and that would soon apply equally to hers. Familiar as Raja was with the military precision of planning a royal schedule set in stone often months in advance, he saw no room for manoeuvre or a change of heart. 'Abandon you? How am I abandoning you?'

Made to feel as if she was being melodramatic, Ruby reddened and pursed her sultry mouth. 'You're supposed to be my husband.'

Taken aback by the reminder, Raja quirked an expressive ebony brow. 'But according to you we're only faking it.'

'Well, you're not faking it worth a damn!' Ruby condemned with furious bite, strands of hair shimmying round her flushed cheekbones, eyes accusing. 'A husband should be loyal and supportive. I don't know how to be a princess yet and if I make mistakes I'm likely to offend people. Hasn't that occurred to you? You can't leave me alone in a strange place. I don't know how to give these people what they expect and deserve and I was depending on you to tell me!'

Unprepared for his gutsy bride to reveal panic, Raja frowned, setting his features into a stern mask. 'Unfortunately arrangements are already in place for us to go our separate ways this afternoon. It is virtually impossible to make last-minute changes to that schedule. We're about to land in Najar, I'm expected home and you're flying on to Ashur by yourself.'

Suddenly mortified by the nerves that had got the better of her composure, Ruby screened her apprehensive gaze and said stiffly as she took her seat with determination again, 'Fine. Don't worry about it—I'm sure I'll manage. I'm used to being on my own.'

Ruby didn't speak another word. She was furious with herself for revealing her insecurity. What on earth had she expected from him? Support? When had she ever known a man to be supportive? Raja had his own priorities and they were not the same as hers. As he had reminded her, their marriage, their very relationship, was a fake. As, to be fair, she had requested. Her soft, full mouth curved down. Clearly if she wasn't sleeping with him she was on her own and that was nothing new....

CHAPTER FOUR

THE INSTANT RUBY stepped out of the plane the heat of the sun engulfed her in a powerful wave, dewing her upper lip with perspiration and giving the skin below her clothes a sticky feeling. In the distance an architectural triumph of an airport building glinted in the sun. A man bowed low in front of her and indicated a small plane about fifty yards away. Breathing in deep and slow to steady her nerves, Ruby followed him.

At the top of the steps and mere seconds in her wake, the prince came to a dead halt, rare indecision gripping him.

'You're supposed to be my husband...loyal and supportive.'

'How can you abandon me?'

His stubborn jaw line clenched. He gritted his teeth. He could not fault her expectations. Would he not expect similar consideration from her? He was also a very masculine guy and it went against the grain to ignore her plea for help. At a time when her role was still so new to her, even a temporary separation was a bad idea. Of course she was feeling overwhelmed and he was well aware that people would be only too willing to find fault when she made innocent mistakes. He strode down the steps, addressed the court official waiting to greet him and politely ignored the surprise, dismay and the sudden burst of speech that followed his declaration of a change of plan. All the signs were that the little plane parked on the asphalt was almost ready to take off and, determined not to miss his chance to join his bride, Raja headed straight for it. His security chief ran after him only to be waved away for so small a craft had only limited room for passengers.

Ruby buckled her belt in the small, stiflingly hot compartment. She had never flown in so small a plane before and she felt utterly unnerved by her solitary state. When a young man approached her with a bent head and a tray to proffer a glass she was quick to mutter grateful thanks and grasp it, drinking down the fragrantly scented chilled drink, only to wince at the bitter aftertaste it left in her mouth. She set the empty glass back on the tray with a strained smile and the steward retreated again.

A split second later, she heard someone else board and Raja dropped down into the seat by her side. Astonished by his reappearance, Ruby twisted round to study him. 'You've changed your mind? You're coming with me?'

Raja basked in the glowing smile of instant relief and appreciation she awarded him.

Ruby recalled him asking her if she was offering him a wedding night. Although she had said no, his change of heart made her worry that they had got their wires crossed. But wasn't that a stupid suspicion to cherish? A guy with his looks would scarcely be so desperate that he would nurture such a desire for an unwilling woman.

The same young man reappeared with a second glass but when he focused on Raja, he suddenly froze and then he fell to his knees in the aisle and bowed his head very low, almost dropping the tray in the process.

Raja reached for the drink. The steward drew the tray back in apparent dismay and Raja had to lean out of his seat to grasp the glass.

'What's wrong with him?' Ruby whispered as the steward backed nervously out of the plane again. As the door slammed shut the engines began revving.

'He didn't realise who I was until he saw me up close. He must have assumed I was one of your guards when I boarded.'

The plane was turning. 'I have guards now?'

'I assume they're seated with the pilot. Of course you have guards,' Raja advanced, gulping back the drink and frowning at the acidic flavour. 'Wajid will have organised protection for you.'

As a wave of dizziness ran over Ruby she blinked and took a deep breath to clear her head. 'I'm feeling dizzy…it's probably nerves. I don't like small planes.'

'You'll be fine,' Raja reassured her.

Ruby's head was starting to feel too heavy for her neck and she propped her chin on the upturned palm of her hand.

'Are you feeling all right?' Raja asked as her head lowered.

'Just very, very tired,' she framed, her hands gripping the arms of her seat while the plane raced down the runway and rose into the air, the craft juddering while the engines roared.

'Not up to a wedding night?' Raja could not resist teasing her in an effort to take her mind off her nerves.

At that crack Ruby's head lifted and she turned to look at him. The plane was mercifully airborne.

The pupils of her eyes had shrunk to tiny pinpoints and Raja stared. 'Have you taken medication?' he asked her abruptly.

'No.' Ruby heard her voice slur. All of a sudden her tongue felt too big and clumsy for her mouth. 'Why?'

Raja could feel his own head reeling. 'There must have been something in that drink!' he exclaimed in disbelief, thrusting his hands down to rise out of the seat in one powerful movement.

'What…you…mean?' Ruby mumbled, her cheek sliding down onto her shoulder, her lashes drooping.

Raja staggered in the aisle and stretched out a hand to the door that led into the cockpit. But it was locked. Blinking rapidly, he shook his fuzzy head and hammered on the door, his arm dropping heavily down by his side again. Everything felt as if it were happening to him in slow motion. His legs crumpled beneath him and he fell on his knees, a bout of frustrated incredulous rage roaring up inside him and threatening to consume him. Ruby was slumped unconscious in her seat, her face hidden by her hair and he was in no state to protect her.

RUBY OPENED HER eyes to darkness and strange sounds. Something was flapping and creaking and she could smell leather along with the faint aromatic hint of coffee. She was totally disorientated. Add in a pounding headache and the reality that her teeth were chattering with cold and she was absolutely miserable. She began slowly to shift her stiff, aching limbs and sit up. She was fully dressed but for her shoes and the ground was hard as a rock beneath her.

'What…where am I?' she mumbled thickly, the inside of her mouth as dry as a bone.

'Ruby?' It was Raja's deep accented drawl and she stiffened nervously at the awareness of movement and rustling in the darkness.

A match was struck and an oil lamp hanging on a tent pole cast illumination on the shadowy interior and the man towering over her. She blinked rapidly, relief engulfing her when she recognised Raja's powerful physique. Adjusting to the flickering light, her eyes clung to his hard bronzed features. In shocking defiance of the cold biting into her bones *he* was bare chested, well-defined hair-roughened pectorals flexing above the corrugated musculature of his abdomen. He was wearing only boxer shorts.

'My goodness, what happened to us?' Ruby demanded starkly, shivering violently as the chill of the air settled deeper into her clammy flesh. 'What are we doing in a tent?'

Raja crouched down on a level with her, long, strong thighs splayed. His stunning bone structure, composed of razor-sharp cheekbones, slashing angles and forbidding hollows, momentarily paralysed her and she simply stared, mesmerised by a glorious masculine perfection only enhanced by a dark haze of stubble.

'We were kidnapped and dumped out in the Ashuri desert. We have no phones, no way of communicating our whereabouts—'

'K-kidnapped?' Ruby stammered through rattling teeth. 'Why on earth would anyone want to kidnap us?'

'Someone who intended to prevent our marriage.'

'But we're *already*—'

'Married,' he slotted in flatly for her, handsome mouth hardening into a look of grim restraint as if being married was the worst thing that had ever happened to him but he was too polite to mention it. 'Obviously the kidnappers weren't aware of that when they planned this outrage. Apparently they assumed that our wedding would take place at the cathedral in Simis the day after tomorrow. In fact I believe a reconciliation and blessing service is actually planned for that afternoon.'

'Oh, my word,' she framed shakily, struggling to think clearly again. 'The kidnappers were trying to *stop* us from getting married? But if we're in the desert why is it so cold?'

'It *is* very cold here at night.' He swept up the quilt lying in a heap at her feet and wrapped it round her narrow shoulders.

'You're not cold,' she breathed almost resentfully, huddling into the folds of the quilt.

'No,' he acknowledged.

'Kidnapped,' she repeated shakily. 'That's not what I came out here for.'

'It may not be a comfort but I'm convinced that no harm was intended to come to you. I was not supposed to be with you. I invited that risk by changing my travel plans at the eleventh hour and boarding the same flight,' the prince explained with sardonic cool. 'The kidnappers only wanted to prevent you from turning up for our wedding, a development which would have offended my people enough to bring protesters out into the streets.'

'So not everybody wants us to get married,' Ruby registered with a frown, shooting him an accusing glance. 'You didn't tell me that some people were so hostile to the idea of us marrying.'

'Common sense should have told you that but the objectors are in a minority in both countries.'

'How do you know all this?'

'Our captors were keen to explain their motives. The drugged drink didn't knock me out for as long as you. I began recovering consciousness as a pair of masked men were dragging us into this tent. Unfortunately I was so dizzy I could barely focus or stand and they pulled a gun on me. I don't think they had any intention of using it unless I managed to interfere with their escape,' he explained heavily and she could tell from his discomfited expression just how challenging he had found it to choose caution over courage. 'It would have been foolish to risk injury out here while you were incapacitated and without protection. I believe the men were mercenaries hired by a group of our subjects to ensure that you didn't turn up for the wedding—'

'*Our*...subjects?' she queried.

'We are in Ashur and the masked men were of Western origin... I think. Members of both royal households were aware of our travel plans so it will be hard to establish where the security leak occurred and who chose to take advantage of it and risk our lives. But it must be done—'

'At least we're not hurt.'

'That doesn't diminish the gravity of the crime.' Raja dealt her a stern appraisal. 'One of us could have had an allergic reaction to the drug we were given. Violence could have been used against us. Although our captors tried to talk as though this was intended to be a harmless prank, you might easily have suffered illness or injury alone out here. In addition, our disappearance will have cast both our countries into a very dangerous state of turmoil and panic.'

'Oh, hell,' Ruby groaned as he finished that sobering speech and she pushed her tousled hair off her brow and muttered in a small voice, 'My head hurts.'

He touched her hand, realised her fingers were cold as ice and concern indented his brow. 'I'll light a fire—there is enough wood.'

'What on earth are we going to do?'

With relaxed but economical movements, Raja began to light a small fire. 'A search for us will already have begun. The Najari air force will mount an efficient rescue mission but they have a very large area to cover. We have food and shelter. This is an oasis and *bedu* tribesmen must come here sometimes to water their flocks. Many of them have phones and could quickly summon help. I could trek out to find the nearest settlement but I am reluctant to leave you alone—'

'I would manage,' Ruby declared.

'I don't think so,' the prince told her without apology as a spark flared and he fed it with what appeared to be dried foliage. 'I will make tea.'

'I could come with you—'

'You couldn't stand the heat by day or keep up with me, which would put both of us at greater risk.'

Stymied by his conviction of her lack of stamina, Ruby dug her toes into the quilt in an effort to defrost them. 'How come you're so calm?'

'When all else fails, celebrate the positive and…we *are* safe and healthy.'

The warm drink did satisfy her thirst and drive off her inner chill though even the effort of sitting up to drink made her very aware of how tired and dizzy she still was.

'Try to get some sleep,' the prince advised.

The thin mat that was all that lay between her and the ground provided little padding. She curled up. Raja tucked the quilt round her as if she were a small child. The cold of the earth below pierced the mat, making her shiver again and, expelling his breath in an impatient hiss, Raja got below the quilt with her and melded his heated body to the back of hers.

'What are you doing?' Ruby squeaked, her slight figure stiff as a metal strut in the loose circle of his strong arms.

'There's no need for you to be cold while I am here.'

'You're not a hot-water bottle!' Ruby spat, unimpressed, her innate distrust of men rising like a shot of hot steam inside her.

'And you're not as irresistible as you seem to think,' Raja imparted silkily.

The heat of her angry suspicion blazed into mortification and if possible she became even more rigid. Ignoring the fact, Raja curled her back firmly into his amazingly warm body.

'I don't like this,' she admitted starchily.

'Neither do I,' Raja confided without skipping a beat. 'I'm more into sex than cuddling.'

Outrage glittered in her eyes in the flickering light from the dying fire. She wanted to thump him but the horrible cold was steadily receding from her body and she was afraid that she would look comically prudish if she fought physically free of his embrace.

'And just think,' Raja remarked lazily above her head. 'All those miserable old diehards who think we shouldn't be getting married will be so pleased to find out we *are* married now.'

'Why?'

'If you were still single your reputation would be ruined by spending the night out here alone with me. As it is you're a married woman and safe from the embarrassment of a scandal, if not much of a catch in the wife stakes.'

Ruby twisted her head around, brown eyes blazing. 'And what's that supposed to mean?'

'A sex ban would exude zero appeal for the average male in either one of our countries.'

'You signed up for it,' Ruby reminded him stubbornly, furious that he could be so basic that he deemed sex with a virtual stranger a necessary extra to a successful civilised relationship with a woman.

Raja was not thinking with intellect alone. In fact his brain had little to do with his reactions for he had a raging hard-on. Strands of fragrant silky blonde hair were brushing his shoulder, her pert derrière braced against his thighs while he had one hand resting just below the swell of a plump breast. He raised a knee to keep her out of contact with the seat of his arousal and tried to think of something, *anything* capable of cooling down the sexual fire in his blood.

CHAPTER FIVE

WHEN RUBY WAKENED she was immediately conscious of the heat and the crumpled state of her clothing. What she wanted more than anything at that moment was access to a long, refreshing shower and opening her eyes on the interior of the roughly made and claustrophobic tent was not a heartening experience. She checked her watch and was taken aback to realise how long she had slept for it was already almost one in the afternoon.

Raja was nowhere to be seen and she sat up in a rush, pushing off the quilt and registering the presence of her suitcase in one corner. Mentally she leafed through what she recalled packing for what she had assumed would be short-term requirements while the majority of her wardrobe was shipped out in advance of her arrival. Just as Hermione had been shipped out, she recalled, her eyes suddenly stinging, for she missed her dog and knew her quirky little pet would be sadly missing her. She scrambled up and looked in vain for her shoes before peering out of the tent in search of Raja. It was not that she needed him, it was just she wanted to know where he was, she told herself staunchly.

That angle forgotten, however, Ruby remained standing stock still to stare out of the tent with a dropped jaw at the view of an alien world that shook her to the core. As far as the eye could see there was nothing but sand and the occasional small bush on a wide flat plain overarched by a bright blue sky and baked by a sun so bright and hot she couldn't look directly at it.

'Coffee? You slept soundly,' Raja commented from the side of the small fire he had lit below the ample tent canopy.

'Like the proverbial log.' One glance in his direction and Ruby's teeth grated together in exasperation. As if it weren't hot as hell already he had to build a fire to sit beside! And there he sat, infuriatingly immaculate in the same long off-white robe he had donned the day before and seemingly as comfortable living in the desert as he might have been in a five-star hotel. Only the reality that he was unshaven marked his departure from his usual standards of perfect grooming.

'Where did you get more water to make coffee?' Ruby was struggling not to care that her hair was probably standing on end and mascara had to be smeared all round her eyes.

'This is an oasis. I established that last night. An underground stream feeds a pool below the cliff and our water supply is secure.' He gestured to the other side of the tent. 'Do you want a drink?'

Ruby flipped round to belatedly note the towering cliff of rock on the far side of the tent. A large grove of flourishing date palms and other vegetation made it clear that a water source had to exist somewhere near by. 'I'd sooner not take the risk. After what happened on the plane, I'm only drinking water that comes out of a bottle,' she told him thinly.

The prince compressed his sensual mouth on the laugh he almost let escape. She looked very small, young and unsure of herself, standing there with tousled hair and bare feet, clearly unsettled by her surroundings but struggling not to reveal the fact. She hated to betray weakness and it was a trait he implicitly understood. Dishevelled though she was, however, her hair still glinted like polished silk and her flawless skin had the subdued glow of a pearl. Her beauty was not dependent on cosmetics or the flattering cut and gloss of designer clothing, he recognised, very much impressed by how good she looked without those trimmings. 'There is no bottled water to be had here.'

'Yes, I know that… I'm not stupid!' Ruby snapped back at him in furious self-defence. 'I just don't do the camping thing… OK? Never did do it, never saw the appeal of it and don't want to be roughing it out here now!'

'That is very understandable,' the prince responded with the utmost cool.

Far from impervious to the likely impression she had to be making on a guy who had probably majored in advanced desert survival skills during the war, Ruby dealt him a dirty look. 'I don't care if you laugh at me!'

Retreating crossly back into the tent because she cared very much indeed, Ruby hauled her case to the ground and opened it. She was grateful she hadn't bothered to lock it because, like her shoes, her handbag in which she would have stowed a key was missing. Only when she saw the state of the tumbled contents did she realise how naive she was being: their kidnappers had clearly rummaged through the contents before unloading it from the plane, doubtless keen to ensure that she hadn't packed a phone. She dug out her wash bag and a towel as well as a change of clothing and a pair of sneakers, suddenly very grateful indeed to be in possession of such necessities. A quick inspection of the tent interior warned her that Raja had not been so fortunate.

Donning fresh underwear and tee, she wrapped a sarong round her waist and tried to move more slowly because the heat was making her perspire. She came to a reluctant halt on the edge of the sparse shade offered by the canopy. 'I have a new toothbrush and a razor you can have and you can share my towel.'

In the mood his wife was in, Raja considered that a surprisingly generous offer. A wolfish grin of apprecia-tion slashed his bold, bronzed features and he looked so ravishingly handsome at that instant that Ruby stared fixedly at him, her tummy flipping like an acrobat on a high wire, the warmth of awareness sending hot co-lour surging into her oval face.

She climbed up the slope and saw the pool that had formed in a gully densely shaded by the massive bulk of the rock formation behind it. Raja strode up from the tent to join her and fell into step beside her, his hand first at her elbow and then at her spine to help her as-cend the rougher ground and to steady her when she wavered. He had incredibly good manners and, un-used as she was to that consideration from a man, she could only be pleased that he was willing to make the effort. She was uneasily aware that so far she had not been the most heartening companion. Even worse in so challenging and harsh an environment she could only be at a loss.

They hovered by the side of the palm-fringed, crystal-clear pool formed by the water seeping out from a crack low in the rock face. Ruby moved first, taking off her sneakers to dip her toes in the water. The temperature was deliciously cool on her skin in the intense heat. Lifting her chin and refusing to be self-conscious, she wasted no time in pulling her T-shirt off and untying the sarong. In bra and knickers she reckoned that she was as well covered as she would have been in a bikini. Raja followed suit, stripping off his long tunic and draping it over a rock beside her clothing. Wide-eyed, Ruby watched the sleek muscles working in his strong back and shoulders and then hurriedly averted her gaze, reminding herself how much she had always hated her stepfather leering at her body. It was a clumsy comparison though, she reflected, for she suspected that Raja might well enjoy her admiration.

Standing thigh deep in the pool, Raja watched Ruby wash, his masculine body quickening with hungrily appreciative male interest. Wet through, her underwear was very revealing. He could see the prominent pink nipples poking through the sheer cups of her bra and he wondered how sensitive she would be if he put his mouth to those delicate peaks. As she waded out of the pool again, the clinging fabric of her panties clearly outlined the cleft between her thighs and the forbidden aspect of what he was seeing was a much more stimulating sight than complete nudity. Hard as steel in response, he studied the rippling surface of the water instead. On a very basic level his thoughts were reminding him that she was his wife, that at the very least he was entitled to look while at the same time his brain was recalling their agreement. No sex, no touching. Why the hell had he ever agreed to that? He reckoned that if he touched her the way he was feeling the force of his desire would frighten her.

Ruby walked out of the water and reached for the towel to dab herself dry, moving out of the shade in the expectation that the sun would dry her off more quickly.

'This is the hottest hour of the day. Cover up or you'll burn,' Raja warned her, knowing that he was burning already in an altogether more primitive way.

Reckoning that he was bone-deep bossy in the same unalterable way that holly leaves were prickly, Ruby ignored the stricture and left off her tee. She knotted the sarong just above her bra and began to comb out her damp hair, her attention quite naturally straying to his sleek powerful physique as he stood in the water that had covered her to the waist. His torso was a streamlined wall of muscle, his bulging upper arms, narrow hips and long thighs whipcord taut with lean tensile strength. As he splashed water up over his magnificent body, droplets glistening like diamonds in the bright light, she noticed the revealing fit of his boxer shorts which clearly defined his manhood. Feeling like a voyeur invading his privacy, she quickly looked away but she was shocked.

Was the presence of her only minimally clad body responsible for putting him in that condition? Her face stung with mortified red at the suspicion. What else was she supposed to think? She might not be irresistible as he had quipped the night before but she evidently did have what it took to awaken the most basic chemistry of all. It also occurred to her that she really had not realised until now that an aroused male would be quite so…*large* in that department.

A heavy ache stirred low within her own body and she was taken aback by the recognition that seeing Raja aroused, and knowing that her body was responsible for that development, excited her. And it was the first time ever that a man had had that astounding effect on Ruby. Indeed as a rule she felt uneasy and apprehensive when boyfriends became too enthusiastic in her arms. But then Ruby had never been comfortable with either her body or her own sexuality. How could she have been? During the years that had seen her steadily transform from child to young woman she had been forced to live with her stepfather's obscene comments and the lecherous looks he had constantly aimed at her developing body. While being careful to ensure that her mother neither heard nor saw anything amiss, Curtis Sommerton had taught his stepdaughter to be ashamed of her femininity. His barely concealed lust had made Ruby feel soiled. Although he had never managed to unleash that lust on her, he had taught her an aversion to the male body and the kind of crude sexist comments that some men found amusing.

The prince draped the damp towel carefully round Ruby's bare shoulders. 'Your skin is very fair. Sit in the shadows while I finish here.'

And because Ruby was getting too hot under the sun and her confusing thoughts preoccupied her she did as she was told in most un-Ruby-like silence. She watched him peer into the tiny compact mirror she had produced for his use and shave and then clean those perfect, even white teeth. Her curiosity about him on a personal level was leapfrogging up the scale at an embarrassing rate. Had she had access to the Internet she would have been searching out information about his social life. He *had* to have one. As much of a pin-up as a movie star, rich as sin and obviously possessed of a healthy male libido, Raja al-Somari had to have women in his life. Did he enjoy discreet affairs? He would have to be discreet because Najar was a conservative country just like Ashur. Did he seek out lovers only when he was abroad? Or did he have a lover stashed away somewhere more convenient? The intimate aspect of her thoughts mortified her. What was it to her, for goodness' sake? Even if he had a constant procession of women eager to provide him with an outlet for his sexual needs, it was none of her business!

Having replaced the long tunic, his black hair curling back damply from his brow, Raja approached her. 'We should eat now.'

He showed her the ancient refrigerator operating off a car battery in the back of the tent.

'You understand this way of life,' Ruby remarked.

'When I was a child my father often sent me to stay with my uncle in the desert. He is the ruling sheikh of a nomadic tribe,' he explained. 'But in Najar there are few true nomads left now. The *bedu* have settled so that their children can attend school and they have easier access to jobs and medical facilities. But the nomadic way of life is still quite popular in Ashur.'

There was only fruit, some vegetables, meat and

bread in the refrigerator and several tins of indistin-
guishable supplies. 'I assume we're not expected to
be here for very long,' Raja commented, handing her
a cup of coffee.

Ruby frowned up at what looked like a red flag rippling on top of the cliff. 'What's that up there?'

'A blanket I tied to a stick. It will be easily visible
from the air and unusual enough to attract attention—'

'You *climbed* up there?' Ruby exclaimed, aghast,
for the cliff rose to a pinnacle of almost vertical rock.

'It was not so difficult.' Raja shrugged a broad
shoulder that dismissed the risk involved in so dangerous a climb. 'I went up to take advantage of the view
and see if there was any sign of human habitation but
there is nothing within sight.'

'Obviously this particular place was chosen because
it was isolated,' Ruby said wryly. 'At least I don't have
any family to worry about me—what about you?'

'A father, a younger brother and two sisters and a
whole host of other relatives. But I'm most worried
about my father. He is not strong. The stress my disappearance will cause will endanger his health,' he
proffered, his wide sensual mouth compressing, his
handsome features taut with concern. 'But there is
nothing I can do about it.'

Her generous heart was troubled by his apprehension. 'I have no relatives in Ashur, have I?'

'None close that I'm aware of. Distant cousins, certainly.'

His ability to efficiently feed them both set Ruby's
teeth on edge. He could cook on an open fire with very
limited ingredients and produce an edible meal while

she would have been challenged to do so even in a modern kitchen. Her mother had been a poor cook and Ruby's own repertoire was limited to the making or heating of simple snacks. While she lived with Stella, a very competent cook, her lack in that field had not seemed important but somehow in Raja's presence it annoyed the hell out of her.

Feeling helpless stung Ruby's strong pride. She hated feeling reliant on Raja and was painfully conscious that to date she had proved more of a burden than a help. That sense of inadequacy drove her into ceaseless activity that afternoon. She tidied up her clothes, ashamed of the fact she had left the garments lying in a tumbled heap beside her suitcase. She folded the quilts, shook the sand off the mats and took care of the few dishes and then she wandered round the grove of date palms busily gathering twigs and dried foliage to keep the fire going. The heat sapped her energy fast and she was filled with dismay at the prospect of what the much higher summer temperatures had to be like to live with. Her hair sticking to the back of her neck, she headed up to the pool to cool off again. The cold water felt glorious. Wrapped in the sarong, she sat down wearily on a rock in the deep shade to knot her hair and hold it off her perspiring face, wishing she had something to tie it back with. She looked across the pool to see her desert prince approaching, all six feet plus of his leanly muscled commanding figure pure poetry in motion, and she pursed her lips.

There he was drop-dead gorgeous and rich and he could cook, as well. She marvelled that he had stayed single so long. Of course that authoritarian streak might be a problem for some. He knew best...*always*. Her shoulders were pink and slightly burned as he had warned before lunch and she wasn't one bit grateful that his forecast had come true but she knew that she ought to be grateful that he was so well able to cope when she was not. He was also equally keen to protect her from her own mistakes.

'Watch out for—'

Ruby lifted her hands in a sudden silencing motion, brown eyes lightening with temper. 'Just let it go, Raja. I'll take my chances against whatever it is! You're just about perfect and you know everything and you could probably live out here all year but I'm afraid I'm not cut from the same cloth.'

'The desert is home to my people and yours,' the prince contradicted in a tone of reproof. 'We design and maintain beautiful gardens and parks in Najar but when our people want to get back to basics they come out into the desert.'

Ruby snatched in a sustaining breath and she kicked a rock with a sneaker-clad foot to expel her extreme irritation.

'Ruby!'

As the rock rolled over and something moved and darted from beneath it Raja almost leapt forward in his haste to haul her out of harm's way. From several feet away, plastered back against the solid support of his hard muscular frame, Ruby stared in horror at the greenish yellow insects rushing out.

'Scorpions. They shelter in dark places during the day. Their sting is very painful,' Raja informed her as she went limp against him, sick with repulsion at how close she had come to injury. He removed her to a safe distance.

'I don't like insects either,' Ruby confided in a shaken rush. 'Especially ones that size and anything that stings—'

'There are also poisonous snakes—'

'Shut up...*shut up!*' she launched at him fiercely. 'I'm not on an educational trip. I don't want to know!'

Raja turned her round and stared down at her, eyes shimmering with reluctant amusement.

'I don't care what you say either,' Ruby added truculently. 'Give it a rest—stop trying to train me into being a stuffy royal who never puts a foot wrong!'

This time Raja al-Somari laughed out loud, his ready sense of humour finally breaking free of his innate reserve, for Ruby was very much an original and not at all like the women he was accustomed to meeting. She didn't flirt—at least if she did, she didn't bother to do it with him. Indeed she used no feminine wiles that he could identify. She staged no enticing poses to draw attention to her body. She made no attempt to appeal to his ego with compliments or to pay him any especially gratifying attention and she had not told him a single story calculated to present her in a flattering light. He had never in his entire life met a woman as uncomplicated as she was and the more he was exposed to her frank, fearless style, the more he liked it.

'So, you do have a sense of humour after all. My goodness, is that a relief!' Ruby exclaimed, shaking her head in emphasis, a wealth of damp strands escaping her loose knot and spilling across her shoulders.

Raja stared down at her stunning face and the teasing smile on her ripe rosy lips. He lowered his handsome, dark head almost jerkily as if he were being yanked down to her level by some mysterious but very powerful outside force. He found her soft, sultry mouth with his and although that kiss started out gentle and searching it heated up at supersonic speed. Desire rose to gush through Ruby in a floodtide. Nothing had ever felt so necessary as the hard pressure of that sensual mouth on hers and the taste of him drowned her senses like a shot of alcohol on a weak head.

Without a word, Raja released her with startling abruptness and pressed a hand to her spine to urge her back down the slope towards the tent.

Ruby had never experienced such a charge of hunger before and, suddenly deprived of that connection with him, she was in a daze. The tip of her tongue snaked out to explore the reddened and swollen contours of her lips and all she could think about was how much she wanted his hot, hungry mouth back on hers again. The strength of that craving shook her. Her nipples were tight and tingling and her legs felt shaky. Putting one foot in front of another was a challenge. And at the same time, gallingly she was desperate to know what he was thinking.

Outside the tent Ruby shot Raja a sidewise glance brimming with curiosity. His hard profile was taut and he skimmed a look back at her, eyes brilliant with a wealth of stormy emotion. That shook her and in response her heart started beating very, very fast. 'Don't play games with me, Ruby,' he spelled out in a roughened undertone.

Games? Ruby was offended by the suggestion and she lifted her chin in denial. 'I don't know what you're talking about—*you* kissed *me*—'

'But you made no objection. When you have said that you don't want me to touch you what else is that but a game?'

'I don't calculate things to that extent. You are so suspicious,' Ruby condemned, flushed and flustered by the reminder and by the embarrassment of her own uncharacteristic behaviour. 'It's being in this situation… I simply forgot and got carried away for a moment.'

'Every action has consequences,' Raja pronounced, rigid with the pent-up force of arousal he was restraining, his lean hands clenching into fists, for his body was not one half as disciplined as his quick and clever brain.

Ruby sank down on a mat inside the tent. It was hot but nothing was as hot and disturbing as the hum of unnatural warmth at the centre of her body, which was shockingly new and demanding. She could not relax. She lifted a hand, watched it tremble and tried and failed to laugh at the state she was in. One kiss and it had been earth-shattering, even more so than the last. Now she felt cheated. She wanted more, she wanted to know what it felt like to make love with a man who attracted her to that extent. The hurricane-force potency of that attraction was certainly a first. She had not experienced anything comparable with other men when intimacy had often felt like more of a threat and a nuisance than a potential source of pleasure. More than once her unenthusiastic response had led to her being asked if she was frigid or gay. She had often had to fight her way out of over-keen encounters. She had had to shout, she had had to defend and justify her boundaries because the easy availability of sex was often taken for granted in relationships. But not once, not once in the five years since she began dating had she actually *wanted* to make love.

And now what was she doing about it? Here she was taking refuge in the tent and avoiding Raja as if she were ashamed of herself or afraid when she was neither, she conceded uncertainly. It was not as though she could fall pregnant either, she reminded herself squarely. Some months earlier her doctor had advised her to agree to a course of contraceptive pills in the hope of correcting an irregular menstrual cycle. Although she had no supply with her in the desert she assumed she would still be protected for some time against conception. She lifted her head high. She had not been playing some sexual game with Raja, she was not a tease and didn't want him thinking that she was. In an impatient movement she scrambled upright again.

Raja was staring into the dying embers of the fire, black lashes lowered and as spectacular even in profile as glossy black fringes, his high cheekbones prominent, sculptured mouth clenched.

'I wasn't playing games,' Ruby declared defiantly.

He flung his proud dark head back and looked straight at her. 'I want you so much I ache…'

And his admission sizzled through Ruby like a hot knife gliding through butter. His confidence shocked her, for she had believed that she was being bold but his words made hers meaningless and little more than a sulky expression of innocence. Indeed almost a lie,

she adjusted uncomfortably, jolted by her sudden unexpected collision with the scorching challenge of his
gaze. Just at that moment she knew that she had sought
him out again quite deliberately and that he was experienced enough to know it.

'A woman hasn't made me ache since I was younger
than you are now,' Raja told her huskily, vaulting upright with an easy grace of movement that tensed every
muscle in her slim body. 'You're very beautiful...'

So was he, but she was too wary and proud to tell
him that that lean dark-angel beauty of his had taken up
residence in her brain and dug talon claws of need and
desire into her very soul. When he kissed her she felt
as dizzy and uncoordinated as though she had drunk
too much alcohol. He made her feel out of control and
she didn't like that but, regardless of that fact, every
time she looked at him it was a tougher challenge to
look away again. She moved closer and somehow he
met her in the middle, a possessive hand closing on her
slight shoulder to hold her in place, his mouth or was
it her mouth eagerly melding with the temptation of
his again. And that crushing kiss was good, *so* good,
her bare toes curled and her nerve endings sang. Her
arms went round him, her fingers spearing into his
hair, and with her eager encouragement his mouth got
rougher and harder, his lean, powerful length sealing
more forcefully to her softer curves.

It was too much: she couldn't breathe, broke her
mouth free to pant for breath and yet immediately
sought him out again with renewed hunger and blindly
impatient hands. In the midst of it he eased back from
her to haul off his robe but just as quickly he pulled

her back into his arms. The sarong fell at her feet but she didn't notice because Raja was already lowering her down on the quilts while pressing taut open-mouthed kisses along the slender expanse of her neck. She squirmed helplessly as the tip of his tongue scored the pulse there and then he nipped at her responsive flesh with his strong white teeth. Need was driving her now, all the while the heat in her pelvis was building and building into a furnace.

Her bra fell away. His palm closed over a small, pert breast and she gasped, back arching as he plunged his mouth down to the swollen pink tip and let his teeth graze the straining nipple. She dragged him up to kiss him again and ran an appreciative palm down over the hair-roughened expanse of his superb torso. He caught her hand in his and brought her fingers down to the rampant length of the shaft straining against his hard flat stomach. A shudder ran through his big frame as she took that invitation and stroked him, moulding the smooth hard heat and promise of him with reverent fingers.

He moved her beneath him and again put his carnal mouth to her tender nipples. He was gentle at first but still she writhed and when he got a little more ardent she cried out, struggling to find herself again in the thunderous, greedy surge of the hunger he had awakened.

'Very beautiful,' Raja groaned in reply. 'And wonderfully passionate...'

The hollow ache between her thighs had her hips shifting back and forth. He traced the tender pink flesh there and she shivered, violently and with longing, driven by feverish want and need. He slid a finger into her and she was hot and wet and tight and he groaned with masculine appreciation, capturing her lips with his again, letting his tongue dart into the sensitive interior of her mouth with a skilful flick that made the blood drum insanely fast through her veins.

He teased the tiny bundle of nerve endings that controlled her entire body and she writhed in the storm of intoxicating sensation. 'Don't stop...whatever you do, don't stop!' she warned him through gritted teeth, reacting to an overload of pleasure that wiped out every thought and consideration and left frantic desire in charge.

Black hair tousled, golden eyes hot as flames, the prince rose over her. 'After this, there is no going back.'

In the merciless grip of unsated need, Ruby could barely focus on his darkly handsome features. 'No going back?' she repeated blankly.

Raja, as eager for completion as she was, was already pressing back her thighs and impatiently splaying his hands below her hips to raise her to him. As he positioned himself and pushed into her a sharp pain arrowed through her and she cried out. He stopped moving to gaze down at her with a bemused frown. 'What's wrong?'

'Nothing...don't stop,' Ruby told him, taut with discomfiture for it had not occurred to her that losing her virginity might hurt. Her more experienced friend, Stella, might have told her a lot of things but that possibility had not been mentioned.

Dark eyes confused, he stared down at her. 'But I hurt you.'

Ruby could feel her face getting hotter and hotter. 'It's my first time…that's all. No big deal.'

It was Raja's turn to be surprised and it was a very big deal on his terms. His bride was a virgin? The level of his ignorance about her annoyed him. He had made the wrong assumptions but not without her encouragement to do so. A slight shudder racked him as he endeavoured to remain still while every fibre of his being craved the completion of sinking into her as far and as fast as he could go.

'It's all right…it really is,' Ruby whispered, deeply embarrassed by the enforced pause in their lovemaking.

The prince lowered his head and pressed a kiss to the rosy invitation of her mouth. For the very first time he allowed himself to think of her as his wife. It was a powerful source of attachment for a man given to ruthlessly guarding his emotions. Lithe as a cat, he shifted inside her and her eyes widened with wondering appreciation as the first swirl of sensation circled her pelvis and melted her inside to hot, liquid honey.

'Oh…' she framed, taken aback by that feeling of exquisite fullness, lips parting, eyes drifting shut on a heady vocal sound of appreciation.

'I want it to be good for you…'

Ruby looked up at him, her entire body buzzing with electrified arousal. 'It's better than good…'

Raja shifted again, initially slow and sure, patiently teaching her his rhythm while he revelled in the velvety grip of her slick passage. In the still heat of the tent, perspiration gleaming on his sleek bronzed length, he pleasured her with long driving strokes. Excitement gripped her as the pace quickened and the only thing that mattered then was the pounding surge of his body into hers. Delirious with the pulsing pleasure, she arched her back and wild tremors tore through her. With a feverish cry she splintered into the electrifying heat of an earth-shattering climax.

Afterwards, Raja held her close, soothing fingers caressing the smooth skin of her abdomen while little quivers, aftershocks of that intense physical crescendo, still coursed through her. 'I'm sorry I hurt you. If I had known that you were not experienced I would have been more gentle.'

Hugging a glorious unfamiliar sense of well-being along with the feeling that she was still floating on a fluffy cloud, Ruby fixed dazed eyes on his face. 'I'm not sure gentle would have been quite so exciting.'

Raja laughed with easy appreciation and vaulted upright. He pulled on his boxers and strode out of the tent. She wondered what he was doing but was too lazy to ask or follow as she lay there with limbs that felt weighted down. At the corner of her mind a kernel of unease was nagging at her, keen to remind her that she had trashed the platonic agreement she had forged with Raja and made their relationship much more personal, much more intimate than she had ever envisaged.

Just at that moment such serious reflections seemed ridiculously irrelevant. They were marooned in the desert in circumstances neither of them could ever have foreseen and, as far as she was concerned, the normal rules no longer applied. It was just sex, she told herself urgently, not worth getting worked up about. Creating a fuss about it would only make her look deeply uncool.

Raja strode back in and knelt down by her side. One glimpse of that strong, dark face and sleek physique and her tummy flipped and her brain seemed to turn to mush. He smiled down at her, and it was, without a doubt, the most spectacular smile. Evidently her approval rating had gone from zero to through the roof. He reached down to uncurl her legs for she was lying coiled in a ball.

'What are you doing?' she muttered in bewilderment.

He didn't answer, he simply showed her. He had soaked the towel in the pool and wrung it out. Beneath her stunned gaze he began to run that very welcome cold, wet cloth over her hot, damp body, cooling her feverish temperature, leaving her fresh and revitalised and unexpectedly touched by his thoughtfulness.

They ate in a surprisingly comfortable silence below the tent canopy. 'I don't think we'll be here for much longer,' Raja admitted quietly. 'Once the fact that we were married in the UK is publicly announced there can be no reason for leaving us here.'

'But that means that someone would have to own up to knowing where we are.'

'There are many ways of passing information without the source being identified,' the man by her side remarked shrewdly.

When she finished her drink and began to get up he rose with her and pulled her up against his powerful frame. Hot eyes raked her flushed and uncertain face and for an instant she was stiff, suddenly disturbingly lost in the brave new world of intimacy she had created with him. The balance of power had changed irrevocably. A low-pitched growl vibrating in his throat, Raja closed a hand into her tumbled hair and kissed her, hard and hungrily, unleashing a passion that was uninhibited. He thrust aside the sarong and cupped her bare breasts, teasing the tips between thumb and finger. An arrowing tingle of damp heat speared between her thighs and she ached. She quivered and clung, wanting and needing again even more than she had the first time.

CHAPTER SIX

RUBY SUFFERED A rude awakening the next morning. Raja was shaking her shoulder, the tent walls were flapping loudly and her ears were ringing with noise.

'Get dressed,' he framed urgently as she blinked in bewilderment. 'We've been found and we're leaving!'

As he strode from the tent she peered out after him and saw a pair of what looked like heavy-duty military helicopters coming in to land. Galvanised into action as she registered that their desert sojourn appeared to be at an end, she yanked open her case in search of something decent to wear. She dressed in haste, choosing cropped trousers and a vest top teamed with a light shirt. As she hastily brushed her hair every movement she made ensured that she remained mortifyingly conscious of the intimate ache between her legs.

The events of the past twelve hours raced through her memory and her slender hands fisted in defensive rejection of her reckless behaviour. As a rule, Ruby didn't *do* reckless. Ruby was usually thoughtful and cautious, never impulsive, yet she had, with very little thought, utterly destroyed the platonic marital agreement she had insisted on. All for what? Great sex, she acknowledged shamefacedly, but in the aftermath even greater regrets.

They had agreed to a fake marriage and now how was their relationship to be defined? The agreement had been broken, the boundaries blurred and their respective roles were no longer clear-cut. Raja's unqualified passion had enthralled her. She had to be honest with herself about that. She found the Najari prince regent incredibly attractive. He fascinated her and he had tempted her from that first kiss back in England. No other man had ever had that effect on her. She had been eager to know what sex was all about, had wanted to feel what other women felt and had sensed from the outset that he might well be the guy who could show her. And he had, unquestionably, shown her. Over and over and over again, she recalled, her face burning. In bed her desert prince ditched all reserve and cool in favour of a scorching-hot sexual intensity that had lit a fire inside her that she could neither resist nor quench.

As Ruby emerged from the tent she saw Raja standing in conversation with several men, all of whom wore military uniform. Every male eye turned towards her and then heads inclined and lowered and a respectful murmur of greeting acknowledged her presence. Raja drew her forward with an assured hand to introduce her to the various air-force personnel before assisting her into the nearest helicopter.

'We will breakfast in Najar—'

'I think I should stay in Ashur for the moment,' Ruby told him quietly. 'I ought to continue on to where I was heading when we were kidnapped.'

The tall black-haired male by her side frowned down at her.

'Naturally you want to let your father see that

you're OK as soon as possible. I'll be fine,' she asserted lightly.

Raja captured her hand in his. 'Where's your wedding ring?'

Ruby glanced down at her bare fingers. 'Oh, dear, I didn't notice. It was very loose and it must've fallen off. I don't think it was still on my finger when we arrived here.'

His wide sensual mouth compressed. 'I will find a replacement.'

A slight hint of amusement on her gaze, Ruby sent him an airy glance as though the matter was too trivial to discuss. 'No hurry...'

His face hardened, inky lashes dropping low over his intent scrutiny. 'We must agree to disagree,' he traded huskily. 'I will see you tonight—'

'Tonight?' Ruby was surprised, having assumed that their separation would last somewhat longer. She was also rather keen to have a decent breathing space in which to regroup.

'Tonight,' Raja confirmed, striding off to speak to the pilot before climbing aboard the second helicopter.

During the flight, when Ruby felt nervous tension beginning to rise at the prospect of what expectations might await her in Simis, the capital of Ashur, she breathed in deep. She reminded herself that she was reasonably intelligent, even-tempered and willing to learn, not to mention being filled with good intentions. She didn't need Raja by her side telling her what to do every minute of the day.

The airport building outside Simis was a large temporary shed. Surrounded by soldiers and police who made her nervous, Ruby was greeted by Wajid Sulieman's familiar and surprisingly welcome face and tucked straight into a waiting car. His concerned questions about her health and how she had managed in the desert brought a smile to her expressive mouth.

'I was lucky to have the prince with me,' she admitted, willing to award honour where it was due. 'How did you find us?'

'Someone contacted the media with your location,' Wajid told her. 'From the moment that we announced that you were missing, people began gathering outside the palace gates to wait for news. There was great anger and concern on your behalf. Some were quick to suspect the Najaris of duplicity and there were protests. It was a very tense situation.'

'I'm sure feelings ran equally high in Najar,' Ruby remarked as the car cut around a horse and cart.

'Even higher. Your husband is a war hero and tremendously popular,' Wajid said. 'It is unfortunate that he was unable to accompany you here but I understand that he will be arriving later.'

'Yes.' Crowds lined the old-fashioned city streets and necks were craned to get a better view of her car. 'Are those people actually waiting to see me?' Ruby whispered incredulously.

'There is great excitement and curiosity about your arrival. It is a positive event after so many years of bad news,' the older man volunteered wryly. 'For the next few days you will be out and about a good deal to allow people to become familiar with you. The photograph taken after your wedding was very well received. I cannot praise Prince Raja highly enough for having had the foresight to organise it.'

'Raja thinks of everything,' Ruby agreed, thinking sunburn, scorpions…sex. A little tremor of heated recollection rippled low in her body and she stiffened, annoyed that even memory could make her so sensually susceptible.

On her short visit to Ashur as a teenager she had seen the imposing grey building that comprised the palace only from the vantage point of the tall wrought-iron gates. A step in the imperious wake of Wajid, she entered the palace from a side entrance where a group of staff bowed low and several introductions were offered. From the hall she was escorted up a staircase.

'Your uncle, the late King Tamim, and his family used the east wing. I thought you might be more comfortable in this more modern corner of the palace.'

Ruby reckoned that only in Wajid's parlance could a decor at least sixty years out of date be deemed modern. 'What was my uncle like?'

'He was rather set in his ways, as was his daughter, Princess Bariah—'

'My cousin.'

'A fine young woman, who was of course destined to marry Prince Raja before the accident that took her life and that of her parents,' the older man remarked in his pedantic manner, quite unaware of Ruby coming to a sudden halt and shooting him a look of dismay.

Her cousin had originally been contracted to marry Raja? Of course that made sense but it was still the first time that that fact had been mentioned to Ruby. And like a bolt from the blue that little fact cut Ruby to the bone. Just at that moment it was a deeply unwelcome reminder that there was nothing personal, private or indeed special about her relationship with the future king of Najar and Ashur, for Raja had been equally willing, it seemed, to marry her cousin. Fate had simply served Ruby up in her cousin's stead. But how had Raja really felt about that sudden exchange of brides? Had he been attached to her royal cousin, Princess Bariah? A sliver like a shard of ice sliced through Ruby, who was affronted and hurt by the idea that she might well have been a second-best choice on her husband's terms. No doubt he would have been equally willing to share a bed with her cousin. How could she have been foolish enough to allow such intimacy without good reason? And how could desire alone ever be sufficient justification?

As she stepped through a door a little dog barked wildly and hurled itself at her legs. Smiling happily, Ruby got down on her knees to pet Hermione, who gave her a frantic squirming welcome before finally snuggling into her owner's arms and tucking her little head blissfully below Ruby's chin. Wajid mentioned the reconciliation service to be held at the cathedral that afternoon, which Ruby had to attend, as well as an evening reception at which she was to meet many important people. She stifled a groan at the thought of her inadequate wardrobe and wondered if the red suit could be freshened up for the occasion.

A knock sounded on the door and a young woman joined them. 'This is Zuhrah, Your Royal Highness, who with the assistance of your personal staff will take care of all your needs,' Wajid explained. 'She speaks excellent English.'

Zuhrah explained that she would look after Ruby's diary and take care of all the invitations she received. Wajid departed while the pretty brunette showed Ruby through the spacious suite of rooms that had been set aside for her use. Over the light lunch that was served in the dining area Ruby mentioned the red suit and Zuhrah wasted no time in going off to track it down. As soon as she had eaten Ruby took advantage of the bathroom—she would never take one for granted again— and enjoyed a long, invigorating shower. Having dried her hair, she returned to the drawing room, clad in a wrap, and asked Zuhrah, who was tapping out notes on a netbook, if her missing handbag had turned up. Apparently it had not and Ruby knew she would have to see a doctor if she wanted another contraceptive pill. But did she need to take that precaution now? Was she planning to continue sleeping with Raja?

She thought not. Her brain said no, a very firm no. A mistake was a mistake and better acknowledged as such. There was another consequence to be feared as well, she reminded herself ruefully. She had missed taking her contraceptive pills while she was in the desert and there had to be a risk that she might already have conceived a child by Raja. What was she going to do if that happened? A chill ran down Ruby's spine at the prospect of such a dilemma. She loved babies but a baby that would be deemed royal would severely complicate her practical marriage and ultimately wreck any hope of them establishing a civilised relationship. She was convinced that if she had a child there was no way that Raja would agree to her taking that child back home to the UK with her again.

The service at the cathedral late that afternoon required nothing more from Ruby than her presence. Police stood outside the historic building with linked arms to hold back the crowds struggling to catch a glimpse of the new princess. The evening reception was a great deal more taxing, however, for while she was perfectly able to make small talk she was embarrassed several times by more probing questions concerning her background than she wished to answer. People were extremely curious about her and as yet she did not have the skill to deflect unwelcome queries. Later she would register that she had known the exact moment when Raja entered the big reception room for a flutter of excitement seemed to run through the gathered cliques. With a muttered apology, Wajid left her side and heads turned away from her, eyes swerving towards the door while a low buzz of comment sounded.

'*Real* royalty,' someone whispered appreciatively within Ruby's hearing. 'And you can definitely tell the difference.'

Mortified heat burnished Ruby's fair complexion. *Real* royalty? Had she performed her role so badly? But then she knew that she could only be a pretend princess by virtue of her birth. How could she be anything else when she had spent all her life to date living as an ordinary person? But she was *trying*, she was trying very hard to be polite, reserved and dignified as Wajid had advised her she must be at all times while carefully avoiding controversial subjects. It was tough advice for a bubbly and naturally outspoken young woman to follow. To Ruby it also felt like trying to be something she was not while putting on airs and graces that went against the grain.

His tall powerful physique sheathed in a dove-grey suit, her husband looked devastatingly handsome. Her *husband*? Why was she thinking of Raja in such terms? He wasn't her husband, not really, she told herself angrily, irritated by the mental mistake. A woman chose her husband with her heart but she had not. Guilty colour mantling her face, Ruby studied that lean, strong, wondrously handsome face and she steeled herself to feel nothing, absolutely nothing. She watched Raja work the room like a professional, smooth and practised and yet charming as well with a word here, a greeting there, for some a smile, for others a more serious aspect. He was a class act socially, everything she was not. Hovering at his elbow, Wajid Sulieman looked as though all his Christmases had come at once.

When refreshments were served, Raja was finally free to join Ruby. Lustrous dark eyes gleaming like polished amber flared down into hers while he rested a light hand at her spine. She went rigid, rejecting the temptation of even that much familiarity while recalling Bariah, who would never have been ill-at-ease in such a social gathering.

'My family were very disappointed not to meet you today,' the prince told her quietly.

'Whereas here everyone is disappointed that I'm not you—you carry the accolade of being *real* royalty, unlike me,' Ruby retorted, only to bite her lip a few seconds after that hot rejoinder had escaped her for she would have preferred to keep that particular thought to herself.

'You are imagining that. A beautiful woman in fashionable apparel is almost always more welcome than a man,' Raja fielded without skipping a beat.

Wajid introduced them to an older couple, who represented a charity that ran an orphanage just outside Simis, which Ruby, apparently, would be visiting the next day. In the wake of that casual announcement, which was news to Ruby, she appreciated how little freedom she now had when it came to how she might choose to spend her time. Her time evidently now belonged to an ever-growing list of duties, engagements and activities, not least of which was her need to learn the language so that a translator did not have to dog her every footstep.

'You're very quiet. What's wrong?' Raja enquired as Ruby mounted the stairs that led back to her suite.

'It's not important.' Ruby pushed open the door and sped through to the bedroom to change into something more comfortable. A maid was engaged in hanging clothes in a closet there, *male* clothes. Her soft full mouth compressing as she recognised that fact, Ruby walked back into the main reception room where Raja was poised by the window.

'You're staying in this suite with me?'

'Married couples usually share the same accommodation,' Raja pointed out evenly.

Temper roused by that tranquil response skittered up through Ruby in an uneasy rush. He made it sound so simple but their relationship was anything but simple. 'I didn't realise that but for that plane crash you would have married my cousin Bariah,' she admitted. 'I hadn't worked that out yet.'

'A marriage would hardly have been included in the peace accord if the royal families did not have a bride and a groom in mind.'

As usual what Raja said made perfect sense and her teeth gritted in frustration. 'I'm sure you would have preferred a proper Ashuri princess!'

Face deadpan, Raja gazed steadily back at her, patently refusing to be drawn on that touchy topic.

Tension roared through Ruby's rigid stance like a hurricane seeking an outlet. 'I *said*—'

'I am not deaf,' Raja cut in very drily. 'But I do wonder what you expect me to say in reply to such an assumption.'

Flushed and furious, Ruby surveyed him. 'Is an honest answer too much for me to ask for?'

'Not at all, but I will not insult either you or your late cousin with the suggestion that I might compare two completely different women and voice a preference for either,' Raja advanced, eyes cool while his strong jawline set hard as iron. 'That is not a reasonable request.'

'Well, as far as I'm concerned, it's perfectly reasonable!' Ruby slung back heatedly.

'But to answer you would be disrespectful.'

'Unlike you I'm only human. Naturally I want to know although I don't know why I'm bothering to ask. Bariah was a real princess and would've had much more in common with you than I have.'

'No comment,' the prince pronounced stonily and with much bowing and scraping the little maid emerged from the bedroom and left the suite.

'Bariah spoke the language, *knew* this country.' Ruby's statement was pained for after spending only hours in the Ashuri palace she was all too conscious of her deficiencies.

'Given time and patience you will learn,' Raja murmured quietly, his lack of tension merely increasing the adrenaline surge ready to charge through Ruby's veins.

Ruby was in no mood to be comforted. 'My cousin would have known automatically how to behave in every situation—'

'Wajid already thinks you're doing a marvellous job,' Raja imparted gently.

As she stiffened defensively her eyes flared bright as topaz gemstones. 'Don't patronise me!'

'I'm going for a shower,' Raja breathed, casting his jacket down on a chair and striding into the bedroom.

Ruby stilled in her restive stalk round the spacious room and shot a startled glance in his direction as she followed him into the bedroom. 'You're actually planning to sleep in here with me?'

In the act of unbuttoning his shirt, Raja dealt her an impatient glance and said nothing.

For a timeless moment Ruby watched a wedge of masculine torso appear between the parted edges of the shirt. 'There are two big sofas in the room next door,' she pointed out, in case he had not yet noticed the possibility of that option.

Raja treated that reminder to the contempt he evidently felt it deserved. His eyes burned hot gold below his black, spiky lashes, his jaw squared, giving his face a dangerous edge.

'All right... I'll take a sofa,' Ruby pronounced, determined to stick to her guns. It was her belief that if she reinforced their separation they would both soon forget those boundaries they had unwisely crossed and return to their original agreement.

Raja elevated a deeply unimpressed and sardonic black brow and stripped off his boxers to walk fluidly into the bathroom. As nude exits went it scored an impressive ten in the cooler-than-cool stakes. While the shower was running, Ruby made up a bed on a sofa for herself, donned her pyjamas, doused the lights and climbed in. Hermione snuggled in next to her feet.

A little while later, a wild burst of barking drove her from the brink of slumber.

'Call off the dog or I will put her out to the kennels,' Raja growled, his face grim in the light spilling from the bedroom.

Ruby leapt off the sofa, snatched the snarling Hermione up into her arms and attempted to soothe her overexcited pet. 'What are you doing in here?'

'Retrieving my wife,' Raja traded in a wrathful tone of warning.

'I'm not your wife, not your proper wife!' Ruby launched furiously back at him, inflamed by that insistence and the label.

'So you're not a real princess or a proper wife. Then what are you?' Raja challenged impatiently, bending down from his considerable height to haul her up into his arms while she clutched Hermione frantically to her chest. 'My sex buddy? A friend with benefits?'

He then went on to employ a third term of description, which was crude enough to make Ruby's soft, full lips fall open in shock and her big, brown eyes flame. 'How *dare* you?'

Raja settled her down on the bed with a good deal more care than she had grounds to expect from an angry man. Hermione tried to bite him. Composed in the face of that attempted attack, he scooped up the animal and put Ruby's pet out of the room. From the other side of the door Hermione whined and scraped the wood.

'Are you planning to do the same to me if I stand up to you?' Ruby enquired furiously. 'I am not sleeping with you again—'

'I'm not very interested in sleeping right now either.' At least six feet three inches tall and magnificently male, Raja threw back the sheet and slid into bed beside her.

'I am not your sex buddy or that other thing you mentioned!' Ruby proclaimed in a rage.

'No, you're my wife,' Raja repeated again, immovably stubborn on that point.

Ruby was taken aback when he got out of bed again and crossed the room to reach for his jacket and retrieve something from a pocket. He returned to bed and reached for her hand.

'What are you doing?' she demanded apprehensively.

'I'm replacing your wedding ring.' And this time the ring on her finger was a perfect fit as well as being very different from its predecessor. The first ring had been a plain gold band but the second struck her as a good deal more personalised for it was a slender platinum ring chased with ornate decoration.

'Don't call me your wife again,' Ruby muttered helplessly, twirling the ring round her finger with a restless hand. 'It makes me feel trapped.'

This time Raja did not hide his anger. His nostrils flared and his dark golden eyes scorched hers like burning arrows, leaving her feeling alarmingly short of breath. 'You should be proud to be my wife,' he told her without hesitation.

Her breath rattled in her tight throat. She had not meant to insult or offend. Without warning things had become terrifyingly personal. 'I'm sure I would be proud if I loved you,' she whispered in a response intended to soothe.

'Love!' Raja loosed a derisive laugh of disagreement. 'What need have we of that with the fire that burns between us?'

Well, so much for the emotional angle, she was thinking irately, for clearly she had not married a romantic guy, when sure fingers trailed across her cheekbone and captured her chin. His other hand curving to her waist, Raja lowered his proud, dark head and claimed her full, pink mouth hungrily with his. There was a split second when she might have pushed him away and her slim body braced and her hands rose in protest against his broad shoulders to do exactly that. But the moist slide of his tongue between her lips and the hand rising below her pyjama top to curve to the plump swell of her breast sent a flood of damp heat to the tender flesh between her thighs and a surge of such hunger that she shivered in shock. The dark force of desire took her by storm, every fibre of her being sitting up, begging and clawing for more.

CHAPTER SEVEN

'WE SHOULDN'T DO THIS!' Ruby gasped in a last-ditch attempt to reclaim control of the situation while she mustered sufficient self-discipline to drag her tingling mouth from the unadulterated magnetic allure of his.

Having already whisked her free of her pyjama bottoms, Raja threw back his tousled dark head and angled his lean hips to let her feel the hard evidence of his erection against her stomach. She quivered, fighting her desire for him with all her might, for at that instant desire had as much of a hold on her as a powerful addiction in her bloodstream.

'You mustn't get me pregnant!' Ruby exclaimed in a sudden panic, anxiety gripping her at the thought of suffering such a far-reaching and serious consequence. Just for a moment she could barely credit that she had ever been stupid enough to run that level of risk.

A hand spread below her hips to raise her to him. 'We took no precautions in the desert,' Raja reminded her with a frown.

'But we don't need to run that risk now. I take contraceptive pills but I missed some when we were there so for the rest of the month I need to take extra precautions.'

Raja found it deeply ironic that the potential pregnancy from which she was so keen to protect herself would have been a source of much rejoicing in both their countries. He suppressed that knowledge, for once uninterested in the bigger picture and concentrating on his own reactions for a change. As he studied her stunning oval face with burnished golden eyes of anticipation, he was startled to discover that he was willing to want whatever would make her happy. 'It's OK. Don't worry about it. I will protect you—'

'We can't be sex buddies…it's indecent—'

'I like indecent,' Raja confided huskily, trailing provocative fingertips very gently along the tender skin of her thigh so that she became even more painfully aware of the awesome strength of her own craving. 'In fact I could live beautifully with indecent.'

To silence the argument he sensed brimming on her lips he tasted her sultry pink mouth with the lingering eroticism that came so naturally to him, sensually teasing the soft fullness of her lower lip before penetrating her mouth in a smooth, explicit thrust. And while he kissed her he was skimming the ball of his thumb against the most sensitive spot on her entire body with a shocking expertise that made her stifle a scream while she writhed and gasped her response.

Before she could catch her breath from that onslaught, Raja leant back from her to rip open a foil packet and make use of a condom. Her heart thudded violently up tempo. She would not let herself think about what she was doing. She was rebelling against everything she knew because she had never wanted anything so much as she wanted him in that moment. And without a doubt she was ashamed of it, ashamed of the wild seething longing that controlled her, befuddling her brain and enslaving her body.

Raja sank into her in a long, slow surge, stroking her tender flesh with his. It felt so indescribably good that she cried out and her inner muscles clenched and convulsed around him. In the throes of extreme pleasure, he shuddered violently, as entrapped in that hunger as she was. 'It's never been like this for me before...' he confided.

Or for her, her brain echoed but speech was beyond her. Her whole body was attuned to every movement of his. With every subtle shift of that lean, powerful physique of his the dark pleasure rose in a sweet suffocating tide. He withdrew and then delved deep, moving faster and faster and her spine arched and she moaned in frantic excitement, defenceless against the feverish beat of exquisite sensation. Her climax finally rippled through her in an unstoppable force and she flamed into countless burning pieces before she dropped back to planet earth again. Another cry was dragged from her as the violent tremors of his final pleasure rocked her slight body with renewed sensitivity and sensation.

Raja eased back from her to study her with appreciation. He bent his head to press a kiss to her cheekbone. 'You're amazing,' he told her breathlessly.

'What have we done?' Ruby lamented out loud, already gritting her teeth, aware that in yielding to her hunger for him she had given way to weakness for the first time in her life. And that acknowledgement hurt her pride, really hurt.

Laughing, Raja described what they had done in the

most graphic terms and she curled a hand into a fist and struck his shoulder in reproach. 'This is not a joke.'

'You're my wife. We had sex. Our desire was mutual and natural and the slaking of it rather wonderful. Why the fuss?' Raja enquired with a slumberous smile of satisfaction while he marvelled at the unfathomable way in which she drew out the lighter side of his nature.

Ruby was jolted by the reality that he was in a totally different frame of mind and mood. He was celebrating while she was filled with regrets. 'It's not that simple—you know it's not. We made an agreement—'

'A foolish agreement destined to be broken from the outset,' Raja countered without an ounce of uneasiness. 'How could we marry and live in such proximity and not surrender to the attraction between us?'

In rejection of that stance, Ruby twisted free of his arms and rolled away to the far side of the bed. 'That's not what you said to me at the time.'

At that precise reminder, an impatient look skimmed across Raja's face. 'Choice didn't come into it—I had to win your agreement to marry me—'

'*Had* to?' Ruby prompted stiffly, her whole attention lodged to him with unwavering force.

Far from impervious to the threat of the drama waiting in the wings, Raja raked his fingers through the black hair falling into curls at his brow and sent her a look of reproach. 'You are not that naive, Ruby. With this marriage we brought the end to a war and created a framework for a peaceful future for both our countries. There is nothing more important than that and I never pretended otherwise. We sacrificed personal freedom for the greater good.'

That grim little speech, voiced without sentiment, froze Ruby to the marrow and felt like an ice spear thrust through her heart. He had torn any possibility of fluffy illusion from their relationship to insist on showing it to her as it truly was. But had she ever been in doubt of what their relationship entailed? A marriage that was part of a peace treaty between warring countries? A royal husband, who had married her because it was his duty to do so? Exactly when had she begun to imagine that finer feelings might be incorporated in that logical and unemotional package?

Scrambling out of bed because she was hugely uncomfortable with any physical reminder of what had just taken place there, Ruby pulled on her wrap and folded her arms. She would be reasonable, totally reasonable and practical just as he was, she told herself urgently. 'You said that we made a foolish agreement. On what grounds do you base that charge?'

'When we made that agreement, we were already strongly attracted to each other.'

'But you didn't argue that at the time,' Ruby protested.

'Sometimes you can be very naive.' Raja sighed, expelling his breath in a measured hiss and stretching back against the tumbled pillows, a gloriously uninhibited vision of male magnificence. 'Why do you think I went to the UK to meet you? My job was to persuade you to marry me as quickly as possible and assume your rightful place as a royal here in Ashur.'

Ruby lost colour as he made that explanation. 'Your...*job*?'

'There is nothing warm and fuzzy about that peace

treaty, Ruby, or the stability that rests on the terms being upheld to the letter of the law. Obviously I was prepared to do pretty much whatever it took to win your agreement,' Raja admitted tautly.

'Obviously,' Ruby repeated, feeling horribly hollow inside as if she had been gutted with a fish knife. 'So, are you saying that you deliberately set out to get me into bed in the desert?'

'I desired you greatly.' Brilliant dark eyes struck challenging sparks off her critical and suspicious scrutiny.

'That's not what I asked you,' Ruby declared. 'I asked you if I was seduced to order, another box to be ticked on your list of duties.'

His clever brow furrowed, his darkly handsome features still and uninformative. 'To order?' he queried huskily.

'Your English is as good as mine, possibly even better!' Ruby snapped, her temper hanging by a fingernail to a cliff edge as she forced herself to seek a clarification that stung her shrinking self like acid. 'Stop faking incomprehension to play for time when I ask an awkward question!'

Unmoved by that indictment, Raja stretched, hard muscle rippling across his broad shoulders and abdomen as he shifted position with the fluidity and grace of a tiger about to spring. 'Is that what I'm doing?' he traded with an indolence she suspected to be entirely deceptive.

Being stonewalled merely aggravated Ruby more and her chin came up, eyes bright with antagonism and resentment now. 'Let me bring this down to the simplest level. Did you or did you not take off your boxers and lie down with me that night for the sake of your precious country?'

Raja very nearly laughed out loud at that demand but restrained the urge, aware it would go down like a lead balloon. 'I am willing to confess that I never had any true intention of allowing our marriage to be a fake. I hoped to make our marriage real from the day of our wedding.'

The barefaced cool with which he made that shattering admission shook Ruby, whose nature was the direct opposite of calculating, to her very depths. 'So, you deceived me.'

'You put me in a position where I could do little else. A divorce between us would be a political and economic disaster. Any goodwill gained by our marriage would be destroyed and offence and enmity would take its place. And how could I continue to rule this country without an Ashuri princess by my side?' he demanded bluntly. 'Your people would not accept me in such a role.'

Unfortunately for him, Ruby was in no mood to recognise the difficulties of his position or to make allowances. Deep hurt allied with a stark sense of humiliation were washing through her slight body in poisonous waves. 'You deceived me,' she said again, her voice brittle with angry bitter condemnation. 'I gave you my trust and you deceived me.'

'I always intended to do whatever it takes to make you happy in our marriage,' Raja breathed in a driven undertone, his dark eyes alight with annoyance and discomfiture, for he was well aware that he had been less than honest with her and that went against the grain with him, as well. 'That is the only justification I can offer you for my behaviour.'

'But if it takes a divorce to make me happy you're going to make it difficult,' Ruby guessed, her face pale and tight with the self-control she was exerting as she turned on her heel. 'I'm sleeping on the sofa tonight.'

As the door eased shut on her quiet exit Raja swore, jolted by a powerful wave of dissatisfaction more biting than any he had ever known. He had wounded her and he had never wanted to do that. Although it would have been very much out of character he badly wanted to unleash his temper and punch walls and shout. But the discipline of a lifetime held, forcing him to stop, think and reason. Pursuing her to continue the altercation in the state of mind she was in would only exacerbate the situation. He had chosen honesty and maybe he should have lied but he believed that the woman he had married deserved the truth from him.

Ironically, Raja believed that he knew what his wife wanted from him. After all, almost every decent woman he had ever spent time with had wanted the same thing from him: eternal devotion and commitment and all the empty words and promises that went along with them. At a young age Raja had learned to avoid getting involved with that kind of woman. His mistress Chloe's unconcealed greed was a great deal easier to satisfy and the main reason why Raja much preferred relationships based on practicality and mutual convenience.

Ruby, however, was very emotional and she would demand more than he had to offer. Ruby would want things that would make him grossly uncomfortable. He looked back down the years to when he had been a student deeply in love for the one and only time in his life. She would want romance and poetry, hand-holding and constant attention and if he even looked at another woman she might threaten to kill herself, he recalled with a barely repressed shudder. He was no woman's lapdog and, although his father was a noted poet in Najar, Raja secretly hated poetry. He groaned in increasing frustration. Why were some women so difficult? So highly strung and demanding? Her metaphoric cup was half empty but in comparison his was almost full to overflowing. Ruby was a very beautiful and very entertaining woman and he had just enjoyed the most fantastic sex with her. That was enough for him and an excellent foundation for a royal marriage between strangers. He was more than content with what they already had together. Why couldn't she be content? And how was he to persuade her of the value of his more rational and reserved approach?

On the sofa, which had all the lumps if not the worn appearance of a piece of furniture that had served beyond its time, Ruby tossed and turned. She was stunned that Raja could admit to telling her a barefaced lie. He had agreed to her terms. He had said the words but he hadn't *meant* them. Clearly he had been diametrically opposed to a platonic marriage and the first chance he got to change that status quo he had snatched at it.

Just as Ruby had snatched at Raja out in the desert, craving the hot, hard passion of that lean, strong body against hers! Lust, that was all it could have been, and she had given way to that lust and without much of a

struggle. It didn't matter how much she blamed the upsetting circumstances of their kidnapping for what had
transpired. In her heart she knew that nothing would
ever have happened between them had she not found
Raja al-Somari downright irresistible in the flesh.

But it seemed that Raja had made love to her for
much more prosaic reasons than mere desire. He had
slept with her to consummate their marriage, to make
it a *real* marriage and ensure that she was less able to
walk away easily. How much did he really find her attractive? Was it even possible that he was the sort of
guy who had set out to bring her down simply because
she defied his wishes and expectations? How many
women had actually said no to Prince Raja with his
fabulous looks and even more fabulous wealth? Had
she only made herself an irresistible challenge?

Her eyes prickled with stinging tears of humiliation
that rolled slowly down her face in the moonlight that
filtered through the windows, which had no curtains.
She had never had the power to guess what went on in
Raja's arrogant, dark head. Their confrontation tonight
had been an education. He had been a total mystery to
her and a dangerously fascinating one at that, she acknowledged painfully.

Possibly she had been overdue for the experience of
meeting a man who affected her more than she affected
him. Had she got too full of herself? Too convinced
she could not be fooled or hurt by a man? She had assumed she could call the shots with Raja and he had
just proved that she could not. The guy she had stupidly
married was much colder, more astute and ruthless than
she could ever be. Raja had manipulated her into doing

what he wanted her to do when she slept with him and in doing so he had crushed Ruby's pride to dust.

Hermione was standing guard over Ruby's sleep when Raja entered the room soon after dawn. With a snarl, the little dog launched herself at him and he caught the animal. He suffered a bite on his arm before he got the frenzied little dog under control and deposited her outside the suite with a word of command to the guards standing outside to take care of her. Raja then strolled quietly back across the room to study his soundly sleeping wife. She didn't take up much space on the sofa and she looked achingly young. Below the tousled mane of blonde hair, only her profile was visible. He could see the silvery tear tracks marking her cheek and he cursed under his breath, his conscience pierced afresh. He had screwed up, he had screwed up royally. He should have kept his mouth shut. Lying didn't come easily to him but the truth had done way too much damage.

Somehow he had to redress that damage and make their marriage work. With no previous experience in the marital department and only a long unhelpful history of unscrupulous mistresses to fall back on, Raja felt unusually weak on the necessary strategy required to make a wife happy. Particularly a wife as unusual as Ruby. An apology would probably be in order. It was not that he had done anything he shouldn't have done, he reasoned in frustration, more a question of accepting that in her eyes he was guilty and that for the sake of better marital relations he had to respond accordingly. He would buy her something as a gift, as well. Flowers? His nostrils flared and he grimaced. Flowers had the same nauseous effect on him as poetry. Diamonds? He had never met a woman who didn't melt when he gave her diamonds...

CHAPTER EIGHT

FROM HER SMALL collection of clothing, Ruby selected a black dress she had bought to wear at her mother's funeral and a beige cotton casual jacket. She would be too warm in the garments but they would have to do because she couldn't wear the red suit again. Some minimal make-up applied to conceal the puffiness of her eyes and her pallor, her hair caught up in a high ponytail for coolness, Ruby forced herself to walk out to the dining area and join Raja for breakfast.

'Good morning…' Raja murmured lazily as if they had not parted at odds the night before.

'Good morning.' One glance at that handsome face and her mouth ran dry and her heart thumped loudly behind her breastbone, while a tiny heated knot of re-action pulled taut in her pelvis and made her clench her thighs together as she took a seat opposite him. Face burning with discomfiture, she suddenly didn't blame herself any more for succumbing to Raja's lethal sex appeal. He was a heartbreakingly beautiful man. Her biggest weakness was her failure to appreciate how clever and calculating he might be, but now that she did know she would be a great deal more cautious.

'I've made arrangements for a new wardrobe to be assembled for you in Najar,' Raja informed her.

'I do need more clothes. I don't own dressy outfits but I wouldn't want anything too expensive or flashy,' Ruby responded thoughtfully as he poured tea for her and she buttered a roll. 'The state this country is in, it wouldn't be appropriate for me to be dressed up like some sort of celebrity.'

'Wajid would disagree with you. He thinks life is too dull here and that you will bring some much-needed colour and the promise that brighter times lie ahead. Here you *are* a celebrity, whether you like it or not, and celebrities dress up.'

Zuhrah joined them along with her male administrative counterpart, Asim, who organised Raja's diary. Ruby's engagements at the orphanage and at a school were discussed and useful sheets of facts tucked into a file for her. She could not help noticing that the heavy-duty visits, like one to a homeless camp and another to a makeshift hospital, fell on Raja's shoulders, Wajid evidently having decided such venues were no place for a lady. A lighter note was struck when a maid appeared with a crystal vase filled with the most exquisite white roses, which she placed on the table.

'Oh, how lovely!' Ruby got to her feet to lean down and draw in the rich opulent perfume of the perfect blooms and only then noticed the gift envelope inscribed with her name. She recognised Raja's distinctive handwriting immediately. Eyes veiling, her facial muscles freezing, she took the card and sat down again to open it with pronounced reluctance.

I am sorry for upsetting you. Raja

Her teeth gritted. She reckoned there was never a truer word written than that apt phrase but she was unimpressed by the apology, for a wife barely able to look at him never mind speak to him was naturally a problem he had to fix. No doubt any effort made towards that objective would be all for the greater good and the peace treaty, as well.

'Thank you,' she said with the wooden intonation of a robot and gave him an even more wooden smile purely for the benefit of their audience of staff. Wajid would have been proud of her, she reflected bleakly. Instead of throwing the vase at her royal husband she had smiled at him, showing a restraint in her opinion that raised her near to sainthood. After all, had he been sincerely sorry would he not just have apologised across the table?

Ruby didn't do a good fake smile, Raja acknowledged wryly while he wondered if it had been accidental or deliberate that at one point she had actually pushed the vase of roses out of her way to lay down her file. And then he could not credit that he had actually spared the brain power to wonder about something so trivial! He left the room to phone his jeweller and explain what he wanted: a diamond of the very highest calibre. Raja did not embarrass easily but her silence over breakfast had embarrassed him. He did not want their differences paraded in front of their staff for inevitably it would lead to gossip and the news that their marriage was in trouble would enter the public domain very soon afterwards.

Wajid accompanied Ruby to the orphanage and revealed that Raja had requested that he do so as soon as he had realised that Wajid had scheduled them to make visits separately.

'His Royal Highness is very protective of you,' Wajid told her with approval. 'When he is unable to be with you he wants you to have every possible means of support.'

It occurred to Ruby that that was paradoxical when Raja seemed to have the power to wound her more than anyone else. His protectiveness meant nothing, she reasoned unhappily. The prince was simply one of those very masculine men who deemed a woman to be more helpless and instinctively expected to have to take care of her. That in the desert she had proven him right on that score still blasted a giant hole in her self-esteem. But why did she feel so unhappy? Why had he hurt her as no other man had ever succeeded in doing since her stepfather had gone out of her life?

It hadn't just been sex for her, Ruby conceded reluctantly, striving to be honest about that. Raja was strong and clever and resourceful and she admired those traits. Add in his looks, boundless sex appeal and equally extensive charm and her defensive barriers had begun crumbling so fast she had barely registered the fact. Of course she had never met the equal of Raja al-Somari before. He came from a different world and culture but he had also been shaped by every educational advantage and great wealth and status. Twenty-odd years earlier, Ruby's mother, Vanessa, had made the mistake of falling in love with just such a man. Was Ruby about to make the same mistake? Not if she could help it.

The limousine in which she was travelling drew up outside the orphanage, a cluster of relatively modern buildings that had mercifully not been targeted by the Najari soldiers. As the older couple she had met at the reception the night before appeared on the steps to welcome them, Ruby had no more time for introspection. She had always loved children. As her visit progressed she was alternately appalled by the scale of loss many of the children had suffered in losing their entire families and then touched by the resilience of their spirits. The orphanage was in dire need of more trained staff, bedding and toys but most of the children were still able to laugh and smile and play.

One little girl attached herself to Ruby almost as soon as she appeared by sliding her tiny hand into hers. About three years old, Leyla had big dark eyes, a tangle of black curls and a thumb firmly lodged in her rosebud mouth.

The orphanage director was surprised by the little girl's behaviour and explained that she was rather withdrawn with the staff. Leyla's parents had died during the war. Unfortunately there was no tradition of adoption in Ashuri society and many people were struggling just to feed their own families. Leyla clinging to her skirt, Ruby spent the most time with the younger children and listened while a story was being told. When the time came for Ruby to leave, Leyla clung to Ruby as if her life depended on it and, lifted from her, wept inconsolably. Ruby was surprised at how difficult she found it to part with Leyla. Just the feel and scent of that warm little body curled trustingly in her arms had made her eyes sting with tears. All of a sudden her own problems seemed to shrink in comparison.

Ignoring Wajid's disapproving expression, Ruby promised to come back and visit in the evening. Their next visit to a temporary school housed in tents was a good deal more brisk but also less formal as Ruby mingled with teenagers and answered their questions as best she could, trying not to wince or stiffen when the court advisor admonished those he considered were being too familiar with his royal companion.

'I don't like formality. I'm more of a hands-on person and that's the only style I'm comfortable with,' Ruby informed the older man as they drove off.

'Royalty should be more reserved,' Wajid preached.

A determined look in her level eyes that Raja would have recognised, Ruby said quietly, 'I'll carry out my engagements as the ordinary person that I am, Wajid. I can only do this kind of thing because I like mingling with people and chatting to them.'

'Princess Bariah would not have dreamt of lifting a crying child,' the older man was reduced to telling her.

'I am not Bariah. I grew up in a different society.'

'One day soon you will be a queen and such familiarity from your subjects would seem disrespectful.'

Aware that a man old enough to be her grandfather was almost certain to cherish a less liberal viewpoint on suitable behaviour, Ruby dropped the subject. But she had not noticed Raja standing on ceremony with their guests at the reception the evening before. He had appeared equally friendly and courteous with everybody.

When she got back to the palace she was so tired she lay down. For quite some time she thought sadly about Leyla. The little girl had touched her heart and she was wishing that there were something she could do to help her before she finally fell asleep for several hours. She wakened when a maid knocked to deliver a garment bag. Unzipping it, she extracted an opulent sapphire-blue evening dress and high-heeled shoes. Her expression thoughtful, she checked the size of both.

Only minutes later, Raja joined her in the bedroom.

'Did you organise this?' she asked, extending the dress.

'Yes. This evening you'll be meeting friends and relatives of your late uncle and his family. You would feel ill at ease if you were underdressed in such a gathering,' Raja forecast smoothly.

'You even got my sizes right,' Ruby remarked, thinking how very, very handsome he was, even when in need of a good shave, for dark stubble clearly accentuated the sensual curve of his sculpted mouth. 'You're obviously used to buying clothes for women.'

A slight frown at that remark drawing his ebony brows together, Raja swung fluidly away to remove his jacket and made no response.

But Ruby was not so easily deflected. 'Are you in the habit of buying for your sisters?'

'They do their own shopping,' Raja admitted.

'So, you are accustomed to buying clothes for the other women in your life,' Ruby gathered, not a bit averse to making him uncomfortable if she could.

'No comment. I'm glad you like the dress.'

Her brown eyes flamed amber. 'Your hide is as tough as steel, isn't it?'

'I never said I was a virgin,' Raja shot back at her with sardonic cool, his strong features taut.

'Oh, I had already worked that out for myself,' Ruby retorted, thinking of how smoothly he had seduced and bedded her.

In retrospect the level of his experience with her sex was obvious to her and to her annoyance that awareness loosed a whole flock of curious questions inside her head. How had she compared to his other lovers? Did he go for blondes, brunettes or redheads or any of the above? Would he even have found her attractive had she not been a long-lost and almost forgotten Ashuri princess? Every question of that ilk that crossed Ruby's mind infuriated her. Why was she letting him make her feel insecure and vulnerable? Now that she knew the truth behind their consummated marriage, she would be better able to protect herself.

'There will not be another woman in my bed while you remain my wife,' Raja volunteered abruptly, his brilliant, dark eyes welded to her expressive face.

'My goodness, do you think I care?' Ruby forced a laugh and then plastered an amused and scornful smile to her lips. 'I couldn't care less what you do. I have to take account of the reality that we're stuck with each other for the foreseeable future so there's no sense in fighting every step of the way.'

'You make a good point,' Raja responded although outrage had shot flames of gold into his gaze when she declared that she didn't care what he did.

'And I'm not asking you to sleep on the sofa tonight and I'm not sleeping on it either. We're adults. I'm asking you to respect that agreement you think is so foolish and forget that we ever had sex.'

Wonderment consumed Raja as she spoke. Forget about the sex? She stood there looking like every fantasy he had ever had in her little black dress with her beautiful eyes, sultry pink mouth and glorious legs tempting him and she thought he could easily return to treating her like a sexless stranger? He *had* deceived her by cloaking his true intentions, he reminded himself fiercely. This was the punishment, the payoff. He had to give her time to adjust to her new role.

'I will do my best,' Raja replied flatly.

He emanated angry vibrations and she wondered why that was. The need to get inside Raja's head and understand what made him tick was, Ruby was discovering, a constant craving. Did he only want to make love to her because he thought that should be his right as a husband? Or would he have wanted her anyway just for herself? And why, when she had never planned to become intimate with him, should that distinction matter to her?

Later he did up the zip on the blue dress and it fit her like a tailor-made glove, the rich colour flattering her fair colouring. As she sat at the dressing table straightening her hair Raja came to her side and handed her a jewellery box. 'It is a small gift.'

Ruby lifted the lid and stared down dumbstruck at the flawless glittering teardrop diamond on a pendant. Small wasn't the right word. It was a *big* diamond and, although she knew next to nothing about the value of jewellery because she had never owned any beyond a wristwatch, she guessed that a diamond that large had to be worth a small fortune.

'Thanks,' she mumbled in shock.

'Allow me.' While she lifted her hair out of the way, Raja clasped the pendant at the nape of her neck. She shivered as his fingertips brushed her sensitive skin and that little knot of sexual hunger in the pit of her stomach tightened up a notch. 'I would've given you earrings but your ears aren't pierced.'

'No, I'm a total unbelievable coward. I once went with a friend and she fainted when they did her ears. She bled all over the place too—it put me right off!' Ruby confided, suddenly desperate to fill the awkward silence.

His shrewd, dark eyes screened in his reflection in the mirror, Raja rested a hand on her taut shoulder. 'Ruby...'

'My mother said my father chose my name, you know,' she volunteered abruptly. 'He said that a virtuous wife was worth more than rubies. It's kind of insulting that the only future he could see for me was as someone's wife.'

'But I am grateful to have you as my wife.'

'Only because I was part of the peace treaty,' Ruby fielded, flatly unimpressed by that declaration. 'Spoils of war and all that.'

TWO WEEKS LATER, the night before Ruby's first visit to Najar, Raja was enjoying a pleasant daydream. A century or so earlier had he acquired Ruby as the spoils of war, she would have belonged to him...*utterly*. It was a heady masculine fantasy to toy with while he was being driven to the orphanage that his wife had contrived to visit alone almost every evening since her initial official visit there. He had Wajid to thank for that information, for Ruby had kept very quiet about where she took off to during their rare moments of leisure.

Ruby took care not to share that time with him. It was yet another vote of no confidence from his wife, who was not his wife in any way that mattered, Raja conceded grimly. They might still share the same bed but she had placed a bolster pillow down the middle of it. That had made him laugh the first night, but within a week the comedy aspect had worn very thin.

His cell phone pinged with a message and he checked, frowning as the snap Chloe had put in of herself shone up at him, all blonde hair and a wide, perfect smile. Ruby did not possess that perfection of feature. Her nose turned up at the tip and she had the cutest little gap between her front teeth. Yet whenever he saw Ruby there was no one else in the room capable of commanding his attention. His handsome mouth curled as he read the suggestive text from his mistress. He had no desire to exchange sexy texts. That didn't excite him. Chloe was becoming a liability. On the other hand if Ruby had felt the urge to send him a suggestive text he would have responded with imagination and enthusiasm, he acknowledged with self-derision. Unfortunately there was as much chance of a sext coming from Ruby as of Ashur sending a rocket to the moon.

Raja, however, remained conscious that he had no real grounds for complaint. His bride was already performing her duties as a future queen with considerable grace and good humour. Her naturally warm personality had great appeal. The Ashuri people liked her easy manner and chatty approach, not to mention her frankness in referring to the days when she had led the life of a young working woman.

Forewarned by a call of his impending unofficial visit, the orphanage director greeted him in the hall and took him straight to Ruby. Ruby was in the nursery with a little girl on her lap, painstakingly reading out a few brief words from a picture book in the basic Ashuri language, which she was working so hard to learn. A cluster of children sat on the floor round her feet.

'The princess is a natural with children. It's unfortunate that the child she is holding—Leyla—is becoming a little too attached to your wife,' the older woman told him in a guarded undertone.

Raja got the message intended. He watched the little girl raise a hand to pat Ruby's cheek and then beam adoringly up at her, her other hand clutching possessively at Ruby's top. He watched Ruby look down at the child and realised that he had a problem that cut both ways, for his wife's lovely face softened into a deeply affectionate smile. Raja would have been elated to receive such a smile but he never had. When Ruby saw him in the doorway, she leapt almost guiltily upright, arms locking protectively round the child in her arms. A staff member approached to take the little girl and Ruby handed her over, visibly troubled when the child began to sob in protest.

'Raja…' Ruby framed in a jerky, almost soundless whisper, for she was so astonished to see him standing there that her voice just deserted her.

Clad in the long off-white tunic called a *thaub* that he wore most days, Raja looked fantastically handsome, the smooth golden planes of his classic masculine features demarcated by the exotic set of his lustrous dark eyes and high cheekbones. Her tummy flipped like a teenager's and she froze, feeling foolish and very much aware that she was hopelessly infatuated with her husband, which was one reason why she avoided his company as much as was humanly possible. He was like an ever-growing fever she was trying to starve into subjection in her bloodstream.

'I had some news I wished to share with you,' Raja imparted lightly. 'Until Wajid mentioned it, I had no idea that this was where you were coming most evenings.'

'I enjoy being with the children. There's no formality here—it's relaxing,' she told him.

'Mrs Baldwin said you're fond of one particular child—'

'Leyla…there's just something about her that grabs my heart every time I see her,' Ruby admitted, opting for honesty. 'I really love spending time with her. She's so sweet and smart.'

Installed in the limo he had arrived in, Ruby said, 'What news wouldn't wait until I got back to the palace?'

'There have been arrests here and in Najar. The members of the royal households who shared our itinerary with the kidnappers have been identified and arrested, as have their supporters.'

Taken by surprise by that information, Ruby frowned and asked, 'Who were they?'

'An aide on my father's staff and a private secretary from Wajid's team here in the palace. Wajid is very ashamed of that link. Be tactful with him if he raises the subject. He is very much aware that the kidnapping could have ended tragically.'

'But we were unhurt,' Ruby hastened to remind him.

Her husband looked grave, his sensual mouth compressing. 'Ruby…tempers run high with memories of the war still so fresh. Fighting could have broken out again. Our lives and those of others were put at risk. The mercenaries whom the perpetrators hired to act for them have fled the country and are unlikely to be apprehended but a prison sentence is inevitable for the citizens involved.'

'I understand.' The justice system was rigid and retribution fell swift and hard on those who broke the laws in their countries. Ruby was already learning to temper her opinions in the light of the society in which she now lived, but it still occasionally annoyed her to depend so much on Raja's interpretation of events and personalities.

Just weeks earlier she had claimed that she intended to be as much involved as Raja in ruling Ashur and could only marvel at her innocence, for the longer she lived in the palace, the more she appreciated how much she still had to learn about the constantly squabbling local factions and the council of elderly men who stalled and argued more than they made decisions. Raja spent a good deal of his time soothing difficult people and in meetings with the Najari investors financing the rebuilding of Ashur. His duties seemed endless and he was working very long hours because he was also dealing with his duties as Regent of Najar from a distance. Unable to offer much in the way of support, Ruby felt guilty.

Indeed the longer she stayed in Ashur, the more confused and unsure of her own wishes Ruby was becoming. She was fully conscious that Raja had married her with the best of intentions and acted as he saw fit in an effort to turn their platonic marriage into a lasting relationship. He had played the hand he had been given without intending to hurt or humiliate her. He wanted her to stay married to him but to date he had put no pressure on her to do so and she respected him for that. Yet while he was bearing the blame for the dissension between them she knew that she had played a sizeable part in her own downfall by being so violently attracted to him. Her decision to surrender to that attraction had badly muddied the water and her thinking processes and encouraged her to want more from him than he was ever likely to give her. When she had specified and demanded a marriage of convenience, how could she blame him for *her* change of heart?

At the same time avoiding Raja and keeping to the other side of the bolster in the bed was beginning to feel a little childish. She was also living on her nerves because her period was currently overdue. She had told herself that her menstrual cycle could just be acting up. But in her heart of hearts she was terrified that her misfiring cycle combined with the new tenderness of her breasts meant that she had fallen pregnant. She had abandoned all restraint in the desert with Raja and it looked as though she might well be about to pay a price for that recklessness.

'The little girl you were with,' Raja commented quietly.

Instantly, Ruby tensed. 'Leyla? What about her?'

'Have you gone to the orphanage every evening?'

'Have you a problem with that?' Ruby countered defensively.

'The child seems very attached to you. Is that wise?'

he prompted gently. 'She will be hurt when you disappear from her life again.'

Annoyance hurtled up through Ruby and she closed her hands together very tightly to control her feelings. 'I have no plans to disappear.'

Sensing her distress at what he had suggested, Raja stretched out a hand to rest it on top of her tensely knotted fingers. 'We're leaving Ashur tomorrow for a couple of weeks. You have many claims on your time now.'

'I... I was thinking of adopting Leyla!' Ruby flung at him, finally putting into words the idea that had been growing at the back of her mind for two weeks and working on her until it began to seem a possibility rather than a wild idea. 'I know you'll probably think I'm crazy but I've become very fond of Leyla. Whatever it takes, I'd very much like to give her a home.'

Astonished by that outspoken admission, Raja studied her. 'But you're planning to divorce me...'

Ruby frowned. 'Well, eventually, yes, *but*—'

'Then I suspect that you have not thought this idea through,' Raja intoned. 'The Ashuri Court of Family Law would not countenance foreign adoption and would wish the child to be raised here where she was born with her own language and people. I doubt that you are willing to offer her that option.'

'I would love her,' Ruby breathed in stark disagreement as the limo drew up outside the side entrance to the palace. 'Leyla needs *love* more than she needs anything else!'

'Love is not always enough,' Raja drawled softly.

In receipt of that hoary old chestnut, Ruby shot him a furious look of disagreement and took the stairs to their suite two at a time. Her heart was hammering like mad behind her breastbone because she was genuinely upset. Having finally got up the courage to voice her hopes with regard to Leyla, she had been shot down in flames. The hard facts Raja had voiced rankled and hurt. Evidently there was no question of her trying to adopt Leyla if she was planning to ultimately divorce Raja. But *was* she planning to divorce him?

Exactly when would she be able to walk away from Raja without that decision impacting on the stability of Ashur? She could not imagine a date even on the horizon when she might leave her marriage without there being a risk of it leading to political upheaval in her late father's country. Her decision to marry Raja had been rash in the extreme, she conceded ruefully. She had not looked into the future. She had failed to recognise that a short-term fix might be almost worse for her country of birth than her refusing outright to marry Raja. A divorce would unleash more political and economic turmoil. Raja was right about that, for she had listened to people talking and seen for herself how much weight rested on their marriage as a symbol of unity and reconciliation. An image of Leyla's tear-stained little face swam before her now and her heart turned over inside her chest.

'What do you know about love?' Ruby demanded, challenging Raja as she poured the mint tea waiting for them on a tray. 'Have you ever been in love?'

'Once was enough,' he admitted sardonically.

Ironically Ruby felt affronted by that admission. He didn't love her but he had fallen for someone else? 'Who was she?'

His lean strong face took on a wry expression. 'Her name was Isabel. We met as students at Oxford. I was besotted with her.' He grimaced, openly inviting her amusement. 'We read poetry and went everywhere together holding hands.'

'People apparently do stuff like that when they're in love,' Ruby remarked stiltedly, well aware that he had never shown any desire to read her a poem or to hold her hand and, as a result, feeling distinctly short-changed rather than amused.

'The romance turned into a nightmare,' Raja confided tight-mouthed, his beautiful dark eyes bleak with recollection. 'She was very jealous and possessive. Everything was a drama with her. If I even spoke to another woman she threw a scene. I was nineteen years old and totally inexperienced with your sex.'

Sipping the mint tea, which she had learned to find refreshing, Ruby was touched by his honesty, for baring his soul did not come naturally to a man accustomed to keeping his own counsel and concealing his feelings. 'At that age you must have found a volatile woman hard to cope with.'

'She threatened to kill herself when I tried to break it off. I stood up to her but she carried through her threat—she *did* take an overdose,' he admitted gravely, acknowledging her wince of sympathy with compressed lips. 'When I said it was a nightmare I wasn't exaggerating. Eventually Isabel's parents put her into a clinic to be treated for depression. It took me a long time to extract myself from my entanglement with her.'

'And of course it put you off what she saw as love,' Ruby conceded thoughtfully, understanding that perfectly, her brown eyes soft as she tried to picture him as a naive teenager spouting poetry and holding hands. 'But Isabel sounds as if she had a very twisted idea of love. It was just your bad luck to meet a woman like that and get burned.'

Raja shrugged a broad shoulder in a fatalistic gesture.

'My mum, though—she got burned twice over,' Ruby volunteered, startling him. 'She lacked good judgement. She just fell in love and believed the man would be perfect. My father married his second wife behind her back and then told Mum he had no choice because he needed a son and she had had to have a hysterectomy after giving birth to me.'

'And the second burning?' Raja queried curiously, for he was already familiar with the first, although he had been given a rather different version.

Ruby grimaced. 'The reason Hermione distrusts men around me—my stepfather, Curtis. He was always trying it on with me—'

'Your stepfather tried to abuse you?' Raja ground out in an appalled tone, black brows drawing together.

Ruby nodded in uneasy confirmation. 'He started bothering me when I was about twelve. By then Mum was going out several nights a week to a part-time job and I was left alone in the house with him.'

Raja was outraged that she had been targeted at such a tender age by a man within her own home where she should have been safe. For the first time he understood what had given Ruby her essentially feisty and independent nature as well as her distrust of his sex. Angry concern in his gaze, Raja was frowning. 'You

didn't tell your mother what he was doing, did you?'
he guessed. 'Why not?'

'Because it would've broken her heart,' Ruby proffered heavily. 'She adored Curtis and she'd had a bad
enough time with my father.'

'Your stepfather never actually managed to touch
you?'

'No, but I lived in terror that he would. It was such
a relief for me when he walked out on us. He made me
very suspicious of men. He also left Mum absolutely
broke.' Ruby set down her cup and began to move towards the bedroom.

'Ruby?'

Ruby glanced back at him warily.

'How much do you want to give Leyla a home?'

Ruby paled and contrived to look both very young
and very determined. 'I've never wanted anything
more...' *Apart from you*, but that was a truth she refused to voice, watching him as he stood there poised,
darkly beautiful and dangerous to her every sense and
emotion.

'I will make enquiries on our behalf—'

'Our?'

'Only a couple could be considered to adopt her.
It would have to be a joint application from us both.'

Astonished by that speech, Ruby trembled with
emotion. 'Is that an offer?'

Raja surveyed her steadily. 'No, it is my assurance
of support in whatever you decide to do.'

And Ruby knew very well what was going unsaid
in that statement. A married couple naturally meant a
couple planning to stay married. Lashes lowering, she

was too enervated to respond and she turned away and went for a shower. Towelling herself dry in the bathroom, she took stock of her situation. She was in love with him. Why not just come clean about that? She was madly, hopelessly in love with Raja al-Somari! Aside from that sense of duty of his, which had hit her pride squarely where it hurt, she liked everything about Raja. His strength, his intelligence, his generosity. His protectiveness, his understanding, his tolerance. He was no longer just a very good-looking, sexy guy, he was the one she had learned to love to distraction even though she had done her utmost to resist his considerable appeal.

The bedroom was empty. But she left the bolster pillow in the foot of the wardrobe where it stayed by day. Tonight she saw no need for a barrier. In fact she was not quite sure which of them had required the restraint imposed by the presence of the bolster the most.

Thirty minutes later, Raja came to bed and the very first thing he noticed was the missing bolster. He slid into the bed in semi-darkness and lay there. There might as well have been a ten-foot wall down the middle of the bed, he reflected wryly. He refused to give her the excuse of believing that there had been any sort of a price attached to his support in the adoption application she was hoping that they would make. He was very much impressed by her commitment to the child, her willingness to become a mother at a young age when so many women would have chosen only to make the most of his unlimited wealth.

Barely a foot away Ruby lay wide awake, as well. She knew that she wanted him quite unbearably. She also knew that suddenly bringing the sex factor back in before other things were sorted out between them would be extremely imprudent but she was still madly hoping that he would take her unspoken invitation.

But the invitation was ignored and it took her a long time to get to sleep. Hours crept past while she thought about Leyla, wondering if they would be allowed to offer the little girl a home and if Raja would learn to love her, as well. She should have discussed the subject more with him. She had to learn how to be half of a couple and wondered why that skill seemed to come so much more naturally to him. It felt as though she had barely slept when she woke up and recalled that this was the day when she would finally meet Raja's family and see Najar for the first time.

CHAPTER NINE

'WAJID SAID THAT adopting an Ashuri child would be a fantastic PR exercise,' Raja revealed with a look of distaste mid-morning the following day as they travelled to the airport for their flight. 'The orphanage director is pleased about our decision because she hopes that our example will encourage people to consider the other children available for adoption.'

'My goodness, you've been busy,' Ruby commented a tad guiltily at his obvious industry with regard to her hopes concerning the little girl. Having woken soon after dawn when Raja always got up, she had felt distinctly nauseous and had returned to bed only to sleep in late and have a rushed breakfast. A stomach upset, she was wondering now that she felt perfectly fine again, or a symptom of a more challenging condition? Could she be pregnant? How soon would she be able to find out? And how could she check discreetly without anyone finding out?

She was startled when the limousine turned in the orphanage gates.

'I think it's time that I met Leyla properly,' Raja announced, recognising her surprise at that change to their itinerary. 'And I believe that you would be glad of the opportunity to see her again before we leave.'

The Baldwins met them on the doorstep to express voluble thanks for the sizeable donation that Raja had made to the orphanage. He had not shared that fact with Ruby and was clearly uncomfortable with the couple's gratitude. They were ushered into an office and Leyla was brought to them there. Her little face lit up when she saw Ruby and she ran in her eagerness to greet her, only to fall to a halt when she saw Raja. He crouched down to a less intimidating height and produced a ball from his pocket. Leyla clutched the ball in a tiny fist while surveying Raja with great suspicion. But Raja was perfectly at home with her, talking to her, smiling and teasing until the child began to giggle and hide her face.

Witnessing that surprising show, Ruby was learning something she hadn't known. 'You're used to kids.'

'I ought to be. My sisters have five children between them and my cousins must have about thirty,' he volunteered, finally standing up with Leyla content to be held in his arms, her thumb stuck in her mouth, her eyes bright.

The effort he was making, the kindness he displayed, Ruby reflected on a tide of quiet appreciation, just made her love him all the more. Suddenly the fact he had taken advantage of her susceptibility to him in the desert no longer mattered and her resentment melted away. Hadn't she encouraged him and taken the final decision? As she had good reason to know he was a very practical and dutiful guy, loyal to his country, his family, faithful to his promises and keen to meet every expectation no matter how unreasonable it might be. And at its most basic, all Raja had ever wanted from her was the willingness to make their marriage work. But the man whom she had resented for that no-nonsense aspiration was also the same one holding the little girl she had come to care for and he was willing for both their sakes to consider making her a part of his illustrious family. And no man Ruby had ever met had been willing to expend even a tenth of Raja's effort and thoughtfulness into making her happy.

ARRIVING IN THE country of Najar was not remotely like flying into Ashur. For a start there was a proper airport that was very large and sophisticated. In fact as Ruby looked out open-mouthed at the busy streets through which they were being driven with a police escort and motorcycle outriders, Najar seemed to have nothing at all in common with Ashur. Towering office blocks, apartment buildings, fancy shopping malls and exotically domed mosques all blended together in a well-designed city with wide, clean streets. She saw at once why Raja had looked at her in disbelief when she had accused him of wanting the throne of Ashur. Her birth country was very much the poor relation, decades behind its rich neighbour in technology and development.

In contrast, the royal palace was still housed in an ancient citadel separated from the aggressively modern city by the huge green public park that stretched outside its extensive walls.

And the palace might be ancient on the outside but, from the inside, Ruby soon appreciated that Raja's family home bore a closer resemblance to a glossy spread from an exclusive design magazine. The interior was so grand and opulent that she was stunned by the eye-watering expanse of marble flooring and the glimpses of fabulously gilded and furnished rooms. Her steps had slowed and she was fingering the plain dark dress she had chosen to wear with her nervous tension rising to gigantic heights when a door opened and a group of women appeared. And, oh, my goodness, Ruby's sense of being intimidated went into overdrive as shrieks of excitement sounded and high heels clattered across the incredible floor. Ruby and Raja were engulfed by an enthusiastic welcome.

Raja drew her forward in her little black chainstore dress. 'This is Ruby...' and she wanted to kick him for not warning her that the women in his family wore haute couture even in the afternoon. Indeed one look at Raja's female relatives and she felt like the ugly duckling before the swan transformation. All of them were dressed as if they were attending a cocktail party. They sported elaborate hairdos, full make-up, jewel-coloured silks and satins and fantastic jewellery.

They entered the room the women had just vacated on a tide of welcoming chatter and questions. Fortunately everybody seemed to speak at least some English. Children joined their mothers in the crowd surrounding Ruby. There was an incredible amount of noise. Most of the men standing around in the big room attempted to act as though they were not as curious about Raja's bride as their womenfolk were. One tall young man made no such attempt at concealment and he strode across the room to seize her hand and shake it with a formality at odds with his wide grin and assessing eyes. 'Raja said you were even more gorgeous than you looked in your photo and he was right. I'm his brother, Haroun,' he told her cheerfully.

Ruby thought that it was heartening to know that Raja paid her compliments behind her back that he would never have dreamt of making to her face. Was he afraid she might get big-headed? Or did compliments fall under the dubious heading of romance? Or did a woman in a platonic relationship just not qualify for such ego-boosting frills? Haroun looked like a smaller, slighter, younger version of his big brother and he was rather more light-hearted, for he was cracking politically incorrect jokes about Ashur within seconds. Drinks and snacks were served by uniformed staff and Raja's sisters, Amineh and Hadeel, were quick to come and speak to her.

'You are very beautiful,' Hadeel, a tall, shapely woman in her mid-twenties, told her with an admiring smile. 'And a much more suitable match for my brother than your unfortunate cousin.'

'Am I?' Ruby studied her sister-in-law hopefully. 'I never met my cousin so I know nothing about her.'

'Bariah was thirty-seven years old and a widow,' Amineh told her wryly.

'But she was also a very good and well-respected woman,' Hadeel hastened to add, clearly afraid that her sister might have caused offence.

Ruby, however, was just revelling in the promise of such indiscreet gossip. She had missed that aspect of female companionship and felt that when Raja's sisters were willing to be so frank with her it boded well for her future relationship with them. Learning that Bariah had been eight years older than Raja and had also been married before was something Ruby could have found out for herself from Wajid, but she had been too proud to reveal her curiosity and ask more questions. She met Amineh's and Hadeel's husbands and a whole gaggle of children followed by a long parade of more distant relatives. Everyone was very friendly and welcoming and she was thoroughly relaxed by the time that Raja came to find her. He explained that his father found large family gatherings very tiring and that he was waiting in the next room to meet her in private.

King Ahmed was in a wheelchair and frail in appearance. He had Raja's eyes and white hair and, although he spoke only a few words of English, his quiet smile and the warm clasp of his hand were sufficient to express his acceptance of Ruby as the latest member of his extensive family. Ruby was surprised to learn that Raja had already told his father about Leyla and their plans. The older man was warmly supportive of their intentions and talked at some length about his sadness over the suffering and disruption inflicted on families during the war.

'I didn't realise that you were so close to your father that you would already have told him about Leyla,' Ruby commented on the way back into the party at the end of their audience with the king.

Raja laughed. 'No matter where I am in the world we talk on the phone every day. I think he would have been very shocked to hear the news about Leyla from anyone else!'

'I wish I'd known my father,' Ruby confided, feeling a slight nauseous lurch in her stomach and tensing slightly, for she had assumed her tummy upset at the start of the day had gone away and she didn't want it revisiting her while she was in company.

Raja paused to look down at her with his dramatic, dark, deep-set eyes. 'The loss was his, Ruby. I fear that you suffered because he and your mother parted on bad terms.'

'Well, after what he did to Mum, naturally they did.'

'The story of your background that I heard suggested that your mother was aware that your father might well take another wife after they were married. It was a lifestyle practised by several of your ancestors over the past hundred years,' Raja told her quietly. 'Perhaps your mother didn't understand what she was getting into when she agreed to marry him.'

'That's very possible...' Ruby focused wide brown eyes on him that were suddenly full of dismay. 'I can't believe I didn't ask you *but*—'

Raja laughed and rested a silencing forefinger against her parted lips. 'No, do not ask me that question, *habibi*. I would be mortally offended. One wife has always been sufficient for the men in my family and the thought of more than one of you is actually quite unnerving.'

'Unnerving? *How?*' Ruby demanded and just at that moment her fractious insides clenched and went to war with her dignity again. Forced to hurry off to the nearest cloakroom, Ruby was so embarrassed by her digestive weakness that her eyes flooded with tears. Her mood was not improved when Raja's sisters insisted on waiting outside the door for her to ensure that she was all right, for she would rather have suffered the sickness without a concerned audience close by.

When the emergency was over, she was ushered into the building that acted as Raja's secluded home within the rambling fortress. He had his own staff, one of whom showed her up a flight of stairs to a superbly decorated bedroom suite. It was a relief to slip off her shoes there and lie down on top of the bed. A drink reputed to soothe a troubled stomach was brought to her and a little while after that as her tension eased and she relaxed she began feeling fine and eventually and surprisingly rather hungry.

A pair of Saluki hounds trotting at his heels, Raja walked in to study her from the foot of the bed. Hermione had accompanied them and the little dog jumped up at the side of the bed to nuzzle her cold nose against Ruby's hand, the Salukis following to make her acquaintance. 'Oh, they're beautiful, Raja!' Ruby exclaimed, leaning out of bed to pat their silky heads. 'Do they belong to you?'

'Yes. Hermione seems to like them well enough. How are you feeling?' Raja asked

'Great now, believe it or not,' she told him with a hesitant smile. 'I'm going to have a shower and then I'd like something to eat. I'm sorry about all the fuss.'

'Are you sure that you're feeling well enough to get up?'

Ruby slid easily off the bed and scolded Hermione for trying to jump up on it. She could not help noticing that Raja's dogs, who had retreated to sit by the door, seemed to be very well trained. 'Very sure.'

'I'll order a meal.'

'Haven't you eaten either?'

'I wanted to see how you were first.'

Ruby checked out the dressing room in search of her wrap and found the closets and drawers were already packed with unfamiliar clothes in her sizes. 'That's some new wardrobe you've bought me!' she called to Raja.

'It won't matter what you wear. You will still outshine every outfit,' Raja responded huskily.

Ruby was surprised by that tribute. A flowing blue negligee set draped over one arm, she emerged from the dressing room to study him, the colour of awareness lighting up her face. Having discarded his traditional robe, he was in the act of changing into designer jeans and a shirt. The fluid grace and strength of that muscular physique of his still had enough impact to take her breath away. It didn't matter how much exposure she had to Raja al-Somari, he still had the power to trip her heartbeat inside her and make her mouth run dry with excitement.

'Shower,' she reminded herself a little awkwardly.

The bathroom was as palatial as the bedroom and the invigorating beat of the water from multi-jets restored her energy levels. She wondered how Raja had tolerated the weak water flow of the old-fashioned shower in their suite of rooms in Ashur. Since her arrival in Najar she had come to realise that he was accustomed to a lifestyle in which every possible modern convenience and luxury was available to ensure the last word in comfort. She admired him for not having uttered a single complaint while he was forced to stay in the palace in Ashur.

When she returned to the bedroom Raja was talking on the phone in Arabic. He glanced up and then stilled to stare, lustrous dark eyes flaming gold at the sight of her. A wealth of blonde hair falling round her lovely face, her slim shapely figure framed by the flowing blue nightwear, she was a picture. With an abstracted final word he concluded his call and pushed the phone into his pocket.

As she met that intense appraisal Ruby's face flushed, her nipples tightening into prominence while a melting sensation of warmth pulsed between her thighs. As he crossed the room, his eyes holding her gaze with a stormy sensuality that filled her with yearning, she was welded to the spot.

Without a word, Raja pushed the tumble of silky blonde hair back from her cheekbone and lowered his head to trace the seam of her closed mouth with his tongue and then pry her lips apart. Fingers stroking her slender neck, he plundered her mouth with a hungry ferocity that blew Ruby away. Staggered by the passion he made no attempt to contain, she angled her head back, snatching in a ragged breath as she looked up at him through her lashes and collided with the smouldering urgency in his stunning eyes. Her tummy flipped. One kiss and she felt as if he had switched a light on inside her, bathing her in warmth and dazzling brilliance.

'I am already so hot and ready for you,' Raja breathed thickly.

Ruby trembled, insanely aware of the surging dampness and the ache at the heart of her body. She was so wound up she couldn't make her throat produce a recognisable sound. But it was also one of those moments when she knew not a shred of doubt about what she wanted to happen next. Her hands lifted of their own volition to unbutton his shirt.

A wolfish smile tilted Raja's handsome mouth. He bent his head to kiss her again with lingering eroticism. 'I will make it so good for you, *aziz*,' he husked in a tone of anticipation that slivered through her like a depth charge of promise.

And the breath rattled in Ruby's tight throat and her knees went weak because she had every faith in his ability to deliver on that score. He would drive her out of her mind with pleasure and she was way past the stage where she could deny either of them what they both needed. She wasn't quite sure when wanting had become a much more demanding *need* and self-denial an impossible challenge. Mesmerised by Raja's raw sensuality, she stretched up to touch his face with delicate fingertips, tracing those slashing angular cheekbones, and those beautiful sculpted lips. She gasped beneath that carnal mouth as it captured hers with delicious masculine savagery. Suddenly, as if her caress had unlocked his self-control to free his elemental passion, he trailed off the peignoir with impatient hands and pushed her back on the bed. Throwing off his shirt, he came down beside her bare-chested.

Breathing shallowly, the level of his hunger for her unhidden, Raja stared down at her. 'I don't know how I've kept my hands off you for so long. It was pure torment.'

As she pushed up on her elbows, feeling marvellously irresistible, Ruby's eyes brightened and she stretched closer to unzip his jeans. The bulge of his arousal made that exercise a challenge and she laughed when he had to help her and then stopped laughing altogether when he drew her hand down to the long, hard length of his erection in an expression of need that was a huge turn-on for her.

She bent her head and took him in her mouth, silky blonde hair brushing his hair-roughened thighs. Watching her, Raja groaned with intense pleasure, knotting his hands in her hair and then finally pulling away at the peak and surprising her.

'Raja…?'

'I want to come inside you,' he told her raggedly. 'And once isn't going to be enough…'

Shivering in reaction to the coiled-tight ache of need in her, Ruby let him move her. Her body was eager and ready, charged by a hunger so strong it made her tremble. He filled her with a single thrust, sinking into her with a power and energy that almost made her pass out with pleasure. She cried out as he lifted her legs onto his shoulders and rose over her to plunge down into her honeyed sheath again and again. Uncontrollable excitement gripped her as he drove her slowly, surely to a delirious climax. At the apex of delight she came apart under him, writhing and sobbing with mindless satisfaction as the wild spasms of pleasure ripped through her in wave after wave. Afterwards he cradled her close, murmuring in his own language, stroking her cheek with caressing fingers while his lustrous eyes studied her with unashamed appreciation.

It was the middle of the night before they ate.

Ruby wakened feeling sick again at dawn and Raja was very insistent on the point that in his opinion it was time for her to see a doctor. He was worried that she had contracted food poisoning. While Ruby lay as still as she could and fought the debilitating waves of nausea Raja made arrangements for a doctor's visit and got dressed.

An hour and a half later, Ruby received the answer to the big question she had been asking herself for more than a week.

'Congratulations,' Dr Sema Mansour pronounced with a wide smile. 'I am honoured to be the doctor to give you such important news.'

Ruby smiled back so hard her facial muscles ached under the strain. 'Please don't tell anyone else,' she urged, although even as she said that she appreciated that it was not a secret that she could hope to keep for long.

'Of course not. It is a confidential matter.' Lifting her doctor's bag, the young female medic, recommended by Princess Hadeel, took her leave.

A light breakfast was served to Ruby in bed and the maid plumped up her pillows first to ensure her comfort. Indeed all the staff involved in her care in the magnificent bedroom displayed a heart-warming level of concern for her welfare. Munching on a piece of roll without much appetite, Ruby stared into space and wondered how Raja would feel once she made her announcement. Last night they had made love and she had felt buoyant at the knowledge that her husband desired her so much.

But starting a family wasn't something they had ever discussed or planned, although he had proved keen to encourage her desire to adopt Leyla.

Ruby had always assumed that some day she would

want children. But until she had met Leyla and Mother Nature had turned her broody, she had believed that the family she might ultimately have lay somewhere far into her future. Leyla, however, had stolen into Ruby's heart and she had experienced such a strong longing to be Leyla's new mum that she had been amazed at herself. And now she was carrying Raja's baby. That hadn't taken long, although it was true that they had been very active in that line in the desert. Ruby flushed hotly at the recollection of a night when she had barely slept, indeed had behaved like a sex addict wonderfully well matched with another sex addict. Wretchedly virile fertile man, she thought ruefully and in shock, for there was no denying that a royal baby in the offing would change everything.

In the short term Ruby had been willing to ditch the concept of divorce and future freedom if it meant she could qualify to adopt little Leyla and raise her as her daughter. In spite of that though, she had still believed somewhere in the back of her mind that there remained a slight possibility that ten years or more down the line she and Raja might be able to separate from each other and lead their own lives without causing too much of a furore within their respective countries. Now with the needs of a second child entering the equation she felt that she had to be a good deal more practical. She had to ask herself if she was willing to subject possibly Leyla and her future child to the rigours of a broken home solely because she wanted a husband who loved her the way she already loved him. Children got attached to their parents living together as a couple. She had seen the heartbreak among school friends when their parents broke up and one parent moved out. Although in many cases there was no alternative to a separation, Ruby felt that she was in a position where she was still lucky enough to have choices to make.

Raja appeared in the doorway, brilliant dark eyes alive with concern, the taut line of his handsome mouth easing with relief when he saw that she was eating. 'It was a stomach upset, probably the result of you being given so much unfamiliar food,' he reasoned. 'Perhaps we should ask one of the chefs to cook English meals for you.'

'No, what we needed was better birth control,' Ruby contradicted, taking tiny sips of tea to moisten her dry mouth while she stared mournfully back at her husband. 'And I'm afraid that ship has sailed.'

Raja was staring fixedly at her, shapely ebony brows quirked, bewilderment stamped in the angles of his strong face. 'Better birth control?'

'We didn't use any in the desert—didn't *have* any to use,' she conceded heavily for so far being pregnant, between the nausea and the sore breasts, was not proving to be a lot of fun. '*And*...you've knocked me up.'

Raja had never bothered to try and imagine how he might hear that he was to become a father for the first time, but had he done so he was certain that not once would the colloquial British phrase 'knocked up' have featured on his dream wife's lips. 'You're...' Shaken by the concept, he had to clear his throat to continue. 'You're *pregnant*?'

'Yes, congratulations, you're a real stud.' Ruby sighed in a tone that would not have encouraged him to celebrate. 'But it's such a shock.'

Raja shifted his proud dark head in agreement. In
receipt of her announcement, which had rocked him
on his feet, he felt a little light-headed. 'I feel rather
foolish,' he admitted wryly. 'This possibility didn't
once cross my mind.'

'Me neither—until afterwards. I worried after we
were rescued,' Ruby told him ruefully.

'You should have told me that you were concerned.
I can't believe it but in the excitement of the situation
I overlooked the risk of such a development,' Raja de-
clared gravely.

'That's not like you,' Ruby remarked helplessly, for
she always got the feeling that Raja worked everything
out to the nth degree and rarely got taken by surprise.
'At the beginning I even suspected that conceiving a
child might have been part of the seduction plan. After
all, once you got me pregnant it would be harder for
me to walk away from our marriage.'

'But not impossible and I wouldn't wish an unwilling mother on any child of mine.' Raja scored impatient
fingers through his cropped black hair, his clear, dark
golden gaze melding to hers in reproach. 'I am not a
Machiavelli. My desire for you was very strong and I
acted on it for the most natural of reasons.'

It disturbed Ruby that she could not work out how
he felt about her revelation that she was pregnant. She
had originally assumed that he would be pleased, which
was why she had announced it in that quirky fashion,
striving to be cool. But now she was no longer so certain of his reaction because his innate reserve concealed his true reaction from her. 'I bet you that Wajid
turns wheelies when he finds out—it's another piece

of good PR, isn't it? Three weeks of marriage and I'm pregnant?'

'And you feel even more trapped than you did already,' Raja assumed, his stubborn jaw line clenching, a muscle pulling taut at the edge of his handsome mouth. 'I know you had already decided that you wanted to offer a home to Leyla, but you are very young to take on the responsibility of parenthood—'

'Raja…girls of fourteen were falling pregnant when I was at secondary school. At twenty-one I'm mature enough or I wouldn't have been talking about trying to adopt Leyla,' Ruby argued, feeling insulted and wondering if he considered her immature.

Raja strolled over to the window and looked out at the lush tranquil garden in the courtyard. His lean classic profile was taut. 'I *do* understand how you must feel. Such massive changes in your life are a challenge to cope with. Be honest with yourself and with me—'

Tension made Ruby sit up a little straighter in the bed. 'Honest about what? And how do you feel?'

'I felt incredibly trapped when I knew I had to get married as part of the peace accord,' he admitted without warning, the words escaping him in a low-pitched driven surge. 'I didn't want a wife I didn't choose for myself. My father reminded me that he didn't even meet my mother before he married her but, as I pointed out to him, he was raised in a different world with exactly that expectation. I never dreamt that I would be asked to make an arranged marriage. I had to man up.'

With that confession, which Ruby was quite unprepared to receive at that moment, she felt as though he had driven a knife into her. It shook her that she had been happy to feel like a victim while ignoring the reality that he might have felt equally powerless on his own behalf. *I didn't want a wife I didn't choose for myself.* That one sentence really said all she needed to know. At heart they had always had much more in common than she was prepared to accept. No doubt he had not shared his feelings on the score of their marriage when they first met for fear of influencing her into a negative response. She could understand that. Yet even so, regardless of how she had felt at the beginning, she had adapted, a little voice pointed out in her head—adapted, without even appreciating the fact, to her new position and responsibilities to live a life that was a great deal more demanding but also more interesting than the life she had left behind her in England.

Paradoxically it had wounded Ruby to hear her husband admit that he too had felt trapped when he had learned that he had to marry her. It was a case of very bad timing to learn that truth at the same time as she told him she had already conceived his child. But perhaps once again she was being unfair to him, Ruby reasoned uncertainly, reluctant to come over all dramatic like his first love. After all, how much enthusiasm could she reasonably expect from him? A baby with a woman he didn't love could only feel like another chain to bind him even though he had already agreed to take on Leyla.

Raja sank down on the side of the bed and reached for her hand. 'We will have two children. We will be a family before we have learned how to be a couple.'

'Not how you would have planned it?' Ruby prompted.

'When it comes to us nothing seems to go as planned and who is to say that what we have now is not all the better for that?' Expression reflective, he sounded more as if he was trying to convince her of that possibility than himself. 'I'm accustomed to change and I will handle this, but you have already had so many challenges to overcome in so short a space of time. This is a tough time for you to fall pregnant.'

Ruby was bewildered. 'I—'

'Naturally I feel guilty. I should have been more careful with you,' Raja breathed curtly. 'You have enough to deal with right now without this added responsibility.'

'You still haven't told me how you feel about the baby. Don't you want it?' Ruby queried anxiously.

Raja dealt her an astonished appraisal. 'Of course I want my own child, but not at the cost of your health and emotional well-being.'

'I'll be fine.' Ruby was disappointed that he had said nothing more personal. 'But most of those fancy clothes you bought me aren't likely to fit in a few months.'

'Not a problem. I like buying you things,' Raja volunteered, his thumb rubbing gently over the pulse in her narrow wrist. 'I want you to spend the next couple of days just acclimatising and catching up on your rest.'

Ruby gave him an impish grin. 'No more all-night sex sessions, then?'

Dark colour highlighted his superb bone structure and his eloquent mouth quirked in reluctant appreciation of that sally. 'Oh, Ruby...' he breathed, his hands gathering her slight body up so that he could kiss her with all the devastating expertise that sent her defensive barriers crashing flat like a domino run.

Feeling daring, Ruby pushed the sheet back. 'You could rest with me,' she muttered in an intuitive invitation.

'I have only fifteen minutes to make a meeting on the far side of the city,' Raja groaned, pausing to extract a second driving kiss, his breathing fracturing as he stared down at her with unalloyed hunger before finally springing up again, adjusting the fit of his trousers to accommodate his response to her. 'You're a constant temptation. I'll see you mid-afternoon and we'll go over the adoption papers we need to lodge to apply for Leyla.'

He found her very attractive, Ruby told herself consolingly. It wasn't love, it was lust, but marriages had survived on less. He was taking the advent of an unplanned baby very much in his stride, but then Raja was the sort of guy who typically rose to every challenge. The very worst thing she could do was brood about what they didn't have as opposed to what they did. In time he might almost come to love her out of habit. What was wrong with that? Did she need the poetry and the hand-holding? It would have been much worse had she fallen in love with a man she couldn't have. A man, for example, who belonged to another woman. Here she was safely married to a very handsome, sexy and exciting man and she was still feeling sorry for herself. Why was that? Was she one of those perennially dissatisfied personalities who always wanted more than she could have?

Ruby was dozing when she heard a mobile phone

going off somewhere very close to her ear. With a sound of exasperation she lifted her head and focused in surprise on the slim cell phone flashing lights and lying semi-concealed in a fold of the bedding. It was Raja's phone. It must have fallen out of his pocket while he was kissing her. She closed a hand round it and immediately noticed the photo of the gorgeous blonde.

And that was that. Ruby suffered not one moral pang rifling through Raja's phone and discovering that someone called Chloe had sent him a series of suggestive texts in English. Obviously a woman who was a lover, a woman who had shared a bed with him, enjoying all the intimacies and no doubt many more than Ruby had ever had with him. In shock Ruby read the texts again. The skank, she thought furiously, appalled by the sexy little comments calculated to titillate the average male. Raja's healthy libido did not require stimulation yet he had been receiving those texts ever since they got married. She went through his phone. If he had sent any texts back to Chloe he had clearly had the wit to delete them.

So, who was Chloe and what was Ruby going to do about her? Was she his most recent girlfriend? Why hadn't he told Chloe to leave him alone? Why hadn't he told her that his relationship with her was over? He had promised Ruby that he would be faithful and that there would be no other woman in his life while he was with her. Suddenly the cocoon of shock that had kept Ruby unnaturally calm was cracking right down the middle…

CHAPTER TEN

DISTRESS FLOODED RUBY and for a horrible timeless period she was too upset even to think straight. Men had cheated on Ruby before but invariably because she refused to sleep with them and it had never hurt so much that she wanted to scream and sob and rage all at the same time.

Yet she had instinctively trusted Raja—why was that? She peered down at the photo. Chloe was a very beautiful woman. Few men would feel obligated to ditch a woman with Chloe's looks and penchant for provocative texts just because they had made an arranged marriage. Why would Raja award Ruby that amount of loyalty when he didn't love her?

I felt incredibly trapped. I didn't want a wife I didn't choose for myself. Today the revelation about the baby had proved such a shock that Raja had at last chosen to be honest with her, sharing what was on his mind and in his heart. All the time that she had subjected him to her bad temper and resentment over the head of their need to marry he had suffered in silence rather than admit that he felt *exactly* the same way. That truth had cut deep. Was Raja planning to keep Chloe in the background of his life while he pretended to be a devoted husband? Was Chloe to be his secret comfort and escape from the exigencies of his royal life and arranged marriage?

The advent of two children was unlikely to lock Raja closer to home and hearth. In all probability children would make him feel more trapped than ever. The demands of a family and all the accompanying domesticity would never be able to compete with the freewheeling appeal of a Chloe, willing to send him sexy texts about what she longed to do to him between the sheets.

Ruby was devastated. She had understood what Raja meant when he had said that they should have had the time to get to know each other as a couple before they considered becoming parents. She also knew that she had literally shot herself in the foot. Tears trickling down her cheeks, Ruby thought about Leyla and yet she knew she could have done nothing different where that little girl was concerned. Her need to give Leyla the love she craved had been overwhelming. But hadn't she railroaded Raja into that commitment with her? She missed the little girl a great deal and could hardly wait for the magical day when she would have the right to take Leyla out of the orphanage and bring her home as her daughter. She had already pictured sharing that special day with Raja but Chloe's texts and the intimate pledges within them might well be much more of an attraction for him.

Having dressed in a denim skirt and tee and slid her bare feet into sandals, Ruby ate a chicken salad in the shaded arbour in the courtyard. Her stomach was mercifully at peace again. It was a beautiful spot with trees, lush greenery and flowers softening the impact of the massive medieval walls that provided a boundary. In the centre water from a tranquil fountain streamed down into a mosaic tiled basin, cooling the temperature. Had she been in a happier mood she would have thought she was in paradise.

She wondered exactly what she was going to say to Raja about those texts. She would have to be blunt and he would have to be honest. How important was Chloe to him? He had to answer that question.

A burst of barking from Hermione warned Ruby that Raja had arrived. Steps sounded on the tiles and Raja appeared, tall and sleek and darkly attractive in a lightweight designer suit.

'I left my phone here?' Lean brown fingers immediately descended on the cell phone lying on the table top and swept it up. 'I've been looking for it. I use my phone for everything...'

Ruby's pensive face tensed. 'I *know*,' she said feelingly. 'I'm going to be totally frank with you—I've read Chloe's texts. Her photo flashed up and I'm afraid I just had to go digging and I'm glad that I did.'

For a split second, Raja was paralysed to the spot, black brows drawing together, lush lashes flying up on disconcerted dark eyes, his dismay unhidden. 'Chloe,' he repeated flatly. 'That's over, done with.'

'If it's over, why was she still texting you as recently as last week?'

Raja was frowning at her. 'Did you read my texts?'

Ruby lifted her chin but her colour was rising. 'We're married. I felt I had the right.'

Faint colour defined his stunning cheekbones. His

proud gaze challenged that assumption. 'Even married I am entitled to a certain amount of privacy.'

'Not if you're going to be married to me, you're not. All right—I snooped. But I stand by what I did,' Ruby told him resolutely and without an instant of hesitation. 'It cuts both ways. Everything in my life is open to you.'

His face was impassive. A smouldering silence stretched between them in the hot, still air and during it a servant delivered mint tea and a plate of the tiny decorative cakes that Raja loved to the table. Dry-mouthed, Ruby poured the tea into the cups, her heart beating very fast.

Raja studied her from semi-screened eyes. Without warning a surprising smile curved his beautiful mouth. 'The idea of you reading those texts embarrasses me,' he admitted.

'Receiving that kind of thing *should* embarrass you,' Ruby told him forthrightly, but the ease of his confession and that charismatic smile reduced the worst of her tension, for she could not credit that he could smile like that if there was anything serious going on between him and Chloe.

'My affair with Chloe is over—it was over the moment you and I consummated our marriage,' he added.

'I'm willing to believe that but, if it's over as you say, why was she still sending you texts like that?' Ruby pressed uncomfortably.

'Think about it,' Raja urged wryly. 'From my point of view, Chloe was a sexual outlet. From hers, my greatest advantage was that I spent a great deal of money on her and she is naturally reluctant to lose that benefit. As I didn't wish to see her again I arranged to pay her a settlement through my lawyer last week. I can only assume that the texts are supposed to tempt me back to her bed. I didn't reply. I thought to reply would only encourage her.'

'She was your mistress,' Ruby remarked uneasily, relieved that no deeper feelings had been involved, but troubled by the obvious truth that he could so efficiently separate sex from emotion. 'That arrangement sounds so...so *cold*.'

'It suited both of us. I didn't want complications or hassle.' Raja shrugged a broad shoulder, his face reflective. 'But now I have you and as long as I have you I have no need of any other woman.'

There was something wonderfully soothing about that statement, voiced as it was with such rock-solid assurance in her ability to replace his sexually sophisticated mistress. The worst of the stress holding Ruby taut drained away.

'I was really upset when I saw those texts,' Ruby admitted reluctantly.

'I regret that you saw them and had reason to doubt my integrity. In that field, you can trust me, Ruby,' he murmured levelly, his sincerity patent. 'I believe in trust and honesty. I would not deceive you with another woman.'

Her eyes stung like mad and she widened them in an effort to keep the tears from overflowing, but some of them escaped, trickling down her cheeks. 'I believe you,' she said in a wobbly voice. 'And I don't know why I'm crying.'

'Hadeel said you might be very emotional over the

next few months because of your hormones,' Raja told her, startling her with that forecast and belatedly adding, 'I told her that you were pregnant.'

Ruby was disconcerted by that admission. 'You've told your family already?'

'Only Hadeel, the sister I am closest to, and she will keep our news a secret until we are ready to share it with the rest of the family. It's such exciting news—I could not keep quiet. I *had* to tell someone!' Raja exclaimed, a mixture of apology, appeal and distinct pride in his delivery that touched her heart.

It was the first sign that she had seen that he was genuinely pleased about the baby and a stifled sob escaped her convulsed throat because inexplicably, even though he had set her worst fears to rest, she felt more like having a good cry than ever. 'I don't know what's the m-matter with me.'

Murmuring soothing things, Raja scooped her up in his arms and carried her back indoors, shouldering open the bedroom door to settle her down onto the comfortable bed.

'Do you want me to start sending you texts like that?' Ruby asked him abruptly. 'I mean, I haven't done anything like that before but I'm sure I could learn the knack.'

Raja dealt her a startled look and then he laughed with rich appreciation of that proposal. 'No, thanks for the offer but I can get by without that sort of thing. To be truthful it's not really my style.'

'Honestly?' Ruby pressed anxiously.

'Honestly. I would much rather do it than talk about it, *aziz*,' he husked with considerable amusement gleaming in his lustrous eyes. 'And of course I have to have you to do it with. That goes without saying.'

'Am I really going to be enough for you?'

'Oh, yes,' Raja asserted. 'More than enough.'

'How can you be so sure?'

'You're special and you were from the start. My first introduction to you was a photo of you when you were fourteen. It was taken outside the cathedral in Simis. Wajid had it in his possession—'

'My goodness, you saw that snap? Mum sent it after we came home from that holiday in Ashur when we were turned away from the palace gates,' Ruby explained. 'I think it was her way of saying that we were perfectly happy whether the royal family ignored us or otherwise.'

'I was very impressed with the photo, and when I saw you for real I was stunned by your impact on me and by how much you challenged me,' Raja confided. 'I only had to look at you to want you. I couldn't take my eyes off you.'

'I couldn't take my eyes off you either,' Ruby said. 'But you admitted earlier that you were very resentful of the need for us to marry...'

'The instant I saw my beautiful bride my fate became instantly more bearable,' Raja told her, laughing at the face she pulled. 'Yes, I'm a very predictable guy—I desired you at first glance and I'm afraid that went a long way towards settling my objections to our arranged marriage.'

Ruby frowned, studying him in disbelief. 'That is just so *basic*.'

Raja spread his hands as if to ask her to hold that

opinion. 'But then when I was least expecting it I fell in love with you…'

'And then you…*what*?' Ruby gasped, utterly bemused by that declaration.

'At first it was just sexual desire that motivated me and then it was your smile, your strength and your sense of fun that had even more appeal. I fell in love without even realising what was happening to me,' Raja declared, gazing at her with hot golden eyes in which possessiveness was laced with pride. 'All of a sudden you became the most important element in my world.'

'I don't believe you. You said you slept with me in the desert because you wanted to make our marriage a real marriage.'

'I slept with you purely because I wanted you. Any other aspirations which I cherished were secondary to that simple fact,' Raja intoned levelly. 'I'm not too proud to admit that I wanted you any way I could get you. I was very hurt when you said later that you didn't care what I did.'

Ruby was beginning to believe but she wasn't prepared to let him off the hook too easily. 'But there was a seduction plan?'

Raja curled her fingers into his palm. 'I couldn't resist you.'

'I was pretty horrible to you in the desert. I mean, it wasn't your fault that we were there but I behaved as though it was.'

'You were scared and trying not to show it. I understood that.' Raja bent his dark, arrogant head and brushed his sensual mouth very slowly and silkily across her soft pink lips. 'And then you gave me your body and there was nothing I wouldn't have done for you, nothing I wouldn't have forgiven.'

'I thought that night was amazing but it can't have been so special to you.'

'It was, *aziz*.' Raja extracted a deep drugging kiss that made her tremble and look up at him with dazed eyes. 'But I think I fell in love with you when you said over that hotel lunch you walked out on that I would have been equally willing to marry a dancing bear. No other woman would ever have said such a thing to me. Or maybe our defining moment came when you said very ungraciously that you would only drink *bottled* water from now on—'

'Stop teasing me.' Her fingers speared into his thick black hair and she kissed him back with all her heart and soul, the longing he could awaken slivering through her in a piercing arrow of need.

'That second night we spent together was extraordinary. It was our wedding night,' Raja pointed out, his brilliant eyes resting appreciatively on her beautiful face. 'And wonderful.'

'Yes, it was, wasn't it?' Ruby agreed, arching up to taste his mouth again for herself and hauling him back down to her again with greedy hands.

'I thought I would never love a woman again and then I met you and it was a done deal right from the start. I was so resentful of the need to marry you until I actually met you. You got right under my skin. I tried to stay in control but it didn't work. And then after we were rescued you made it clear that you wanted nothing more to do with me. The flowers and the diamonds didn't make much of an impression and that's about all

I had in my repertoire. You vanished every evening and only spoke to me when you had to. I'm not used to being ignored.'

'It probably did you the world of good. I felt stupid.' Ruby wrinkled her nose. 'I'd demanded a platonic marriage and then got intimate with you the first chance I got. I didn't know how to behave after that.'

'I lay in that bed every night burning for you.' Raja groaned, his body shuddering against hers in recollection. 'I have never felt so frustrated and yet so aware that I would be putting unfair pressure on you if I made another move.'

'I did need breathing space.' Ruby rubbed her cheek comfortingly against his hand in a belated apology, hating the idea that he had been unhappy, as well. 'I wanted you as well but I had so many other things—like my new royal life—to worry about. I was exhausted and living on my nerves and afraid that it would be a mistake to trust you too much.'

'The greatest mistakes were mine. I was too impatient, too hungry for you.' Raja sighed, discomfiture darkening his beautiful eyes and stamping his features with regret. 'I should never have touched you in that tent. I rushed you into something you weren't ready for and almost lost you in the process.'

'You can't plan stuff like that. I fell in love with you too,' Ruby murmured, looking at him with loving eyes, revelling in the tenderness of his embrace and loving his strength and assurance. 'But I was so scared I was going to get hurt, that I was falling for a guy who would never feel the same way about me.'

'I won't hurt you, *aziz*. You are my beloved and I can only be happy if you are happy with me—'

'Obviously you got over that trapped feeling—'

'I trapped you with me,' Raja pointed out, dropping the mask of his reserve completely. 'I felt so guilty about letting you fall pregnant. That shouldn't have happened. I was selfish, thoughtless. I should have abstained from sex when I couldn't protect you.'

'That night was worth the risk. I would make the same choice again,' Ruby told him, running a caressing hand across the muscular wall of his warm hard torso and smiling with satisfaction when he pushed against her and sought out her mouth again with barely restrained passion.

'Some day I would like to take you back into the desert and show you its wonders.'

'You were enough of a wonder for me,' Ruby countered, in no hurry to recapture the magic of sand and scorpions, before he kissed her breathless and all sensible conversation was forgotten.

'I really do love you,' he told her some time later when they had sated their desire and they lay close and satisfied simply to be together.

'I love you too but words are cheap—you didn't give me the poetry or the hand-holding,' she complained with dancing eyes.

'Not the poetry, please,' he groaned, wincing at the prospect. 'I don't have a literary bone in my body.'

Unconcerned, Ruby squeezed the fingers laced with hers and kissed his stubborn jaw line, loving the scent of his skin. She was very happy and she would settle quite happily for the hand-holding.

EPILOGUE

A LITTLE LESS than two years later, Ruby smiled as Leyla told her brother, Hamid, to put away his toys and began showing him how to go about the task.

A lively little girl of five years, Leyla was very protective of her little brother but bossy, as well. For the sake of peace, Hamid toddled across to the toy box on his sturdy little legs and dumped a toy car in it, ignoring the rest of the cars scattered across the rug. Of course, even as a toddler Hamid was accustomed to the reality that servants would cheerfully tidy up after him and go out of their way to fulfil his every need and wish.

Hamid, the heir to the united throne of Najar and Ashur, was treated like the eighth wonder of the world in both palaces. Hamid might easily have become spoilt by overindulgence but Raja was very aware of the potential problem and he was a strict but loving father. With his black curly hair and big dark eyes, Ruby's son was the very image of his father and an energetic child with a quick temper and a wilful streak. Ruby tried not to laugh as Leyla tried to pressure her brother into lifting more cars and he sat down and refused to move another step in silent protest.

Ruby still felt surprised to be the mother of two

young children, nor did it seem possible to her that she and Raja had already reached their second wedding anniversary. The two years had flown by, packed with events and precious moments. Leyla's adoption had been a joy. Ruby still remembered the memorable day when she and Raja had collected the little girl from the orphanage and explained that they would now be acting as her mother and father and that she would be living with them from then on. A decree from the throne had made Leyla an honorary princess so that she would not be the odd one out among any siblings born to her adoptive parents. Happily many of the other inmates of the orphanage had also found adoptive homes since then.

Hamid's birth a couple of months later had provided an excuse for huge public celebrations in Najar and Ashur. Their son was the next generation of their ruling family and a very welcome reminder of all that had changed between the two countries. Ashur was no longer a devastated country on the edge of economic meltdown. Slowly but surely the infrastructure had been rebuilt and the unemployment figures had steadily fallen while more liberal laws had encouraged the development of trade and tourism. As the standard of living improved accordingly the Ashuri people had become more content and travel between the two countries had become much more common.

Raja and Ruby enjoyed great popularity. Ruby had never got the chance to have much input into the ruling aspect of their royal roles because soon after Raja's father, King Ahmed's death the previous year elections had been held to pick a government and the monarchy now held more of a constitutional role. Raja had been devastated by the older man's demise and he and Ruby had grown even closer when he shared his grief with her.

Ruby had never even dared to dream that she might be so happy in her marriage. But Raja made her feel incredibly happy and secure. He was wonderfully patient and loving with the children and endlessly supportive of her. Living with Raja, she felt irresistible and very much loved.

Tall, breathtakingly handsome and still very much the focus of his wife's daydreams, Raja appeared in the doorway of the nursery and smiled at Ruby, making her heart lurch in response. 'It's time for us to leave.'

Ruby emerged from her reverie as Hamid and Leyla pelted over to their father and jumped into his arms. Raja hugged the children and then set them down with the suggestion of firmness, nodding to the staff waiting to take over and extending a hand to Ruby to hurry her away.

'Why won't you tell me where we're going?' she pressed as he walked her out of the palace and led her over to the helicopter parked on the landing pad he had had built.

'It's an anniversary surprise,' he told her again.

When she realised that the helicopter was flying over the desert her heart sank a little. A surprise including a tent would not be welcome. As the craft began to land a glimpse of a familiar rock formation made her soft mouth curve down.

Raja sprang out and swung round to assist her out.

'I've organised electric and a bathroom but I'm afraid there's no supermarket,' he teased her.

Ruby blinked in astonishment at the vast tented structure within view. 'What on earth?'

'The sort of desert lifestyle you can enjoy, *habibi*,' Raja pronounced with satisfaction. 'Every convenience and comfort possible has been organised so that we can celebrate our wedding anniversary and remember how we first came together here...'

'That is so romantic.' In the shade of the tent canopy, Ruby turned in the circle of his arms, her eyes tender. She knew that for his sake she was going to pretend to enjoy every moment of the desert sojourn he had arranged for them.

'I would have done this last year but Hamid was so young I knew you wouldn't want to leave him even for a night,' he explained earnestly.

As she entered the main body of the tent Ruby's jaw dropped at the opulence. There was carpet and proper seats and even overhead fans to cool the interior. There was a proper bedroom and when she found the bathroom at the back of the structure she beamed at him in wondering approval. 'You really do know the way to a girl's heart,' she told her husband. 'How the heck did you arrange all this without me finding out about it?'

'With a great deal of ingenuity and secrecy. I've been planning it for weeks,' he confessed, closing his hands over hers to draw her close and kiss her with hungry fervour. 'Happy anniversary, Your Majesty. May we enjoy many many more together...'

Gazing up into his brilliant dark golden eyes, Ruby felt dizzy with love and longing and thought with a little inner quiver of bathing naked in the cliffside pool with him later. She knew her demand for a bathroom had persuaded him that she wouldn't wish to revisit that particular experience but she was already planning to surprise him with her contrariness.

'I love you so much,' Raja breathed huskily.

'You were going to get all your favourite food for dinner tonight—now you're going to miss out—'

'No, we won't. We have a chef coming in a few hours to take care of our evening meal,' Raja whispered.

'You think of absolutely everything.' Ruby was entranced and she leant up against his lean, muscular chest, listening to the solid reassuring thump of his heartbeat. 'That's one of the reasons I love you. You cross every t and dot every i—'

Tipping up her chin, Raja sealed his mouth to hers and the world spun dizzily on its axis for Ruby. He swept her up in his arms and carried her through to the comfortable bed awaiting them. Happiness bubbling through her, she made the most of his passion, which was only another one of the many reasons why she loved him to distraction.

* * * * *

Irish author **Abby Green** threw in a very glamorous career in film and TV—which really consisted of a lot of standing in the rain outside actors' trailers—to pursue her love of romance. After she'd bombarded Harlequin with manuscripts they kindly accepted one, and an author was born. She lives in Dublin, Ireland, and loves any excuse for distraction. Visit abby-green.com or email abbygreenauthor@gmail.com.

Books by Abby Green

Harlequin Presents

Forgiven but Not Forgotten?
Exquisite Revenge
One Night with the Enemy
The Legend of De Marco
The Call of the Desert
The Sultan's Choice
Secrets of the Oasis
In Christofides' Keeping
The Virgin's Secret

One Night With Consequences

An Heir Fit for a King

The Chatsfield

Delucca's Marriage Contract

Billionaire Brothers

The Bride Fonseca Needs
Fonseca's Fury

Blood Brothers

When Falcone's World Stops Turning
When Christakos Meets His Match
When Da Silva Breaks the Rules

Visit the Author Profile page
at Harlequin.com for more titles.

Abby Green

The Call of the Desert

This is for India Grey, Natalie Rivers
and Heidi Rice—I couldn't do this job without any
of you and it wouldn't be half as much fun,
thank you. (My phone company also extends its
thanks for keeping them in business.)

CHAPTER ONE

'THE EMIR OF BURQUAT. His Royal Highness Sheikh Kaden Bin Rashad al Abbas.'

Kaden looked out over the thronged ballroom in London's exclusive Royal Archaeology Club. Everyone was staring at him and a hush had descended on the crowd, but that didn't bother Kaden. He was used to such attention.

He walked down the ornate marble steps, one hand in his trouser pocket, watching dispassionately as people were caught staring and turned away hurriedly again. Well, to be more accurate, the men turned away and the women's looks lingered—some blatantly so. Like that of the buxom waitress who was waiting at the bottom of the stairs to hand him a glass of champagne. She smiled coquettishly as he took the glass but Kaden had already looked away; she was far too young for his jaded heart and soul.

Ever since he'd been a teenager he'd been aware he possessed a certain power when it came to women. When he looked in the mirror, though, and saw his own harsh features staring back at him, he wondered cynically if all they felt was the seductive urge to wipe away that cynicism and replace it with something softer. He had been softer...once. But it was so long ago now that he could hardly remember what it had felt like. It was like a dream, and perhaps like all dreams it had never been real.

Just then a movement on the other side of the room caught his eye, and a glimpse of a shiny blonde head amongst all the darker ones had his insides contracting. *Still. Even now.* He cursed himself and welcomed the sight of the club's managing director hurrying towards him, wondering angrily why he hadn't yet mastered such arbitrarily reflexive responses to the memory of something that had only ever been as flimsy as a dream.

JULIA SOMERTON'S HEART was palpitating, making her feel a little dizzy.

Kaden.

Here.

In the same room.

He'd descended the stairs and disappeared into the throng of people, despite his superior height. But that first image of him, appearing in the doorway like some sleek, dark-haired god, would be etched on her retina for ever. It was an image that was already carved indelibly onto her heart. The part of her heart that she couldn't erase him from, no matter how much she tried or how much time passed.

She'd noted several things in the space of that heart-stopping split second when she'd heard his name being called and had looked up. He was still as stupendously gorgeous as he'd been when she'd first met him. Tall, broad and dark, with the exotic appeal of someone not from these lands—someone who had been carved out of a much more arid and unforgiving place. He'd been too far away for her to see him in any detail, but even from where she'd stood she'd felt the impact of that black gaze—eyes so dark you could lose yourself for ever. *And hadn't she once?*

Some small, detached part of herself marvelled that he could have such an effect on her after all this time. Twelve long years. She was a divorcée now, a million miles from the idealistic girl she'd once been. When she'd known him.

The last time she'd seen Kaden she'd just turned twenty—weeks before his own twentieth birthday. Something she'd used to tease him mercilessly about: being with an *older woman.*

Her heart clenched so violently that she put a hand to her chest, and one of her companions said with concern, 'Julia, dear, are you all right? You've gone quite pale.'

She shook her head, and placed her drink down on a nearby table with a sweaty hand. Her voice came out husky, rough, 'It must be the heat… I'll just get some air for a minute.'

Blindly Julia made her way through the crowd, pushing, not looking left or right, heading for where patio doors led out to a terrace which overlooked manicured gardens. She only vaguely heard her colleague call after her, 'Don't go too far—you've got to say your piece soon!'

When she finally reached the doors and stepped out, she sucked in huge lungfuls of air. She felt shaky and jelly-like—at a remove from everything. She recognised shock. It was mid-August and late evening. The city air was heavy and oppressively warm. The faintly metallic scent of a storm was in the atmosphere. Huge clouds sat off in the distance, as if waiting for their cue to roll in. The garden here was famous for its exotic species of plants which had been brought back by many an adventurer and nurtured over the years by the dedicated gardeners.

But Julia was blind to all that.

Her hands gripped the wall so hard her knuckles shone white in the gathering twilight. She was locked in a whirlpool of memories, so many memories, and they were as bright and as painfully bittersweet as if it had all happened yesterday.

Ridiculously tears pricked her eyes, and an awful sense of loss gripped her. Yet how could this be? She was a thirty-two-year-old woman. Past her prime, many people would say, or perhaps coming into it, others would maintain. She felt past her prime. The day she'd flown away from the Emirate of Burquat on the Arabian Peninsula something inside her had withered and died. And even though she'd got on with her studies and surpassed her own dreams to gain a master's degree and a doctorate, and had married and loved her husband in her own way, she'd never truly *felt* again. The reason for that was in the room behind her, a silent malevolent presence.

God, she'd loved him so much—

'Dr Somerton, it's time for your speech.'

An urgent voice jarred her out of the memories. Dredging up strength from somewhere deep inside her, from a place she hadn't needed to visit in a long time, Julia steeled herself and turned around. She was going to have to stand up in front of all these people and speak for fifteen minutes, all the while knowing he was there, watching her.

Remembering?

Perhaps he wouldn't even remember… Perhaps he'd struggle to place her in his past. Her mouth became a bitter line. He'd certainly had enough women to make her blur into the crowd—not to mention a marriage of his own. She hated to admit that she was as aware of his exploits as the next person on the street who read the gossip rags on their lunchbreaks.

Maybe he'd wonder why she looked familiar. Acute pain gripped her and she repressed it brutally. Perhaps he wouldn't remember the long nights in the desert when it had felt as if they were the only two people in the world underneath a huge blanket of stars. Perhaps he wouldn't remember the beautiful poignancy of becoming each other's first lover and how their naive lovemaking had quickly developed beyond naivety to pure passion and an insatiable need for one another.

Perhaps he wouldn't remember when he'd said to her one night: *'I will love you always. No other woman could ever claim my heart the way you have.'*

And perhaps he wouldn't remember that awful day in the beautiful Royal Palace in Burquat when he'd become someone cold and distant and cruel.

Reassuring herself that a man like Kaden would have consigned her to the dust heap of his memories, and stifling the urge to run from the room, Julia pasted a smile on her face and followed her colleague back into the crowd, trying desperately to remember what on earth she was supposed to talk about.

'Ah, Sheikh Kaden, there you are. Dr Julia Somerton is just about to speak. I believe she used her research in Burquat for her masters degree. Perhaps you met her all those years ago? She's involved in fundraising now, for various worldwide archaeological projects.'

Kaden looked at the red-faced man who'd forced his way through the crowd to come and join him, and made a non-committal response. The man was the managing director of the club, who had invited him with a view to wooing funds out of him. Kaden was trying to disguise the uncomfortable jolt of shock to hear the name *Julia*. Despite the fact that he'd never met another Julia in Burquat, he told himself that there might have been another student by that name and he wouldn't have necessarily been aware, considering his lack of interest in all things archaeological after *she'd* left.

This was his first foray back into that world and it would be ironic in the extreme if he was to meet *her*. She had been Julia Connors, not Somerton. Although, as an inner voice pointed out, she could be married by now. In fact, why wouldn't she be? *He* had been married, after all. At the memory of his marriage Kaden felt the usual cloud of black anger threaten to overwhelm him. He resolutely pushed it aside. He was not one to dwell on the past.

And yet one aspect of his past which had refused to dissolve into the mists of time was facing him right now. If it *was* her. Unaccountably his heart picked up pace.

A hush descended over the crowd. Kaden looked towards the front of the room and the world halted on its axis for a terrifying moment when he saw the slim woman in the black cocktail dress ascending the steps to the podium. *It was her.* Julia. In a split second he was transported back to the moment when he'd realised that, because of lust, he'd placed her on a pedestal that she had no right to grace. And only that realisation had stopped him making the biggest mistake of his life.

Shaking his mind free of the disturbingly vivid memory, Kaden narrowed his eyes on Julia. Her voice was husky; it had caught him from the first moment they'd met. She'd been wearing a T-shirt and dusty figure-hugging jeans. Her long hair had fallen in bright tendrils over her shoulders. A safari-style hat had shaded her face from the sun. Her figure had been lithe and so effortlessly sensual he'd lost the power of speech.

If anything she was more beautiful than that first day he'd seen her. Time had hollowed out her cheeks, adding an angularity that hadn't been there before. *She'd only been nineteen.* Her face had still held a slight hint of puppy-plumpness. As had her body. From what he could see now, she looked slimmer, with a hint of enticing cleavage just visible in the V of her dress. In fact, there was a fragility about her that hadn't been there before.

She was a million miles from that first tantalising dusty image he held in his mind's eye; she was elegance personified now, with her long blonde hair pulled back into a low ponytail. The heavy side parting swept it across her forehead and down behind one ear. Her groomed appearance was doing little, though, to stop the torrent of carnal images flooding Kaden's mind—and in such lurid detail that his body started to harden in response.

He would have anticipated that she'd have no effect on him. Much like any ex-lover. But the opposite was true. This was inconceivable. He had to concede now, with extreme reluctance, that no woman since this woman had exerted such a sensual hold over him. He'd never again lost control as he had with her—every time.

And he'd never felt the same acrid punch of jealousy to his gut as when he'd seen her in another man's arms, with another man's mouth on hers, tasting her... feeling her soft curves pressed against him. The vividness of that emotion was dizzying in its freshness, and he fought to negate it, too stunned by its resurgence to look too closely into what it meant.

This woman had been a valuable lesson in never allowing his base nature to rule his head or his heart again. Yet the years of wielding that control felt very flimsy now he was faced with her again.

More than a little bewildered at this onslaught of memories, and irrationally angry that she was here to precipitate them, Kaden felt his whole body radiate displeasure. Just then a rumble of laughter trickled through the gathered crowd in reaction to something she'd said. Kaden's mouth tightened even more, and with that tension making his movements jerky he said something about getting some air and stalked towards the open patio doors.

As soon as Julia's speech was over he was going to get out of there and forget that he'd ever seen her again.

JULIA STEPPED DOWN off the dais. She'd faltered during her speech for long seconds when she'd noticed Kaden head and shoulders above the rest of the crowd, at the back of the room like a forbidding presence, those dark eyes boring through her. And then with an abrupt move he'd moved outside. Almost as if disgusted by something she'd said. It had taken all her powers of concentration to keep going, and she'd used up all her reserves.

To her abject relief she saw her boss at the fundraising foundation come towards her. He put a hand to her elbow and for once she wasn't concerned about keeping distance between them. Ever since her divorce had come through a year ago Nigel had been making his interest clear, despite Julia's clear lack of encouragement. Tonight, though, she needed all the support she could get. If she could just get through the rest of the relentless schmoozing and get out of there perhaps she could pretend she'd never seen Kaden.

Nigel was babbling excitedly about something as he steered her away, but she couldn't even hear him above the din of chatter and the clink of glasses. People were making the most of the *gratis* champagne reception. Julia craved that sweet oblivion, but it was not to be.

With dread trickling into her veins and her belly hollowing out, she could already see where they were headed—towards someone at the back of the room, near the terrace. Someone with his back to them: tall, broad and powerful. Thick ebony-black hair curled a touch too much over the collar of his jacket, exactly the way it had when she'd first met him.

Like a recalcitrant child she tried to dig her heels

into the ground, but Nigel was blithely unaware, whispering confidentially, 'He's an emir, so I'm not sure how you have to address him. Maybe call him Your Highness just in case. It would be such a coup to interest him in the foundation.'

In that split second Julia had a flashback to when she'd met Kaden for the first time. She'd only been working on the dig for a couple of weeks, had still been getting used to the intense heat, when a pair of shoes had come into her line of vision. She'd barely looked up.

'*Don't* step there. Whoever you are. You're about to walk on top of a fossil that's probably in the region of three thousand years old.'

The shoe had hovered in mid-air and come back down again in a safer spot, and a deep, lightly accented voice had drawled seductively, 'Do you always greet people with such enthusiasm?'

Julia gritted her teeth. Since she'd arrived she'd been the object of intense male interest and speculation. She was under no illusions that it was most likely because she was blonde and the only female under fifty on the dig. 'If you don't mind, I'm in the middle of something here.'

The shoes didn't move and the voice came again, sounding much more arrogant and censorious. 'I *do* mind, actually—I am the Crown Prince and you will acknowledge me when I speak to you.'

She'd completely forgotten that the Emir was due to visit with some important guests that day—and *his son*. Dismay filling Julia, she put down her brush and finally looked up, and up, and up again, to see a tall, broad figure standing over her. The sun was in her eyes so all she could make out was his shape—which was formidable.

Taking off her gloves, she slowly stood, and came face to face with the most handsome man she'd ever seen in her life. Robes highlighted his awe-inspiring height and broad shoulders. He wore a turban, but that couldn't hide the jet-black hair curling down to his collar, or the square cut of his jaw. The most mesmerising dark eyes.

Feeling more than a little overwhelmed she took off her hat and held out her hand…

'And this is Dr Somerton, who you just heard. As our funds manager she's been instrumental in making sure that funding reaches our digs all over the world.'

Past merged into present and Julia found that she was holding out her hand in an automatic response to the introduction. She was now facing Kaden, and much as she'd have loved to avert her gaze he took up a lot of space, completely arresting in a dark suit with a snowy-white shirt open at the neck, making him stand out from the men in the crowd who were more formally dressed. He looked darker, and infinitely more dangerous than any other man there.

There was no such thing as sliding towards middle age with a receding hairline and expanding gut for him. He oozed virility, vitality, and a heady, earthy sexual magnetism far more powerful than she remembered. There was not a hint of softness about him, or his face. He was all lean angles. The blade of his slightly crooked nose highlighted a sense of danger and a man in his vigorous prime. She remembered the day he'd got that injury, while playing his country's brutal national game.

Her heart squeezed as she recalled that moment and saw the new harshness stamping the lines of his face. She wondered how long it had been there. Her eyes slid down helplessly...his mouth hadn't changed. It was as sensual as she remembered, with its full lower lip and the slightly thinner, albeit beautifully shaped upper lip. She'd used to love tracing that line with her finger. Heat flared in her belly. *And with her tongue.* It was a mouth which held within it the power to inspire a need in the most cynical of women to make this man *hers*.

The strength of that need washed through Julia, and dismay gripped her. She couldn't still want this man— not after all these years. Her hand hovered in mid-air as the moment stretched out between them. He was looking at her as intently as she was looking at him, but it was no consolation. There was no polite spark of recognition, only an extreme air of tension. He knew her, but clearly did not relish meeting her again.

Julia realised that just as his big hand enveloped her much smaller one, and a million and one sensations exploded throughout her body.

FAR TOO INNATELY civilised to be deliberately rude and ignore Julia's hand, as he perversely longed to do, Kaden reached out to take it. He instinctively gritted his jaw against the inevitable physical contact but it was no good. At the first touch of his fingers to that small, soft hand he wanted to slide his thumb with sensual intent along the gap between her thumb and forefinger in a lover's caress. He wanted to curl his fingers around her palm and feel every delicate bone.

He wanted to relearn this woman in an erotic way that was so forceful it set off a maelstrom of biblical proportions inside him. And somewhere in his head he wondered when had just shaking a woman's hand ever precipitated such an onslaught of need.

A voice answered him: about twelve years ago, in the searing heat of the afternoon sun amongst dusty relics, when this same woman had stood before him with a shy smile on her face, her hand in his. And, much to his chagrin, Kaden felt his intention to walk away and forget he'd seen her again dissolve in a rush of lust.

CHAPTER TWO

A MINOR EARTHQUAKE was taking place within Julia's body, and Kaden seemed loath to let her hand go—about as reluctant as she was for him to let it go. The realisation shamed her, and yet to her horror she couldn't seem to muster up the energy to extricate her hand from his. She noticed the look in his eyes change to something ambiguous, and every cell in her blood jumped and fizzed in reaction.

An emotion which felt awfully poignant and *yearning* was threatening. She struggled to remember where she was, and with whom, but it was almost impossible. The reality that it was *Kaden* in front of her was too much to take in. All she could do was react.

As suddenly as Julia had registered the changed intensity in Kaden's gaze locked onto hers it was gone, and his eyes moved to take in their companions. Julia had forgotten all about them. Her hand was dropped as summarily as if he had flung it away from him, and a dark cloud of foreboding seemed to blot out the sultry evening just visible through the open patio doors. She shivered in response, and wanted to hug her arms around her body.

Nigel was saying nervously, 'His Royal Highness the Emir of Burquat,' and Julia was wondering a little hysterically if she should be curtseying. She didn't trust her voice to speak and then Kaden's black gaze was back on her.

'Dr Somerton.'

His voice was so achingly familiar that she longed to be able to hold on to something for balance, only dimly registering the cool tone.

A small anxious-looking man with a red face was beside Kaden. Julia recognised him as the director of the club. He was talking, but his voice seemed to be coming from far away,

'Perhaps you have met before, Doctor? When you were in Burquat during your studies?'

A sharp pain lanced Julia and she looked at Kaden, not sure what to say.

His mouth turned up in a parody of a smile and he drawled, 'I seem to have some vague recollection. What year were you there?'

The slap of rejection was so strong it almost made Julia take a step back. The awful sense of isolation she'd felt when she'd left Burquat was as fresh now as twelve years ago. That this man could transport her so easily back to those painful emotions was devastating. Perhaps he could tell just how excruciating this was for her—hadn't she all but thrown herself at him that last day? Perhaps he thought he was sparing her some embarrassment now?

She forced an equally polite and distant smile to her lips. 'It's so long ago now I can barely recall it myself.'

She switched her brittle-feeling smile to the other men. 'Gentlemen, if you don't need me for this discussion I'd appreciate it if you would excuse me. I just got back from New York this afternoon, and I'm afraid the jet lag is catching up with me.'

'Your husband is waiting for you at home? Or perhaps he's here in the room?'

Shock at the bluntness of Kaden's question slammed into Julia. How dared he all but pretend not to know her and then ask such a pointedly personal question? Her jaw felt tight. 'For your information, *Your Highness*, I am no longer married. My husband and I are divorced.'

Kaden did not like the surge of emotion that ripped through him at her curt answer. He had had an image of her returning to a cosy home to be greeted by some faceless man and had felt a blackness descend over his vision, forcing him to ask the question. Even realising that, he couldn't stop himself asking, 'So why are you still using your married name?'

Julia's face tightened. 'I'm involved in various contracts and it's simply been easier to leave it for the moment. I have every intention of changing it back in the future.'

It was as if Kaden was enclosed in a bubble with this woman. The other men went unnoticed, forgotten. Unbidden and unwelcome emotion was clouding everything.

At that moment Nigel, Julia's boss, moved perceptibly closer to her, taking her elbow in his hand, staking a very public claim.

Only moments ago she'd welcomed his support and his tacit interest as a barrier. Now Julia chafed and made a jerky move away, causing Nigel's hand to drop. She could feel his wounded look without even seeing it, and her head began to throb. The club's director who still stood beside Kaden, was looking a bit bewildered at the obvious tension in the air, which was making a lie of the fact that she and Kaden claimed to barely know one another.

She knew she'd only been introduced as a polite formality. She wasn't expected to take part in Nigel's wooing of new donors. Her job started when they had to decide how those funds would be best used. If she'd known for a second that Kaden was due to be here this evening, she would have made certain not to come.

Determined to succeed this time, Julia stepped away from the trio of men on very shaky legs. 'Please, gentlemen—if you'll excuse me?'

Ignoring the dagger looks from Nigel, and the dark condemnation emanating from Kaden like a physical force, she turned on her heel and walked away. It seemed to take an age to get through the crowd. She was almost at the door when she felt a hand on her arm, but it didn't induce anything more than irritation and she reluctantly turned to face Nigel. His handsome face was red.

'Are you going to tell me what that was all about?'

Once again Julia pulled her arm free and kept walking. 'It was about nothing, Nigel. I'm tired and I want to go home, that's all.'

She hoped the panic she felt at being there for one second longer than was absolutely necessary didn't come through in her voice. She reached the cloakroom and handed in the ticket for her jacket, noticing a visible tremor in her hand.

'So you two obviously know each other, then? I'd

have to be deaf, dumb and blind to fail to notice *that* atmosphere.'

Julia sighed. 'We knew each other a long time ago, Nigel.' She turned and put on her jacket, which had just been handed to her, and pointed out gently, 'Not that it's any of your business.'

His face became mottled. 'It *is* my business when the most potentially lucrative donor we've had in years could get scared off because he's had some kind of previous relationship with my funds manager.'

Julia stopped and faced Nigel, forcing herself to stay civil. 'I'm sure he's mature enough not to let a tiny incident like this change his mind about donating funds to research. Anyway, it's all the more reason for me to leave and stay out of your way.'

She turned to go and Nigel caught her hand. Gritting her teeth at his persistence, Julia turned back, her stomach churning slightly at the sweaty grip of his hand—so far removed from the cool yet hot touch from Kaden.

He was conciliatory. 'Look, I'm sorry, Julia. Forgive me? Let me take you out to dinner this week.'

Julia fought back the urge to say yes, which would be the easy thing to do, to placate him. Seeing Kaden had upset any equilibrium she thought she might have attained since her divorce had become final. Since she had last seen *him*. And that knowledge was too frightening to take in fully.

She shook her head. 'I'm sorry, Nigel. I have thought about it…and I'm just not ready for dating.' She pulled her hand from his and backed away. 'I'm really sorry. I'll see you tomorrow in the office.' Already she could imagine his sulky mood at being turned down and dreaded it.

She turned and walked quickly to the door. Her heart was hammering, and all she wanted was to escape to the quiet solace of her house where she could get out of her tailored dress and curl up. She wanted to block out the evening's events and the fact that her past had rushed up to meet her with the force of a sledge-hammer blow.

As soon as Julia had turned and walked away Kaden should have been putting her out of his mind and focusing on the business at hand, as he would have with any other ex-lover. But he wasn't. He found that the urge to go after her was nigh on impossible to resist. Especially when that obsequious man who'd had the temerity to put his hand on her had followed her like a besotted lap dog.

Kaden made his excuses to the still bewildered-looking director of the club and forged his way through the crowd, ignoring the not so hushed whispers as he passed people by. His blood was humming. He felt curiously euphoric, and also uncultivated—like a predator in the desert, an eagle soaring high who had spotted its prey and would not rest until it was caught.

It was an uncomfortable reminder of how he'd felt from the moment he'd first met Julia, when sanity had taken a hike and he'd given himself over to a dream as dangerous as any opiate could induce. But this feeling was too strong to deny or rationalise.

The fact that she represented a lapse in emotional

control he'd never allowed again only caught up with him when he reached the lobby and saw it was empty.

She'd disappeared.

So what was this desolation that swept through him? And what was this rampant need clawing through him to find her again? He was done with Julia. He'd been done with her a long time ago.

Disgusted with himself for this lapse, Kaden called up his security, determined to get out of there and do what he'd set out to do all along: forget that he'd ever seen Julia Connors—he scowled, *Somerton*—again.

He had no desire to revisit a time when he'd come very close to letting his heart rule his head, forgetting all about duty and responsibility in the pursuit of personal fulfilment. He didn't have that luxury. He'd *never* had that luxury.

JULIA COULD SEE the tube station entrance ahead of her, not far from the building she'd just left behind. The night-time London air was unbearably heavy around her now, making a light sweat break out over her skin and on the nape of her neck under her hair. Thunder rolled ominously in the distance. A storm had been threatening all evening, and if she'd been in better humour she might have appreciated the symbolism. The clouds that had been squatting in the distance were now firmly overhead—low, dark and menacing.

What was making the weather feel even more ominous was the fact that she'd been having disturbing dreams of Kaden lately. Maybe, she wondered a little hysterically, she was hallucinating?

Hesitating for a moment, Julia stopped and looked

back. But the building just sat there, innocently benign, lights blazing from the windows, laughter trickling out into the quiet street from the party. She shuddered despite the heat. She wasn't going back now anyway. She couldn't face Nigel again. *Or* Kaden's coolly sardonic demeanour. As if nothing had ever happened between them.

Part of her longed to just jump in a cab, but her inherently frugal nature forbade it. Out of the corner of her eye she saw a sleek black shape slow to a crawl alongside her—just before she heard the accompanying low hum of a very expensive engine. At the same time as she turned automatically to look, lightning forked in the sky and the heavens opened. She was comprehensively drenched within seconds, but had become rooted to the spot.

Everything seemed to happen in slow motion as she registered the Royal Burquati flag on the bonnet of the car. She noticed the tinted windows, and the equally sleek accompanying Jeep, which had to be carrying the ubiquitous security team.

As she stood there getting soaked, unable to move, Julia was helplessly transported back to a moment in the hot, winding, ancient streets of Burquat City, when, breathless with laughter, her hand clamped in Kaden's, they'd escaped from his bodyguards into a private walled garden. There, he'd pushed her up against a wall, taken away the veil hiding her face and kissed her for the first time.

It was only when the back door of the car opened near her and she saw the tall figure of Kaden emerge that reality rushed back. Along with it came her breath and her heartbeat, and the knowledge that she hadn't been hallucinating.

The rain seemed to bounce off him, spraying droplets into a halo around him. The sky was apocalyptic behind him. And still that rain was beating down.

Julia backed away, her eyes glued to him as if mesmerised.

'Julia. Let me give you a lift.'

Her name on his tongue with that exotic accent did funny things to her insides. A strangled half-laugh came out of Julia's mouth. 'A lift?' She shook her head, 'I don't need a lift—I need to go home. I'll take the tube.'

She dragged her gaze from his and finally managed to turn around. Only to feel her arm caught in a hard grip. Electric tingles shot up and down her arm and into her groin just as more lightning lit up the sky. She looked up at Kaden, who had come to stand in front of her. So close that she could see his jet-black hair plastered to his skull, that awesomely beautiful face. Those black eyes. Rain ran in rivulets down the lean planes, over hard cheekbones.

'What do you want, Kaden? Or should I address you by your full title?' Bitterness and something much scarier made her feel emotional. 'You gave a very good impression back there of not knowing who I was. I'm surprised you even remember my name.'

Through the driving rain she could see his jaw clench at that. His black gaze swept her up and down. Then his hand gentled on her arm, and perversely that made her feel even shakier. With something she couldn't decipher in his voice he said, 'I remember your name, Julia.' And then, with easy solicitude, 'You're soaked through. And now I'm soaked. My apartment isn't far from here. Let me take you there so you can dry off.'

Panic mixed with something much more hot and primal clutched Julia's gut. Go with Kaden to his apartment? To *dry off*? She remembered the way his look had changed earlier to something ambiguous. It was a long time since she'd felt that curl of hot desire in her abdomen, and to be reminded of how this man had been the only one ever to precipitate it was galling. And that he could still make it happen twelve years on was even more disturbing.

She shook her head and tried to extricate her arm. 'No, thank you. I don't want to put you out of your way.'

His jaw clenched again. 'Do you really want to sit on a tube dripping wet and walk home like a drowned rat?'

Instantly she felt deflated. She could well imagine that she *did* resemble a drowned rat. Mascara must be running down her cheeks in dark rivers. He was just being polite—had probably seen her and hadn't wanted to appear rude by driving past. His convoy would have been far too conspicuous to go unnoticed.

'I can take a taxi if I need to. Why are you doing this?'

He shrugged minutely. 'I wasn't expecting to see you…it's been a surprise.'

She all but snorted. It certainly was. She had no doubt that he'd never expected to see her again in his lifetime. And thinking of that now—how close she'd come to never seeing him again—Julia felt an aching sense of loss grip her. And urgency. She wouldn't see

Kaden after tonight. She knew that. This was a fluke, a monumental coincidence. He was just curious—perhaps intrigued.

He'd been her first lover. Her first love. *Her only love?*

Before she could quash that disturbing thought Kaden was manoeuvring her towards the open door of his car, as if some tacit acquiescence had passed between them. Julia felt weak for not protesting, but she knew in that moment that she didn't have the strength to just walk away. Because meeting him again *didn't* mean nothing to her.

He handed her into the plush interior of the luxury car and came around the other side. Once his large, rangy body was settled in the back seat alongside her he issued a terse command in Arabic, and the car pulled off so smoothly that Julia only knew they were moving because the tube station passed them in a blaze of refracted light through the driving rain.

KADEN SAT BACK and looked over at Julia. He could see her long dark lashes. Her nose had the tiniest bump, which gave her profile an aquiline look, and her mouth…

He used to study this woman's mouth for hours. Obsessed with its shape, its full lower lip and the perfect curve of its bow-shaped upper lip. He'd once known this profile as well as his own. *Better.*

She wore a light jacket, but the rain had made her clothes heavy and the V in the neckline of the dress was being dragged downwards to reveal the pale swells of her breasts. He could see a tantalising hint of the black lace of her bra, and evidence of her agitation as her chest rose and fell with quick breaths.

Rage at his uncharacteristic lack of control rose high. He'd fully intended to leave and put her out of his mind, but then he'd seen her walking along the street, with that quick, efficient walk he remembered. Not artful or practised, but completely sensuous all the same. As if she was unconscious of how sexy she was. He'd forgotten that a woman could be unconsciously sexy. Before he'd known what he was doing, he'd found himself instructing his driver to stop the car.

Sexual awareness stunned him anew. It shouldn't be so overwhelmingly fresh. As if they'd hardly been apart. For a long time after she'd left Burquat Kaden had told himself that his inability to forget about her was because of the fact that she'd been his first lover, and that brought with it undeniable associations and indelible memories.

But he couldn't deny as he sat there now, with this carnal *heat* throbbing between them, that the pleasure they'd discovered together had been more than just the voluptuous delight of new lovers discovering unfamiliar terrain. It had been as intensely mind—blowing as anything he'd experienced since. And sitting beside Julia was effortlessly shattering any illusion he'd entertained that he'd been the one to control his response to women in the intervening years. They just hadn't been *her*. That knowledge was more than cataclysmic.

Julia could feel Kaden's eyes on her, but she was determined not to look at him. When they'd been together he'd always had a way of looking at her so intently... as if he wanted to devour her whole. It had thrilled her

and scared her a little in equal measure. His intensity
had been so dark and compelling. She'd felt the lash of
that dark intensity when it had been turned against her.

If she turned and saw that look now…

She raised her hand to her neck in a nervous reflex
and felt that it was bare. The wave of relief that coursed
through her when she realised what she'd just done was
nothing short of epic. She always wore a gold necklace
with the detail of an intricate love knot at its centre. It
had been bought from a stall in the souk in Burquat.
But its main significance was that Kaden had bought it
for her, and despite what had happened between them
she still wore it every day—apart from when she was
travelling, for fear of losing it.

The only reason she wasn't wearing it now was because she'd been in such a rush earlier, upon returning
from the US, that she'd forgotten to put it back on. The
knowledge burned within her, because she knew that
it somehow symbolised her link to this man when no
link existed any more. If he had seen the necklace—
Her mind seized at the prospect. It would have been
like wearing a badge saying *You still mean something
to me*. And she was only realising herself, here and
now, how shamefully true that was.

'We're here.'

The car was drawing to a smooth halt outside an
exclusive-looking building. A liveried doorman was
hurrying over to open the car door, and before Julia
knew it she was standing on the pavement watching
as Kaden came to join her. The rain had become a
light drizzle, and Julia shivered in clothes that felt un-

comfortably damp against her skin, despite the heavy warmth of the night.

Kaden ushered Julia in through the open doors. The doorman bowed his head deferentially as they passed. Julia felt numb inside and out. Shock was spreading, turning her into some sort of automaton. Sleek doors were opening, and then they were standing in an opulently decorated lift. The doors closed again, and with a soft jolt they were ascending.

A sense of panic was rising as she stood in that confined space next to Kaden's formidable presence, but before she could do anything the door was opening again and Julia was being led straight from the lift into what had to be the penthouse apartment. It was an old building, but the apartment had obviously been refitted and it oozed sleek modernity with an antique twist. It was decorated in understated tones of cream and gold, effortlessly luxurious. The tall windows showcased the glittering city outside as Kaden led her into a huge reception room and turned to face her.

Julia looked away from the windows to catch Kaden's dark gaze making a leisurely return up her body. Heat exploded in her belly, and when his eyes met hers again she found it hard to breathe.

He backed away to an open door on the other side of the room and said coolly, 'There is a bedroom and en suite bathroom through here, if you want to freshen up and get dry.'

Julia followed his tall form, feeling very bedraggled. She was aware of trailing water all over the luxurious carpet. He turned again at the open door, through which she could see a set of rooms—a smaller sitting room leading into a bedroom.

'I'll have your clothes attended to if you leave them in the sitting room.'

Julia looked at him, and a curious kind of relief went through her. 'You have a housekeeper here?'

Kaden shook his head, 'No, but someone will attend to them, and I'll leave some dry clothes out for you.'

How could she have forgotten the myriad silent servants who were always present to do the royal bidding, no matter what it was? Like erecting exotic Bedouin tents in the desert in a matter of hours, just for them. Her belly cramped. Still in a state of shock, she could only nod silently and watch as Kaden strode away and left her alone.

She walked through the opulent rooms until she came to the bedroom, where she carefully closed the door behind her, leaning back against it. She grimaced at herself. Kaden was hardly likely to bash the door down because he was so consumed with uncontrollable lust. She could well imagine that his tastes no longer ran to wet and bedraggled archaeologists.

Shaking her head, as if that might shake some sanity back into it, she kicked off her shoes and pushed away from the door. She explored the bathroom, which held a glorious sunken bath and huge walk-in shower. She caught a glimpse of herself in the mirror and her eyes grew big. She did indeed look as if she'd been dragged through a hedge backwards and then hosed down with water. Her long blonde hair hung in rats' tails over her shoulders and was stuck to her head. Mascara had made huge dark smudges under her eyes.

With a scowl at herself, she peeled off her drenched clothes. She got a towel from the bathroom to protect the soft furnishings and left them in the outer sitting room, half terrified that Kaden would walk back through the door at any moment. She scuttled back through the bedroom into the bathroom. With a towel wrapped around her she gave a longing glance to the bath, but stepped into the shower instead. Taking a bath in Kaden's apartment felt far too decadent a thing to do.

As it was, just standing naked under the powerful hot spray of water felt illicit and wicked. To know that Kaden was mere feet away in another room…also naked under a hot shower… With a groan of disgust at her completely inappropriate imagination, Julia turned her face upwards. She resolved to get re-dressed in her wet clothes if she had to, and then get out of there as fast as she could.

KADEN HAD SHOWERED and changed into dry clothes, and now stood outside the rooms he'd shown Julia into. He dithered. He never dithered, but all he could see in his mind's eye was the seductive image of Julia standing before him in those wet clothes. She should have looked like a drowned rat, but she hadn't. That cool, classic English beauty stood out a mile—along with the delicate curves of her breasts, waist and hips.

The burning desire he'd felt in the car hadn't abated one bit, and normally when he was attracted to a woman it was a straightforward affair. But this wasn't just some random woman. This woman came with long silken ties to the past. *To his heart.* He rejected that rogue thought outright. She'd never affected his heart. He'd thought she had…but it had been lust. Overwhelming, yes, but just lust. Not love.

He'd learnt young not to trust romantic love. His father had married for love. But after his mother had died in childbirth with his younger sister his father had silently communicated to him that love only brought pain. It had been there in the way that his father had become a shadow of his former self, wrapped up in grief and solitude. Kaden had always been made very aware that one day he would rule his country, so he could never afford to let such frivolous emotions overwhelm *him* the way they'd taken over his father's life.

Kaden's father had married again, but this time for all the *expected* reasons. Practicality and lineage. Unfortunately his second wife had been cold and manipulative, further compounding Kaden's negative impressions of marriage and love. Any halcyon memories he might have had of his mother and father being happy together had quickly faded into something that felt like a wispy dream—unreal.

Yet when Kaden had met Julia he'd been seduced into forgetting everything he'd learnt. Guilt weighed heavily on him even now. And that sense of betrayal. If he hadn't seen her with that other man…if he hadn't realised how fickle she was…

Kaden cursed himself for this sudden introspection.

In his hands he held some dry clothes. He knocked lightly and heard nothing. So he went in. The bedroom was dimly lit and the door to the bathroom was slightly open. As if in a trance he walked further into the bedroom and laid the dry clothes down on the bed. He'd picked up Julia's wet clothes on the way through.

Her scent hit his nostrils now and his eyes closed. Still the same distinctive lavender scent. A dart of anger rose up, as if her scent was mocking him by not having changed.

Before his mind could become clouded with evocative memories a sound made him open his eyes to see Julia, framed in the doorway of the bathroom, with only a towel wrapped around her body and another towel turban—like on her head. Steam billowed out behind her, bringing with it that delicate scent.

Lust slammed into Kaden like a two-ton lorry. Right in his solar plexus. Long shapely legs were bare, so were pale shoulders and arms. Kaden cursed himself for bringing her here. The last thing he needed right now was to be reopening doors best left shut.

He said, with a cool bite in his voice, 'I'll send these out to be dried.' He indicated the clothes on the bed. 'You can change into these for now. They should fit.'

Julia's eyes, which had widened on seeing him, moved to the clothes on the bed. He saw her tense perceptibly. She shook her head, a flush coming into her cheeks, and put out a hand. 'I'll change back into my own clothes and go home.'

An image of her walking out through the door made Kaden's self-recrimination dissolve in an instant. He held the clothes well out of Julia's reach. 'Don't be silly. You'll get pneumonia if you put these back on.'

Julia's eyes narrowed and she stretched her hand out more. 'Really—I don't mind. This wasn't a good idea. I should never have agreed to come here.'

CHAPTER THREE

SILENCE THICKENED AND grew between them. Julia couldn't fathom what was going on behind those darker than dark eyes. And then Kaden moved towards her and she stepped back. Her heart nearly jumped out of her chest.

He pointed out silkily, 'But you did come. What are you afraid of, Julia? That you won't be able to control yourself around me?'

A few seconds ago she'd seen a look of something like cool distaste cross his face, and yet now he was acknowledging the heat between them. Baiting her. Her heart was thumping so hard she felt sure it would be evident through the towel wrapped around her.

A long buried sensation rushed through her like a tangible force—what it had felt like to have his naked body between her legs, thrusting into her with awesome strength.

For a moment she couldn't breathe, then she said threadily, 'Just give me my clothes, Kaden. This really *isn't* a good idea.'

But Kaden ignored her, was already stepping back and away, taking her clothes with him and leaving the fresh ones on the bed. She looked at them. Jeans and a delicate grey silk shirt. Rage filled her belly at being humiliated like this.

She indicated the clothes with a trembling hand. Too much emotion was coursing through her. More than she'd felt in years. 'I won't wear your mistress's cast-offs. I'll walk out of here in this towel if I have to.'

Kaden turned. He was silhouetted in the doorway, shoulders broad in a simple white shirt. Black trousers hugged his lean hips. Julia hadn't even noticed his still damp hair. She'd been so consumed by his overall presence.

He said, with a flash of fire in his eyes, 'Be my guest, but there's really no need. Those clothes belong to Samia. You remember my younger sister? You're about the same size now. She's been living here for the last couple of years.'

Immediately Julia felt petulant and exposed. She blushed. 'Yes, I remember Samia.' She'd always liked Kaden's next youngest sister, who had been bookish and painfully shy. Before she could say anything else, though, he was gone and the door had shut behind him.

Defeated, Julia contemplated the clothes. She took off the towel and put them on. There were even some knickers still in a plastic bag, and Julia could only figure that someone regularly stocked up Samia's wardrobe. The jeans were a little snug on her rear and thighs, and she felt extremely naked with no bra under the silk shirt. Her breasts weren't overly large, but they were too big for her to go bra-less and feel comfortable. There wasn't much she could do. It was either this or dress in the robe hanging off the back of the bathroom door. And she couldn't face Kaden in just a robe.

She went back into the bathroom and dried her hair with the hairdryer. It dried a little frizzy, but there was not much she could do about that either. And, anyway, it wasn't as if she wanted to impress Kaden, was it? She scowled at the very thought.

Fresh resolve to insist on leaving fired her blood, and she picked up her shoes in one hand and took a deep breath before emerging from the suite, steeling herself to see Kaden again. When she did emerge though, it was to see him with his back to her at one of the main salon windows, looking out over the view. Something about his stance in that moment struck her as acutely lonely, but then he turned around and his sardonic visage made a mockery of her fanciful notion.

She hitched up her chin. 'I'll get a taxi home. I can arrange to get my clothes from you another time.'

Kaden's hand tightened reflexively on the glass he held. He should be saying *Yes, I'll call you a taxi*. He should be reminding himself that this was a very bad idea. But rational thought was very elusive as he looked at Julia.

Her hair drifted softly around her narrow shoulders. Like this, with the veneer of a successful, sophisticated woman stripped away, she might be nineteen again, and something inside him turned over. The grey silk shirt made the grey of her eyes look smoky and mysterious. He could remember thinking when he'd first met her that her eyes were a very icy light blue, but he had then realised that they were grey.

The silk shirt left little to the imagination. Her bare breasts pushed enticingly against the material, and under his gaze he could see her nipples harden to two thrusting points. His body responded forcibly. The jeans were too tight, but that only emphasized the curve of her hips and thighs. He wanted her to turn around so he could see her lush derrière. She'd always had a voluptuous bottom and generous breasts in contrast to her otherwise slender build.

Heat engulfed him, and he struggled for the first time in years to cling on to some control. Once again when it came to it…he couldn't let her go.

Julia was on fire under Kaden's very thorough inspection. 'Please…' She wasn't even really aware of what she was saying, only that she wanted him to stop. 'Don't look at me like that.'

He smiled and went into seduction mode. 'Like what? You're a beautiful woman, Julia. I'm sure you're used to having men's eyes on you.'

Julia flushed at the slightly narrowed dark gaze, which hinted at steel underneath the apparent civility. The memory of what had happened just before she'd left Burquat flashed through her head and brought with it excoriating heat and guilt. And nausea… Kaden's eyes had been on her in her moment of humiliation. Even now she could remember the way that man had pulled her so close she'd felt as if she were suffocating, when all she'd wanted— She slammed the door on that memory.

She shook her head, 'No, actually, I'm not. And this is not appropriate. I really should be leaving. So if you'll just call me a taxi…?'

Kaden smiled then, and it was the devil's smile. She sensed he'd come to some decision and it made her incredibly nervous.

'What's the rush? I'm sure you could do with a drink?'

Julia regarded this suddenly urbane pillar of solicitude suspiciously. Her shoes were unwieldy in her hand. She felt all at once awkward, hot, and yet pathetically reluctant to turn and never see Kaden again. That insidious yearning arose...the awareness that tonight was a bizarre coincidence. Fate. Surely the last time she would ever see him?

As much as she longed to get as far away as possible from this situation, and this man, a dangerous curiosity and a desire for him not to see how conflicted she was by this reunion made her shrug minutely and say grudgingly, 'I suppose one drink wouldn't hurt. After all, it has been a long time.'

He just looked at her. 'Yes, it has.' Hardly taking his eyes from hers, he indicated a bottle of cream liqueur on the sideboard and asked, 'Do you still like this?'

Julia's belly swooped dangerously. He remembered her favourite drink? She'd only ever drunk it with him, and hadn't touched it in twelve years. She nodded dumbly and watched as his large, masculine yet graceful hands deftly poured the distinctive liquid. He replaced the bottle on the sideboard and then came and handed the delicately bulbous glass to Julia.

She took it, absurdly grateful that their fingers didn't touch. Bending her head, she took a sniff of the drink and then a quick sip, to disguise the flush she could feel rising when the smell precipitated a memory of drinking it with Kaden one magical night in his family's summer palace by the coast. It was the night they'd slept together for the first time.

For a second the full intensity of how much she'd loved him threatened to overwhelm her. And he'd casually poisoned those feelings and in one fell swoop destroyed her innocent idealism. Feeling tormented, and wondering if this avalanche of memories would ever go back into its box, she moved away from Kaden's tall, lean body, her eyes darting anywhere but to him.

She sensed him move behind her, and then he appeared in her peripheral vision.

'Please, won't you sit?'

So polite. As if nothing had happened. As if she hadn't given him her body, heart and soul.

Slamming another painful door in her mind, Julia said quickly, nervously, 'Thank you.'

She followed him, and when he sat on a plush couch, easily dominating it, she chose an armchair to the side, putting her shoes down beside her. She was as far away from him as she could get, legs together primly. She glanced at him to see a mocking look cross his face. She didn't care. This new Kaden intimidated her. There was nothing of the boy she'd known. They'd both just been teenagers after all…until he'd had to grow up overnight, after the death of his father.

Now he was a man—infinitely more commanding. She'd seen a glimpse of this more formidable Kaden the last time they'd spoken in Burquat, but that had been a mere precursor of the powerful man opposite her now.

Julia felt exposed in her bare feet and the flimsy shirt. It was too silky against her bare flesh. Her nipples were hard, tingling. She hadn't felt this effortlessly aroused once during her marriage, or since she'd been with Kaden, and the realisation made her feel even more exposed. She struggled to hang on to the fact that she was a successful and relatively sophisticated woman. She'd been married and divorced. She was no naive virgin any more. She could handle this. She had to remember that, while he had devastated *her*, he'd been untouched after their relationship ended. She'd never forget how emotionless he'd been when they said goodbye. It was carved into her soul.

Remembering who the clothes belonged to gave her a moment of divine inspiration. With forced brightness she asked, 'How *is* Samia? She must be at least twenty-four by now?'

Kaden observed Julia from under hooded lids. He was in no hurry to answer her question or engage in small talk. It was more than disconcerting how *right* it felt to have her here. And even more so to acknowledge that the vaguely unsettled feeling he'd been experiencing for what felt like years was dissipating.

She intrigued him more than he cared to admit. He might have imagined that by now she would be far more polished, would have cultivated the hard veneer he was used to in the kind of women he socialised with.

Curbing the urge to stand and pace out the intense conflict inside him as her vulnerability tugged at his jaded emotions, Kaden struggled to remain sitting and remember what she'd asked.

'Samia? She's twenty-five, and she's getting married at the end of this week. To the Sultan of Al-Omar. She's in B'harani for the preparations right now.'

Julia's eyes widened, increasing Kaden's levels of inner tension and desire. He cursed silently. He couldn't stand up now even if he wanted to—not if he didn't want her to see exactly the effect she had on him. He vacillated between intense anger at himself for bringing her here at all, and the assertion that she would not be walking out through his front door any time soon.

Kaden was used to clear, concise thinking—not this churning maelstrom. It was too reminiscent of what had happened before. And yet even as he thought that the tantalising prospect came into his mind: why not take her again? Tonight? Why not exorcise this desire which mocked him with its presence?

'The Sultan of Al-Omar?' Julia shook her head, not liking the speculative gleam in Kaden's eyes. Blonde hair slipped over her shoulders. She tried to focus on stringing a sentence together. 'Samia was so painfully shy. It must be difficult for her to take on such a public role?'

An irrational burst of guilt rushed through Kaden. He'd seen Samia recently, here in London before she'd left, and had felt somewhat reassured by her stoic calm in the face of her impending nuptials. But Julia was reminding him what a challenge this would be for his naturally introverted sister. And he was surprised that Julia remembered such a detail.

It made his voice harsh. 'Samia is a woman now, with responsibilities to her country and her people. A marriage with Sultan Sadiq benefits both our countries.'

'So it is an arranged marriage, then?'

Kaden nodded his head, not sure where the defensiveness he was feeling stemmed from. 'Of course— just as my own marriage was arranged and just as my next marriage will be arranged.' He quirked a brow.

'I presume your marriage was a love match, and yet you did not fare any better if you too are divorced?'

Julia hid the dart of emotion at hearing him say he would marry again and avoided his eye. Had her marriage been a love match? In general terms, yes— it had. After all, she and John had married willingly, with no pressure on either side. But she knew in her heart of hearts that she hadn't truly loved John. And he'd known it too.

Something curdled in her belly at having to justify herself to this man who had haunted her for so long. She looked back at him as steadily as she could. 'No, we didn't fare any better. However, I know plenty of arranged marriages work out very well, so I wish Samia all the best.'

'Children?'

For a moment Julia didn't catch what Kaden had said it had been uttered so curtly. 'Children?' she repeated, and he nodded.

Julia felt another kind of pain lance her. The memory of the look of shame on her husband's face, the way he had closed in on himself and started to retreat, which had marked the beginning of the end of their marriage.

She shook her head and said, a little defiantly, 'Of course not. Do you think I would be here if I had?' And then she cursed herself inwardly. She didn't want Kaden analysing why she *had* come. 'My husband— *ex*-husband—couldn't... We had difficulties... And you? Did you have children?'

That slightly mocking look crossed his face again, because she must know well that his status as a childless divorcee was common knowledge. But he just shook his head. 'No, no children.'

His mouth had become a bitter line, and Julia shivered minutely because it reminded her of how he'd morphed within days from an ardent lover into a cold stranger.

'My ex-wife's mother suffered a horrific and near-fatal childbirth and stuffed my wife's head with tales of horror and pain. As a result Amira developed a phobia about childbirth. It was so strong that when she did discover she was pregnant she went without my knowledge to get a termination. Soon afterwards I started proceedings to divorce.'

Julia gave an audible gasp and Kaden saw her eyes grow wide. He knew how it sounded—so stark. His jaw was tight with tension. How on earth had he let those words spill so blithely from his mouth? He'd just told Julia something that only a handful of people knew. The secret of his ex-wife's actions was something he discussed with nobody. As were the painstaking efforts he'd made to help her overcome that fear after the abortion. But to no avail. Eventually it had been his wife who had insisted they divorce, knowing that she could never give him an heir. She hadn't been prepared to confront her fears.

Kaden's somewhat brutal dismissal of a wife who hadn't been able to perform her duty made a shiver run through Julia. The man she'd known had been compassionate, idealistic.

To divert attention away from the dismay she felt at recognising just how much he'd changed, she said quickly, 'I thought divorce was illegal in Burquat?'

Kaden took a measured sip of his amber-coloured drink. 'It used to be. Things have changed a lot since you were there. It's been slow but steady reform, undoing the more conservative laws of my father and his forebears.'

A rush of tenderness took Julia by surprise, coming so soon after her feeling repelled by his treatment of his wife. Kaden had always been so passionate about reform for his country, and now he was doing it.

Terrified that he would see something of that emotion rising up within her, Julia stood up jerkily and walked over to the window, clutching her glass in her hand.

She took in the view. Kaden had told her about this apartment, right in the centre of London. Pain, bittersweet, rushed through her. He had once mentioned that she should move in here when she returned to college in London—so that he could make sure she was protected, and so she would be waiting for him when he came over. But those words had all been part of his seductive patter. Meaningless. A wave of sadness gripped her.

She didn't hear Kaden move, and jumped when his deep voice came from her right, far too close. 'Why did you divorce your husband, Julia?'

Because I never loved him the way I loved you. The words reverberated around her head. Never in a million years had she imagined she would be standing in a room listening to Kaden ask her that question.

Eventually, when she felt as if she had some measure of control, she glanced at him. He was standing with one shoulder propped nonchalantly against the wall, looking at her from under hooded lids. With one hand in his pocket, the glass held loosely in the other, he could have stepped straight out of a fashion magazine.

He looked dark and dangerous, and Julia gulped—because she felt that sense of danger reverberate within her and ignite a fire. She tried to ignore the sensation, telling herself it was overactive hormones mixed in with too many evocative memories and the loaded situation they were now in. She looked back out of the window with an effort. She felt hot and tingly all over, her belly heavy with desire.

'I...we just grew apart.' She shook her head. 'It seemed like a good idea, but it never really worked. And our difficulty with having children was the last straw. There wasn't enough to keep us together. I'm glad there were no children. It wouldn't have been the right environment to bring them into.'

Julia had never told Kaden that she was adopted, or about her own visceral feelings on the subject of having children. She'd never told anyone. It was too bound up in painful emotions for her. And perhaps she hadn't told him for a reason—because on some level she'd been afraid of his judgement, and that what they shared hadn't been real. She'd been right to be afraid.

She was aware of tension emanating from Kaden and didn't want to look at him, afraid he might see the emotion she felt she couldn't hide. Her face always gave her away. He was the one who had told her that as he'd held her face in his hands one day...

Suddenly from out of the still ominously cloudy sky came a jagged flash of lightning. Julia jumped so violently that liquid sloshed out of her glass. Immediately shocked and embarrassed by her overreaction, she stepped back. 'I'm sorry…'

Kaden was there in an instant. He took the glass out of her hand, placing it down on the table alongside his own. He was back in front of her before she could steel herself not to react. His dark eyes looked her up and down and then rested on her chest. As if mesmerised, Julia followed his gaze to see where some of the drink had landed on her shirt, right over one breast, and now the material was clinging to the rounded slope.

Panicky, Julia stepped back, 'I'll get a cloth… I don't want Samia's shirt to get ruined.'

A big hand snaked out and caught her upper arm. 'Leave it.'

Kaden's voice was unbearably harsh, and in that instant the air between became even heavier and more charged. As if the tension and atmosphere between them was directly affecting the weather, a huge booming roll of thunder sounded outside.

Julia flinched, eyes glued to Kaden's with some kind of sick fascination. Faintly she said, 'I thought the storm was over.'

With a move so smooth she didn't even feel it happening Kaden put his hands on her arms and pulled her closer. Their bodies were almost touching.

'I think the storm is just beginning.'

For a second confusion made Julia's head foggy. She didn't seem to be able to separate out his words, or even understand what Kaden was saying. And then she realised, when she saw how hot his gaze had become and how it moved down to her mouth. Desire was stamped onto the stark lines of his face and Julia's heart beat fast in response. Because it was a look that had haunted her dreams for ever.

Desperately trying to fight the urge to succumb to the waves of need beating through her veins, she shook her head and tensed, trying to pull back out of Kaden's grip. His hands just tightened.

'Kaden, *no*. I shouldn't be here…we shouldn't have met again.'

'But we did meet. And you're here now.'

Julia asserted stiffly, 'I didn't agree to come here for this.'

Kaden shook his head, and a tiny harsh smile touched his mouth. 'From the moment we stood in front of each other in that room earlier the possibility of *this* has existed.'

Bitterness rang in Julia's voice. 'Even when you pretended not to know me?'

More lightning flashed outside, quickly followed by the roll of thunder. The unmistakable sound of torrential rain started to lash against the window.

'Even then.'

Nothing seemed to be throwing Kaden off. Had he somehow magically dimmed the lights in the room? Julia wondered frantically, feeling as though reality was slipping out of her grasp. The past was meshing into the present, and the future was fast becoming irrelevant.

Julia tried again. 'The possibility of this stopped existing twelve years ago in Burquat—or have you forgotten when you informed me our *affair* was past its sell-by date?' Bitterness laced her voice, but she couldn't pretend it wasn't there, much as she would have loved to feign insouciance. The rawness of that day was vivid.

Kaden's hands were steady. 'I don't wish to discuss the past, Julia. The past bears no relationship to this moment.'

'How can you say that? The past is the reason I'm standing here now.'

Kaden shook his head, eyes glowing with dark embers, effortlessly stoking Julia's desire higher and higher, despite what her head might be saying.

'I would have wanted you even if tonight was the first time we'd met.'

His flattery did nothing for Julia's ego. The evidence of how unmoved he was by the past broke something apart inside her. Of course it had no effect on him now. Because he felt nothing for her—just as he'd never really felt anything for her.

Julia tensed as much as she could. She had to get out of there. Things were spiralling out of all control. 'Well, the past might not be relevant to you, but it is to me, and I think this is a very bad idea.'

Kaden's eyes flashed, showing Julia a glimpse of the emotion that thickened the atmosphere between them, no matter how he might deny it. '*This* is desire, pure and simple. We're two single consenting adults and I want you.'

Julia looked up, helpless to pull away or articulate any kind of sane response. Which should be *no*. How was it possible that this desire hadn't abated one bit? That if anything it felt stronger? There were so many layers of meaning here, and Kaden wanted to ignore all of that. As if they had never met before.

He lifted a hand and slid it around the back of her neck, under the fall of her hair, and pulled her even closer. Huskily he said, 'I didn't expect this. I didn't expect that if I ever saw you again I would feel this way. Perhaps this was meant to be…a chance encounter to burn ourselves free of this insatiable desire.'

Insatiable desire. That was exactly how it felt— how it had always felt between them. Moments after making love Julia had always been ashamed of how quickly she'd craved Kaden's touch again, and only the fact that it had been mutual had stopped her shame from overwhelming her.

As he said, he hadn't expected to see her again. And she could well believe that he'd not expected to desire her again. But he did, and obviously resented it. Why wouldn't he? He'd turned his back on her, and he'd bedded plenty of women far more beautiful than Julia since then. It must be galling to meet your first lover and realise you still wanted her. That made Julia feel acutely vulnerable. But it was too late.

Kaden had pulled her even closer, and now her soft belly touched his hard-muscled form—far harder than she remembered—and his head was lowering to hers. She tried to stiffen, to register her rejection, but everything was blocked out when she felt the explosive touch of Kaden's mouth to hers. Did it coincide with another clap of thunder outside or was that in her head?

Her heart spasmed in her chest, as if given an electric shock, and as his mouth moved and fitted to hers like a missing jigsaw piece she fell down into a dark vortex of desire so intense that it obliterated any kind of rational thought. Her hands had gone automatically to his chest, but instead of pushing him away they clung. The feel of powerful muscles under his shirt was intoxicating.

Time stood still. Everything stood still except for their two hearts, beating fast. Blood was rushing through veins and arteries, pumping to parts of Julia's body that hadn't been stimulated in a long, long time.

Kaden was seduction incarnate. His hands moved over and down her back, cupping her bottom in the tight jeans, floating sensuously over the silk shirt. With an easy expertise he certainly hadn't displayed when she'd known him before he coaxed her mouth open and his tongue stroked along hers, making a faint mewl come from the back of her throat.

Through the heat haze in her head and her body Julia felt something urgent trying to get through to her. Kaden's touch was all at once achingly familiar, and yet so different from how she remembered. They'd been so young, and their passion had been raw and un-tutored. The man who held her in his arms now was not raw and untutored. He was a consummate seducer, well-practised in the art. His body was different too. Muscles were filled out and harder.

It was that realisation that finally broke the spell cast around Julia. Plus the fact that within a mere hour of meeting Kaden again she was kissing him like a sex-starved groupie.

Wrenching herself away in one abruptly violent move, Julia staggered backwards, looking at Kaden's flushed face and glittering eyes. 'I don't know you. You're a stranger to me now. I don't do this... I don't make love to strangers.'

Something dark crossed Kaden's handsome features. He drawled, 'From what I recall, you found it remarkably easy to make love to relative strangers.'

With the memory of that incident so vivid, Julia lashed out. 'It was just a kiss, Kaden. A stupid kiss. It meant nothing... It was just—' She stopped abruptly. Had she really been about to blurt out that she'd only allowed that man to kiss her because she'd felt so desperately insecure after days of silence from Kaden? That she'd pathetically wanted to try and prove to herself that his touch alone couldn't be the only touch she'd ever crave?

She clamped her mouth shut, burning inside. This man would never know that her experiment had backfired spectacularly—on more levels than one.

She had to claw back some sense of sanity. Some sense of the independent woman she'd become. Her voice was shaky. 'This is not a good idea, Kaden. The past is the past and we should not be revisiting it.'

Kaden felt tight and hot inside. With ruthless effort he excised the image of her kissing that man from his mind. What on earth had prompted him to bring up that kiss? The last thing he wanted was for Julia to know that he remembered the incident. And yet it was like the stain of a tattoo on his memory, the jealousy fresh.

She was avoiding Kaden's eye. He might have appreciated the dark humour of the situation if he'd been in a better mood: merely *kissing* her just now had had a more explosive effect on his libido than anything he'd shared with a woman in years. If ever. Her chest was rising and falling rapidly. Some more buttons had opened on her shirt, exposing the shadowy line of her cleavage, and his erection just got harder. If that was possible.

The fact that what she said was right irked him beyond belief. He knew with a soul-deep certainly that to explore this desire with *this* woman had danger written all over it. He had a sense of having escaped the fire years before, only to be standing right on its edge again.

But stronger than that was this life-force rushing through his veins, along with the very carnal urge to sate himself. It was heady, and it made him feel as if he was awakening from a long sleep. He could no more turn back from it than he could stop breathing. He struggled to control himself. The rawness of what he was feeling was rising up, and Kaden ruthlessly drove it down, back to depths he'd never plumbed and had no intention of doing so now.

He crossed the room to where Julia stood. She looked up. Those grey eyes were dark and troubled. A line of pink slashed each cheek, and her lips were full and tender-looking. In a completely instinctive gesture he reached out and tucked some hair behind her ear, only realising as he did it that he'd used to do that all the time. His jaw clenching hard was the only sign that he'd recognised this tell-tale gesture which was at such odds with the dark emotion seething through his gut. *Jealousy*. He had to distance himself from their past, focus on the present.

'If we had met at any other time we wouldn't have been available, and yet this desire would still have blown up. It would have made a mockery of the fact that twelve years had gone by. And of our marriages.'

He went on, his deep voice mesmerising, 'But we're both free and single now, two consenting adults.'

Julia knew she should run—and fast. Get away and pray to God that she never saw Kaden again. But her feet wouldn't move. The way he'd casually reached out to tuck her hair behind her ear had broken something apart inside her, bringing with it an onslaught of memories of so many moments when he'd done that. It had been the first physical gesture he'd made to her.

Fatefully, knowing that on some level she was making a momentous decision by *not* leaving, Julia couldn't seem to turn away. She felt curiously lethargic—as if she'd been running towards something for a long time, only to have finally reached her destination. She wanted this man with a hunger she'd known only once before...for *him*.

She'd fully expected that if they ever met again that he would act as dismissively as he had earlier...and yet here she was. He wasn't pretending not to know her now. He was looking at her as if she was the only woman on the planet. That elusive feeling of home and connection that she'd only ever found with him whispered to her like a siren song, calling her to seek it again.

Desperately she fought it—going that way again could only end in worse devastation. Clinging furiously to some last vestige of pride, to the illusion that she had control, she backed away. 'Just because we've met again, it doesn't mean anything, Kaden. It doesn't mean that we have to end up...in bed.'

For a long tense moment they just looked at each

other, and then, after another ear-splitting crack of thunder, the electricity went off.

Julia gasped and Kaden cursed. 'The storm must have outed the power. Wait here. I'll get some candles.'

Julia felt Kaden move away from her and took a deep, shaky breath. The darkness seemed to envelop her in a cloak of collusion. It made her want to forget the outside world, forget to remember their history. To give in to what he was offering. She wanted him so badly she shook.

Desperately she tried to remember the awful excoriating pain of the moment when he'd coolly informed her that all they'd shared had been a summer fling, that he had a life of responsibilities that didn't include her. But it was like trying to hold on to a wispy cloud. All she knew was the exhilaration rushing through her blood, the heightened awareness of desire.

Through the silence of the apartment she heard a crash somewhere and a colourful curse. They were sounds that *should* have been restoring her sanity, making her more determined to leave. But instead they were only firing her desire. She heard a movement and saw flickering light. This was it.

Kaden came back into the room, and in the soft glow Julia could only look at him and marvel at the shadows which made his face seem even more mysterious, his eyes two dark pools. He put down the candle and came closer and closer, until his body was just inches away from hers. His heat enveloped her, along with his exotic masculine scent. It made her think of hot nights in the desert, and of even hotter things.

'Julia, I don't want to analyse why this has happened like this. I don't want to discuss the past... I just want you.'

She looked up at Kaden. So many feelings were rushing through her like a torrent, but one above all others. She wanted him too. She'd dreamt for years of seeing him again. He'd cast her out without a moment's hesitation, and when she'd heard about his nuptials something in her had died. So she had given in and accepted John's proposal, believing it was futile to love a ghost.

But he wasn't a ghost any more. He was flesh and blood and standing right in front of her. And then he reached out a hand and cupped her jaw, his thumb stroking her cheek. She was undone. When he pulled her closer she didn't resist. Because she couldn't.

CHAPTER FOUR

KADEN FOUND HIMSELF relishing the other-worldliness that enforced darkness imposed, surrounding them in this cocoon. Julia's eyes were huge, her breaths coming short and rapid, and as he lowered his head so that his mouth could drink from hers he felt an inalienable sense of rightness. It was too strong to deny or question or rail against. His mouth settled over Julia's, his arms pulled her close, and when he felt her breasts crushed against his chest he was lost.

The outside world—the lashing rain against the windows and the intermittent thunder and lightning—all faded into the background as flames of heat started licking around them.

After what seemed like an aeon had passed Kaden pulled back. Julia was stunned, her limbs jelly-like. Her mouth felt swollen and her heart was hammering as if she'd just run half a marathon. Her hands were around Kaden's neck, his breath was harsh, and she could feel the hard ridge of his erection against her belly.

He just said coarsely, 'Julia.'

She didn't stop him when he shifted slightly so that he could pick her up into his arms. 'Take the candle,' he instructed roughly.

Half in a daze, Julia looked down to see the flickering candle on a table. She reached down to pick it up in its stand and then Kaden was striding out of the room, the soft light guiding their way to a door which he all but kicked open. In the shadowy half-light Julia could pick out a huge bed and unmistakably masculine furnishings. Kaden's bedroom.

A sliver of sanity returned, and Kaden must have felt her tense, because he looked down into her face and said implacably, 'There is no going back from here.'

Her breath was suspended for a long moment, and then the enormity of meeting Kaden again struck home. How fleeting this night would be. The weight of her yearning for this man was heavy on her shoulders, and it was too strong to deny, much as the tiny sliver of sanity she had left might be urging her to. Slowly. Fatefully, she shook her head. 'I don't want to go back.'

He carried her over to the chest of drawers, where she put down the candle, then let her slide down his body, his hands touching her from shoulder to waist to hip. He pushed some of her hair back over one shoulder and bent his head to her neck, pressing a kiss there. Julia's head fell back. It was too heavy to hold up. Her blood was hot as it pumped through her veins.

Kaden's fingers came to her shirt and he started to undo the buttons in the slippery fabric. She shivered slightly when the air whispered over her bare skin. Soon her shirt hung open. Kaden drew back and stood to his full height.

He was downright intimidating in the dusky light, with no help from an obscured moon, but he was also *thrilling*. He was a big man all over. Julia watched with a drying mouth as he coolly started to open his own buttons. Part of her wanted to be as bold as she'd once been and brush his hands aside so that she could do it. But this wasn't the past. She was more cautious now, no matter how time seemed to be blurring here tonight.

His shirt was open, and with an economy of movement he pulled it off, revealing his awe-inspiring chest. It was broad and tautly muscled, and he had filled out since she'd seen him last. Coarse dark hair covered his pectorals, leading downwards in a dark line to just above his belt.

A finger to her chin lifted her face back up and Julia flamed guiltily. She'd all but been licking her lips at the prospect of seeing him fully naked for the first time in years.

Instead of pushing her shirt off her shoulders and arms, Kaden's big hands came to her waist, spanning it easily. His action pushed the shirt off her breasts, revealing them to his incendiary gaze. She could see a pulse throb in his neck and her belly quivered. Hot, wet heat moistened her sex in readiness.

Kaden breathed out. 'So beautiful...you're so damn beautiful.'

He cupped one fleshy weight in his hand and a thumb moved back and forth rhythmically over the tight peak. Julia moaned, and didn't even realise she was pushing her breast into his hand to increase the friction.

With a languorous movement he brought his thumb to his mouth and sucked it deep, before moving it back and repeating the action, moistening the hard tip. Julia moaned even louder, her breath coming short and fast.

Excitement was building, ratcheting her inner tension upwards.

'Kaden...please.'

'Please what?' he asked, almost casually. 'Do you want me to put my mouth on you? Do you want me to taste you?'

Julia was almost weeping. 'Yes...'

Kaden's head came down and his mouth closed unerringly over her already deeply sensitised nipple. Silky hair brushed the hot skin of her breast, adding to the exquisite sensation. He sucked so hard that Julia cried out, her fingers arrowing through his hair, holding him in place. His other hand was moulding and cupping the flesh of her other breast, readying it too for his ministrations.

His mouth moved to the second peak and Julia's legs all but buckled. Ruthlessly, with an arm around her waist, Kaden clamped her to him, not letting her fall, all the while subjecting her to something on the knife-edge of pleasure and pain.

Julia was fast losing sight of any reality. She was made up of sensations, a slave to this man and his touch. He was so much more confident than she remembered. He knew exactly what to do, where she ached to be touched.

As abruptly as he'd started torturing her with his mouth he stood back again, and with his hands clamped on her waist he drew her into him with an urgency that sent blood rushing to her pelvis. His head bent, mouth finding hers, tongue delving deep and seeking hers. The friction of her sensitised breasts against his chest was delicious torture. Through the haze of desire and excitement Julia felt a wild surge of exhilaration at being with this man again. It was as if now she'd given in to it she could fully appreciate the experience.

Blindly obeying the deep call of her blood, Julia let her hands seek and fumble with Kaden's belt and zip, undoing them with a feverish intensity. While their mouths still clung, Julia pushed his trousers down over his lean hips. She could feel Kaden step out of them and kick them away. And then her hands were on his boxers.

He drew back at that, and she could see his eyes glittering. Her breasts were heavy. Her blood was on fire. Not taking her eyes off his, she put her fingers between his hot skin and the material and pulled them down. It was only when they snagged that she looked. The bulge of his erection was formidable. Running a finger around the rim of his boxers, unaware of the look of torture on Kaden's face, Julia stopped just where she could feel the smooth head of him.

Slowly she pulled the boxers out, free of his erection, and then they too were slid down over his powerfully muscled thighs. It reminded Julia again of the national sport that Kaden so loved to play, which had broken his nose at least once. It had looked barbaric to her: men stripped to the waist, using a crude form of shortened hockey stick to whack a ball between two goals. Part of the play was to crash into one another and divert each other from the ball. It was visceral, exciting and undeniably violent. And Kaden excelled at it.

But now she couldn't take her eyes off his impressive erection, springing free from the cradle of black hair. Moisture beaded the tip enticingly, and she could feel her own body moisten in answer.

His voice broke the spell. 'I'm feeling a little underdressed here.'

Julia's wide gaze clashed with his as he pushed her shirt off her shoulders, down her arms, from where it slithered to the floor in a pool of grey silk. Then his efficient hands were on her jeans, flicking open the button and pulling down the zip. Julia barely had a chance to get her breath before she felt him tugging them down over her hips and thighs.

Any embarrassment because the jeans were too small was lost when she saw how his gaze roved hungrily over her body. She sucked in a shaky breath when he took her by the hand to lead her to the bed. The candlelight and the dark, ominous sky outside made everything seem even more unreal. But the heat between her and Kaden was very real.

As he pushed her back onto the bed she realised with an illicit thrill that his touch was all at once familiar and yet that of a stranger. He was truly a man now, and she sensed a hunger in him that hadn't been there before, an easy dominance.

He joined her on the cool sheets and all rational thought fled. Pulling her into his body, touching her chest to chest and down, he kissed her again, deeply, as if he couldn't get enough of kissing her. Julia sank back into the covers, relishing the latent strength in Kaden's powerful form. His hand smoothed its way down, over her chest and to her belly. Fingers seeking even further until they encountered her pants.

With a perfunctory movement they were dispatched,

and Kaden pushed her thighs apart, his hand seeking between her legs to where her body told of its readiness for him.

One finger stroked in and out of her moist heat. Julia's hands gripped Kaden's shoulders. She couldn't breathe, and almost arched off the bed when one finger was joined by another one, opening her up, stretching her, preparing her for his own body. Julia's hand sought his erection and wrapped around it, squeezing and moving up and down—a silent plea for him to stop torturing her. She couldn't speak, couldn't articulate anything.

Kaden shifted and was moving down her body, pressing kisses along her belly until his mouth was at the juncture of her legs and his tongue was tasting her as he'd once shocked her by doing all those years ago. She gasped, but ruthlessly he held her thighs wide apart, baring her to his mouth and that wickedly stabbing tongue.

He reached one hand up to find her breast and rolled a nipple between his fingers. Without anything to cling on to, Julia felt her body tighten in a spasm of pleasure so intense she didn't even notice when Kaden moved again, so that his huge body now lay between her legs.

Shattered from the intensity of the strongest orgasm she could remember having, she could only lie there in a stupor as Kaden took himself in his hand and stroked the head of his erection back and forth against her moistened sex. Her body was already greedy for him, her muscles still clenching as if trying to suck him in.

At some point he'd had the sense to don protection, and Julia was exceedingly grateful—because all concerns for practicalities had gone out of the window.

Torturously he let himself be sucked in slowly, sheathing the head in her heat before pulling out. Julia moaned softly, her eyes glued to Kaden's harsh face. He looked so stark, like a pagan god stripped bare of all civility. And then he leaned over her on both hands and with one cataclysmic thrust seated himself in her fully. All the way to the hilt. Julia gasped at his size, but the fleeting pain quickly morphed to an intense pleasure, as if her body recognised him and was rejoicing.

'You...' he said roughly. 'You are the only one who has ever made me feel like this...'

Julia asked brokenly, 'Like what?'

'Like I'm not even human any more.'

And with that he started up a remorseless rhythm, stroking in and out, his thrusts so long and full that Julia pulled up her legs to allow him to slide even deeper. There had not been one second of hesitation on her part in allowing him into her body. It had taken her husband months to woo her, for her to trust him enough to sleep with him. She'd still been so shaken by what had happened in Burquat... But here with Kaden it felt so natural and right she couldn't fight it.

The tremors of her last orgasm were still dying away as new tremors started up, even more intense than the last time. Sweat beaded her brow and dampened her skin. And Kaden still moved between her legs and inside her, as if he wanted to wring out this pleasure for as long as possible. Julia knew she wouldn't last. Head flung back, she arched upwards and splintered all over again, just as Kaden's thrusts increased, and when the storm in her body abated he gave a guttural groan and sank over her, his huge body stilling.

DURING THE NIGHT Julia woke briefly to see that the storm had finally died away. The candle had gone out and she was tucked against Kaden's chest, his arms tight around her like a vice. The moon peeked out from behind a cloud.

The storm outside might have abated, but another storm was starting up inside her.

What on earth had she done?

Her thoughts must have made her tense, because she could feel Kaden stirring behind her. He shifted them so that she lay on her back, looking up into slumbrous long-lashed eyes. She felt extremely vulnerable. She'd never expected to see him again, much less—

'Kaden... I—'

But he cut her off by putting a finger over her mouth. He shook his head, a lock of silky black hair flopping over his forehead, making him look sexily dishevelled. 'Don't say a word. I don't want to hear it.'

He took her mouth with his, and within seconds the conflagration that had burnt them before was starting up again. Julia's mind was screaming at her to stop, but the call of her blood was too strong. Kaden didn't even move over her this time. He gently shifted her so that she was on her side and lifted up one of her legs, pulling it back over his thigh. She gasped out loud when she felt him surge up and into her from behind, his arm snaking around her midriff and holding her firm as he thrust upwards.

His other hand cupped a breast, trapping a nipple between his fingers, and Julia helplessly fell into the fire all over again.

WHEN JULIA WOKE next she knew it was morning. She could sense the bright sunlight on her face. She was replete and lethargic. And at peace. *At peace?* The words resounded in her head as she registered her nakedness and the pleasurable ache throughout her body.

Almost superstitiously, she didn't open her eyes. She didn't need to; the pictures forming behind her closed lids were too lurid. Images formed into a set of scenarios: seeing Kaden at the top of the stairs after he'd been announced at the club; standing in front of him and registering that sardonic coolness; the rain; coming back here; the lights going out…and then heat. Nothing but heat. Maybe it had all been a dream. God only knew she'd had a few like it…

'I can tell that you're going through exactly what I went through when I woke. And, yes, every second of it happened for real.' The voice was dry, mocking, and not a dream.

Julia's eyes flew open and she squinted in the bright light. Mercifully the sheet was up over her breasts. She pulled it up higher and could see Kaden now, standing at the window, looking gorgeous and pristine in a dark suit, drinking nonchalantly from what looked like an espresso cup.

He gestured with his other hand to a small breakfast table. 'There's coffee there for you too, and some orange juice and a croissant.'

Her stomach churned. It was excruciating to be facing Kaden like this. She'd been so *easy*. She came up on one arm and bit her lip, looked down. Her eyes were watering, and she couldn't tell if it was from the bright sunlight or looking at Kaden. The storm from last night had well and truly passed, and already the bitter recrimination was starting.

What on earth had she been thinking? Had one thunderstorm rewired her entire brain?

He moved forward then, and put down his cup. He came closer to the bed. Julia sat up awkwardly. Kaden's eyes were very black and intense on her, and already she could feel the heat of renewed desire deep within her.

'I'm here until the end of the week, when I have to fly to Al-Omar for Samia's wedding. I'd like to see you again, Julia.'

Julia didn't know what to make of the maelstrom that erupted inside her at his words. She'd been expecting him to tell her casually to let herself out of the apartment when she was ready. 'You want to see me again?'

He shrugged, oozing insouciance and an ease with this morning after situation. Another indication of the urbane seducer he'd become. 'I don't see why not. I think we have unfinished business…why not finish it?'

Julia's mouth twisted. 'You mean have an affair for a few days and then walk away?'

His mouth thinned. 'It doesn't have to be as crass as that. You can't deny the attraction is as strong as ever. Why not indulge it to its natural conclusion? I don't see it lasting for longer than a few days.'

That warm spread of desire suddenly cooled. Julia

sat up straighter, pulling the sheet around her carefully. She felt seriously dishevelled and at a disadvantage in front of Kaden like this. She attempted her haughtiest look. 'I'm extremely busy this week. I don't know if I have time to fit in an...*affair*.'

Kaden's face became mocking. 'I don't plan on spending the *days* with you, Julia, I was thinking more along the lines of the evenings...and the nights.'

Instantly she castigated herself. Of course he wasn't talking about having *conversations*. She stood up, clinging on to the sheet like a lifeline.

'It's a crazy idea, Kaden. Last night was...' She bit her lip. 'It should never have happened.'

He strolled closer, and Julia would have moved back if she could—but the bed was at the back of her legs. Up close to him in her bare feet, she was reminded of how huge he was—and how utterly gorgeous. Once again the juxtaposition between the boy and the man was overwhelming. But his hands were shoved deep in his pockets, and she sensed an underlying tension to his otherwise suave manner.

He took one hand out then, and touched his knuckles to her chin. She gritted her jaw against his touch. His dark eyes roved her face and she couldn't make out any emotion. It made her wonder at the depths this civility hid from her.

Steel ran through his voice, impacting her. 'Well, it did happen, Julia. And it's going to happen again. I'll pick you up from your house this evening at seven.'

And with that he stepped back and strolled away.

Julia's mouth opened and closed ineffectually. She couldn't get over his easy arrogance that she would just fall in with his wishes. 'You…' she spluttered. 'You can't just seriously think that I will—'

He turned at the door. 'I don't think, Julia. I *know.*' He arched a brow. 'I believe you said you were busy this week? You'd better get a move on. You'll find your clothes hanging in the closet. Help yourself to whatever you need. One of my cars will be waiting outside. You will be taken wherever you wish to go.'

Kaden turned and left the room, shutting the door behind him. He didn't like the way he'd just had to battle to control himself enough not to topple Julia back onto that bed and take her again. And again. She'd looked tousled and thoroughly bedded, and far too reminiscent of memories he'd long suppressed. And he was *still* ignoring the voice in his head urging him to walk away, to forget he'd seen her again. He *should* have been able to leave last night as a one-off, an aberration. But he couldn't do it.

He was well aware that he'd just acted like some medieval autocrat, but the truth was he hadn't wanted to give her a chance to argue with him. To have her tell him that she was refusing to see him again, or point out again that this shouldn't have happened. He might have appreciated the fact that this was the first time a woman was clearly less than eager to share his bed if he'd been able to think past the urgent lust he still felt.

Standing in front of Julia just now, he'd not been able to think beyond the immediate future. He'd had a vision of being in London for the next few days, and the thought of not seeing her again had been repugnant.

He tried to rationalise it now. Their desire was clearly far from sated, but he had no doubt a couple of nights would be more than enough to rid himself of this bizarre need to reconnect with an ex-lover. *An ex-lover who almost had you in such thrall that you forgot what your priorities were.*

Kaden scowled, but didn't stop. By the time he reached his waiting car his face was as dark as thunder, tension vibrating off him in waves.

MINUTES LATER JULIA was still standing looking at the closed door, clutching the rumpled sheet, her mouth half open. And to her utter chagrin she couldn't drum up anything other than intense excitement at the thought of seeing Kaden again. Even after he'd so arrogantly informed her that it would suit him to have an affair while he was in London, to fill his time. Pathetic.

Last night ran through her brain like a bad movie, and all she could remember was the wanton way she'd succumbed to his caresses over and over again. The way she'd sought him out, her hand wrapping around him, eager to seduce him.

She groaned out loud and finally stumbled towards the bathroom. That was nearly worse. His scent was heavy in the air, steam still evident from his recent shower. She could see that glorious body in her mind's eye—naked, with water sluicing down over taut, hard muscles and contours.

She tore off the sheet and turned on the shower, relishing the hot pounding spray, but try as she might she couldn't stop older memories flooding her brain, superseding the more recent and humiliating ones. Pandora's box had been well and truly opened. All she could think of now were the awful last weeks and days in Burquat. Even under the hot spray, Julia shivered.

A few weeks before she'd been due to return to England to complete her studies, Julia and Kaden had returned from a trip to the desert where they'd celebrated her birthday. She'd been so in love with him, and she'd believed that he'd loved her too. He'd *told* her he loved her. So why wouldn't she have believed him?

But, as clear as if it was yesterday, she could remember watching him walk away from her when they got back to Burquat. For some reason she'd superstitiously wished for him to turn around and smile at her, but he hadn't. That image of his tall, rangy body walking away from her had proved to be an ominous sign. She'd not seen him again until shortly before she was due to leave Burquat.

That very night it had been announced that the Emir wasn't well, and so Kaden had in effect become acting ruler. Heartsore for Kaden, because she'd known he was close to his father even though he'd been a somewhat distant figure, she'd made attempts to see him. But she'd been turned back time and time again by stern-looking aides.

It was as if he'd been spirited away. Days had passed, Julia had made preparations to go home and there had still been no sign or word from Kaden. She'd put it down to his father's frailty and the huge responsibility he faced as the incumbent ruler. She'd never realised until then how different it would have been if he had already been ruler. Much to her shame, she hadn't been able to stop the feeling of insecurity growing when there was no word, even though she'd known it was selfish.

A few nights before she'd been due to leave, Julia had given in to the urging of some fellow archaeology students and gone out for a drink, telling herself it was futile to waste another evening pining for Kaden. She hadn't been used to drinking much normally, and all she could remember was standing up at one point and feeling very dizzy. One of her colleagues had taken her outside to get some air. And it was then that he had tried to kiss her.

At first Julia had rejected his advances, but he'd been persistent…and that awful insecurity had risen up. What if Kaden had finished with her without even telling her? What if he wasn't even going to say goodbye to her? Even stronger had been the rising sense of desperation to think that Kaden might be the only man who would ever make her feel whole, who would ever be able to awaken her sensuality. The thought of being beholden to one man who didn't want her terrified her. The way she'd come to depend on Kaden, to love him, had raised all her very private fears and vulnerabilities about being adopted…and rejection.

He *couldn't* be the only one who would ever make her feel anything again, she'd determined. So she had allowed that man to kiss her—almost in an attempt to prove something to herself.

It had been an effort in futility from the first moment, making instant nausea rise.

And that was when she'd seen Kaden, across the dark street, in long robes and looking half wild, with stubble darkening his jaw. She'd been so shocked she hadn't been able to move, and then…too late…she'd started to struggle. Kaden had just looked at her with those dark implacable eyes, and then he'd turned and left.

The following day the death of Kaden's father had been announced.

Only by refusing to move from outside the state offices had Julia eventually been allowed to see Kaden before she left the country a few days later. She'd stepped into a huge, opulent office to see Kaden standing in the middle of the room, legs splayed, dressed in ceremonial robes, gorgeous and formidable. And like an utter stranger.

She'd been incredibly nervous. 'Kaden… I…' She'd never found it hard to speak with him, not from the moment they'd first met, but suddenly she struggled to get two words out. 'I'm so sorry about your father.'

'Thank you.' His voice was clipped. Curt.

'I…I've tried to see you before now, but you've been busy.'

His mouth thinned. 'From the looks of things you've been busy yourself.'

Julia flushed brick red when she remembered her tangled emotions and what they'd led her to do. 'What you saw the other night…it was nothing. I'd had a bit too much to drink and—'

Kaden lifted a hand, an expression of distaste etched on his face. 'Please, spare me the sordid details. It does not interest me in the slightest how or when or where you made love to that man.'

Julia protested. 'We didn't make love. It was just

a stupid kiss… It stopped almost as soon as it had started.'

Kaden's voice was icy. 'Like I said, I'm really not interested. Now, what was it you wanted to see me about? As you said yourself, I'm very busy.'

Julia immediately felt ashamed. Kaden was grieving.

'I just…I wanted to give you my condolences personally and to say…goodbye. I'm leaving tomorrow.'

A layer of shock was making her a little numb. Not so long ago this man had held her in his arms underneath a blanket of stars and said to her fervently, *'I love you. I won't ever love another woman again.'*

Nausea surged, and Julia had to put her hands against the shower wall and breathe deep. She hadn't thought of that awful evening for a long time.

And yet it wouldn't go away, the memory as stubborn as a dark stain. She could remember feeling compelled to blurt out, 'Kaden…why are you behaving like this?'

He'd arched a brow and crossed his arms. 'Like what?'

'Like you hardly know me.'

His face had been a mask of cool civility. 'You think six months of a summer fling means that I *know* you?'

Julia could remember flinching so violently that she'd taken a step backwards. 'I didn't think of it as a fling. I thought what we had was—'

He had slashed down a hand, stopping her words, his face suddenly fierce. 'What we had was an affair, Julia. Nothing more and nothing less than what you were engaging in with that man the other night. You are not from this world.' His mouth had curled up in an awful parody of a mocking smile. 'You didn't seriously think that you would ever become a permanent part of it, did you?'

Of course she hadn't. But her conscience niggled her. Deep within her, in a very secret place, she'd harboured a dream that perhaps this was *it*. He'd even mentioned his London apartment. Bile rose as she acknowledged that perhaps all he'd meant by that was that he'd give her the role of convenient mistress.

Horror spread through her body as the awful reality sank in. It was written all over every rejecting and rigid line of his body. Everything she'd shared with Kaden had been a mere illusion. He'd been playing with her. A western student girl, here for a short while and then conveniently gone. Perfect for a summer fling. And now he was ruler, a million miles from the carefree young man she thought she'd known.

Shakily she said, 'You didn't have to tell me you loved me. You could have spared yourself the platitudes. I didn't expect to hear them.' And she hadn't. She truly hadn't. She knew she loved this man, but she hadn't expected him to love her back…and yet he had. Or so she'd been led to believe.

Kaden shrugged and looked at a cuff, as if it was infinitely more interesting than their conversation. He looked back at her with eyes so black they were dead. 'I went as far as you did. Please don't insult my intelligence and tell me that you meant it when *you* said it. You can hardly claim you did when within days you were ready to drop your pants for another man.'

Julia backed away again at his crude words, shaking

her head this time, eyes horrifically glued to Kaden. 'I told you, it wasn't like that.'

She realised in that moment that she'd not ever known this man. And with that came the insidious feeling of worthlessness she'd carried ever since she'd found out she was adopted and that her own birth mother had rejected her. She wasn't good enough for anyone. She never had been...

To this day Julia couldn't actually remember walking out of that room, or the night that had followed, or the journey to the airport the next day. She only remembered being back in grey, drizzly autumnal England and feeling as though her insides had been ripped out and trampled on. The feeling of rejection was like a corrosive acid, eating away at her, and for a long time she hadn't trusted her own judgement when it came to men. She'd locked herself away in her studies.

Her husband John had managed to break through her wall of defences with his gentle, unassuming ways, but Julia could see now that she'd fallen for him precisely because he'd been everything Kaden was *not*.

When she thought of what had happened last night, and Kaden's cool assertion that he would see her later—exactly the way a man might talk to a mistress—nausea surged again, and this time Julia couldn't hold it down. She made it to the toilet in time and was violently ill. When she was able to, she stood and looked at herself in the mirror. She was deathly pale, eyes huge.

What cruel twist of fate had brought them together like this again?

And yet even now, with the memory of how brutally he'd rejected her still acrid like the bile in her throat,

Julia felt a helpless weakness invade her. And, worse, that insidious yearning. Shakily she sat down on the closed toilet seat and vowed to herself that she would thwart Kaden's arrogant assumption that she would fall in with his plans. Because she didn't know if she could survive standing in front of him again when he was finished with her, and hearing him tell her it was over.

CHAPTER FIVE

KADEN SAT IN his car outside Julia's modest-sized town house. He was oblivious to the fact that his stately vehicle looked ridiculously out of place in the leafy residential street. His mind and belly were churning and had been all day. Much to his intense chagrin he hadn't been able to concentrate on the business at hand at all, causing his staff to look worried. He was *never* distracted.

He'd struggled to find some sense of equilibrium. But equilibrium had taken a hike and in its place was an ever-present gnawing knowledge that he'd been here before. In this place, standing at the edge of an abyss. About to disappear.

Kaden's hand tightened to a fist on his thigh. He was not that young man any more. He'd lived and married and divorced. He'd had lovers—many lovers. And not one woman had come close to touching that part of him that he'd locked away years before. When Julia had turned and walked out of his study.

He shook his head to dislodge the memory, but it wouldn't budge. That last meeting was engraved in his mind like a tattoo. Julia's slate-grey eyes wide, her cheeks pale as she'd listened to what he'd said. The burning jealousy in his gut when he'd thought of her with that man. It had eclipsed even his grief at his father's death. The realisation that she was fallible, that she was like every other woman, had been the start of his cynicism.

Most mocking of all though—even now—was the memory of why he'd gone looking for her on that cataclysmic night of his father's death. Contrary to his father's repeated wishes, Kaden had insisted that he wanted Julia. He'd gone to find her, to explain his absence and also to tell her that he wanted her to be his queen some day. That he was prepared to let her finish her studies and get used to the idea and then make a choice. Fired up with love—*or so he'd thought*—he hadn't been prepared for seeing her entangled in that embrace, outside in the street, where anyone could have seen her. *His woman.*

He could remember feeling disembodied. He could remember the way something inside him had shrivelled up to nothing as he'd watched her finally notice him and start to struggle. In that moment whatever he'd felt for her had solidified to a hard black mass within him, and then it had been buried for good.

Only a scant hour later, when Kaden had sat by his dying father's bed and he had begged Kaden to *'think of your country, not yourself'*, Kaden had finally seen the future clearly. And that future did not include Julia.

It had been a summer of madness. Of believing feelings existed just because they'd been each other's first lover. He'd come close to believing he loved her, but had realised just in time that he'd confused lust and sexual obsession with love.

As if waking from a dream, Kaden came back to

the car, to the street in suburban London. He looked at the town house. Benign and peaceful. His blood thickened and grew hot. Inside that house was the woman who stood between him and his future. On some level he'd never really let her go, and the only way he could do that was to sate this beast inside him. Prove that it was lust once and for all. And this time when he said goodbye to her she would no longer have the power to make him wake, sweating, from vivid dreams, holding a hand to his chest to assuage the dull ache.

JULIA FELT AS if she was thirteen all over again, with butterflies in her belly, flushing hot and cold every two seconds. She'd heard Kaden's car pull up and her nerves were wound taut waiting for the doorbell. What was he doing? she wondered for the umpteenth time, when he still didn't emerge from the huge car.

Then she imagined it pulling away again, and didn't like the feeling of panic *that* engendered. She'd vacillated all day over what to do, all the while knowing, to her ongoing sense of shame, that she'd somewhere along the way made up her mind that she wasn't strong enough to walk away from Kaden.

By the time she'd returned from work, with a splitting headache, she'd felt cranky enough with herself for being so weak that she'd decided she *wouldn't* give in so easily. She would greet Kaden in her running sweats and tell him she wasn't going anywhere. But then she'd had an image of him clicking his fingers, having food delivered to the house and staying all night. She couldn't forget the glint of determination in his eye that morning. And the thought of having him here in her private space for a whole night had been enough to galvanise her into getting dressed in a plain black dress and smart pumps.

The lesser of two evils was to let him take her out. She'd thank him for dinner, tell him that there couldn't possibly be a repeat of last night, and that would be it. She'd never see him again. She was strong enough to do this.

She'd turned away from her furtive vigil at the window for a moment, so she nearly jumped out of her skin when the doorbell rang authoritatively. And all her previous thoughts were scrambled into a million pieces. Her hands were clammy. Her heart thumped. She walked to the front door and could see the looming tall, dark shape through the bubbled glass. She picked up her bag and cardigan and took a deep breath.

When she opened the door she wasn't prepared for the hit to her gut at seeing a stubble-jawed Kaden leaning nonchalantly against the porch wall, dominating the small space. He obviously hadn't shaved since that morning, and flames of heat licked through her blood. He was so intensely masculine. He was in the same suit—albeit with the tie gone and the top button of his shirt open.

His eyes were dark and swept her up and down as he straightened up. She tingled all over. Julia wished she'd put her hair up, it felt provocative now to have it down. Why had she left it down?

Kaden arched a brow. 'Shall we?'

Julia sucked in a breath and finally managed to move. 'Yes…' She pulled the front door behind her, absurdly glad that Kaden hadn't come inside, and fum-

bled with the keys as she locked it. Kaden was waiting
by the door of the car and helped her in. His hand was
hot on her bare elbow.

The car pulled off smoothly and Julia tried to quell
her butterflies. Kaden's drawling and unmistakably
amused voice came from her right.

'Are we going to a funeral?'

She looked at him and could see him staring pointedly at her admittedly rather boring dress. She fibbed.
'I didn't have time to change after work.'

His eyes rose to hers and he smiled. 'Liar,' he
mocked softly.

Julia was transfixed by that smiling mouth, by the
unbelievably sensuous and wicked lines. Her face
flamed and her hand moved in that betraying reflex
to her throat. She stopped herself just in time. She felt
naked without his necklace. It was the first time she'd
not worn it at home. Her hand dropped to her lap, and to
hide her discomfiture she asked, 'Where are we going?'

To her relief Kaden released her from his all too intent gaze and looked ahead. 'We're going to the Cedar
Rooms, in the Gormseby Hotel.'

Julia was impressed. It was a plush new hotel that
had opened in the past few months, and apparently
there was already a year-long waiting list for the restaurant. Not for Kaden, though, she thought cynically.
They'd be tripping over themselves to have him en-
dorse their restaurant. Yet she was relieved at the idea
of being in a public place, surrounded by people, as if
that would somehow help her resist him and put up the
fight she knew she must.

Kaden was struggling to hang on to his urbanity beside Julia. Her dress was ridiculously boring and plain, but it couldn't hide her effortless class, or those long shapely legs and the enticing swell of her bosom. Her hair was down, falling in long waves over her shoulders, and she wore a minimum of make-up. Once again he was struck that she could pass for years younger. And by how beautiful she was. She had the kind of classic beauty that just got better with age.

The minute she'd opened the front door her huge swirling grey eyes had sucked him into a vortex of need so strong that he'd felt his body responding right there. Much as it had in that crowded room last night. A response he'd never had to curb for any other woman, because he'd always been in strict control.

With Julia, though, his brain short-circuited every time he looked at her. It only fired up his assertion that this was just lust. With that in mind, and anticipating how urgent his desire would be by the time they got to dessert, he made a quick terse call in Arabic from his mobile phone.

By THE TIME they were on their desserts Julia had given up trying to maintain any kind of coherent conversation. The opulent dining room was arranged in such a way that—far from being surrounded by the public—she and Kaden were practically in a private booth. And it was so dark that flickering candles sent long shadows across their faces. It was decadent, and not at all conducive to remaining clear-headed as she'd anticipated.

Their conversation had started out innocuously enough. Kaden had asked her about her career and why she'd taken the direction she had. She'd explained that her passion for fund distribution had grown when she'd seen so much misused funding over the years, and she'd seen it as the more stable end of archaeology, considering her future with a husband and family. To her surprise his eyes hadn't glazed over with boredom. He'd kept looking at her, though, as if he wanted to devour her. Desperately trying to ignore the way it made her feel, she'd asked him about Burquat.

It sounded like another country now—vastly different from the more rigidly conservative one she'd known. Once again she was filled with a rush of pride that his ambition was being realised.

Scrabbling around for anything else to talk about, to take the edge off how intimate it felt to be sitting here with him, Julia said, 'I saw something in the papers about drilling your oil fields. There seems to be great interest, considering the world's dwindling oil supplies.'

'We're certainly on the brink of something huge. Sultan Sadiq of Al-Omar is going to help us drill the oil. He has the expertise.'

'Is that part of the reason why he's marrying Samia?' Julia felt a pang of concern for Kaden's younger sister. From what she remembered of her she was no match for the renowned playboy Sultan.

Kaden's mouth tightened. 'It's a factor, yes. Their marriage will be an important strategic alliance between both our countries.'

Kaden sat back and cradled a bulbous glass of brandy. He looked at Julia from under hooded lids. She felt hunted.

'So…your boss—Nigel. Are you seeing him?'

Julia flushed, wondering what kind of woman Kaden had become used to socialising with, *sleeping* with. She swallowed. 'No, I'm not.' Not sure why she felt compelled to elaborate, she said, 'He's asked me out, but I've said no.'

'You've had no lovers since your husband?'

Julia flushed even hotter and glared at Kaden. 'That's none of your business. Would you mind if I asked *you* if you've had any lovers since your divorce?'

He was supremely relaxed, supremely confident. He smiled. 'I have a healthy sex life. I enjoy women…and they enjoy what I can give them.'

Julia snorted indelicately, her imagination shamefully providing her with an assortment of images of the sleek, soignée women she'd seen grace his arm over the years. 'No doubt.' And then something dark was rising up within her, and she said ascerbically, 'I presume these women are left in no doubt as to the parameters of their relationship with you, much as you outlined to me this morning?'

Kaden's face darkened ominously. 'I took your advice a long time ago. Women know exactly where they stand with me. I don't waste my breath on platitudes and empty promises.'

For some perverse reason Julia felt inexplicably comforted. As if Kaden had just proved to her that no woman had managed to break through that wall of ice. And yet…how would *she* know? She was the last woman in the world he would confide in. And she was obviously the last woman in the world who could break through the icy reserve she'd seen that last evening in Burquat.

She realised then just how provocative the conversation was becoming, and put down her napkin. 'I think I'm ready to go now.'

Kaden rose smoothly to his feet and indicated for Julia to precede him out of the booth. With his head inclined solicitously he was urbanity incarnate, but Julia didn't trust it for a second. She knew the dark, seething passion that hummed between them was far from over.

When they reached the lobby Julia turned towards the main door, her mind was whirring with ways to say goodbye to Kaden and insist on getting a taxi. At the same time her belly was clenching pathetically at the thought of never seeing him again. Kaden caught her hand and her mind blanked at the physical contact. She looked up at him, and that slow lick of desire coiled through her belly. She cursed it—and herself.

'I've booked a suite here for the night.'

Julia straightened her spine and tried to block out the tantalising suggestion that they could be in bed within minutes. 'If your aim is to make me feel like a high-class hooker then you're succeeding admirably.'

Kaden cursed himself. Never before had he lacked finesse with a woman. He wanted Julia so badly he ached, and he'd booked the room because he'd known he wouldn't have the restraint to wait until he got back to his apartment or her house. But she was as stiff as a board and about as remote as the summit of Everest. He had a good idea that she had every intention of walking away from him. He didn't like the dart of panic he felt at acknowledging that.

Julia watched Kaden's face. It was expressionless except for his jaw clenching and his eyes flashing. A dart of panic rose; to willingly spend another night with this man was emotional suicide.

'Kaden, I don't know what you think you're doing, but I came here tonight to have dinner with you. I do not intend repeating what happened last night. There's no point. We have nothing to say to each other.'

In a move so fast her head spun, he was right in front of her. He said roughly, '*We* may have nothing to say to each other, but our bodies have plenty to say.'

He put his hands on her arms and pulled her close. She sucked in a breath when she felt the burgeoning response of his body against her. Immediately there was an exultant rush of blood to her groin in answer. Any thoughts of emotional suicide were fading fast.

And it was then that she noticed they were standing in the middle of the lobby and attracting attention. How could they not? Kaden was six feet four at least, and one of the most recognisable men on the planet. Even if he wasn't, his sheer good looks would draw enough attention.

He intuited the direction of her thoughts, and his eyes glinted down at her. 'I have no problem making love to you here and now, Julia.'

To illustrate his point he pulled her in even tighter and brought his mouth down so close that she could feel his breath feather along her lips. Instinctively her mouth was already opening, seeking his.

He whispered, 'We have unfinished business, Julia. Are you really ready to walk away from this? Because I'm not.'

And with that he settled his mouth over hers, right in the middle of that exclusive lobby, in front of all those moneyed people. But for all Julia was aware they might have been in her house. What undid her completely was that his kiss was gentle and restrained, but she could feel the barely leashed passion behind it. If he'd been forceful it would have been easier to resist, but this kiss reminded her too much of the Kaden she'd once known...

His hands moved up to cradle her face, holding her in place while his tongue delved deep and stroked along hers, making her gasp with need.

Eventually he drew back and said, 'The reason I booked the room was because I knew I wouldn't be able to wait until I got you home. Not because I wanted you to feel like a high-class call girl. Now, we can continue this where we stand, and give the guests the show of their lives, or we can go upstairs.'

Julia's hands had crept up to cling on to Kaden's arms. She felt the muscles bunch and move and looked up into those dark eyes. She could feel herself falling down and down. There was no space between them. No space to think. She didn't have the strength to walk away. Not yet.

Hating herself, she said shakily, 'OK. Upstairs.'

With grim determination stamped all over his darkly gorgeous features, Kaden held her close and walked her across the lobby to the lifts. Her face flamed when she became aware of people's discreet scrutiny, and Julia realised that within the space of twenty-four hours her carefully ordered and structured life had come tumbling down around her ears—so much so that she didn't even recognise herself any more.

And the worst thing about this whole scenario: she was exhilarated in a way she hadn't felt in a long time.

FOR THE SECOND morning in a row Julia woke up in an unfamiliar room and bed. But this time there was no pristine Kaden in a suit, watching her as she woke. The bed beside her was empty, sheets well tousled. She knew instantly that she was alone, and didn't like the bereft feeling that took her by surprise. Their scent mingled with the air, along with the scent of sex. In a flash the previous night came back in glorious Technicolor.

They'd said not a word once they'd got to the room. They'd been naked and in bed within seconds, mutually combusting.

They'd made love for hours, insatiably. Hungering for one another only moments after each completion. Julia was exhausted, but she couldn't deny the illicit feeling of peace within her. She sighed deeply. She knew Kaden was going to Al-Omar the next day for Samia's wedding.

Then she spotted something out of the corner of her eye. She turned her head to see a folded piece of stiff hotel paper. She opened it up and read the arrogantly slashing handwriting: *I'll pick you up at your place, 7.30. K*

Julia sighed again. One more night in this strange week when everything felt out of kilter and off balance and slightly dream-like. She'd love to be able to send a terse note back with a curt dismissal, but if last night had proved anything it was that the fire had well and truly been stoked and she was too fatally weak to resist.

All of the very good reasons she had for saying no—
her very self-preservation, for a start—were awfully
elusive at the prospect of seeing Kaden for a last time.

WHEN THE DOORBELL rang that evening Julia was flustered. She opened the door, and once again wasn't
prepared for the effect of the reality of Kaden on her
doorstep.

'Hi… Look, I've just got back from work.' She indicated her uniform of trousers, shirt and flat shoes.
'I need to shower and change. Today was busy, and
then there was a problem with the tube line, and—'
She stopped abruptly. She was babbling. As if he cared
about the vagaries of public transport.

Kaden took a step inside her door before she knew
what was happening, dwarfing her small hallway, and
said easily, 'We're in no rush. You get ready; I'll wait
down here.'

Julia gulped, and her hand went nervously to her
throat again. But of course the necklace wasn't there.
Every morning she had to consciously remember not to
put it on. Self-recrimination at her own weakness made
her say curtly, 'I won't be long. There's fresh coffee in
the kitchen if you want to help yourself.'

And with that she fled upstairs and locked herself
into her en suite bedroom. Lord, she was in trouble.

Kaden prowled through the hallway. From what he
could see it was a classic two-up-two-down house, with
a bright airy kitchen extending at the back, which was
obviously a modern addition. He hated this weakness
he felt for the woman upstairs. Even now he wanted

to follow her into the shower and embed himself in her tight heat.

Last night had been very far removed from the nights he'd shared with other women. He was always quickly sated and eager to see them leave, or leave himself. But it had only been as dawn was breaking and his body was too weak to continue that he'd finally fallen asleep.

When he'd woken a couple of hours later all he'd had to do was look at Julia's sleeping body to want to wake her and start all over again. Right now he didn't feel as if an entire month locked in a hotel room would be enough to rid him of this need.

His mind shied away from that realisation, and from more introspection. It was perhaps inevitable that his first lover should make a lasting impression, leave a mark on his soul. The chemistry between them had been intense from the moment they'd met over that fossil at the city dig. Kaden's mouth twisted. It had been as if he'd been infected with a fever, becoming so obsessed with Julia and having her that he hadn't been able to see anything else.

He hadn't even noticed his own father's growing frailty. Nor even listened to his father's pleas until they'd been uttered with his last breath.

With a curse he turned away from the view of the tiny but perfect garden. What was he doing here, in this small suburban house? His movements jerky, he found a cup and poured himself a strong black coffee, as if that might untangle the knots in his head and belly.

He wandered through to the bright and minimalist sitting-room. He wondered, with an acidic taste in his mouth, if this had been the marital home. He couldn't see any wedding photos anywhere, but stopped dead when he saw the panoramic photo hanging above the fireplace, his insides freezing in shock.

It was a familiar view—one of his favourites. A picture taken in the Burquati desert, with the stunning snow-capped Nazish mountain range in the distance. He had a vivid memory of the day Julia had taken this picture. His arms had been tight around her waist and she'd complained throatily, 'I can't keep the camera steady if you hang on to me like you're drowning!'

And he'd said into her ear, overcome with emotion, 'I'm drowning, all right. In love with you.'

The shutter had clicked at that moment, and then she'd turned in his arms and—

'I'm sorry—I tried to be as quick as I could.'

Kaden's hand gripped the coffee mug so tightly he had to consciously relax for fear of breaking it into pieces. He schooled his features so they were a bland mask which reflected nothing of his inner reaction to the memory sparked by the picture.

He turned around. Julia was wearing a dark grey silky dress that dipped down at the front to reveal her delicate collarbone and clung to the soft swells of her breasts, dropping in soft, unstructured folds to her knee. Her legs were bare and pale, and she wore high-heeled wedges. He dragged his eyes up to hers. She'd tied her hair back into a ponytail and it made her look ridiculously innocent and young.

Julia's body was reacting with irritating predictability to Kaden's searing look. When she'd walked in she'd noted with dismay that he'd spotted the photograph.

It was one of her favourite possessions. Her husband John had used to complain about it, having taken an instant dislike to it, and she'd hidden it away during their marriage. It was almost as if he'd intuited that she'd lost her heart in that very desert. At that very moment.

Kaden indicated behind him now, without taking his dark eyes off hers. 'The frame suits the photo. It turned out well.'

She fixed a bright smile on her face, resolutely blocking out the memory of that day. 'Yes, it did. I'm ready to go.'

Kaden looked at her for a long moment and then threw back the rest of his coffee. He went into the kitchen, where he put the cup in the sink, rinsed it and then came into the hall. Julia already had the door open, and allowed Kaden to precede her out so she could lock up.

Like the previous night, she asked him, once in the back of the car, 'Where are we going?'

'I thought we'd go to my apartment this evening. I've arranged for a Burquati chef to cook dinner. I thought you might appreciate being reminded of some of our local dishes.'

Sounding a little strangled, Julia answered, 'That sounds nice.'

AND IT WAS. Julia savoured every morsel of the delicious food. She'd always loved it. Balls of rice mixed with succulent pieces of lamb and fish. Tender chicken breasts marinaded for hours in spices. Fresh vegetables fried in tantalising Burquati oils. And decadent sweet pastries dripping with syrup for dessert, washed down with tart black coffee.

'You haven't lost your appetite.'

Julia looked across the small intimate table at Kaden. He was lounging back in his chair like a sleek panther, in a dark shirt and black trousers. She felt hot, and her hand went in that telling gesture to her neck again. She dropped it quickly. 'No. I've never lost my healthy appetite.' She smiled ruefully and the action felt strange. She realized she hadn't smiled much in the past few days. 'That's why I run six miles about three times a week—to be able to indulge the foodie within me.'

Kaden's eyes roved over her. 'You were definitely a little…plumper before.'

There was a rough quality to his voice that resonated deep inside Julia. She could remember Kaden's hands squeezing her breasts together, lavishing attention on the voluptuous mounds.

'Puppy fat,' she said, almost desperately.

Abruptly she stood up, agitated, and took her glass of wine to go and stand by the open doors of the dining room, which led out to an ornate terraced balcony overlooking the city. She needed air and space. He was too intense and brooding. The tension between them, all that was not being acknowledged about their past history, was nearly suffocating. And yet what was there to say? Julia certainly didn't need to hear Kaden elaborate again on why he'd been so keen to see the back of her…

She heard him move and come to stand beside her. She took a careful sip of wine, trying to be as nonchalant as possible, but already she was trembling with wanting him just to take her in his arms and make her forget everything. One last night and then she would put him out of her mind for good.

'I want you to come to Al-Omar with me for Samia's wedding.'

Julia's head whipped round so fast she felt dizzy for a moment. 'What?' she squeaked. 'You want me to come...as your date?'

He was looking impossibly grim, which made Julia believe that she hadn't just had an aural hallucination. He nodded. 'It'll be over by Sunday.'

Julia felt bewildered. She hadn't prepared emotionally for anything beyond this night. 'But...why?'

Kaden's jaw tightened. He wasn't sure, but he was damn hopeful it would mean the end of his burning need to take this woman every time he looked at her. And that it would make all the old memories recede to a place where they would have no hold over him any more. That it would bring him to a place where he could get on with his life and not be haunted by her and the nebulous feeling of something having gone very wrong twelve years before.

He shrugged. 'I thought you might enjoy meeting Samia again.'

Julia looked at Kaden warily. His expression gave nothing away, but there was a starkness to the lines of his face, a hunger. She recognised it because she felt it too. The thought of *this*—whatever it was between them—lasting for another few days out of time was all at once heady and terrifying.

She'd once longed for him to come after her, to tell her he'd made a mistake. That he *did* love her. But he hadn't. Now he wanted to spend more time with her. Perhaps this was as close as she would ever get to closure? This man had haunted her for too long.

She stared down at her wine glass as if the ruby liquid held all the answers. 'I don't know, Kaden...' She looked back up. 'I don't know if it's such a good idea.'

Kaden sneaked a hand out and around the back of her neck. Gently he urged her closer to him, as if he could tell that her words were a pathetic attempt to pretend she didn't want this.

'This is desire—karma—unfinished business. Call it what you will, but whatever it is it's powerful. And it's not over.'

Kaden's hand was massaging the back of her neck now, and Julia felt like purring and turning her face into his palm. She gritted her jaw. 'I have to work tomorrow. I can't just up and leave the country. I'll... have to think about it.'

His eyes flashed. Clearly he was unused to anything less than immediate acquiescence. 'You can do whatever you want, Julia. You're beholden to none. But while you're thinking about it, think about *this*.'

This was Kaden removing the wine glass from her hand and pulling her into him so tightly that she could feel every hard ridge of muscle and the powerful thrust of his thighs and manhood. Cradling her face in his hands, he swooped—and obliterated every thought in her head with his kiss.

CHAPTER SIX

'WOULD YOU LIKE some champagne, Dr Somerton?'

Julia looked at the impeccably made-up Burquati air hostess and decided she could so with a little fortitude. She smiled tightly. 'Yes, please.'

The woman expertly filled a real crystal flute with champagne, and then passed a glass of what looked like brandy to Kaden, who sat across the aisle of his own private jet.

It was dark outside. It would take roughly six hours to get to B'harani, the capital of Al-Omar. They'd been scheduled to leave that afternoon, but Kaden had been held up with business matters—hence their overnight flight.

Julia's brain was already slipping helplessly back into the well-worn groove that it had trod all day. *Why* had she decided to come? A flush went through her body when she remembered back to that morning, as dawn had been breaking. She'd been exhausted. Kaden had been ruthless and remorseless all night. Each orgasm had felt like another brick dismantled in the wall of her defences.

Kaden had hovered over her and asked throatily, 'So, will you come to Al-Omar with me?'

Julia had sensed in him a tiny moment of such fleeting vulnerability that she must have imagined it, but it had got to her, stripping away any remaining defences. Stripping away her automatic response to say no and do the right thing, the logical thing. Lying there naked, she'd been at his mercy. To her ongoing shame, she'd just nodded her head weakly, reminding herself that this was finite and soon she would be back to normal, hopefully a little freer of painful memories.

'You don't need to look like you're about to walk the plank. You're going to be a guest at the society wedding of the year.'

Julia clutched the glass tightly in her hand now and looked at Kaden. Since she'd got into his car just a couple of hours ago outside her house he'd been on the phone. And he'd been engrossed in his laptop since boarding the flight. But now he was looking at her.

Unbidden, the words tumbled out. 'Why are you doing this? Why are we here?' *Why have you come back into my life to tear me open all over again? And, worse, why am I allowing it to happen?*

It was as if she had to hear him reiterate the reasons why she was being so stupid. Kaden's dark eyes held hers for a long moment and then dropped in a leisurely appraisal of her body. Julia was modestly dressed: a plain shirt tucked into high-waisted flared trousers. Her hair was coiled back into a chignon. It should have felt like armour, but it didn't. Kaden's laser-like gaze had the power to make her feel naked.

His eyes met hers again. 'We are doing this to sate the desire between us. We're two consenting adults taking pleasure in one another. Nothing more, nothing less.'

Julia swallowed painfully. 'There's more to it than that, Kaden. We have a past together. Something you seem determined to ignore.'

Kaden turned more fully in his seat, and Julia felt threatened when she saw how cynicism stamped the lines of his face. And something else—something much darker. Anger.

'I fail to see what talking about the past will serve. We had an affair aeons ago. We're different people now. The only constant is that we still want each other.'

Affair. Julia cursed herself for opening her mouth. Kaden was right. What on earth could they possibly have to talk about? She was humiliatingly aware that she wanted him to tell her that he hadn't meant to reject her so brutally. She didn't feel like a different person. She felt as if she was twenty all over again and nothing had changed.

Incredibly brittle, and angry for having exposed herself like this, she forced a smile. 'You're right. I'm tired. It's been a long day.'

Kaden frowned now, and his eyes went to her throat. 'Why do you keep doing that? Touching your neck as if you're looking for something?'

Julia gulped, and realised that once again in an unconsciously nervous gesture her hand had sought out the comforting touch of her necklace. Panic flared. She wasn't wearing it, but she'd broken her own rule and brought it with her, like some kind of talisman. She blushed. 'It's just a habit…a necklace I used to wear. I lost it some time ago and I haven't got used to it being gone yet.'

His eyes narrowed on her and, feeling panicky, Julia

put down her glass and started to recline her chair. 'I think I'll try to get some sleep.'

Kaden felt the bitter sting of a memory, and with it an emotion he refused to acknowledge. It was too piercing. He'd once given Julia a necklace, but he had no doubt that wasn't the necklace she referred to. It was probably some delicate diamond thing her husband had bought her.

The one he'd given her would be long gone. What woman would hold on to a cheap gold necklace bought in a marketplace on a whim because he'd felt that the knot in the design symbolised the intricacies of his emotions for his lover? His lover. Julia. Then and now.

He cursed himself and turned away to look out at the inky blackness. He should have walked away from her in London this morning and come to Al-Omar to make a fresh start. He needed to look for a new bride to take him into the next phase of his life. He needed to create the family legacy he'd promised his father, and an economically and politically stable country. It was all within his grasp finally, after long years of work and struggle and one disastrous marriage.

He glanced back to Julia's curved waist and hips and his blood grew hot. He still wanted her, though. She was unfinished business. His hands clenched. He couldn't take one step into the future while this hunger raged within him and it *would* be sated. It had to be.

ARRIVING IN B'HARANI as dawn broke was breathtaking. The gleaming city was bathed in a pinky pearlescent light. It was festooned with flags and decorations, and streets were cordoned off for the first wedding procession, which would take place later that day.

Kaden had barely shared one word with Julia as they'd sped through the streets to the imposing Hussein Castle. There, they'd been shown to their opulent suite, and Kaden had excused himself to go and see his sister.

Now Julia was alone in the room, gritty-eyed with tiredness and a little numb at acknowledging that she was back on the Arabian Peninsula with Kaden. She succumbed to the lure of a shower and afterwards put on a luxurious towelling robe. The massive bed dressed in white Egyptian cotton was beckoning, and she lay down with the intention of having a quick nap.

When she woke, some time later, the sun was high outside and she felt very disoriented when she saw Kaden emerge from the bathroom with a tiny towel slung around his hips. He was rubbing his hair with another towel, and he was a picture of dark olive-skinned virility, muscles bunching and gleaming.

Julia sat up awkwardly. 'Why didn't you wake me?'

He cast her a quick glance. 'You were exhausted. There's nothing much happening till this evening anyway. The civil ceremony took place this morning, and Sultan Sadiq and Samia are doing a procession through the streets this afternoon. This evening will be the formal start of the celebrations, with more over the next two days. On Sunday they will marry again in a more western style.'

'Wow,' breathed Julia, while trying to ignore the sight of Kaden's half naked body. 'That sounds complicated.'

Kaden smiled tightly, seemingly unaware of his

state of undress. He flung aside the towel he'd been drying his hair with, leaving it sexily dishevelled. 'Yes, quite. In Burquat things are much more straightforward. We just have a wedding ceremony in front of our elders at dawn and then a huge ceremonial banquet which lasts all day.'

Against her best effort to focus on what he was saying, Julia couldn't stop her gaze from dropping down Kaden's exquisitely muscled chest. He really had the most amazing body—huge but leanly muscled. The towel around his hips looked very precarious, and as she watched, wide-eyed, she could see the distinctive bulge grow visibly bigger.

Her cheeks flamed and her gaze jumped up to meet Kaden's much more mocking one. His hand whipped aside the towel and it fell to the floor along with the other one. Gulping, she watched as he walked to the bed. He lay alongside her and pushed aside the robe, baring her breasts to his gaze. Once again Julia was a little stunned at this much more sexually confident Kaden and how intoxicating he was.

Weakly, she tried to protest, 'What if someone comes in?'

'They won't,' he growled, and bent his head to surround one tight nipple with hot, wet, sucking heat.

Julia moaned and collapsed back completely. Kaden's other hand slid down her belly, undoing the tie on the robe as he dipped lower and between her legs, to where she was already indecently wet and ready.

He removed the robe and within seconds she was naked too, with Kaden's body settled between her legs, his shoulders huge above her. She could feel him flex the taut muscles of his behind and widened her legs, inviting him into more intimate contact. When he thrust into her Julia had to close her eyes, because she was terrified he would see the emotion boiling in her chest. As he started up with a delicious rhythm Julia desperately assured herself that this was just about sex, not emotion. She didn't love him any more. She couldn't... Because if she did, the emotional carnage was too scary to contemplate.

LATER THAT EVENING Julia paced the sitting room, barely aware of the gorgeous cream and gold furnishings, carpet so thick her heels sank into it.

She'd been whisked off that afternoon to be pampered in readiness for the banquet—something she hadn't expected. And while there she'd had a selection of outfits for her to pick from. Too unsure to know whether or not she could refuse, she'd chosen the simplest gown. Deep green in colour, it was halter-necked, with a daringly low-cut back. She'd been returned to the suite and now, made-up and with her hair in an elaborate chignon, she felt like a veritable fashion doll.

And there was no sign of Kaden. Julia paced some more. Being dressed up like this made her intensely uncomfortable. She'd caught a glimpse of herself in the mirror and for a moment hadn't even recognised the image reflected back. Her eyes were huge and smoky grey, lashes long and very black. Her cheeks had two spots of red that had more to do with her emotions than with artifice.

The door suddenly clicked, and Julia whirled around to see Kaden striding in, adjusting a cufflink on his shirt. The breath literally left her throat for a moment. It was the first time she'd ever seen him in a tuxedo and he looked…stunning. It nearly made her forget why she was so incensed, but then he looked at her with that irritating non-expression. The irrational feeling of anger surged back.

She gestured to the dress. 'I agreed to come with you to a wedding. I'm not your mistress, Kaden, and I don't appreciate being treated like one.'

He put his hands in his pockets and looked her up and down, and then, as if he hadn't even heard her, he said, 'I've never seen you look so beautiful.'

To Julia's abject horror her mind emptied and she stood there, stupidly, as Kaden's black gaze fused with hers. She read the heat in its glowing depths. She'd always veered more towards being a tomboy, and had truly never felt especially *beautiful*. But now, here in this room, she did.

It made the bright spark of anger fade away, and she felt silly for her outburst. Of course Kaden didn't see her as his mistress. She couldn't be further removed from the kind of women he sought out.

She half gestured to the dress, avoiding Kaden's eye. 'I didn't mean to sound ungrateful. It's a lovely dress, and the attention…wasn't all bad.' She looked back up. 'But I don't want you to get the wrong idea. I don't expect or even want this kind of treatment. I'm not like your other women. This…what's happening here…is not the same…'

He took his hands out of his pockets and came close. Julia stood her ground, but it was hard. Black eyes glittered down into hers. A muscle throbbed in his jaw and she saw how tightly Kaden was reining in some explosive emotion.

'No, you're not like my other women. You're completely different. Don't think I'm not aware of that. Now, let's go or we'll be late.'

After a tense moment she finally moved. Kaden stood back and allowed Julia to precede him out of the room. Feeling off-centre, he didn't touch her as they walked down the long corridor. She wasn't and hadn't ever been like any other woman he'd been with. It was only now that he was noticing the disturbing tendency he'd always had to judge the women he encountered against his first lover—noticing the faint disappointment he always felt when they proved themselves time and time again to be utterly different. Materialistic. Avaricious. *Less.*

He was used to being ecstatically received whenever he indulged a woman, and wondered if this was some ploy or game Julia was playing—affecting uninterest. But with a sinking feeling he knew it wasn't. Years ago she'd have laughed in his face if he'd so much as attempted to get her into a couture dress. She'd been happy in dusty jeans and shirts. That crazy safari sunhat.

There'd only been one moment when she'd worn a dress. When he'd presented her with a cream concoction of delicate lace and silk that he'd seen in a shop window and hadn't been able to resist. As dresses went, it hadn't been sophisticated at all, but Julia had put it on and paraded in front of him as shyly as a new bride. It had been the first and only time she'd worn a dress, and that had been the night that he'd realised just how deeply—Kaden shut the door on that unwanted thought that had come out of nowhere. His insides clenched so hard he could feel them cramp.

Breathing deep, he brought his focus back to the here and now. To the woman by his side who was blissfully unaware of his wayward thoughts. He was vitally aware of the smooth curve of Julia's bare back in the dress. The pale luminescence of her skin. And the vulnerable part of her neck, which was revealed thanks to her upswept hair.

The dim hum of the conversation of hundreds of people reached them as they rounded a corner. Kaden took Julia's arm in his hand and felt her tension. Good. He wanted her to be tense. And unsettled. And all the things he was. They walked across a wide open-air courtyard and pristine Hussein servants dressed all in white opened huge doors into the glorious main ballroom.

JULIA HAD BEEN in plenty of stately homes and castles on her travels, but this took her breath away. She'd never seen such opulence and wealth. The huge ballroom was astounding, with an enormous domed ceiling covered in murals, and immense columns which opened out onto the warm, evocatively dusky night.

Waiting to greet them were the Sultan and his new bride—Kaden's sister Samia. As they approached, Julia saw Samia's face light up at seeing Kaden. She'd blossomed from a painfully shy teenager into a beauty with great poise. She'd always had a strong bond with her older brother, being his only full sibling, daughter of their father's first beloved wife. Their father had married again, and Julia remembered Kaden's stepmother as a cold, disapproving woman. She'd gone on to have three daughters of her own, but no sons which, Kaden had once told Julia, made her extremely bitter and jealous of Kaden and Samia. Certainly Julia could remember avoiding her malevolent presence at all costs.

Samia transferred her look to her then, and Julia attempted a weak smile. Samia looked at her with a mixture of bewilderment and hostility. It confused Julia, because she'd imagined that Kaden's younger sister would barely remember her.

But she didn't have time to analyse it. Kaden gripped her hand, and after a few perfunctory words dragged her into the throng. Still shaken by Samia's reaction, Julia asked, 'Why did Samia look at me like that? I'm surprised she even recognised me.'

Kaden sent her a dark glance that was impossible to comprehend and didn't answer. Instead he took two glasses of champagne from a passing waiter and handed her one. Raising his glass in a mocking salute, he said, 'Here's to us.'

He clinked his glass to Julia's and drank deeply. She couldn't stop an awful hollow feeing from spreading through her whole body. She sensed that he was regretting having brought her here. No doubt he would prefer the balm of a woman well versed in the ways of being a compliant and beautiful mistress. Suitably appreciative of all he had to offer. All Julia wanted to do was to get out of there and curl up somewhere comforting and safe.

Several people lined up then, to talk to Kaden, and Julia became little more than an accessory while they fawned and complimented him on the news that the vast Burquati oil fields were to be drilled. Once again Julia had a sense of how much had changed for Kaden since she'd known him.

Before long the crowd were trickling into another huge banquet room for dinner, and she and Kaden followed. He was deep in conversation with another man, speaking French.

During the interminable dinner Julia caught Samia's eyes a few times, and still couldn't understand the accusing look. Kaden was resolutely turned away from her, talking to the person on his other side, which left Julia trying to conduct a very awkward conversation with the man on her left, who was infinitely more interested in her cleavage and had not a word of English.

Kaden was acutely aware of Julia, and how close her thigh was to his under the table. He had to clench his fist to stop himself from reaching out and touching it, resting his hand at the apex of her thighs, where he could feel her heat.

He felt constricted. His chest was tight. It had been ever since he'd seen Samia's reaction to Julia. Samia was the chink in his armour. She was the only one who knew the dark place he'd gone to when Julia had left Burquat. It made him intensely uncomfortable to remember it. He reassured himself now, as he had then, that it had only been because he'd physically ached for her, his lust unquenched.

He knew he shouldn't be ignoring Julia like this. It was unconscionably rude. But he was actually afraid that if she looked at him she'd see something that he couldn't guard in his eyes. Samia's reaction had been like rubbing sandpaper over a wound, surprising in its vividness.

Assuring himself that it was nothing—just another trick of the mind where Julia was concerned—Kaden finally gave up trying to pretend to be interested in what his companion was saying, made an excuse, and resolutely ignored Samia's pointed looks in his direction. They were like little lashes of a whip.

He turned to Julia and could see from the line of her back that she was tense, that her jaw was gritted. Instinctively he put his hand around the back of her neck, and felt her tense even more in reaction. He moved his fingers in a massaging movement and she started to relax. Kaden had to hold back a smile at the way he sensed she resented it.

Immediately a sense of calm and peace washed over Kaden, and for once he didn't castigate himself or deny it. He gave himself up to it. The rawness subsided.

After what felt like an interminable moment Julia finally turned to look at him, and as his gaze met hers his body responded with predictable swiftness.

'Kaden…?'

He looked at her, and in that moment some indecipherable communication seemed to flow between them. Her eyes were huge, swirling with emotion, and Kaden couldn't find the will to disguise his own response. The room faded and the din of conversation became silent.

Julia wanted to ask Kaden to stop looking at her like that…as if they were nineteen again and he wanted to discover the secrets of her soul. But she couldn't open her mouth. She didn't want to break the moment.

The clatter of coffee and liqueurs being served finally seemed to break through the trance-like state, and in an abrupt move Kaden took his hand off her neck, reached for her hand and stood up.

Julia gasped and looked around. A couple of people had started to drift away from the table, but many still sat. Kaden tugged at her and she had no choice but to stand. People were looking.

'Kaden...what are you doing? It's not over yet.'

His eyes were so black Julia felt as if she might drown in them for ever.

'It is for us. I can't sit beside you for another minute and not touch you.'

And with that he pulled her in his wake as he strode away from the table. Before she knew what was happening they were outside the ballroom. She could barely catch her breath, and when she stumbled a little he turned and lifted her into his arms.

'Kaden!' she spluttered, as they passed servants who looked away diplomatically, as if they were used to seeing such occurrences all the time.

She couldn't deny the thrill of excitement firing up her blood. Kaden was acting like a marauding pirate. He carried her all the way back through a labyrinthine set of corridors to their room, and only once inside the door, which he kicked shut with his foot, did he let her down. He wasn't even breathing heavily. But Julia was, after being carried so close to his hard-muscled chest.

In the bedroom, he let her down on shaky legs. He pushed her up against the firmly shut door, crowding her against it and saying, 'We'll have to endure enough pomp and ceremony over the next two days, but every spare minute will be spent in this room. *That's* the focus of this weekend.'

The sheer carnality stamped on his face and the hint of desperation in his voice stopped Julia from thinking too deeply about the hurt that lanced her—as if for a moment there, when he'd been looking at her at the table, she'd got lost in a fantasy of things being different.

And then his urgency flowed through to her—the realisation that even now time was slipping out of their hands. Overcome with an emotion she refused to look at, she took his face in her hands and for the first time felt somewhat in control. Kaden was right. Focus on the now, the physical. Not on the past. Or on a future that would never exist.

'Well, what are you waiting for, then?' And she kissed him.

SOME HOURS LATER, Kaden was standing by the open French doors of the bedroom. B'harani lay before him like a twinkling carpet of gems. Soaring minarets nestled alongside modern buildings, and he knew that this was what he wanted to create in Burquat too. He'd already started, but he had a long way to go.

He sighed deeply and glanced back at the woman asleep in the bed amongst tumbled sheets. She was on her back, the sheet barely covering her sex, breasts bare, arms flung out, cheeks flushed. Even now his body hardened in helpless response. He grimaced. He'd taken her up against the door, her legs wrapped around his waist, with no more finesse than a rutting animal. And yet she'd met him every step of the way, her body accepting him and spurring him to heights he'd not attained in years.

Since her.

It all came back to her—as if some sort of circle was in effect, bringing them helplessly back to the beginning and onwards like an unstoppable force.

JULIA WOKE SLOWLY, through layers and layers of sleep and delicious lethargy. With an effort she opened her eyes and saw the tall, formidable shape of Kaden leaning against the open doors which led out to a private terrace. He was looking at her steadily, no expression on his face.

Helpless emotion bubbled up within her—especially when she saw the vast star-filled Arabian sky behind him. She had so much she wanted to say, but the past was all around her, in her. The lines were blurring ominously.

Instinctively she put out a hand and said huskily, 'Kaden…'

For a long moment he just stood there, arms crossed, trousers slung low on narrow hips, top button open. He was so beautiful. And then he gritted out, 'Damn you, Julia.'

He strode back into the room, all but ripped off his clothes and came down over her like an avenging dark angel. All the inarticulate words she wanted to say were stifled by Kaden's expert touch and quickly forgotten.

WHEN JULIA WOKE on Sunday morning she ached all over. But it was delicious. Kaden was not there, and she found a note on his pillow to inform her that he'd gone riding.

When she thought of how Samia had been looking at her for the past two days she felt guilty, and she had no idea why.

The previous day, evening and night had passed in a dizzying array of events and functions all leading up to the grand ceremony today, which would be held in front of hundreds of guests and the media.

With a sigh Julia got up, went to the bathroom and stepped into the shower. Once finished, and dressed in a robe with a towel around her damp hair, she stepped out onto the open terrace to see that breakfast had been left for her on a table. She grimaced at the dewy fresh rose in an exquisite glass vase. That was a touch Kaden wouldn't welcome.

All that existed between her and Kaden was this intense heat. They couldn't even seem to hold a coherent conversation before things became physical. And she didn't doubt that was exactly how Kaden wanted it.

Julia assured herself stoutly that that was just fine. She picked up a croissant and walked to the wall, from where she could see the stunning city of B'harani spread out before her.

Her heart swelled—not for this city in particular, but for this part of the world. If any city held her heart it was Burquat, high on its huge hill, with its ancient, dusty winding streets and mysterious souks. But the air here was similar, and the heat...

She heard a sound behind her and turned to see Kaden standing at the doors. Her heart leapt. He was dressed in faded jeans which clung to powerful thighs and a sweaty polo shirt, boots to his knees. Damp hair stuck to his forehead.

As she watched, he started to pull off his shirt with such sexy grace that she dropped the croissant and didn't even notice. How could she feel so wanton and hot, mere hours after—?

Kaden threw down his top and came to Julia, hemming her in against the wall with his arms. His mouth found and nuzzled her neck. He smelled of sweat and musk and sex.

Julia groaned and said, half despairingly, 'Kaden...'

He pulled one shoulder of her robe down and kissed her damp skin. 'You missed a bit here...I think we need to remedy that.'

With that awesome strength he picked her up, and within minutes they were naked and in the shower.

MUCH LATER, WHEN the daylight was tipping into dusk outside, Julia woke from a fitful sleep. She felt disorientated and a little dizzy, even though she was lying down. Flashes of the day came into her head: the lavish wedding ceremony in the ornate ceremonial hall, Samia looking pale and so young, her husband tall and dark and austere, reminding Julia of Kaden.

And then, after a token appearance at the celebration, Kaden pulling her away, bringing her back here, where once again passion had overtaken everything. Her body was still sensitive, so she couldn't have slept for long.

She heard a noise and turned her head to see Kaden sitting at a table in the corner of the palatial room, with his slim laptop open in front of him. That lock of hair

was over his forehead, and he sipped from a cup of
what she guessed was coffee.

There was something so domestic about the scene
that Julia's heart lurched painfully. And she knew right
then with painful clarity that she had to be the one to
walk away this time. She couldn't bear to stand before
Kaden again and have him tell her it was over.

As if he could hear her thinking, he looked over. He
was already half dressed, in black pants and a white
shirt. His look was cool enough to make her shiver
slightly, and he glanced at his watch. 'We have to be
ready in half an hour for the final banquet.'

Julia shot up in the bed, clutching the sheet. 'You
should have woken me.' With dismay she thought of her
dress for this evening that was already in the wardrobe.
It was another couture gown, and she was going to require time to repair the damage and restore herself to
something approximating normality. If she could ever
feel normal again.

Feeling absurdly grumpy, Julia marched into the
bathroom and locked the door behind her.

Kaden sat back in the chair and frowned, looking
at the tangled sheets of the bed. The truth was he'd felt
so comfortable here in the room, with Julia sleeping
in the bed just feet away, that he'd forgotten all about
waking her. His skin prickled at that. He'd felt that way
before…with her, but never with another woman. Even
with his own wife he'd insisted on separate bedrooms
and living quarters. He knew now that if the situation
had been reversed and he'd been married to Julia it
would have been anathema not to share space with her.

If he'd married Julia.

That all too disturbing thought drove him up out of his chair and to the phone. He picked it up and gave instructions to the person on the other end.

WHEN JULIA EMERGED from the bathroom there was a pretty young girl dressed all in white waiting for her. She said shyly, 'My name is Nita. I'm here to help you get changed.'

Too bemused even to wonder where Kaden had disappeared to, Julia let Nita help her, and within half an hour she was dressed and ready again. At precisely that moment Kaden reappeared at the bedroom door, resplendent in another tuxedo. He held out his arm for Julia, who took it silently.

This time her dress was a deep purple colour. A tightly ruched strapless bodice gave way to swirling floor-length silk which was covered in tiny crystals. The effect was like a shimmering cloud as Julia walked alongside Kaden.

She could feel the ever-present tension in his form beside her, and marvelled at the irony of the whole situation. She was arguably living every little girl's fantasy, here in this fairytale castle, yet with the bleakest of adult twists.

She had to end this tonight—before he did. Before he could see how helplessly entangled she'd already become again.

A FEW HOURS LATER, when the crowd had watched Sultan Sadiq lead his new wife from the ceremonial ballroom, Julia was exhausted, and more than relieved when Kaden took her hand to lead her from the room.

Her traitorous blood was humming in anticipation as they neared the bedroom. But she forced ice into her veins.

When they reached the room she extricated her hand and went and stood apart from him. He was surveying her warily, and she realised just how little they'd really communicated all weekend—as if he had been deliberately trying to avoid any conversation or any kind of intimacy beyond sex. It galvanised her.

She hitched up her chin. 'The couple I was talking to earlier are leaving Burquat tonight, on a private flight back to England. They've offered me a seat on the plane if I'm ready to go in an hour.'

Julia was vaguely aware of tension coming into Kaden's form. 'You can't wait until tomorrow morning, when I am going to take you home?'

She shook her head, almost dizzy with relief that she was taking control of things. That Kaden wasn't coming closer, scrambling her brain. 'There's no need. I need to get back. I've got work this week. I've got a life, Kaden. I think it's best if we just say this is over, here and now. What's the point in dragging it out?'

Kaden was seeing a red mist over his vision. So many conflicting things were hitting him at once. No woman had ever walked away from him, for one thing. But a dented ego had never been his concern. It was Julia, standing there so poised and cool, as if ice wouldn't melt in her mouth. When only hours before she'd been raking his back with her nails and sobbing for him to release her from exquisite pleasure.

Jerkily Julia moved to the drawers and picked up what looked like a jewellery box. She was already gathering her things to start packing. Filled with something that felt scarily close to panic, Kaden took a step forward and noticed how skittishly she moved back. Her face had an incredibly vulnerable expression but he blocked it out, and it was only then that he noticed— at the same time as she did—that some jewellery had fallen from the box after her skittish move.

He watched as she bent to pick up the trinkets and then, as if in slow motion, something gold fell back to the floor. Before he even knew what he was doing he'd stepped forward and picked the piece up.

Julia stood up. Her heart had stopped beating. It was like watching a car crash in slow motion. Kaden straightened. The distinctive gold chain with its detail of a love-knot looked ridiculously delicate in his huge hand. He didn't even look at her.

'You still have it.'

Julia didn't have the strength to berate herself for having brought it. She swallowed and said, far more huskily than she would have liked, 'Yes, I still have it.'

Even now her fingers itched to touch the tell—tale spot where it usually sat, and she clenched her hand into a fist. Kaden looked at her and his face was unreadable, those black eyes like fathomless wells.

'You always touch your throat...' He reached out his other hand and touched the base of her neck with a long finger. 'Just here...'

Julia gulped, and could see his eyes track the movement. With dread in her veins and a tide of crimson rising upwards she could only stand still as Kaden carefully stepped closer and opened the necklace, placing it around her neck and closing it as deftly as he had the day he'd bought it for her.

She felt the weight of the knot settle into its familiar place, just below the hollow at her throat. Kaden took his hands away, but didn't move back. Julia couldn't meet his eyes. Mortified and horrifically exposed.

Kaden looked at it for a long moment, and then he stepped back. When she raised her eyes to his they were blacker than she'd ever seen them. His face was set in stark lines. 'If you're sure you want to go home now, I'll see that Nita comes to help you.'

Julia shook her head, feeling numb. She wasn't sure how to take Kaden's abrupt *volte face*, when moments ago he'd looked as if he was about to tip her back onto the bed and persuade her to stay in a very carnal way. Now he looked positively repulsed. It had to be the necklace. He was horrified that she still had it, and what that might mean. Memories, the sting of rejection—all rushed back.

'It's fine. I don't need help.'

Kaden saw Julia's mouth move but didn't really hear what she was saying. All he could hear was a dull roaring in his head, the precursor to a pounding headache. And all he could see was that necklace. It seemed to be mocking him. He could still feel its imprint on his hand.

A tightness was spreading in his chest. He had to get out of there *now*. He backed away from Julia. Gathering force within him was the overwhelming sensation of sliding down a slippery slope with nothing to hold onto.

Julia watched the play of indecipherable expressions cross Kaden's face. She felt like going over and thumping him. She wanted to wring some sort of response out of him… But then she felt deflated. How could she wring a response out of someone who had no feelings?

She swallowed painfully. 'I… It's been—'

She stopped as he cut her off. 'Yes,' he agreed grimly. 'It has. Goodbye, Julia.'

And with that he turned and was gone, and all Julia's flimsy control shattered at her feet—because she felt as if she'd just been rejected all over again.

LESS THAN AN hour later Kaden was in his own private plane, heading back to Burquat. He'd actually had a meeting lined up the following morning, with some of Sultan Sadiq's mining advisors, but had postponed it. The fact was he'd felt an overwhelming need to get as far away from B'harani as possible, as quickly as possible.

He looked down at his hand. It was actually shaking. All he could see, though, was that necklace, sitting in his hand, and then around Julia's neck. It was obviously the necklace she went to touch all the time. It hung in exactly that spot, and when he'd put it on she'd looked *guilty*.

The question was too incendiary to contemplate, but he couldn't help it: who would keep and wear a cheap gold necklace for twelve years? It was the only piece of jewellery, apart from his ex-wife's wedding rings, that he'd ever given to a woman, and he remembered the moment as if it was yesterday.

Kaden's mind shut down… He couldn't handle the implications of this.

He watched the B'harani desert roll out below him,

and instead of feeling a sense of peace he felt incredibly restless. His hands clenched to fists on his thighs, he didn't even see the air hostess take one look at his face and beat a hasty retreat.

Kaden assured himself that for the first time since he'd met Julia he was finally doing the right thing. Leaving her behind in his past. Where she belonged.

CHAPTER SEVEN

'YOU ARE DEFINITELY PREGNANT, Julia. And if the dates
you've told me are correct I'd say you're almost three
months gone—at the end of your first trimester.'

Julia's kindly maternal doctor looked at her over her
half-moon glasses,

'Why didn't you come to me sooner? You must have
suspected something, and we both know your periods
are like clockwork.'

Julia barely heard her. Shock was like a wall between her and the words. Of course she'd suspected
something for the last two months, but she'd buried
her head in the sand and told herself that fate couldn't
be so cruel—not after years of trying for a baby with
her husband. Hence the reason why her doctor knew
her so well.

But then the problem hadn't been on her side. It had
been her husband's.

The doctor was looking at Julia expectantly, and
she forced herself to focus. 'I just... I couldn't believe
what it might be.'

Her doctor smiled wryly. 'Well it's a baby, due in
about six months if all goes well.' She continued gently, 'I take it that as you're divorced the father is...?'

'Not my ex-husband, no.' Julia bit her lip. 'The

father is someone I once knew, long ago. We met again recently...'

'Are you going to tell him?'

Julia looked at her friend. 'To be honest? I don't know yet...what I'm going to do.'

The doctor's manner became more brisk. 'Well, look, first things first. I'll book you in for a scan, just to make sure everything is progressing normally, and then we can take it from there— OK?'

One month later

KADEN PACED IN his office. The ever-present simmering emotions he'd been suppressing for about four months were threatening to erupt. Julia was here. Outside his office. Right now. She'd been waiting for over an hour. He would never normally keep anyone waiting that long but it was *Julia*, and she was here.

He ran a hand through his hair impatiently. What the hell did she want? His heart beat fast. Did she want to continue the affair? Had she spent the last months waking in the middle of the night too? Aching all over? He felt clammy. Would she be wearing that necklace?

He clenched a fist. Dammit. He'd hoped that by now he'd have chosen a wife and be in the middle of wedding preparations, but despite his aides' best efforts every potential candidate he'd met had had something wrong with her. One was too forward, another too meek, too sullen, too avaricious, too fake... The list was endless.

And now he couldn't ignore the fact that Julia Somerton had come to Burquat, going unnoticed on the flight lists because of her married name. In Burquat all repeat visitors were noted. She'd made her way to the castle and now she was sitting outside his door.

His internal phone rang and he stalked to his desk to pick it up. His secretary said, 'Sire, I'm sorry to bother you, but Dr Somerton is still here. I think you should see her now. I'm a little concerned—'

Kaden cut her off abruptly, 'Send her in.'

JULIA FINALLY GOT the nod from Kaden's secretary, who was dressed not in traditional garb, as everyone used to be when she'd been here last, but in a smart trouser suit, with a fashionable scarf covering her hair. She'd been solicitous and charming to Julia, but Julia had noticed her frequent and concerned looks and wondered if she really looked so tired and dusty.

Her flight from London had left at the crack of dawn, and the journey from Burquat airport in a bone-rattling taxi with no air-conditioning had left her feeling bruised and battered. Thankfully, though, the incessant morning sickness she'd been suffering from had finally abated in the last month, and she felt strong enough to make the journey. Physically at least. Mentally and emotionally was another story altogether.

She knew that she'd lost weight, thanks to the more or less constant morning sickness, and she was pale. She couldn't even drum up the energy to care too much. She wasn't coming here to seduce Kaden. When he'd said that clipped and cold goodbye in B'harani after seeing the necklace it couldn't have been more obvious that he'd been horrified. She'd watched his physical reaction and known that any desire had died a death there and then.

Julia stopped herself from touching her neck now, and reminded herself that the necklace was safely back in the UK. She stood up and walked to the door. The secretary had told her to leave her suitcase by her desk. Julia hadn't even booked into a hotel yet, but she'd worry about that after.

The door swung open and she took a deep breath and stepped into Kaden's office. The early evening sunlight was in her face, so as the door shut behind her all she could see was the formidable outline of Kaden's shape.

She put a hand up to shade her eyes and tried to ignore the wave of *déjà-vu* that almost threatened to knock her out. The last time she'd been in this room—

'To what do I owe the pleasure, Julia?'

So cool.

Julia forced herself to breathe deep and focus on getting the words out. 'I came because I have to tell you something.'

Kaden finally stepped forward and blocked the light, so now Julia could see him. She felt her breath stop at being faced with his sheer male beauty again. And also because he had a beard—albeit a small one. His hair was longer too. He looked altogether wild and un-tamed in traditional robes, and her heart took up an unsteady rhythm.

Stupidly she asked, 'Why do you have a beard?'

He put up a hand to touch it, almost as if he'd for-gotten about it, and bit out, 'I've spent the last ten days in the desert, meeting Bedouin leaders and councils.

It's a custom among them to let their beards grow, so whenever I go I do the same. I haven't had time to shave yet. I just got back this morning.'

Julia found this unexpected image of him so compelling that her throat dried. He was intensely masculine anyway, but like this... Her blood grew hot even as she looked at him. And he was looking at *her* as if she'd just slithered out from under a rock.

He quirked a brow. 'Surely you haven't come all this way to question me on my shaving habits?'

A wave of weakness came over her then, and Julia realised she hadn't eaten since a soggy breakfast on the plane—hours ago. She cursed herself. She had to be more careful. But in fact, whether fatigue or hunger, whatever it was created a welcome cushion of numbness around her.

She looked at Kaden again and willed herself to be strong, straightening her spine. 'No, I've come for another reason. The truth is that I have some news, and it affects both of us.' She continued in a rush, before she could lose her nerve. 'I'm pregnant, Kaden. With your baby... Well, actually, the thing is, it's not just one baby. If it was I might not have come all this way. But you see, I'm almost four months pregnant with twins... and the thought of two babies was a bit much to deal with on my own...and I know I could have rung, but I tried a few times...but that's when you must have been away in the desert and I didn't want to leave a message...'

Kaden lifted a hand. He'd gone very still and pale beneath his tan. 'Pregnant? Twins?'

Julia nodded, hating herself for babbling like that.

She'd wanted to be ultra-calm and collected, but now she was in front of Kaden she felt as if she was nineteen again. She wanted to run into his chest and have him hold her—but that scenario was about as likely as a sudden snow shower inside the palace.

'You look like you've *lost* weight—not as if you're pregnant.' He sounded almost accusing.

Julia stifled a slightly hysterical laugh when she thought of the sizeable bump under her loose top. She was already wearing stretch-waisted jeans.

His hand dropped. His eyes narrowed. He looked even wilder now. 'And you say these babies are mine?'

At that insulting insinuation Julia actually swayed on her feet. Kaden came around his desk so fast it made her feel even dizzier. She put out a hand, as if that could stop him.

'Do you really think I came all this way for the good of my health? Just to pass off some other man's babies as yours?' Her voice rang with bitterness. 'Believe me, I've been actuely aware of the awful irony of this situation for months of sleepless nights now. One baby I could have coped with. I wasn't even sure if I was going to tell you. But two babies…'

Kaden's eyes raked her from head to toe. His lip practically curled. 'I used protection.'

Julia's chin went up. 'There is a failure rate, and clearly it failed.'

The enormity of what Julia was saying, and to whom hit her then like a ton weight. Two babies. Who would be unwanted and unloved by their father. It was so much the opposite of what she'd once dreamt of with this man that the pain lanced her like a sharp knife right through the heart.

Everything was becoming indistinct and awfully blurry. That numbness was spreading. But in the face of his overwhelmingly hostile response Julia had to assert her independence. She had a horror of him assuming she'd come for a hand-out.

Faintly, Julia tried to force oxygen to her brain and to be articulate. 'These are your babies, Kaden, whether you like it or not. And now that I've told you I'll leave. I don't expect anything from you. I just wanted you to know that they exist…or will exist in about five months, all being well.'

She turned on her heel, but it seemed to take an awful long time—as if everything had gone into slow motion. And then, instead of getting closer to the door, she seemed to be moving further and further away. With a cry of dismay as black edges appeared on her peripheral vision, Julia felt herself falling down and down. Only faintly did she hear a stricken '*Julia!*' and feel something warm and strong cushion her back before the blackness sucked her down completely.

'WHY IS SHE taking so long to come round?' Kaden asked the wizened palace doctor impatiently. He didn't like the metallic taste of fear in his mouth. 'Shouldn't we go straight to the hospital? I told you she's pregnant.'

The doctor was unflappable and kept his fingers on Julia's wrist, checking her pulse. Kaden had laid her down on the couch in his office before bellowing for his secretary to call Dr Assan. She'd been so limp and lifeless, her cheeks paler than he'd ever seen, dark bruises under her eyes.

And he'd kept her waiting all that time—after a long journey. She was pregnant. His conscience stung him hard.

Dr Assan looked at Kaden pacing near to him. 'We're just waiting for the paramedics to come and then she will be taken to the hospital for a full examination. But as far as I can tell she is fine—probably just tired and dehydrated. You said she flew from England today?'

'Yes—yes, I did,' Kaden agreed irritably. He was used to things happening quickly, and even though it was only a couple of minutes since she'd collapsed time seemed to have slowed down to the pace of a snail.

With a granite-like weight in his chest, he cursed himself for lashing out just now and insinuating that he might not be the father. Of *course* he believed her when she said the babies were his. She'd looked shell-shocked, not avaricious. He knew with a bone-deep certainty that she wasn't mercenary enough to make a false claim of paternity.

In five months' time he would have a ready-made family.

The thought was overwhelming.

Just then a knock came to the door, and in the flurry of activity Kaden concentrated on what they were doing to Julia. When they produced a stretcher to carry her out to the ambulance Kaden reacted to a surge of something primal, and waded in and picked her up into his arms himself, ignoring the paramedics.

Dr Assan motioned for them to follow Kaden as he

strode out with Julia in his arms. Kaden was oblivious to the sea of people hurrying after him. He was only aware of the swell of Julia's pregnant belly against his chest, and something powerful rose up within him. His gut clenched tight. In his arms Julia stirred, but he didn't even break his stride as he looked down to see those pools of grey on him. Dazed and confused.

For a moment he forgot everything and reacted only to those eyes, and to the sensation of relief rushing through him. 'Don't worry, you're safe, and I'm going to take care of you.'

JULIA WAS WARM and secure in a dark place. But someone kept prodding her and shining a light in her eyes. Instinctively she moved away from the light, but it kept following her until eventually she opened her eyes, and then it blinded her. She squeezed her eyes shut again, but heard a kindly voice saying, 'Julia, you need to wake up now. You've given us all quite a fright.'

In her hazy consciousness she heard an echo of Kaden's voice. *Don't worry...I'm going to take care of you...*

Without really knowing where she was or what was happening, she spoke from a place of urgent instinctive need, 'Kaden...where is Kaden?'

A moment of silence, and then she felt his presence. A hand on hers. The relief was overwhelming. 'I'm right here.'

And at his touch and his voice it all came back. She wasn't nineteen any more. She was thirty-two, and pregnant with his babies. And he didn't want her—or them. Instantly she was cold and wide awake. Her eyes opened to see Kaden towering over her where she lay in a hospital bed, austere and remote in his robes and with that beard. She pulled her hand away, knowing that he must be hating her so much right now.

She looked to the man who had to be the doctor. 'What happened?'

'You're severely dehydrated and fatigued. You'll need to be supervised on a drip for at least twenty-four hours. But apart from that everything is fine, and your babies are fine too. You just need rest and sustenance.'

Julia immediately put a hand to the swell of her stomach and felt Kaden take a step back from the bed. She couldn't bear to look at him and see the censure in his eyes. The disgust he must feel that she was here, with this unwelcome news. The last woman in the world he would have picked to be the mother of his children.

She wondered again if she should have come, and her own doctor's words came back to her. 'Julia, twins are a monumental task for anyone to take on board. You should not do this by yourself. You *must* include the father.'

Kaden's doctor patted her hand and said, 'I'll leave you alone now to rest.'

He left the room and the silence was oppressive. Kaden walked around so that he was in Julia's line of vision. She felt acutely vulnerable, lying on the bed in a hospital robe.

'Where are my things?' she asked, as if that would postpone the painful conversation that was due.

'Your bag is still with my secretary and your clothes are here.'

Julia bit her lip. 'I can't believe I collapsed like that. I had no idea—'

He exploded. 'How could you not have known you were so weak and dehydrated? For God's sake, you're pregnant. Are you not taking care of yourself?'

Julia could actually feel any colour she'd regained drain from her face. She'd known Kaden must be angry, but to see it like this....

He cursed and ran a hand through his unkempt hair. Somehow it only had the effect of making him look even more gorgeous. His black eyes came back to her, and to Julia's utter shock he looked contrite.

'I'm sorry. I had no right to speak to you like that. This has all been a bit of a shock...to say the least.'

Julia's heart thumped. 'I'm sorry that I couldn't warn you first. It just seemed too huge to send via text...' She blushed. 'I don't even have your mobile number...and I didn't think it appropriate to leave a message with your aides.'

His eyes narrowed on her face. 'You said if it hadn't been twins you might not have told me?'

Julia avoided his eye guiltily, fingers plucking at the bedspread. 'I don't know what I would have done, to be honest. It was pretty clear at our last meeting that neither one of us wanted to see each other again.'

His mouth tightened. 'Yes...but once a baby is involved...he or she...they are my heirs. Part of the royal Burquati dynasty. If you had kept my child from me I would never have forgiven you.'

Julia looked at him, curling inwards at his censure. 'I'm sure I would have told you about the baby, even though I know a lasting reminder of our...our meeting again was the last thing you wanted or expected.'

Kaden's eyes flashed. For a long moment he didn't speak, and then he said, 'That's beside the point now. We'll just have to make this work.'

Julia's eyes narrowed on Kaden as a shiver of foreboding went down her spin. 'What do you mean?'

'What I mean, Julia, is that we will be getting married. As soon as possible.'

KADEN HADN'T EVEN realised he was thinking of such a thing until the words came out of his mouth, but to his utter surprise he felt a wave of equanimity wash over him for the first time in months.

Julia just looked at Kaden where he stood at the foot of the bed. Dominating. Powerful. Implacable. Inevitability and a sense of fatalism made her feel even weaker even as she protested shakily, 'Don't be ridiculous, Kaden. We don't have to get married just because I'm having your baby.'

He folded his arms, and corrected her. '*Babies*. And, yes, we do.'

'But...' Julia's mind was feeling foggy again. She was glad she was lying down. 'The people won't accept me as your wife...'

His mouth tightened. 'They're conservative. It might take a while for them to accept you, but they will have no choice. You will be my sheikha—the mother of my children.'

Julia wondered how it could be possible for her to feel dizzy when she was lying down, but the room was spinning and those black edges were creeping back.

She heard Kaden swear again, and he moved towards her, but by the time he'd reached her she'd slipped back down into the comforting numbness of the black place.

One week later

'YOU ARE MUCH IMPROVED, my dear. You should get out and enjoy some of the sunshine. Sit in the garden, breathe the fresh air. I'll go and get Jasmine to come and help you.'

Julia smiled at the kindly Dr Assan and watched him leave. He'd been on standby since she'd returned to the palace from the hospital nearly four days before, and had been checking up on her at regular intervals.

For the last few days all she'd done was eat and sleep. And tried to block out Kaden's proposal—if she could even call it that. He hadn't mentioned it again. He'd come in and out of her bedroom and not said much at all, usually just looked at her broodingly.

Julia sighed deeply now and sat up. Her room was stupendously luxurious. Kaden had obviously had the palace redecorated in the intervening years, because before it had always had a very rustic and ascetic feel. Now, though, it might have come straight from the pages of an interior design magazine.

It hadn't completely lost that rustic feel. For instance it didn't share the de luxe opulence of the Hussein Castle in B'harani. But it was just as impressive. The palace itself looked as if it had been carved out of the hill it stood on, soaring majestically over the small city. Vast courtyards opened out into colourful gardens, where peacocks picked their way over glittering mosaics.

The interior stone floors were minimalist, but covered in the most exquisitely ornate rugs. The walls
were largely bare, apart from the occasional silk wall
hanging or flaming lantern. Windows were huge and
open, with elaborate arches framing stunning views
of the city.

Julia had a suite of rooms comprising a bedroom,
bathroom and sitting room. With every mod-con and
audio visual requirement cleverly tucked away so as
not to ruin the authentic feel.

Outside the French doors of her sitting room lay
a private courtyard filled with flowers. There was a
pond, and a low wall which overlooked the ancient
hilly city. In the near distance could be seen the blue
line of the Persian Gulf. Seagulls wheeled over head,
and the scent of the sea was never far away.

Julia felt incredibly emotional whenever she looked
out over the city. From the moment she'd first come
to Burquat the country and its people had resonated
deep within her. She felt at home here. Or she had until
that night—

'Dr Somerton? I'll help you get ready to go outside.'

Julia glanced around from where she'd been sitting on the edge of the bed to see Jasmine, the pretty
young girl who'd been helping her every day. She knew
she'd only worry Dr Assan if she didn't go out, and she
craved some air, so she smiled and let Jasmine help her.

Clothes had materialised one morning—beautiful
kaftans and loose-fitting trousers to wear underneath—
and Jasmine laid out a set now, in dark blue. They were
comfortable and easy to wear in the heat—especially
now that her bump seemed to be growing bigger by

the day. It was as if her coming to Burquat had precipitated a growth spurt.

The palace had many gardens, but Julia's favourite
so far was the orchard garden, filled with fruit-bearing
trees. Branches were laden with plums and figs, and a
river ran through the bottom of the garden, out of the
palace grounds and down into the city. It was peaceful and idyllic.

Jasmine left her alone to walk there after showing
her where a table and chair had been set up for her
to rest in the shade. Julia couldn't believe how kind
everyone was being to her. Certainly the oppressive
atmosphere she remembered from Kaden's father's
time had lifted, and she had to wonder if that was because Kaden's stepmother had also died, and some of
the older, more austere aides were no longer part of
Kaden's retinue.

She sat down and took a sip of fresh iced lemonade,
savouring the tart, refreshing bite.

'I hope you don't mind if I join you.'

It wasn't a question. Julia looked up to see Kaden
standing nearby, and her belly automatically clenched.
He'd shaved off his beard and had a haircut, but he
looked no less wild or uncultivated despite the custom-
made suit he now wore. He alternated between western
and traditional dress easily.

She shook her head. As if by magic a man appeared
with another chair, and through the trees some distance
away Julia could see a man in a suit with an earpiece,
watching over his precious Emir.

He sat down, his huge body dwarfing the chair,

and helped himself to some lemonade. 'You're looking much better.'

Julia fought not to blush under Kaden's assessing
gaze as it swept down over her body, and wished she'd
put her hair up and some make-up on. Then she remembered how quick he'd been to let her go in B'harani
and looked away, afraid he might see something of her
emotions. Once again she felt humiliated heat rise at
remembering that he'd seen the necklace.

'I'm feeling much better, thank you. All of your
staff have been so kind. I should be well enough to
return home soon. I'll have to organise a plane ticket
back to the UK.'

He shook his head. 'You're not going home, Julia.
I'm already arranging to have your belongings packed
up and sent here. We can rent out your house in London
while you decide what you want to do with it.'

Julia looked at Kaden and her mouth opened. Nothing came out.

He leaned forward, his face grim. 'We are getting
married, Julia. Next week. Your life is here now—
with me.'

Panic bloomed in her gut, but it had more to do with
the prospect of a lifetime facing Kaden's cool censure
than the prospect of a lifetime as his wife. 'You can't
keep me here if I decide I want to go home. That would
be kidnapping.'

'It won't be kidnapping because you'll be staying of
your own free will. You know it's the right thing to do.'

Julia reacted. 'Is it really the right thing to agree to a
marriage just for convenience's sake?' She laughed a lit-

tle wildly. 'I've already been through one unhappy marriage. I'm not about to jump headfirst into another one.'

Kaden was intent, his face stark. 'This isn't about just you—or me. It's about the two babies you are carrying. And it's about the fact that everyone knows you're here and that we were once lovers. The news of your pregnancy will soon filter out, and I want us to be married before that happens. For your sake and our babies' sakes as much as mine.'

Our babies. Her eyes were wide. She felt control of her own existence slipping out of her grasp. She knew she must have gone pale again, but at least she felt stronger now.

As much as she didn't want to admit it, his words resonated within her on a practical level—bringing up two children on her own would be next to impossible with no familial support to speak of. Both her adoptive parents had died some years previously. Her divorce had wiped out any savings and a meagre inheritance. How could she afford childcare for two children unless she worked like a demon? And what kind of a life would that be for her children?

But Kaden's words also impacted on her at a much deeper and more visceral level. Growing up knowing she was adopted had bred within Julia an abiding need to create her own family. To have children and give them the assurance of their lineage and background that she'd never had. Her adoptive parents had loved her, of course... But she'd never really got over the stain of being unwanted by her birth mother and father. Irrationally she felt it was a reflection on *her*, something *she'd* done. And she had carried it down through the years to make what had happened with Kaden so much more devastating. But he was the last person she could confide in about this...

The haunting call of the *muezzin* started up in the city nearby and it tugged on her heart. She'd once fantasised about living here for ever with Kaden, but this was like a nightmare version of that dream.

As if sensing her turmoil, Kaden came out of his chair and down on one knee beside Julia. He took her hand in his. For a hysterical moment she thought he was going to propose to her, but then he said, 'You said it yourself when you came here—two babies change everything. I won't allow them to be brought up on another continent when their heritage is here, in this country. It's *two* babies, Julia. How can you even hope to cope with that on your own? They deserve to have two parents, a secure home and grounding. I can provide that. They will have roles to fulfil in this country—one of them will be the next Emir, or Queen of Burquat. Who knows? They might even rule together...'

Julia moved back in her seat. The thought of him seeing how his touch affected her was terrifying. 'They also deserve to have two parents who love one another.'

Kaden's face became cynical as he dropped her hand and spat out, '*Love?* You speak of fairytales that don't exist. We will make this work, Julia, because we have to. We don't need love.'

She saw the conflict in his eyes and on his face. His mouth was a thin line.

He stood up, instantly tall and intimidating. 'I'll do whatever I have to to make this work. You know this is the only way. I will be a good husband to you, Julia. I will support you and respect you.' A flash of heat sparked between them. 'And I will be faithful to you.'

A WEEK LATER Julia looked at herself in the floor-length mirror in her dressing room. The dawn light hadn't even broken outside yet. According to Burquati tradition, they would exchange vows and rings in a simple civil ceremony as dawn broke.

At any other time Julia would have found the prospect impossibly romantic. As it was all she could think about was Kaden's grim avowal: *'I'll do whatever I have to to make this work.'*

She was wearing an ivory gown, long-sleeved and modest, but it clung to every curve and moved sinuously when she walked. Thankfully the heavy material skimmed over her bump, so it wasn't too glaringly obvious. A lace veil was pinned low on the back of her head, and Jasmine had coiled her hair into a loose chignon. She wore pearl drop earrings, and Kaden had presented her with a stunning princess cut diamond ring set in old gold the day before, telling her it had been his mother's engagement ring, to be kept for his own bride.

The thought of wearing a ring that his first wife had also worn made her feel sullied somehow, but she hadn't had the nerve to say anything to a closed-off and taciturn Kaden. It couldn't be clearer that he was viewing this marriage as a kind of penance.

If she was stronger... Julia sighed. It was more than strength she needed to resist the will of Kaden. And deep within her she had to admit to a feeling of security at knowing that at least her babies would live lives free of shadows and doubts. She wasn't even going to admit to another much more personal and illicit feeling…of peace. Julia quickly diverted her thoughts away from *that* dangerous area.

She thought of the whirlwind it had been since she'd tacitly agreed to this marriage. And of the very muted fanfare that had greeted the public announcement a few days ago. At dinner on the evening their nuptials had been announced, Julia had voiced her building concern to Kaden; the reality of what might be expected of her had started sinking in. 'Wasn't your mother half-English? The people will be used to a foreign Sheikha, won't they?'

Kaden had avoided Julia's eye, and that had made her instantly nervous. 'Unfortunately the track record of Sheikhas here hasn't been good since my mother died. Both my wife and my stepmother never really connected with the people. As for my mother… They accepted her, yes…after a rocky start. The truth is that my father went against his own father's wishes to marry for love. The only reason he was allowed to marry my mother was because she came from a lineage on her father's side that went back as far as our own.'

He'd looked at her then, with a carefully veiled expression. 'It took the people some time to accept her, but they did, and when she died they were just as devastated as my father. He never came to terms with her death during Samia's childbirth. It changed him…made him withdraw and become more cynical… He blamed himself for having pursued his own selfish desires in bringing her here.'

Julia had protested. 'But it was just an awful tragedy.'

Kaden had abruptly changed the conversation then.

Julia had hardly slept since that night, more and more aware of how hard it was likely to be for her to be accepted by the Burquati people, and wondering how far Kaden was prepared to test his people's limits of acceptance to keep his heirs safe—and here.

CHAPTER EIGHT

KADEN PACED BACK and forth in the huge ceremonial ballroom of the palace. He was dressed in the royal Burquati military uniform. His chief aides and the officiator for the wedding ceremony waited patiently. He looked out of the window for the umpteenth time and saw the faint pink trails in the clear sky that heralded the dawn breaking. The thought of how delicate Julia had looked at dinner the previous evening. She'd hardly said a word, and her eyes had been huge, full of shadows, with the faintest purple smudges underneath.

He bit back a curse, hating the urgency rushing through his blood that had nothing to do with protocol and much to do with his disturbing need to see Julia.

He hadn't felt like this on his first wedding day. He'd been battling an almost dread feeling of suffocation that day. But since his marriage had ended he'd put that down to a presentiment of what had happened with his wife, and nothing to do with the lingering memory of another woman.

A sound came from the other end of the room and Kaden turned. His mind was emptied of all thought. Julia was a vision in ivory edged with pale gold as she walked towards him, with Jasmine holding her dress behind her. Her face was obscured by a long veil, and his eyes dropped to where the swell of her belly told the story of why they were getting married.

Something so fierce and primal gripped him in that moment that he had to clench his jaw and fists to stop shaking with it as Julia came to a stop just inches away. She was looking down, and Kaden longed to tell everyone to leave so that he could pull back the veil and tip her face up to his.

Instead he reached for her hand and lifted it up, bringing it to his mouth. Her head lifted and he could see the shape of her face, the flash of grey eyes, as he kissed her palm. Her perfume was soft and delicate, winding around him like a silken tie, bringing with it evocative memories and whispers of the past.

In that moment he hated her for coming back into his life, for reawakening a part of himself that he'd thought buried for ever. The only part of him that had ever been vulnerable, and the only part of him that had believed a different future was possible for him. It hadn't been.

With Julia's hand still in his he turned to the officiator and said curtly, 'Let's get started.'

WHAT FELT LIKE aeons later Julia was sitting beside Kaden at the massive dining table and her face felt as if it was frozen in a rictus grin. Her heart hurt. From the moment Kaden had said, *'Let's get started'* earlier, he'd been curt to the point of dismissal.

She dreaded to think what the photographs would look like—Kaden tall and stern, and her like a rabbit in the headlights. Only a few of months ago she'd been independent and strong, living her life, and now she'd morphed into someone she barely recognised. All because of this man coming back into her life like a tornado.

A small voice mocked her: *she'd been with him every step of the way.*

Julia straightened her spine. She wasn't going to let Kaden ignore her like this. She turned towards him, where he sat beside her. He was looking out over the sea of some five hundred guests with a brooding expression. She knew none of them except for his three youngest sisters, who had travelled from their schools and colleges for the weekend. Samia and her husband had been unable to attend, and Julia had felt a little relieved, not sure if she could take Samia's hostility again.

'Kaden?'

He turned, and Julia sucked in a shocked breath when she saw the look of pure bleakness on his face. But in an instant it was gone, and replaced with something she thought she'd never see again. *Heat.* He took one of her hands and brought it to his mouth. His touch sent her pulse skyrocketing and a flood of heat between her legs.

She tried to pull her hand back, seriously confused, forgetting what she'd wanted to say in the first place. 'Kaden...?'

'Yes, *habiba*?'

She felt very shaky all of a sudden. 'Why are you looking at me like that?'

He arched a brow. 'Is this not how a man is supposed to look at his wife?'

Feeling sickened, Julia wrenched her hand free from his. He was faking it. Of course. In front of his guests.

Julia muttered something about the bathroom and got up, barely noticing Kaden's frowning look as she hurried away, head down.

Kaden watched Julia walk away, eyes glued to the graceful lines of her body in the stunning dress. The veil was long gone, and her hair was coiled at the nape of her neck. She was like a warmly glowing pearl against this backdrop. And for a moment, before she'd called him, he'd been drawn back into the memory of their time in the desert just before everything had changed.

He'd once dreamed of exactly this moment—having Julia by his side as his Queen, his heart full to bursting with pride and love... And then she'd called his name and he'd realised that it wasn't like the dream. That dream had existed in the mind of a foolishly romantic young man who hadn't known any better. *This* was reality, and reality was a long way from any dream.

Cursing himself, he could still feel desire like a tight coil in his body. A desire he'd curbed for too long. Kaden threw down his napkin and stood up. They'd had speeches and ceremonial toasts. Everyone now expected the Emir to take his leave with his wife. Striding out of the room, servants scurrying in his wake, Kaden felt his blood growing hotter by the second.

JULIA HAD MADE her way out of the crowded room feeling stifled and extremely emotional. Jasmine had appeared as if from nowhere to guide her back to her rooms. She still didn't even know her own way around the palace!

When Jasmine showed her into the suite it took a minute before she realised that the distinctively masculine furnishings weren't familiar. She turned to Jasmine, who was waiting patiently for instructions.

'These aren't my rooms.'

Jasmine inclined her head deferentially. 'Sheikh Kaden told me to move your things in here. You will be sharing his rooms from now on.'

Julia's heart fluttered in her chest. She wasn't sure what Kaden was playing at, but she told Jasmine she wouldn't need her further. When the girl had left, emotion started rising again, and blindly Julia made her way out to Kaden's outdoor terrace. Much grander than her own.

It was dusk, and the call of an exotic bird pierced the air as Julia gripped the wall and looked out over Burquat. She could see people coming and going about their business far below, a line of blue which indicated the sea. She smelled the tang of salty air.

And all Julia could think of was how far Kaden was willing to go to make sure everyone believed he desired his wife, and how the immense crowd of guests had looked at her warily, with few smiles. An overwhelming feeling of aloneness washed over her. She put a hand to her bump and thought of her babies. *They* would be protected from this awful feeling of isolation. But she couldn't help, for one weak and self—indulgent moment, feeling sorry for herself. And she couldn't help the tears springing into her eyes and overflowing.

Kaden came into his rooms silently, and immediately saw Julia standing outside. The line of her back looked incredibly slim and tense, and the coil of her hair was shining in the dusky light. A curious feeling of peace mixed with desire rushed through his veins.

He moved forward and saw that Julia heard him. She tensed even more, and didn't turn around. Irritation prickled over his skin. 'Julia?'

Julia was frantically swallowing and trying to blink back tears, her cheeks stinging. The thought of Kaden witnessing her turmoil was too much, but she heard him come closer, and then his hands came onto her shoulders and he was turning her around.

She looked down in a desperate bid to hide, but he tipped her chin up. She looked at him almost defiantly through the sheen of tears. He frowned, eyes roving over her face. 'You're crying.'

Kaden was not prepared for the blow he felt to his solar plexus. Julia's face was pale and blotchy, wet with tears. Eyes swimming, dark pools of grey. Her mouth trembling.

'It's nothing,' she said huskily, lifting a hand to wipe at her cheek.

Kaden took her hand away and cupped her face. His chest felt so constricted he could hardly breathe. His thumbs wiped away the lingering tears.

'What is it?'

Julia bit her lip, clearly fighting for control. 'It's just all…a bit much. Finding out about my pregnancy, coming here…my life changing overnight.'

A solid mass of something dark settled into Kaden's chest. Clearly this was not what she'd envisaged for herself. He felt the sting of guilt. He'd seduced her. And changed their lives.

'Julia…you will not want for anything ever again. You or our babies. You can be happy here.'

She gave a half-strangled laugh. 'When your people look at me as if I'm about to do something scandalous?'

He grimaced. 'They just need time, that's all. There's been so much change in Burquat…my divorce…'

Julia was finding it hard to breathe with Kaden so close and holding her face. She couldn't bear for him to see her desire on top of this. She tried to pull his hands down but they were immovable. She looked into his eyes. 'Kaden…it's OK. You don't have to pretend here. No one is watching. And I don't expect to share your rooms. I'll go back to my own.'

'Pretend what?'

Julia avoided his gaze. 'Pretend to…want me.'

Kaden frowned. Pretend to want her? Could she not feel how on fire he was for her? And then the notion that perhaps she didn't want *him* sent something cold to his gut. He moved his hands and took her wrists. He could feel the hammering of her pulse. A sigh of relief went through him.

'Julia, look at me.'

With obvious reluctance she lifted her head. Her eyes were clear now, but no less troubled.

'What on earth made you think that I didn't want you?'

Now she frowned, a flush coming into her cheeks. 'That last night in B'harani…you were so quick to leave…' She stopped when she thought of his reaction to the necklace, and then said hurriedly, 'Not that

I wanted it to go on. I was happy for it to be over. But I just thought…'

'That I didn't desire you any more?'

She nodded, and Kaden moved close to her again, lifting her hands and trapping them against his chest, where she would feel the thundering beat of his heart. Standing so close to her like this was exquisite torture. A deep contentment flowed through him that he wasn't even aware of. He thought of the necklace then, of how seeing it had made him feel. But instead of dousing his desire, or making him want to flee, it actually made him feel even hotter.

Julia's cheeks flushed even more when Kaden moved so close that his erection pressed against her lower belly. Sensation exploded behind his eyes, through his body, and he had to bite back a groan. He said throatily, 'Does that feel like the response of a man who doesn't desire you?'

He marvelled. How could she not know? He felt as if every time he looked at her she must see the extent of his hunger. She was so different from any other woman he'd known. He'd almost forgotten that a woman like her could exist, and had a fleeting image of how bleak his life would have been if he'd not met her again.

Julia's eyes dropped to Kaden's mouth. She was transfixed. Almost without realising what she was doing, she extricated her hand from his grip and reached up to trace the sensuous line of his lips.

Kaden's hand went around the back of her neck, under the heavy fall of her hair, massaging the tender skin and muscles. His other hand was on her waist, big and possessive. Her breathing was already coming quickly, and she was telling herself to try and stay clear…but it was impossible.

Kaden dropped his head to hers. They were so close now that his breath feathered along her mouth. 'I've never wanted another woman the way I want you.'

Julia looked into his eyes and saw the flame in their depths. She reached up and pressed her mouth to his softly, chastely. For a moment he did nothing, and then with an urgency that made her blood exult in her veins he brought her even closer and fused his mouth to hers, opening her up to him so that his tongue could explore and seek a deeper intimacy.

Julia's hands and arms wound around Kaden's neck, fingers tangling in the silky hair brushing his collar. She could feel the swell of her belly pressing into him, the stab of his erection against her, and something deeply feminine and primal burned within her. This was *her* man.

Perhaps their desire was the one pure, true thing between them? Perhaps they could build on this? Perhaps one day the fact that he'd rejected her once would fade away?

All of these thoughts and other incoherent ones raced through her head in time with her heart, but she just wanted to lose herself in the release only he could give.

He drew back and took in a deep, ragged breath, eyes looking wild. Julia's mouth was burning.

'Wait… I want you so badly, Julia… But can we? I mean, is it safe?'

For a moment she didn't understand what he was saying, and then she felt him place a hand to her belly.

Something inside her melted even more. Blushing, because she was aware of the rampant need inside her, she said, 'Dr Assan told me that it would be OK if we wanted to…you know…'

Kaden clamped her face in his hands and said, 'Thank God.'

And then they were kissing again, and that helpless emotion was bubbling up within Julia. There was a desperation about their kiss, as if they'd been separated for years. As if something had broken open.

He broke the kiss only to lift her up into his arms and carry her into the dimly lit bedroom, with its huge king-size bed. Julia kept her eyes on Kaden, as if to look away might break the spell.

With a kind of reverence Kaden divested Julia of her jewellery and started to take off her clothes, undoing her dress at the back so that it fell open and then down to the floor in a pool of silk and satin at her feet, heavy under its own weight.

She stood in her underwear with her head tipped forward as Kaden took the pins out of her hair so that it tumbled around her shoulders. She could feel him open her bra, and shivered deliciously when his finger traced the line of her spine all the way down to her buttocks. Her breasts were heavy, nipples tight and tingling.

Gently he turned her to face him again, and pulled the open bra down her arms and off. She felt self-conscious for a moment, aware of her bigger breasts and her rounded belly. But under Kaden's hot gaze all trepidation fled. He cupped her breasts, eyes dark and molten as he moved his thumbs over the taut peaks. They were more sensitive now, and Julia groaned softly.

Her hands were shaking with need as she reached out to take off Kaden's jacket and shirt. The buttons were elaborate and proved too much for her clumsy ministrations.

Kaden took her hands away and she watched, dry-mouthed, as bit by bit his glorious torso was revealed. Stepping close, she pressed a kiss to one flat nipple, tugging gently with her teeth and then smoothing it with her tongue. Kaden's hand speared her hair, holding her head. Julia exulted in his rough breathing, in the way his chest filled to suck in more air.

Her hands had found his belt and buckle. Urgently she opened them and pushed his trousers and briefs down to the floor, freeing his impressive erection. Drawing back for a moment, she looked down, feeling dizzy with desire. She reached out a hand and touched him, stroking the hard length, feeling the decadent slide of silky skin over steel.

'Julia…'

Kaden sounded hoarse. Julia acted on pure instinct and bent her knees until she knelt before him on the floor. Still holding him, she took the tip of him into her mouth, tongue swirling around him. Fresh heat flooded through her at doing something so wanton, and she only dimly heard Kaden say harshly, 'Stop… *God*, Julia, if you keep doing that I won't—'

She felt Kaden gently pull her head away. She looked up, and the feral, almost fierce expression on his face reminded her of a wild and beautiful animal. He pulled her to her feet. 'You don't know what you do to me. I won't last…and I want you too much. I need to be inside you. *Now*.'

Within what felt like seconds they were on Kaden's bed, with not a stitch of clothing between them. Kaden's hands smoothed down over Julia's curves, her belly. She reached for him. 'Kaden, I need you.'

His hand dipped between her legs, feeling for himself that she was ready, and if Julia hadn't been so turned on she would have been embarrassed by the triumphant glitter in Kaden's eyes.

He settled his lean hips between her legs, one hand on her thigh, pushing it wider, careful not to rest his weight on her belly. Julia arched her back, nipples scraping against his chest.

And then, just when she was about to plead and beg, she felt him slide into her, inch by delicious inch, filling her and stretching her. Eyes wide, she looked at him as he started to thrust, taking them higher and higher.

Time was transcended. All that existed was this blissful union. And Julia was borne aloft on a wave of ecstasy so overpowering that it seemed to go on for ever, her whole body pulsing and clenching for long seconds even after Kaden's seed had spilled deep inside her. After a timeless moment he extricated himself and pulled her tight into his chest, arms wrapped around her. Julia wondered for one lucid moment before she fell asleep if this was a dream.

Kaden lay awake beside Julia. His heartbeat was still erratic, and a light sweat sheened his skin. Julia was curled into his chest, bottom tucked close into the cradle of his thighs. Already he was growing hard at the feel of her lush behind. Once again he was struck with the immutable truth that no other woman had this effect on him after making love. He felt all at once invincible, and yet more vulnerable than he'd ever felt.

One hand was on Julia's belly, his fingers spread across the firm swell. He put the feelings welling up inside him down to knowing that she was pregnant—with *his* babies, his seed. Undoubtedly that was what had imbued their lovemaking with a heightened intensity.

But as Kaden finally let sleep claim him his overriding feeling wasn't one of peace at being able to put the experience into a box. It was the same disconcerting one he'd had in B'harani, when he'd seen Julia holding that necklace. He felt as if he was sliding down that slippery slope again, with nothing to hold on to, and there was a great black yawning abyss at the bottom, waiting to suck him down.

A few hours later, as dawn broke outside, Kaden woke sweating and clammy, his heart racing. He'd just had a vivid dream of nightmare proportions. He'd been surrounded by a crowd of faceless people and held back by hundreds of hands as he was forced to watch Julia make love to another man. He'd wanted to rip that man limb from limb. He felt nauseous even now, as it came back in lurid detail.

He looked to where Julia lay sleeping on her side on the other side of the bed and felt all at once like holding her close and running fast in the opposite direction.

Two weeks after that cataclysmic wedding night Julia was wondering if it had been a dream. It *felt* like a dream, because they hadn't made love since then. Kaden had been cool the following morning at breakfast, while Julia had felt as if she'd survived an earth-quake.

He'd informed her, while barely meeting her eyes, 'Unfortunately local elections are coming up this week, which means that we'll have to postpone a honeymoon.'

Julia's insides had curdled in the face of this remote man. How could she have been seduced so easily into thinking she'd seen something of the young man she'd fallen in love with?

'That's fine with me,' she'd answered stiffly. 'I hadn't expected anything else.'

And then he'd said, 'I've arranged for you to have lessons in Burquati history and royal protocol. You'll be well prepared for any public engagements. I should be able to accompany you until you get your bearings. The lessons will give you a broad overview of every-thing you need to know, and some tuition in our lan-guage.'

Now Kaden shifted on the other side of the dinner table, and Julia glanced up guiltily to see him assess-ing her. His eyes dropped to her hand.

'Why aren't you wearing your engagement ring?'

Julia looked at the plain gold wedding band on her finger and flushed. 'I was afraid I might lose it.'

She saw his sceptical look, and then felt a surge of adrenaline. The fact that he'd clearly been avoiding coming to bed until she was asleep for the past two weeks, while she lay there aching for him to touch her, was inciting hot anger.

She lifted her chin. 'The truth is that I don't like the idea of wearing a ring that was given to your first wife.'

'Why would you feel that?'

She frowned. 'You said that it was your mother's ring, which was to be given to the woman you married... I just assumed—'

He cut her off. 'I gave Amira a different ring—one that she kept when we were divorced...' His mouth tightened. 'I believe it fetched a nice price at auction in London a few months ago. Clearly her generous divorce settlement is fast running out.'

Julia was disconcerted, her anger fading. 'Why didn't you give your mother's ring to her?'

Kaden looked at Julia, and those big grey eyes threatened him on so many levels. He shrugged nonchalantly, very aware that this was exposing him. He hadn't given the ring to Amira because it hadn't felt right. And yet with Julia there'd been no hesitation.

'It didn't suit her colouring. It meant nothing significant.'

Julia was stung. Well, she'd got her answer. He'd given it to *her* because it suited her colouring. The fact that she hungered so desperately for him mocked her, when she knew more certainly than ever that the only reason she was here at all was because of the heirs she carried. He couldn't even bring himself to make love to her again.

Wanting to disguise how hurt and vulnerable that made her feel, she said, 'How do I know that once I have these babies you won't try to extricate yourself from *me*? You cast your first wife out just because she couldn't give you an heir. Obviously you weren't committed enough to pursue other options. Perhaps it's just the heirs you care about? Maybe a wife is superfluous to your needs?'

Kaden's mouth tightened with anger. 'For your information, I did all I could to make my marriage work. Amira was the one who insisted on a divorce, because she knew she could never give me an heir. She wouldn't even discuss options. And I'm still paying for ongoing treatment to get her over her phobia.'

Julia felt deflated when she thought of the fact that if his wife had been more amenable they might still be married. Cheeks flaming, she said, 'I'm sorry. I had no right to assume I knew what had happened. It must have been...very painful.'

Kaden emitted a curt laugh. 'I wasn't in love with her, Julia. It was an arranged marriage.' His voice sounded surprisingly bitter. 'She had the right lineage.'

Julia glanced at him, pushing down the lancing pain at this evidence of his cynicism. 'And now you've got the heirs, but a wife with all the wrong lineage.'

He just looked at her with those black eyes, and for the first time Julia felt something rising up within her—something she couldn't keep suppressing.

She fiddled with her napkin and avoided Kaden's eye. 'Speaking of lineage, there's something you should probably know.' She rushed on before she could lose her nerve. 'I'm adopted, Kaden. I was adopted at birth. I know who my birth mother is, but she doesn't want to know me. For all I know she could even be dead by now.'

Julia was breathing fast, aghast that she'd just blurted out the stain on her soul like that.

Kaden said carefully, 'Why did you never tell me this before?'

Julia shrugged minutely, still avoiding his eye. 'I don't talk about it—ever.'

'Why not? It's not a bad thing. Plenty of people are adopted. I would have considered adoption myself if Amira had been open to the idea.'

Shock at Kaden's easy acceptance made her look up. His eyes were dark, assessing. Not cold and judgemental. Julia felt as if she was being drawn into those eyes. His reaction was loosening something that had always felt tight inside her.

'From the day my parents told me I was adopted, when I turned thirteen, I always felt...*less*.' She grimaced. 'My parents went out of their way to assure me they loved me, but to know that someone else had had you first...and let you go because they didn't want you...' Even now Julia shivered.

'What about your father? You say your birth mother didn't want to know you?'

'The records from the agency showed that my parents hadn't been married. I found out that my father had emigrated to Australia almost immediately after my birth. He was too far away to trace, so I focused on my mother. I was too impatient to write, so not long before I came here to work on the dig I tracked down her phone number and called her...'

Julia smiled tremulously. 'She knew exactly who I was. It was as if she'd been waiting for my call.' Her smile faded. 'But then she just said, *'Don't call here again. I don't want to have anything to do with you. I gave you up once and it's done'.*'

The pain in Julia's heart was acute. She only realised

she was crying silent tears when Kaden took her hand across the table, enveloping her in warmth.

'It sounds to me as if giving you up was an incredibly traumatic experience for her. Perhaps it's something she simply couldn't deal with.'

Julia brushed away the tears and attempted a smile. 'I know… I saw a counsellor attached to the adoption agency before I contacted her, so I was warned about the reaction I might get. But somehow I'd hoped for the kind of thing you see in the movies—the great reunion. Stupid…'

Kaden was shaking his head, his hand tightening on hers. 'Not stupid at all. It's very human. I'm sorry, Julia…really sorry you went through that. I can't imagine what it's like to grow up not knowing where you've come from.'

Feeling very exposed and brittle at Kaden's sensitivity, Julia pulled her hand back from his and put it on her belly, saying lightly, 'At least these little ones won't ever have to face that.'

Kaden was grim. 'No, they won't.'

The evidence of Kaden's grimness made Julia's emotions see-saw all over the place. She desperately wanted him to hold her…to make love to her and help her forget her pain which was far too close to the surface. But he hadn't touched her in two weeks, and wasn't likely to any time soon.

In a bid to escape before he could see the extent of how this affected her, she stood up. 'I'm quite tired this evening… If you'll excuse me…?'

Kaden stood too. 'Don't forget about the visit to the new hospital wing tomorrow.'

'Oh…'

Julia *had* forgotten about her first public function tomorrow. She was due to cut the ribbon on a new wing of the national hospital. Immediately her concerns about going out in public rose up.

Kaden said, 'I'll be with you tomorrow. All you'll have to do is smile and wave. They won't expect any more. They'll just want to see you.'

Julia turned to walk away from the table, but Kaden caught her wrist. She looked back. She could feel her pulse throbbing against his hand and flushed.

She took her wrist from his grip. After everything she'd just shared, the deep vulnerability she felt was acute enough to be a physical ache within her. She forced a smile. 'I'll be fine. I'm looking forward to it.'

She left the room, feeling Kaden's black eyes boring into her back.

KADEN WAVED AWAY the staff that came in to clear the plates from the private and intimate dining room not far from their suite of rooms. He needed to be alone, to digest everything Julia had just told him. Suddenly restless, he stood up, his long robes falling around him.

He paced back and forth, as if that might dampen the ever-present burn of desire, made worse now after feeling Julia's hectic pulse. It was all jumbled up in his head: his need to lose himself in her body; his equal need to keep his distance; the almost overwhelming need to protect her from ever being hurt again as she so evidently had been by her birth mother.

Julia had looked so vulnerable just now, and he hated the thought of exposing her to the crowds tomorrow. But he couldn't avoid it. He felt inordinately protective, but told himself it was a natural response because she was pregnant, and not because of what she'd revealed about her birth.

He'd had no clue about her adoption. From what she'd told him about herself years before he'd guessed she came from a solidly middle class background. When she hadn't talked about family too much he'd just put it down to English reticence. The fact that she'd made that painful contact with her birth mother just before she'd come to Burquat was uncomfortable for him to dwell on.

For a second Kaden had a glimpse into how rudderless *he* might have felt if he hadn't grown up knowing exactly where he'd come from. The sliver of isolation that washed through him at contemplating that scenario made him want to call Julia back, so that he could hold her close and never let her go again.

He immediately rejected that urge. His hand clenched to a fist. *This* was what he'd been avoiding ever since their wedding night. This rising tide of emotions that he refused to look at or acknowledge. The depth of passion on that night had stunned him. And that awful dream...which had obviously been precipitated by sleeping with Julia. Perhaps here in Burquat the memories were too close to avoid.

The truth was that when Julia touched him he became something else—someone else. It was too reminiscent of how she'd made him feel before. He'd never forget that struggle with his father before he'd died. His total absorption in himself and meeting his own needs...and then the awful shock of seeing her with that man, the excoriating jealousy. Realising how much he'd lost sight of himself and who he was, who he had to be. Exactly what his father had warned him against.

Kaden strode over to the drinks cabinet, poured himself a measure of neat whisky and knocked it back. The burn made him reach for another one, as if that might douse the unquenchable desire, the tangled knot of feelings his wife so effortlessly evoked. He'd told himself that when he'd met her again in London he'd just wanted to bed her. And when she'd arrived to tell him about her pregnancy he'd thought only of the babies.

Now those assertions rang like the hollow untruths they were. Since he'd seen Julia again things had gone a lot deeper than he liked to admit.

The truth was, it was easier to avoid Julia and any chance of intimacy than face her and those grey eyes which made him feel as if he was coming apart at the seams every time he looked at her. Now more so than ever.

CHAPTER NINE

JULIA WAS TREMBLING with nerves by the time they pulled up in Kaden's chauffeur-driven state car outside the hospital the following morning. She was dressed in a silvery grey long tunic, with matching pants underneath and a shawl to match. Her hair was tied back in a loose low bun, make-up and jewellery discreet. The tunic hid her pregnancy quite well—they'd agreed to wait another few days before making the announcement.

She took a deep shaky breath at the sight of the crowds amassed behind cordons, and then felt her hand being taken in a strong, warm grip. She almost closed her eyes for a second at the wave of longing that went through her. She turned to look at Kaden. His eyes were intent, compelling.

'I'll be right by your side. Just be yourself. They won't be able to help but respond to you.'

'But I'm not a public person, Kaden… I've given speeches to rooms full of archaeologists, but never anything like this. They'll expect me to be something I'm not.'

Something fierce crossed Kaden's face and he said, 'They will accept you, Julia, because you're my wife and I've chosen you.'

Julia felt sad, and pulled her hand away. She bit back the words trembling on her tongue. *You wouldn't have chosen me if you'd had a choice.*

Kaden's door was opened then, and with a last look he got out. The crowd went wild. He wore long cream robes and a traditional headdress. Julia's heart clenched amidst her trepidation. He reminded her so much in that moment of the young man she'd first met.

He was coming round the car. He'd instructed the driver to let him open her door. And then he was there, against the bright searing sun, holding out a hand. Julia took a deep breath and stepped out, clutching Kaden's hand. The roar of the crowd dipped ominously.

Security guards shadowed them as they walked towards the hospital. Julia tried to smile, but the crowd was blurring into a sea of faces that all looked suspiciously unfriendly. She was reminded of the aides who had surrounded Kaden after his father's death, when she hadn't been able to get close to him. She stumbled slightly and his arm came around her waist.

'OK?'

She looked up. 'Yes, fine.'

She drew on all her reserves as they got to the top of the steps and were greeted by officials from the hospital. They were exceedingly polite, but with a definite reserve. Kaden gave a short heartfelt speech about the new unit, which was specifically for heart disease, and then they turned towards the huge ribbon over the main doors.

Julia was handed a pair of scissors and cut it. Everyone clapped and cheered, but she couldn't help but notice the reticence of the crowd ever since she'd appeared at Kaden's side.

After being shown around inside by the doctors and officials they re-emerged, and Kaden led her towards the crowds. He said, 'We'll do a short walkabout. It's expected.'

Urged forward, Julia went towards a little girl, who pushed forward shyly to hold out some flowers. She bent down and took them, saying thank you in their native language. But Julia noticed the mother pull the child back, her lips pursed in disapproval, eyes dark and hard.

Another woman who held a baby visibly turned away, and adjusted a shawl over the baby's face so that Julia couldn't see it. As if to protect it from her gaze. Amongst her shock at the people's obvious rejection of her Julia felt a welling desire to have them look at her with open faces and smiles. She realised that she desperately wanted to be able to connect with them.

Kaden was taking her hand and pulling her back to the car. When they got in Julia was a little shell-shocked.

Kaden was grim as the car pulled away. 'I'm sorry about that. They're wary after Amira and my stepmother...they'll come round.'

'It's OK,' Julia replied faintly, feeling more hurt than she'd thought possible. She'd not even known till then how important the Burquati people's opinion of her was. 'I can understand that they wanted to see you with someone more suitable.'

Kaden was silent beside her, and Julia didn't want

to look at him and see disappointment in his second wife etched into his face.

When they got back to the palace Kaden stopped Julia and said, 'I've got to go into the desert for a couple of days to meet with the newly elected Bedouin council.'

Julia looked at him against the backdrop of the magnificent central courtyard and felt a hollowness echoing through her. This was how it would be between them. Distance and polite civility.

She nodded. 'Fine. I'll see you in a couple of days. I've got lessons to get on with in the meantime.'

Julia turned away, and Kaden had an irrational urge to grab her back, throw her into the car and drive them far away. He wanted to be going into the desert with *her*, the way they'd used to. Sneaking off like fugitives, spending nights in a hastily erected tent under the stars. No thought in the world beyond exploring each other and sating mutual desire. And talking for hours.

An ache welled up inside him, and this time he couldn't ignore it. He had a sudden overwhelming need for those memories not to be tainted by what had happened twelve years before. For Julia to look at him the way she'd used to, with such open love and warmth. But the reality was clear. If Julia had ever had any feelings for him they were long gone. She was bound to him for ever, and she couldn't help but hate him for that. He'd seen the way that woman in the crowd had shielded her baby from Julia, as if she were some sort of witch. And Julia had just smiled.

With a jerky move, Kaden got back into the car which would take him to a helicopter to fly him into the desert. In that moment he'd never felt such bleakness surround him, and pain for subjecting Julia to the cold disapproval of his people when he knew just how deep her vulnerability went.

As Kaden flew over the desert a short time later the helicopter dipped abruptly for a moment in an air pocket. The pilot apologised and Kaden smiled tightly. That physical sensation mirrored exactly how he felt emotionally, and it wasn't comfortable.

JULIA SPENT THE next two days working hard with her own secretary to encourage meetings with locals. She was determined to do what she could to bridge the gap, and wanted to avoid having any free time to brood about Kaden and the distance between them. She had to admit, though, that talking to him about her adoption had been cathartic. Thoughts of it and her birth mother no longer came with the heavy oppressive weight they'd used to.

To her delight she'd managed to set up a few coffee morning events at the palace, to meet with local women's groups and dicuss various issues. Julia had always had an interest in the more anthropological end of archaeology, so the prospect of meeting Burquati people and coming to learn their customs excited her.

She was in the middle of her first coffee morning when she saw Kaden again, and she nearly dropped her cup. He stood in the doorway, tall and gorgeous in long robes, jaw dark with stubble. He'd obviously just returned. She could swear her heart physically clenched as she saw him again.

All the women immediately bowed and went silent.

He inclined his head. 'I'll leave you to it. I'm sure you're discussing far more important things than I will be at my cabinet meeting later.'

He smiled, but to Julia it looked slightly strained. His eyes skated over her, giving her no more nor less attention than the other women. The awful yearning for him to acknowledge her with more than that inclusive glance nearly overwhelmed her, and she had to shove the hurt down deep.

He left, and after a moment of pregnant silence the women started chattering in a mixture of English and Burquati. Julia had been struggling to connect with the women, who'd seemed very suspicious, but suddenly they were all smiles and laughs.

Her secretary smiled at her sympathetically, misreading her anguish. 'Don't worry. It'll just take some time.'

Julia smiled wanly and went to join in again, feeling prickly because, if truth be told, she was jealous of these women. Kaden could come and charm them so effortlessly when he couldn't even be bothered to touch her any more!

JULIA WAS LYING in bed that night, unable to sleep. Kaden hadn't returned to their suite all evening, and she'd eaten dinner alone. She knew she couldn't continue like this, with Kaden holding her at arm's length and looking at her as if she might explode at any moment like a ticking bomb.

When she heard his familiar step she tensed. He came into the moonlit room, treading quietly.

Julia came up on one elbow and said huskily, 'I'm awake.'

He stopped, and all she could see in the gloom was his huge shape. Predictably, despite her tangled head and emotions, her body reacted to the sight of him. Softening, melting.

She sat up and pulled her knees towards her to try and hide her agitation. 'Why didn't you come to dinner?'

Kaden started to disrobe. Julia could see gleaming flesh revealed bit by bit, and her belly clenched helplessly with desire.

His voice was cool. 'I got held up with a phone call to Sadiq, discussing the oil wells. They're expecting a baby too. Not long after us.'

'Oh...' Julia didn't know what to say. Kaden seemed to be determined to avoid any further discussion.

He came to the bed and lifted back the covers, getting in and lying down. Tension vibrated between them like a tangible thing.

Julia turned to face him, feeling her hair slip over her shoulders. 'Kaden...we need to talk. It's obvious that this isn't working out.'

Kaden didn't like the flare of panic. He'd been reacting all day to the gut-wrenchingly urgent need he'd had to see Julia immediately on his return from the desert. And then, when he had seen her, the relief had sent him away again just as quickly, for fear she'd read something into his reaction that he didn't want her to see.

He felt as if he was clinging on to the last link that was rooting him in reality. That was rooting him in what he knew and had accepted for twelve long years.

His distance from Julia for the past couple of days had restored some clarity, some perspective, and a sense that perhaps he wasn't going mad... Except earlier, and now, it was back with a vengeance. Any illusion of control gone.

His whole body was rigid against the effortless pull of Julia beside him. Her soft scent was like a siren's call to his blood. He turned his head and saw her outline: the slim shoulders, the curve of her breasts, the swell of her belly under the soft cotton of her vest. She wore vests and shorts to bed, attire he'd never seen another woman wear, and yet it inflamed him more than the slinkiest negligée he'd ever seen.

He turned away from temptation and forced out, 'What isn't working out?'

His clear reluctance to talk made the tiny flame of hope Julia had harboured that they might discuss this fade away. She was overwhelmed for a moment by the sense of futility, and lay down too. She said in a small voice, 'Nothing. It doesn't matter.'

For a moment there was nothing but thick silence, and then, in a move so fast she gasped, Kaden was looming over her, eyes like black pools. 'Tell me, Julia. What were you going to say?'

He was fierce, when only moments before his rigid control had been palpable. She smelt the slightest hint of whisky on his breath, and somehow suspecting that he was in some sort of turmoil too made her feel simultaneously tender and combative. And something in her exulted that he was finally reacting.

Before she could say anything, though, something

in the atmosphere shifted and his fingers touched her throat. He said huskily, 'You're wearing the necklace.'

Julia froze all over, going clammy. Some of her things had arrived from London earlier and she'd found the necklace. She'd put it on, feeling some silly need to connect with something she'd always found comforting. She'd fully intended to take it off.

She immediately sought to protect herself from his scrutiny and drew back minutely. 'It's OK. You don't have to get the wrong idea...'

His voice was a lot harsher than a moment ago. 'What does it mean, Julia? Why have you kept it all this time?'

Julia knocked his hand away and scrambled inelegantly out of the bed, feeling far too vulnerable lying so close to a naked Kaden.

She lashed out in her own anger for exposing herself like this and in anger at Kaden for questioning her. 'I just saw it and put it on. It doesn't mean anything. It certainly doesn't mean that I don't know what this marriage is about. It's about the fact that I'm pregnant with your precious heirs—nothing more, nothing less.'

Kaden uncoiled his big body from the bed and walked around to Julia. Acting on the irrational panic rising within her that she was about to come apart completely, Julia reached up and grabbed the necklace with her hand. She yanked at it, breaking the delicate chain instantly, and flung it aside onto the ground.

Inside she was weeping. Outwardly she hitched up her chin. 'See? It means *nothing*.'

Kaden looked at where she'd thrown the necklace and then back to her. The air crackled between them.

In an abrupt move he pulled her into his body and said fiercely, 'You don't have to resort to dramatics to make your point. I get the message. From now on there will be no doubt as to what this marriage is about.'

Julia closed her eyes as Kaden's mouth fused to hers, his arms like a vice around her. Their bodies strained together. Tears burned the backs of her eyes, but she would not let Kaden see the helpless emotion. It was hot and overflowing, but as Kaden lowered her onto the bed and came down over her she shut her mind to all the mocking voices which told her that she was fooling no one but herself.

THE FOLLOWING DAY Kaden was standing alone on an open terrace in the palace. He'd been having a meeting with an architect about the palace's preservation, but the architect had long gone. The city of Burquat was laid out before him. Cranes dotted the skyline— evidence of much necessary modernisation.

Kaden didn't see the view, though. His thoughts were inward. He smiled grimly to himself. He'd been right to fear touching Julia again. It was as if he'd known it would be the final catalyst in his coming undone. His own useless defence system had crashed and burned spectacularly last night, like a row of elaborate dominoes falling down with one small nudge.

Julia had only had to wear that necklace for him to see clearly for the first time in years.

His jaw tightened. Even then he hadn't been able to give in, still fighting right to the end… He'd had to make her say it, make her tell him how she really felt. As if he needed the concrete proof of her words and to feel the pain that came with them. Because he knew he deserved it. Perhaps that was what he'd been protecting himself against all along—the truth of *her* feelings. Not just his own.

He'd held something very precious a long time ago, and he'd broken it for ever. Kaden looked down and opened his fist to reveal the necklace, its chain in two pieces.

CHAPTER TEN

JULIA WAS IN their private dining room, where Kaden had said he'd meet her for lunch. She was standing at the open French doors but seeing nothing of the glorious view. A couple of weeks had passed since that night. When Julia had woken the morning after she'd been alone. She'd immediately got up to look for the necklace but hadn't found it. Her sense of loss was profound, but she was too nervous to mention it to anyone or ask for help in searching for it. The last thing she wanted was for Kaden to know she was scrabbling around looking for it at any given opportunity.

She'd had to realise with a heavy heart that perhaps she needed to be rid of it because it symbolised something she'd never really had or would have—Kaden's love.

Kaden hadn't avoided her at night since then. They'd made love. And yet his touch was more...reticent. As if he was scared he'd hurt her. It seemed to compound the yawning chasm growing between them, so much worse than before.

How could they have gone three steps forward only to go about a hundred back?

'I'm sorry to have kept you waiting.'

Julia whirled around to see Kaden in the doorway.

Even though he'd left their bed only hours before, she blushed. She schooled her reaction and walked to the table. Just as she put out a hand to touch her chair she felt a kick in her womb, forcible enough to make her gasp and touch her bump, which was now big enough to be obvious to everyone.

Instantly Kaden was at her side, holding her arm. 'What is it?'

As much in reaction to his touch as the kick, Julia said shakily, 'I'm fine...it was just a kick—the first real kick I've felt.'

Another one came then, and she couldn't stop a smile spreading across her face. Feeling the babies move was dissolving any inhibitions. She reached instinctively for Kaden's hand and brought it to her belly, pressing it down, praying that they would kick again. She looked at Kaden, and as always the ever-present awareness seemed to hum between them.

When the seconds stretched and there were no more kicks Julia flushed. She felt exposed. Kaden was too close, looking at her too assessingly. She pulled his hand away,

'They've stopped...'

Instantly the connection was broken, and Kaden stalked to the other side of the table and sat down. Staff appeared as if by magic and served them. Their conversation was stilted, centring around a charity fête that Julia was due to attend that afternoon.

When they'd finished eating Julia wiped her mouth, preparing to go.

Kaden said, 'You don't have to go to the fête this afternoon if you don't want to. Unfortunately I can't get out of my meeting with the foreign minister. He's due to fly to the US tomorrow.'

Julia smiled tightly. 'It'll be fine. I need to get used to going to these things on my own sooner or later.'

Kaden leaned forward and took her hand in his. Julia's eyes widened.

'I know this is hard for you, but already I can see a difference in people's attitudes. You're winning them round.' He grimaced then. 'I'm sorry that you have to go through this when you'd never have willingly signed up for this life.'

Julia's face burned. Little did he know that she'd often dreamt of being by his side.

She took back her hand and pushed back her chair. 'The car will be waiting.'

Kaden watched her leave the room and cursed himself. He clenched his fist and just stopped himself from bringing it crashing down on the table. He kept thinking about the moment after their wedding, when he'd found her sobbing her heart out. Guilt burned in his gut, compounded now by the way he'd felt when he'd seen that beatific smile lighting up her face. He'd felt jealous that something else could make her happy. Jealous of his own babies!

The moment hadn't lasted long before she'd withdrawn again to that cool, polite distance which only dissolved when they were in bed.

He didn't need to be reminded that Julia hadn't smiled like that once since she'd met him again. As if he didn't know why. She was stuck in a marriage of convenience with a man who had brutally rejected her when she'd been at her most vulnerable just to protect his own cowardly heart. Julia was humbling him every day with her innate grace and stoic acceptance of a difficult situation. Of a life she didn't want.

Kaden knew that he had to be fully honest with her. She deserved to know everything. Later, he vowed. When she got home he would tell her. *Everything*. And whatever her reaction was...he would have to deal with it.

TWO HOURS LATER Kaden was sitting at his desk listening to his minister for foreign affairs talk, but not taking anything in. He was wondering where Julia was now. Had she reached the fête? Was she feeling awkward? Was she smiling in that slightly fixed way which signified she was shy or uncomfortable? His gut clenched at the thought of anyone being rude or unfriendly to her.

Only last week he'd watched her host another of her coffee mornings, this time outside in the palace grounds. He'd been inordinately proud of the way she'd listened to people, really devoting her time to them. A million miles away from his ex-wife and stepmother who had both been brought up specially schooled to be in this world.

'Sire?'

They'd announced the news of Julia's pregnancy a few days ago, now that she was showing more obviously, and he was hoping it would have an effect on people's interaction with her. Surely the prospect of—?

'Sire!'

'Hmm?' Kaden looked at his minister, a little dazed for a moment, and then saw that his secretary was also in the room. He frowned. He hadn't even noticed her come in. 'Yes, Sara?'

He only noticed then that she was deathly pale and trembling. The hair went up on the back of his neck for no reason.

'Sire, I'm sorry to disturb you, but I've just heard— there's been a terrible multi-vehicle accident on the main freeway to Kazat, where the fête is. We've been trying to call your wife and the driver, but there's no response from them or the bodyguards. We don't have news yet as the emergency services haven't reached them.'

Kaden heard her words and tried to react, to move. But it was as if his limbs were instantly weighted down with wet cement. He couldn't get up. He could feel his blood draining south and put his hands on his desk to hold on to something.

His secretary started crying and the foreign minister stood up. 'Sire, I'll get your car immediately.'

Kaden stood up then, even though he couldn't feel his own legs, and said with an icy calm which belied the roaring in his brain, 'Not the car. Too slow. Get the helicopter ready and make sure there's a doctor and a paramedic on board. *Now*.'

What felt like aeons later, but what was in fact only thirty minutes, Kaden's helicopter pilot was setting down in a clearing beside the freeway. All Kaden could see was a tangled mass of vehicles, a school bus on its side, with steam billowing out of its engine, and lines of cars blocking the freeway.

The flashing lights of the first emergency vehicles were evident, and there were people blackened from smoke and fire rushing everywhere. And amongst all that twisted metal and heat was Julia. Kaden's mind shut down and he went into autopilot. He simply could not contemplate anything beyond the next few seconds.

The blast of heat nearly pushed him backwards when he got out of the chopper, but Kaden ignored it and waded straight into the carnage. He shouted at the young, scared-looking doctor with him, 'Stay beside me!'

All around them people were wandering around looking dazed, with blood running down their faces, holding hands and arms. But to Kaden's initial and fleeting relief there seemed no serious-looking injuries. He focused on the school bus on its side, and as he went towards it, acting on instinct, he finally saw the Royal car. It was skewed at an angle near the bus, ploughed into the steel girder which ran down the middle of the highway, and near it, on its roof, was the security Jeep.

Kaden's heart stopped. He ran towards the car, and when he got there, his lungs burning, ducked his head into the back seat. It was empty. He felt sick when he saw the trail of blood that led out of the car.

He stood up. *'Julia!'*

Nothing. Panic at full throttle now, he went towards the other side of the school bus and stopped dead in his tracks, a mixture of overwhelming relief and incoherent rage making him dizzy. Julia was handing a small child to her driver, who was in turn handing it to someone else. Adults who looked like teachers were standing in groups with other children, crying. Julia's kaftan was ripped and bloody.

He went towards her and she saw him. 'Oh, Kaden—

thank God! Please…you have to help us. There are still some children trapped inside, and the engine is leaking petrol.'

She looked half crazed, which he could see was due to shock and adrenaline, and in the periphery of his vision he could see people standing with phones, taking videos and photos. Very deliberately he put his hands on Julia's arms and bodily moved her out of harm's way. He looked at the doctor and said, 'She's over five months pregnant. If anything happens to her you'll be held personally responsible.'

Julia protested. 'But, Kaden, there are still children—'

He cut her off. '*You* stay here. *I* will go and get the children. If you move one inch, Julia, so help me God I will lock you in the palace for the rest of your life.'

Through a haze of shock and panic Julia could only feel limp with relief as she watched Kaden stride back to the bus, climb up and reach in to help pull the children out. Within minutes they were all accounted for, and Julia had already instructed the now terrified-looking doctor to go and help the injured children instead of babysitting her. She was helping too, ripping material off her dress to tie around bleeding arms and legs.

She felt herself being lifted upwards and was turned into Kaden's chest. His eyes burned down into hers. 'Are you OK? Are you in pain anywhere?'

Julia shook her head. Some of the shock was starting to wear off, so she was aware of how deranged Kaden looked. She put it down to the accident. 'I'm fine. We need to help these people…'

But her words were muffled against Kaden's chest

as he pulled her into him and hugged her so tightly
that she couldn't breathe. Eventually he pulled back.
'We're getting out of here right now. I need to get you
to the hospital.'

Julia protested. 'I'm fine—what about all these people? The children? They need help more than me!'

But Kaden wasn't listening. She could see an emergency medical plane circling overhead, and more choppers landing. The scene was swarming with emergency
staff now, and the young doctor was busy.

When she still resisted, Kaden uttered an oath and
turned and picked her up into his arms. Julia opened
her mouth, but closed it again at the stern set of his features. He looked as if he was going to murder someone,
and she felt a pang when she recalled what he'd said
to the doctor. *'She's over five months pregnant...'* He
must be livid with her for putting their babies at risk.

She was in the chopper and secured within minutes,
and then they were lifting up and away from the may-
hem. Julia was comforted to see that the emergency
vehicles were already speeding back towards the city,
and other choppers were loading up with patients.

Kaden couldn't speak because of the noise but Julia
was glad. She wasn't looking forward to what he had
to say.

'KADEN, WHY DON'T you just spit it out? You're giving me a headache, pacing around like a bear with a
sore head.'

He stopped and glared at her, his jeans and shirt
ripped and dusty. 'You're a national hero. Do you know

that? With one fell swoop the entire nation is in love with you.'

'What do you mean?' Julia was confused.

Kaden picked up the remote and turned on the TV. A rolling news channel was showing images of the crash, and then it zoomed in on Julia, where she was handing a small child to someone.

She glanced at Kaden. He'd gone grey.

He switched the TV off and muttered thickly, 'I can't even watch that.'

Tears stung Julia's eyes. 'I'm sorry, but I couldn't just ignore what was happening. I know these babies are important to you, but surely your own people are important too?'

He just looked at her. 'What are you talking about?'

Julia put her hand on her bump. She'd just had a scan with Dr Assan and been reassured that all was fine. 'The babies. I presume that's why you're so angry with me...for putting them in danger?'

Kaden raked a hand through his hair and ground out, 'I'm not angry with you for putting the babies in danger. I'm *livid* with you for putting *yourself* in such danger.'

He came close before Julia could fully take in his words and sat down, pulling a chair close to the bed and taking her hands in his with a tight grip. 'Do you have any idea what I went through before I got to you?'

Julia shook her head slowly. An ominous fluttering feeling was starting up in her chest.

'I think I aged about fifty years, and made blood promises to several gods. So if some strange-looking person turns up and demands our firstborn baby don't be surprised.'

'Kaden...' Julia was feeling more shaky now than when she'd been at the crash. 'What are you talking about? You're not making sense.' And yet at the same time he was making a kind of sense she didn't want to think about.

'What I'm talking about, *habiba*, is the fact that for the longest thirty minutes of my life I didn't want to go on living if anything had happened to you.'

Feeling suspiciously emotional, and very vulnerable, Julia couldn't take her eyes off Kaden.

He continued. 'I was going to talk to you this evening when you got back...I don't want to tire you now...'

Concern was etched onto his face, and Julia said fiercely, 'I'm fine. Talk.'

Kaden looked down, and then back up at Julia. 'I'm not sure where to start... There's so much I have to say... But I think first I need to tell you the one truth that is more important than anything.'

Julia held her breath as Kaden gripped her hand tighter.

'I want you to know that I'm not saying this now because of the crash, or because of the after effects of adrenaline and shock. I had arranged for us to go to the summer palace this evening, for a belated honeymoon. You can ask Sara. She was organising it.'

'Kaden...' Julia said weakly. She couldn't look away from the dark intensity of his eyes.

He took a deep, audibly shaky breath. 'I love you, Julia. Mind, body, heart and soul. And I always have.

From the moment we met in the middle of that dig. I did a wonderful job of convincing myself twelve years ago that I hadn't ever loved you, but as soon as I saw you again the game was up…and eventually I had to stop lying to myself.'

Julia looked at Kaden in shock. She could hear her heart thumping. Her mouth opened.

Kaden shook his head and said, 'Don't say anything—not yet. Let me finish.'

Julia couldn't have spoken, even if she'd wanted to. Her mouth closed. She could feel the babies moving in her belly, but that was secondary to what was happening right now.

'The day you left twelve years ago was possibly the worst day of my life.' He winced. 'Barring today's events. I felt as if I was being torn in two—like Jekyll and Hyde. For a long time I blamed the grief I felt on my father's death—and that was there, yes. But a larger part of my grief was for you. There's something I have to explain. When we returned from that last trip to the desert I went to my father. I told him that I was going to ask you to marry me. All I could think about was you—you filled up my heart and soul like nothing I'd ever imagined, and I couldn't imagine not being with you for ever.'

Julia could feel herself go pale as she remembered that heady time. And then her confusion when Kaden had abandoned her. She shook her head. 'But why did you not come to see me? Tell me this…?'

Kaden's jaw clenched. 'Because that night my father had his first heart attack. Only those closest to him knew how serious it was. We sent out the news that he wasn't well, but we hid the gravity of the situation for fear of panicking the people. I became acting ruler overnight. I was constantly surrounded by aides. I couldn't move two steps without being questioned or followed. And I suspect that after what I'd told my father he instructed his aides to keep an eye on me and not let me near you.

'I think he saw history repeating itself. His second wife had been a bad choice, unpopular with the people. He knew how important it would be for me to marry well and create a stable base, and here I was declaring my intention to ask *you* to marry me and to hell with the consequences.'

Kaden sighed. 'I stuck to my guns. I was still determined to ask you to marry me. I decided that while you were finishing your studies I'd give you the time to think about whether or not you really wanted this life...'

Julia felt tears prickle at the back of her eyes. She knew how she would have answered that.

Kaden's voice was gruff. 'The first chance I had I got away on my own and went to find you. One of your tutors told me you were all out that night in a bar...'

Julia squeezed Kaden's hand, willing him to believe her. 'You have to know what you saw meant nothing... it was just a stupid kiss. It was over the moment it started. I was feeling insecure because I hadn't heard from you, and I think I wanted to assure myself that you couldn't be the only man who could make me feel. I was afraid we were over and I'd never see you again.'

To Julia's intense relief Kaden picked up her hand and kissed her palm. 'I know that now...and I can see how vulnerable you must have felt—especially so soon after that blow from your birth mother…' He grimaced. 'I, however, was blindingly jealous and hot-headed. It felt like the ultimate betrayal. Especially when I'd been pining for you for what felt like endless nights, dreaming of proposing to you even if it meant going against my father's wishes. And then to see you in another man's arms…it was too much. The jealousy was overwhelming. I'd been brought up to view romantic love suspiciously. My father became a shadow of himself after my mother died, and he never stopped telling me that my duty was first and foremost to my country. He was most likely trying to protect me…but when I felt so betrayed by you it only seemed to confirm his words. I convinced myself that it wasn't love I felt. It was lust. Because then it wouldn't hurt so much.'

Kaden shook his head. 'I returned to the palace and that night my father had his final heart attack. I got to him just before he slipped away, and his last words to me were pleas to remember that I was responsible for a country now, and had to look beyond my own personal fulfilment. By then I was more than ready to listen to him.'

'Oh, Kaden…I had no idea.' Pain cut through Julia as she saw how the sequence of events had played out with a kind of sickening synchronicity.

Kaden let her hands go and stood up, pacing away from Julia, self-disgust evident in every jerky movement. He turned round and looked haunted. 'When you came to me before you left and tried to explain you got the full lash of my guilt and jealousy. I couldn't be rational. All I could see was you and that man. It haunted me even when we met again. The depth of the feelings I had for you always scared me a little, and I never resolved them years ago. I buried them, and that's why it took me so long to come to my senses...'

Julia felt incredibly sad. 'We were so young, Kaden. Maybe we were just too young to cope with those feelings.'

Kaden raked a hand through his hair. 'That's why Samia looked at you with such hostility at her wedding. She was protecting me because she was the only one who saw the dark place I went to after you left. I never explained anything to her, so she assumed you'd broken my heart. When in fact I did a pretty good job of breaking yours.'

'And your own...' Julia bit her lip to try and keep a lid on the overwhelming feelings within her. Tears blurred her vision, and despite her best efforts a sob broke free.

Kaden was standing apart, hands clenched at his sides, looking tortured.

She shook her head. 'I just...I can't believe you're saying all this...' Another sob came out and she put a hand to her mouth. Tears were flowing freely down her face now.

Kaden clearly wanted to comfort her, but was holding back because he didn't know if she wanted him. 'God, Julia...I'm so sorry. What I've done is—'

'Kaden, don't say anything else. Just hold me, please.'

Julia wasn't even sure if her words had been entirely coherent, but Kaden moved forward jerkily, and after a moment he was sitting on the bed and enveloping her in his strong embrace.

Julia's hands were clenched against his chest. She couldn't stop crying, and kept thinking of all those wasted years and pain. Ineffectually she hit at his chest, and he tensed and pulled her even closer, as if to absorb her turmoil. Eventually he drew back and looked down, his face in agony. Seeing that made something dissolve inside Julia.

'Don't let me go, Kaden…'

He shook his head and said fiercely, 'Never. I'll never let you go ever again.'

When the paroxysm of emotion had abated Julia pulled back in the circle of his arms and said shakily, 'I've always loved you. I never stopped. You and no one else. From the moment I saw you again in London all the feelings rushed back as if we'd never even been separated.'

Kaden shook his head, clearly incredulous. 'How can you? After everything… You don't have to say this… You don't want to be here. You've been forced into this life.'

Julia touched his face and smiled tremulously. 'I wouldn't want to be anywhere else in the world. I was resigned to my fate, loving you while knowing you'd never love me back.'

Kaden's eyes shone suspiciously. 'Oh, my love… that's what *I* expected. I love you so much that if anything had happened to you today…'

He went pale again, and the full enormity of what Kaden had gone through hit Julia when she thought of how *she* would have felt if their places had been switched.

Fervently she said, 'Let's go home, Kaden. I want to go home with you and start living the rest of our lives together. I don't want to waste another moment.'

EPILOGUE

Seven months later

JULIA and Kaden were hosting a christening for their twins and for Samia and Sadiq's baby son, who was just a few weeks younger than the twins. The ceremony had finished in the ancient chapel in the grounds of the archaeological dig site. Julia was standing with Samia now, and they were watching Kaden cradle his dark-haired baby daughter Rihana with all the dexterity of a natural. His brother-in-law Sadiq was holding his son Zaki with similar proficiency.

Samia and Julia's first proper meeting had been awkward, but as soon as Kaden had set Samia straight she'd rounded on him and castigated him for letting her think the worst of Julia for years. Now they were fast becoming good friends.

'No doubt they're discussing the merits of eco-friendly nappies,' Samia said dryly.

Julia snorted. 'Kaden nearly fainted earlier when he smelt Tariq's morning deposit.'

Samia giggled and linked arms with Julia. They'd just been made godmothers to each other's babies. 'Come on—let me introduce you properly to Iseult and Jamilah. You'll love them. Jamilah, the dark-haired one, is Salman's wife. She's got an inner beauty to match her outer beauty, which makes it annoyingly hard to hate her.'

Julia chuckled. She'd only been briefly introduced to Sheikh Nadim of Merkazad and his stunningly pretty red-haired wife, and his brother Salman and *his* wife Jamilah. Both couples also had babies, who were crawling or toddling around, being chased by one or other of their parents.

Just as they approached the other women, though, Kaden cut in and handed Rihana to Samia. 'Here you go, Auntie. I'm stealing my wife for a minute.'

Samia took her baby niece eagerly. 'Be careful—you might not get her back. And I think Tariq has already been stolen by Dr Assan.'

They'd made Dr Assan their son's godfather, and he was showing him off like a proud grandfather.

Kaden took Julia's hand and led her out through a side door. He was dressed in gold and cream ceremonial robes, and Julia wore a cream silk dress. She let herself be led by Kaden through the shade of the old trees to the other side of the dig, feeling absurdly happy and content.

Kaden glanced back and smiled. 'What are you looking so smug about?'

Julia smiled mysteriously, her heart full. 'Oh, nothing much.'

Kaden growled. 'I'll make you tell me later, but first…'

They'd reached the corner, and Julia recognised the spot where they'd first met. Kaden brought her over to the ancient wall, and it took a moment before she could see what he was directing her attention to. A new stone had been placed amongst the older ones, and it held within it a fossil and an inscription.

She gasped and looked at him. 'That's not the same fossil—?'

He smiled. 'Read the writing.'

She did. The inscription simply read: *For my wife and only love, Julia. You hold my heart and soul, as I will hold yours, for ever. Kaden*

It also had the date of the day they'd met. She looked at Kaden, feeling suspiciously teary, and saw that he was holding out his palm. She looked down and saw a familiar chain of gold. Her necklace. She picked it up reverently.

He sounded gruff. 'I got it mended after that night.'

Julia's eyes had filled with proper tears now, and Kaden said mock sternly, with his hands cupping her face and jaw, 'I won't have tears marking this spot.'

Julia smiled through the tears. 'Kiss me, then, and make me happy.'

'That,' Kaden said, with love in his eyes and on his face, 'I can most definitely do.'

And so they kissed, for a long time, on the exact spot where they'd first met almost thirteen years before.

* * * * *

We hope you enjoyed reading this
special collection from Harlequin®.

If you liked reading these stories,
then you will love
Harlequin Presents® books!

You want alpha males, decadent glamour and
jet-set lifestyles. Step into the sensational,
sophisticated world of **Harlequin Presents**,
where sinfully tempting heroes ignite a fierce
and wickedly irresistible passion!

Enjoy eight new stories from
Harlequin Presents every month!

Available wherever books and
ebooks are sold.

H HARLEQUIN

Presents®

Glamorous international settings…
powerful men…passionate romances.

www.Harlequin.com

STEPHP

THE WORLD IS BETTER
WITH
Romance

Harlequin has everything from contemporary, passionate and heartwarming to suspenseful and inspirational stories.

Whatever your mood, we have a romance just for you!

Connect with us to find your next great read, special offers and more.

 /HarlequinBooks

@HarlequinBooks

www.HarlequinBlog.com

www.Harlequin.com/Newsletters

HARLEQUIN

A *Romance* FOR EVERY MOOD™

www.Harlequin.com

SERIESHALOAD2015

HARLEQUIN®

A *Romance* FOR EVERY MOOD™

JUST CAN'T GET ENOUGH?

Join our social communities
and talk to us online.

You will have access to the latest
news on upcoming titles and special
promotions, but most importantly,
you can talk to other fans about your
favorite Harlequin reads.

Harlequin.com/Community

 Facebook.com/HarlequinBooks

Twitter.com/HarlequinBooks

Pinterest.com/HarlequinBooks

HARLEQUIN®

A Romance FOR EVERY MOOD™

Love the Harlequin book you just read?

Your opinion matters.

Review this book on your favorite book site, review site, blog or your own social media properties and share your opinion with other readers!

HARLEQUIN®

A *Romance* FOR EVERY MOOD™

Stay up-to-date on all your
romance-reading news with the
Harlequin Shopping Guide,
featuring bestselling authors, exciting new
miniseries, books to watch and more!

The newest issue will be delivered right to you
with our compliments! There are 4 each year.

Signing up is easy.

EMAIL

ShoppingGuide@Harlequin.ca

WRITE TO US

HARLEQUIN BOOKS
Attention: Customer Service Department
P.O. Box 9057, Buffalo, NY 14269-9057

OR PHONE

1-800-873-8635 in the United States
1-888-343-9777 in Canada

Please allow 4-6 weeks for delivery of the first issue by mail.